PRAISE for *In the Shadows With Catherine the Great*

"I couldn't wait to turn the page to see what happens next."

In the Shadows, a meticulously researched, accurate account of life at the Imperial Court of Russia in the 18th century, serves as a model of what a historical novel should be. Judith Rypma's familiarity with Russian life leading up to and including the beginning of the reign of Catherine the Great shines through on every page. This novel is an engaging way to introduce readers to the complicated treacherous history of Russia in the 18th century; it also is a mini "refresher course" for experts in the field. Even though I must have taught this very history for over 40 years, I couldn't wait to turn the page to see what happens next.

Dr. Edward Alan Cole
Professor Emeritus of Russian Intellectual History

"Pushkin's *Captain's Daughter* Meets Gabaldon's *Outlander*."

Most attempts to return the time of Catherine the Great have been either carefully or creatively done. Judith Rypma somehow manages to do both in her well-written historical novel, *In the Shadows*, the first in a planned series. It's a story of secrets—of a young American who finds love and identity as she is mysteriously transported back into Enlightenment-era Russia, and of the young princess whose loves and ambitions shaped one of the great world empires. Along the way, readers are exposed to the sparkling, precarious court life of prerevolutionary Europe; to celebrated Russian imperial sites; to the enchanting world of royal gems, and to perhaps the thorniest coup of the 18th century. Our two heroines experience the times in full: royal privilege, love, heartache, smallpox, and intrigue. But drawing on a rich resource base, Rypma does more. *In the Shadows* takes us on a journey of discovery into what made Catherine the remarkable woman and ruler she was, and what it would be like to try and make a life, as well as an impact, as a woman in what was very much a man's world. Parallels about Russia, power, and gender today suggest themselves throughout the novel. Heartily recommended!

Dr. Scott Van Lingenfelter
Author, *Russia in the 21st Century*

"I cannot wait for the sequel."

With her latest novel, Judith Rypma lets us time travel with her intrepid heroine back to Imperial Russia as an insider during the early reign of Catherine II as she transforms into "the Great." Characters come alive on every page as they weave their way through the intrigues, romances, and misadventures while the court travels from palace to palace. In inexperienced hands, the historical details that make up the foundation of the novel could potentially bore readers; on the contrary, Rypma's well-researched background as a renowned scholar of Russian language and literature; a poet and novelist of note; and a former travel journalist add to the sparkle of prose—not unlike the many jewels that adorn her heroine. Vivid characterization, expert plotting, and accessible writing make this novel a pleasure to read. I cannot wait for the sequel.

Dr. Christine A. Rydel
Prof. of Russian Language & Literature, retired
Editor, Ardis Publishers

"It is a book written with love—and a book meant to be loved."

This fascinating look at 18th-century Russia through the eyes of two charming protagonists is an elegantly written novel that offers a fresh look at two nations. The author's passion for Russian culture and her careful, thorough research provide a thought-provoking alternative to the destructive tendency to cancel otherness in today's political climate. Above all, it is a book that takes seriously the history of a country outside Rypma's own culture. I am proud to have had the rare opportunity to witness much of the author's research on some of her numerous trips to Russia to collect information and examine artifacts. It is a book written with love—and a book meant to be loved.

Prof. Svetlana Shimberg
Leningrad State University Pushkin, Russia

Another Historical Time Travel Book by Judith Rypma

The Amber Beads (Black Opal Books)

When Julie inherits the contents of her great grandmother's farmhouse, she discovers mostly piles and piles of hoarded junk. However, after fiddling with an amber necklace she discovers in a locked storage room, she finds herself suddenly and inexplicably whisked back in time to the court of the last ruling Romanovs and a Russia in the midst of World War I. As the events of 1917 kindle a flame that becomes the roar of revolution, they not only touch her life and that of her new family but force her to cope with new ways of seeing the world, her cultural heritage, and even the complications of a unique and complicated love. And how—or will—she ever make it back to the present?

Reviews for *The Amber Beads:*

"Rypma has created a history lesson in vivid detail, giving us much more than just the events, but the attitudes and emotions of the people at that time—a glimpse into the past so real, it makes you think you've gone back in time with Julia. A wonderful read."

Taylor Jones

"*The Amber Beads* is both a coming-of-age story and a cunning history lesson. With powerful descriptions, charming characters, and a solid ring of truth, Rypma pulls you in until you feel right there in the scene . . . struggling to survive in war-torn Russia. It takes a talented author to do that."

Regan Murphy

Available from Black Opal Books, Barnes & Noble, Amazon, and local bookstores

IN THE SHADOWS
WITH CATHERINE THE GREAT

JUDITH A. RYPMA

Published by Leonora Books

For R.M.

The gemstone who has been there for me
throughout this massive undertaking, and
whose feedback and support provided
precious gifts.

TABLE OF CONTENTS

PROLOGUE

During rare moments alone, I marvel at my circumstances. I've grown up in a democracy, not an autocracy; the fact that I am suddenly a high-class servant with no rights and virtually no freedom is disturbing. Yet what choice do I have? I am a prisoner in another time. All I can do for now is live the life into which I've been thrust, for however long that may be. Sometimes, curled up beside one of the other maids of honor amidst an eighteenth-century Russian winter, I weep for what I have lost.

CHAPTER 1

(SOPHIE) 1729-1743

"It was the irritant around which the pearl took shape—she was only a girl."
—Gina Kaus

Princess Sophia August Frederika von Anhalt-Zerbst generally sneaked in an extra prayer to muffle the incessantly clanging church bells beside her nursery. Yet the seven-year-old barely noticed the day she was on her knees praying and suddenly toppled onto her side.

Seized by a rattling cough, sharp chest pains, and eventually fever, she baffled the physicians who anxiously attempted everything from prescribing potions and plasters to dribbling the spittle of a virgin down her spine.

Sophie, Figchen, Fige, Fike—the nicknames assigned to her—found herself bedridden for hellish weeks. Weeks softened only by visits from her new governess Babet, who told stories collected by someone named Perrault: tales of princes, castles, and magic. Occasionally Babet encouraged her to memorize passages by great thinkers like Racine and Moliere.

When Sophie did rise from bed, she felt relieved she'd be able to walk and run again.

One glimpse of her mother's horrified expression convinced her otherwise.

"What is wrong with her shoulder? And her back!" Johanna cried hysterically. "It is lopsided!"

When her mother—who insisted on being called by her first name or Princess Johanna—commanded her to turn around, Sophie heard audible gasps.

"It's a letter Z!" a maid whispered loudly.

"What are we to do?" Johanna hissed to her husband, Prince Christian August. "She is flawed!"

"The doctor will know."

"But what if he cannot cure this abomination? It's bad enough she resembles an ugly duckling. No one will want a cripple!"

Sophie knew her dull brown hair and plain features could not compare with other girls her age, let alone her mother's beauty. Johanna resembled a sugary pastry, all pink and blonde froth with frosty blue eyes.

Catherine's birth in the provincial court of a Prussian duchy headquartered in the town of Stettin should've been cause for joy. Instead, Johanna, a seventeen-year-old princess reluctantly married to a man twice her age, complained to anyone who'd listen: "A mere girl!"

"We will have others."

"Christian, what if it's another *girl*?" She spat out the word.

When later she gave birth to two boys in succession, she devoted the time and attention she'd refused Sophie to her sons. Mostly Johanna fawned over the coveted first son, Wilhelm Christian, treasuring him as if he were a long-coveted jewel. Sadly, though, since birth he'd remained flawed, with crooked legs and a weak stamina, fragile as one of the opals his young mother so dearly prized. When little Sophie asked what was wrong with him, her mother slapped her or cuffed her on the ear.

Only today had she shown such interest in Sophie.

Sophie approached the mirror. Her spine *did* appear to zigzag in a letter Z down her now twisted torso.

"Christian, swear the servants to secrecy. If word gets out . . ."

"Let us wait for the doctor before we worry unnecessarily."

The puzzled physician eventually summoned a hangman. Although executioners were highly regarded as healers possessing an intimate knowledge of the human body, the law forbade them to practice medicine. For his second clandestine visit, the hangman furtively smuggled in a special device. "You will wear this until your flawed back straightens," he pronounced. "It goes beneath your gown so no one will know."

It turned out to be a harness strapped over her shoulder and encasing her back. The tight, unwieldy contraption felt horribly uncomfortable, but Sophie at least could drag herself around the fortress, regardless of being wrapped in a carapace like some giant insect.

Now no one would suspect her deformity except for Babet, her parents, and a few trusted servants who helped her dress.

Mostly Sophie huddled with books, imagining herself temporarily wrapped in a chrysalis, like a caterpillar anticipating emergence. She need only await the day she could spread her butterfly wings and fly.

She had no idea she'd be commanded to wear the device for months and then years with no noticeable improvement. It would be a lesson in patience, in quiet dishonor, in humiliation.

Sophie's father always greeted her affectionately when he arrived home. Trim in his blue Prussian general's uniform and straw-hued waistcoat, he ruffled Sophie's hair while protecting her from the sword dangling at his side. Yet after he'd settled wearily into their damp home, he seemed diminished from that proud officer who'd entered the front door. When his wife inevitably greeted him with a litany of complaints—nearly always about money—his face fell. His kind eyes appeared tired, and his mouth formed a straight line. Johanna had married away from the elegant Brunswick Court where she'd grown up and couldn't accept dropping several societal levels.

Sophie shrugged off the grumblings. To her, their somewhat crumbling fortress in a port city was a modest castle. She didn't resent faded furniture and tapestries, shabby curtains, dreary walls, frayed gowns, silver plate with tin edges, even coarse linen chemises. She sympathized with the underpaid servants who scrubbed and rescrubbed threadbare carpets with sauerkraut to coax back color. Who patiently stuffed and re-stuffed the filling in stained furniture. Who darned and re-darned everyone's stockings.

Throughout her early childhood, lack of attention had enabled Sophie to escape with less supervision than most princesses. She played in public gardens with commoners' children or sneaked down to the docks where ships on the River Oder unloaded coffee and cloth from across the Baltic. Once they spied a vessel unloading a group of men so tall they could only be for King Frederick William's special regiment of giants.

Her freedom had ended, however, when, after trading Sophie's governesses like playing cards, Johnna finally gambled on Mademoiselle Babet Cardel—a French Huguenot refugee spinster willing to work for minimal pay and promising to teach her young charge French.

Under Babet's tutelage, life became more structured, but at least Sophie had found someone besides her father who genuinely appeared to care for her.

The harness worked exceptionally well when Sophie was forced to sit ramrod straight for hours to endure lessons by a succession of other tutors. The little princess soaked up history, geography, and the classics, particularly enjoying Homer, Ovid, and Aristotle. Her French dancing master rolled his eyes at her efforts, however, and Babet attempted fruitlessly to teach her the rudiments of singing.

"I'm afraid you are what we call tone deaf," she sighed. "Nonetheless, you excel in most of your other studies. Except music."

"They roar like bulls!" she complained about the music instructors. The screeching hurt Sophie's ears, and every twilight the church organ next door thundered its discordant displeasure—perhaps with her prospects for salvation.

Those prospects were explored thoroughly by her religion instructor, Herr Wagner, who drilled the fear of hell into her daily. She despised the Lutheran pastor, although deep down experienced guilt over her hatred.

"Thank you," Sophie murmured, striving for politeness the first week of their teacher-student relationship when he presented her with an enormous German Bible. Thumbing through it, she noticed hundreds of verses and longer passages underlined in red ink.

"This will be your homework," Herr Wagner announced. "You will eventually memorize every section marked in red. There will be no mistakes."

Sophie despaired of ever learning this much. Worse yet, each underlined passage contained doomsday warnings of vengeance, treachery, hell, and the consequences of more sins than she could imagine committing in a lifetime.

Nevertheless, she resigned herself to memorizing each passage word for word, including all the admonitions about eternal damnation that seemed to bleed off the pages.

When she made an occasional error, Herr Wagner threw up his hands and hollered, as if pronouncing the Last Judgment.

Secretly she referred to her religion tutor as a Blockhead, but at times she ran to her room and knelt at her bed to pray for forgiveness and that she would not be punished for her errors by going to hell.

Rather than confining herself to rote memorization, she occasionally asked questions about passages. "If you must accept Christ to enter heaven, what about all the people born before He was?"

"Damnation," the Blockhead replied promptly.

"But what about Plato and Aristotle and Marcus Aurelius and all the good philosophers who lived before Jesus? Why should they be damned?"

"Little girls should not question the Good Book. It is not ours to challenge the words of Christ and the Apostles. Just recite what you've been assigned."

"But what does this word mean? *Circumcision?*"

He threw up his hands and summoned Babet to intervene, demanding his pupil be flogged for impertinence.

Babet refused. Sophie was sent to her room to pray, although her governess shielded a smile when Herr Wagner pointed out the word Sophie had inquired about.

For hours she begged on her knees for God to redeem her blackened soul, weeping as if her heart would break.

She never did get a definition of circumcision.

Every summer after Sophie recovered, Johanna immersed her daughter in the world of her own childhood at the Court of Brunswick: an atmosphere of constant balls, banquets, operas, concerts, carriage drives, and hunting parties. During these court rituals, the girl was compelled to dress as a miniature lady, young head perched on a slender neck as she trailed Johanna. As much as Sophie despised fussing with her appearance and kissing wealthy ladies' hems, she tried to be obedient as a foal; a long train instead of a tail trailed behind the swirl of perfume left in Johanna's wake.

She also absorbed culture in the small Prussian arts center, where walls boasted paintings by Van Dyck and Rembrandt. Lords and ladies began to compliment her intelligence, noticing that Sophie had a wise observation about everything.

Despite sensitivity to her appearance, she comforted herself with Babet's assurances that she possessed perfect teeth and a winning smile, although even Babet joked about her charge's sharp chin: "If you don't keep it tucked in, that thing could become a dangerous weapon!"

The only time Sophie was deemed useful occurred when Johanna needed her company on an errand. Sophie never knew to which castle corner these clandestine trips would lead, but quickly realized Johanna had a secret vice—one furtively shared by other members of the nobility, although diametrically opposed by the Church. They generally uncloaked and removed their hoods inside a room lit by cheap tallow candles and a tiny window, where they would face a fortune teller, a medium, a palm reader, or a soothsayer. Johanna, obsessed with the futures of noble children and particularly her own sons, willingly paid each seer a pile of coins.

On one occasion, a monk deemed clairvoyant—amazingly smuggled into this bastion of Calvinism and Lutheranism—seemed bored. Johanna had asked about a little girl to whom she'd taken a fancy: Princess Marianna of Brunswick-Bevern. "Do you see her wearing a crown?" she persisted.

The monk stared wordlessly at Johanna, and then without warning turned his head to where Sophie sat in the shadows.

"Her!" he said loudly.

"Me?" Sophie, half asleep, glanced up.

"No, no, not *her*," Johanna corrected the monk. "I'm talking about Princess Marianna."

"On *this girl* my prophesy is for not one, but three crowns above her forehead!"

Johanna winced, then uttered a brittle laugh.

Sophie, astonished and intrigued, nonetheless dismissed anything the man from the old faith predicted.

"Delightful as these fantasies might be," Johanna said sharply, "I will hear no more about this!" When she started to retrieve her payment, the much quicker monk reached out from beneath his robe and scooped up the coins.

"Imagine all that money wasted on some ridiculous prediction about you when there are so many eligible princesses in Europe!" Johanna muttered as they left.

Sophie knew beyond a shadow of a doubt that her mother would never mention the three crowns again.

Despite Johanna's aversion to Sophie's appearance, she hadn't given up considering her a marriage commodity. Sophie occasionally overheard her name linked to eligible royals: the intelligent and promising

Prince Henry of Prussia; a distant cousin, Wilhelm of Saxe-Gotha, and Duke Karl Peter Ulrich of Holstein-Gottorp—the eleven-year-old heir to the Swedish throne and orphaned grandson of Russia's former Peter the Great—who'd grown up in Prussia.

It was to be evaluated as the latter's marital prospects that titled girls secured invitations to meet him at various dates the summer of 1739. When it was ten-year-old Sophie's turn, she observed her second cousin with little interest. He was frail for his age, though not awful to observe.

As days passed, it became apparent that beneath the boy's somewhat polished manners lurked an irritable temper. His incorrigible behavior manifested itself particularly when he overindulged in spirits. Sophie couldn't blame him entirely, given what she'd observed of his handlers and tutors, who constantly barked orders and corrections.

"I hate them all," he whispered when they finally were seated together at dinner.

"Why?"

"They won't permit me to do anything I want!"

"I often feel the same way," Sophie offered.

"Watch this," he nudged her, and signaled for another refill of wine.

"That's enough! You are just a child!" a voice behind them immediately chastised the duke. Karl Peter gave a high-pitched laugh, and in one gulp downed the entire goblet of French cabernet. An hour later, he toddled unsteadily from the table, the oversized military uniform he perpetually paraded around in covered with red wine stains; more wine drooled from his mouth.

Sophie shrugged off this potential suitor, viewing him as a spoiled, petulant, vain, and irritable boy—even a pitiable one. The idea of someday being Queen of Sweden, whatever that entailed, lured her for a short time, yet she could not imagine marriage to this boy to win it.

❧

"There is simply no place in decent society for them!" Johanna commented about her unmarried relatives.

"Do you mean your sister?" Sophie asked.

"Of course. She may be a prioress in a convent, but she has never known love. Or anything else."

"What is 'anything else'? And she loves her dogs, doesn't she?"

"Those stinky pugs she crams into her room? You cannot love animals! And they stink worse than the River Oder."

"She must have a dozen."

"Sixteen! Can you imagine? Is that where you want to end up? Married to a bunch of malodorous dogs?"

"What if I don't *want* to get married?"

"Ridiculous! There are no options for unmarriageable young ladies of the gentry."

"What about my Aunt Sophie?"

Johanna laughed shrilly. "Certainly, daughter. You can live exactly like Canoness Sophie Christiana if you'd like. See if I care!"

The canoness, her father's sister, divided *her* love between the church and dozens of rescued birds she hoarded in an aviary in her room. "At least she doesn't live under the thumb of a husband!" Sophie dared suggest.

Johanna cuffed her on the ear. "Shut up! You will marry or burn."

"But Babet—"

"Babet is a mere governess. Is that what you want? Do you think you are so smart—or perhaps stupid enough—that you would relegate yourself to a life like that?"

Stung, Sophie retreated to the gardens outside. She cared little about her marital future and saw nothing whatsoever wrong with Babet's life. Still, perhaps having her own home would bring some freedom. To do what she wanted. To be her own person.

No such discussion of her brothers' prospects ever occurred. The focus on the oldest, Prince Wilhelm, revolved around his persistent fragile health. Although eligible to marry and destined to inherit Anhalt-Zerbst, he must be carried everywhere due to his uselessly dangling leg. His mother invested fruitlessly in physician after physician, as well as the touted healing powers of countless mineral spas.

Sophie felt guilty at her own vibrant health. The harness was long gone, and when visiting their country estate at Anhalt, she dashed up and down four flights of stone stairs to see how many trips she could make before Babet returned from a nighttime privy trip. When her governess checked on her, Sophie would have the covers pulled up over her head, feigning sleep.

As years dragged, mother and daughter continued to co-exist like competing oysters. They remained each other's irritants—Johanna the colorful interior swirl determined not to be upstaged, and her daughter the grain of sand yearning to evolve as a polished, lovely pearl someone someday might pry open and allow to shine.

Sophie imagined floating through time, adrift on a shell bed of rainbows.

In May 1740, King Frederick William of Prussia died. Known for ruling military fashion over his strictly regulated kingdom, he'd heavily colonized East Prussia with over three hundred new towns. One of the first world rulers to introduce compulsory education, he'd also worked tirelessly to manage Prussia's mines, ports, forests, and infrastructure.

Nevertheless, he was neither respected nor loved by his subjects. With an ugly temper and massive appetite that transformed his legs into barrel size, he offered little to admire about his person. He'd grown huge stuffing himself with a special two-pronged fork utilized for a haunch of venison, eight dozen oysters, or giant portions of pork. Eventually he'd ordered his dining table cut away to accommodate his enormous stomach.

There was much speculation about Prince—now King—Frederick II. Sophie had met him once, recalling a short, intense young man with little tolerance for court formalities. Rather than worry about finery or politics or war, he delighted in philosophy and the arts. Nor was it a secret that his father had beaten him and his sister mercilessly since they were old enough to walk.

No one expected much of the twenty-eight-year-old—only that he'd be a welcome change from his father. Sophie wondered what it would be like to be dragged to your own coronation when you'd rather be reading. To have everyone's expectations of you so low you couldn't hope to gain respect without some miracle. Perhaps Frederick II had some secret potential inside him that would later blossom, the way one spring day unspectacular lilac bushes suddenly exploded in a brilliant outburst of tiny white and lavender stars.

One point did not escape her. It obviously was not enough to be a good ruler, as proven by the expressions of joy she'd witnessed on the streets when the king died. His son, unproven as a monarch, was already loved and respected. Apparently, you needed to be both, since without the people's affection, your accomplishments would be dismissed.

Princess Johanna couldn't stop gloating. "Can you imagine? Princess Elizabeth has seized the throne of all the Russias!"

Sophie vaguely knew Elizabeth was Peter the Great's second daughter, ruling a vast, wild terrain of Arctic cold. She'd also heard that the coup had toppled a mother who was regent for a baby emperor named Ivan VI, and that mother and son had been exiled or locked away someplace.

For Johanna, it was an opportunity to regain prestige. The new empress had been destined to be her sister-in-law—and Sophie's aunt—because Elizabeth had been engaged to Johanna's brother Karl August. Tragically, the bridegroom had died of smallpox just before the wedding. Ever since, rumors persisted that Elizabeth had never recovered from her grief and now refused to marry.

Johanna immediately sat down to write a congratulatory letter to the newly crowned monarch. Sophie paid little attention.

"Your father has had an apoplexy," Johanna said in such a preternaturally calm voice that it took Sophie several moments to digest the news.

Terrified, she raced to her parents' room.

Prince Christian August recognized his daughter, tried to speak, and failed. Sophie took his hand, turning away so he would not see tears streaming down her cheeks.

The stroke had paralyzed his entire left side.

"I won't leave you," Sophie promised, and settled at his bedside each spring day for hours. She read aloud, encouraged him to practice speaking, and attempted to raise his spirits with jokes and stories. He seemed particularly soothed when she recited lengthy biblical passages.

Johanna, settled in another room, glanced in every couple of days.

Fortunately, her father recovered quickly, just in time to help his family deal with a greater tragedy: after a lifetime of frail health, Sophie's brother Wilhelm died. Crippled and pampered all his life, the twelve-year old nonetheless expired of scarlet fever.

Johanna was inconsolable, her grief assuaged only by focusing on her current pregnancy. When a few months later she delivered a daughter, she at once wrote again to the new Russian empress. She eagerly named the newborn after Elizabeth and asked the empress to serve as godmother.

Elizabeth reciprocated months later with a diamond-wreathed portrait of herself. Best of all, Elizabeth addressed the woman who'd just missed becoming her sister-in-law as *cousin*.

The family had barely learned to cope with Christian August's stroke and the death of young Wilhelm when another misfortune occurred: Christian August's first cousin, with whom he'd served as co-ruler of Zerbst, died.

"What will happen now, Papa?" Sophie asked. She'd long wondered how two people could share one throne.

"I suppose I will be sovereign ruler," he said in his new, slower voice.

"What will change?"

"Silly girl," Johanna said sharply. For the first time since her eldest son's death, she seemed her old self. "We'll leave Stettin and move to Zerbst so your father can assume sole regency."

In the chaos of packing, they scarcely noticed that in faraway Russia, the childless Empress Elizabeth had summoned her nephew Karl Peter from Prussia. She ordered him to renounce claim to the Swedish throne; to abandon his Protestant religion for the Orthodox faith; and, as the new heir to the Russian throne, to adopt the name Grand

Duke Peter Fyodorovich.

Zerbst was situated far southeast of Stettin in the heart of what was formally referred to as Prussia. In November the family found themselves welcomed into a city boasting not only medieval towers, walls, and even moats, but—to Johanna's delight—a baroque castle complete with liveried servants and a painted carriage. To Christian, Sophie, and Babet's joy, the sixty-year-old castle also harbored two ancestral treasures: letters from Martin Luther and a Luther Bible illustrated with colored woodcuts.

Zerbst consisted of attractive gabled houses, a renowned brewery, and best of all for Princess Johanna, twenty thousand residents who bowed or curtsied to her.

In contrast with the bullying king he'd served most of his life, Christian August governed with an intense interest in his people's welfare. Sophie meant to absorb all she could about the nature of governing, as her father's promotion had made her heir in her own right to the domain of Jever, traditionally ruled by the princesses of Anhalt-Zerbst.

She accompanied her parents to her potential future domain, situated near the North Sea coast of Lower Saxony, the following summer. Afterward they travelled on to Varel, where they were met on horseback by the remarkable, albeit plain Countess von Bentinck, daughter of the dowager Countess von Altenburg.

Sophie had never witnessed a woman who rode like a man. The countess's high spirits also impressed the young princess. After stripping off leather gloves and changing out of her riding habit, the countess danced and sang her way into Johanna's apartments. Despite her distaste for music, Sophie eagerly joined in to learn the peasant folk dances, earning a parental scolding for inappropriate behavior.

In the countess's apartments, Sophie noticed a large portrait of a handsome man. "Who is that?"

"My husband," the countess said airily. "In fact, had he not been, I should have loved him madly."

"I don't understand."

"It is never a good thing to allow yourself to love a man—or a woman—more than you are loved. It puts you at too much risk."

A boy about three years old sat nearly hidden in the corner. Sophie swallowed her surprise at his beauty, since the nearly thirty-year-old countess was, although interesting and intelligent, physically unappealing, with a strapping, manly appearance that seemed to fit her hearty manner and exuberant, forthright personality.

"This is your son?"

"He is the brother of my dear Fraulein Donep." The countess placed her bonnet on the boy's curly locks. "Doesn't he look just like me?"

Fraulein Donep turned out to be the Countess von Bentinck's special and likely romantic lady friend. Although nowhere in evidence, the husband turned out to be alive and well, separated rather than divorced from his wife. The little boy turned out to be the countess's own child—a result of an adulterous relationship with a lowly footman.

All these inappropriate behaviors and half-truths only deepened Sophie's fascination with the woman. When the countess permitted Sophie to mount a horse, the girl developed an instant passion for riding and yearned to get proficient enough to race across the meadows.

Fearing the influence of the unconventional countess on their daughter, her parents cut their visit as short as politely possible.

Sophie did not forget her new friend, and several times risked severe punishment by sneaking off to visit her. Countess von Bentinck impressed her young admirer with her unique combination of spontaneity, intelligence, disregard for societal approval, self-direction, charm, and independence.

Sophie could chatter about little else to Babet. "I love that a woman can be forced to marry according to societal expectations, and still be independent of her husband."

Babet said little to dissuade her charge from this fascination.

"She also speaks her own mind, not just parroting back what she has memorized." Sophie made a face, recalling the endless recitations Herr Wagner required.

"Indeed, she is free in spirit." Babet grinned despite her disapproval. "Not unlike another young lady I know well. You are kindred souls. Hopefully not, however, in certain of her life decisions," she hastened to add.

When Babet came upon her staring sightlessly at one of her favorite readings—a new novella by Madame de Villeneuve recounting how a young girl was forced to live with a fearsome beast—she asked Sophie how she liked the book.

"I'm enjoying it, although I've noticed how often in such stories a beautiful woman is forced to commit herself to an ugly creature."

"But she does get to live in a palace. And I think you'll enjoy the happy ending. Is that why you're wearing that scowl?"

"No, I was contemplating Countess von Bentinck. It seems to me she is a woman who has made some noise in the world. If only she were a man, she would be considered an exceptional one."

"I don't disagree."

"I believe that someday women, too, will make some noise in the world," Sophie said dreamily.

Babet only nodded.

CHAPTER 2

(MARIA MEEKHOF) 1999

I am in Russia. This is the only thing I'm certain of right now, except to recall how much I didn't want to come in the first place. My aunt—Professor Roberta Meekhof—insisted I accompany her to St. Petersburg for a conference the summer before my final year of high school.

Now suddenly everything seems peculiar. This morning I dressed in faded jeans and a t-shirt to go to a museum, yet now find myself suddenly shivering in snowy darkness and wearing a fur-trimmed cloak and matching muff. Behind me towers a decrepit wooden building where men in old-fashioned military uniforms huddle to warm hands over a fire.

I've no clue who they are or how I got here, let alone gained a totally different wardrobe in a totally different climate and time of day. Nor does this feel like any dream I've ever had.

Someone throws on extra logs, the shooting flames momentarily illuminating faces I don't recognize. Nor can I make out any of their garbled words. *Well of course*, I chide myself. I'm in a foreign country.

And where is my aunt? We parted an hour ago at the Hermitage, agreeing to meet in late afternoon.

Before I can stroll to the fire to get answers or at least warmth, one of a bevy of women clustered around me yanks me back and shakes her head disapprovingly.

I can barely see her face in the darkness, although she reminds me a bit of my aunt: always firm when she believes in something strongly.

She was that way last month after she announced this trip.

"You took me to Moscow when I was eleven. I don't need to go again," I protested.

"St. Petersburg is entirely different. I want you to experience some of what I've dedicated my life to studying. Next summer you'll be getting ready for college and working full time. Besides, this is a major conference, Maria."

I'd have to go, of course, since Aunt Roberta has been my guardian and adoptive mother since both my parents died ten years ago this summer, when I was seven. And wouldn't most people jump at a chance like this?

Still, I continued to fight the idea. "You'll be presenting your paper and lecturing all day and half the night. What am *I* supposed to do there?"

"You can visit some sights on your own. I'll book you on some tours so you can understand the layout." She is like that, almost always willing to give me independence to pursue my own interests and not hovering over me as if I'm a rebellious teenager. Which I'm not—and never have been. Except, that is, for not wanting to come on this trip.

Deep down I do feel obligated and grateful to my father's sister. Despite being a never-married woman with a hectic schedule, she's managed to do an awesome job raising me while keeping up her responsibilities as a professor. I know she loves me as much as I do her.

Yet things did not go smoothly between us after she announced this trip. She accepted none of my excuses, starting with my total disinterest in a country she never stops talking about; Russia is *her* life, her job: not mine. *Mine* consists of school, guys, shopping, swimming, reading novels (few historical), and hanging with friends.

I stomped to my room, and for weeks we barely spoke of anything except the embassy's lengthy visa applications. Eventually she allowed me to invite a friend, but I couldn't get anyone to agree—let alone their parents, who still see Russia as the Big Bad Soviet Union.

Since arriving, I've seen my aunt rarely. As the tours she booked for me progress, I *have* grown fascinated with St. Petersburg's labyrinthic canals, romantic parks, and elaborate pastel buildings. On walks along the main thoroughfare, Nevsky Prospekt, I even count building colors: watermelon, banana, ivory, pistachio, tangerine, mango, turquoise, robin's egg, lavender, pale rose, raspberry.

One of my favorite places must be the Church of the Savior on Spilled Blood, which the guide explains occupies the site where Alexander II was assassinated when 19th-century revolutionaries bombed his carriage. The spectacular interior boasts thousands of minerals, including precious and semi-precious stones, which comprise the columns, floor, mosaics, ceilings, and every inch of space. It feels as if I'm standing inside a jewelry box.

Of course, the entire city is a dream-like fantasy, with elaborate bridges, manicured parks, gilded spires and cupolas, and sculpture-covered facades. This is not what I expected after admittedly devoting all of ten minutes researching the city online. Fortunately, I have my new camera to capture all the places I observe.

I feel good as I wash up after my third morning tour, making a face at myself—almost my mother's face, with dark brows and lashes, butterscotch hued eyes, and delicate features. She was Parisian, which is how she met my father at a conference in Quebec where he, too, taught high school French. When I was seven, the two of them left on a small aircraft with friends headed over Lake Michigan to Wisconsin. They never returned.

In the lobby Aunt Roberta scribbles notes on a stack of papers. She did the same thing on our three flights, while from Chicago to Helsinki I sullenly played games on the seatback's computer screen to avoid conversation.

Sensing me beside her, Aunt Roberta stuffs everything in a small backpack. "Ready for lunch?"

I smile at the backpack, knowing I'm still a long way from convincing her to switch to electronic devices. Bookcases, desks, and file cabinets clutter our home, with Aunt Roberta on the verge of becoming what I'd label an academic hoarder.

We stroll to a non-descript building with a basement cafeteria. I don't even try to convince Aunt Roberta I'd prefer fast food. The cashier ladles out whatever I point to, charging us based on the food's weight.

"So," my aunt says casually while we eat. Too casually, so I know something serious is coming.

"Have you given any more thought to universities?"

I poke at some odd mayonnaise salad filled with carrots, peas, ham, and eggs. "No, not really."

"The deadline is this fall. You know I'm *hoping* you'll pick Michigan State—and not just because we'd save a heck of a lot with my faculty discount."

She smiles self-consciously. We both know my grades will bring plenty of scholarship offers. Anticipating my usual reply, she adds, "You don't necessarily have to declare a major. Maybe just get some of your gen eds out of the way and see if something strikes your fancy, so to speak."

"Well, it *would* be nice if I knew. I mean if I had something that really made me feel passionate. Like you did."

"It didn't start that way. I only knew I liked history, and then narrowed it down my senior year to Slavic history. I didn't suspect I'd become a Petrine scholar until finishing my master's. Even then I didn't make the final decision until I started my doctorate."

Professor Roberta Meekhof specializes in Peter the Great and the early 18th century. I cannot imagine ever finding anything so specific to interest me.

"Perhaps something on this trip will inspire you." She winks, reminding me once again that she has the exact same shade of hazel eyes my father had.

"I'm actually having fun," I admit, and am rewarded with a delighted smile. With her shoulder-length dark brown hair and smooth skin, my aunt still looks almost as young as some of her grad students.

For the last few days, Aunt Roberta manages to free up her schedule to take me on a few more excursions. We zip across the river in a hydrofoil to a magnificent massive palace called Peterhof; meander the city aboard a canal boat, and tour a museum filled with Russian art works. I'm drawn to the portraits of former imperial monarchs, particularly the majestic empresses garbed in elaborate gowns and regalia.

"Peter was succeeded by a series of females, unusual in world history," my aunt explains when she notices my interest. She lapses into her professorial tone: "He changed the law of succession, making it possible for an emperor to appoint his own heir, regardless of gender.

Then he named his own wife, Catherine the First. Thanks to him, Russia had nearly a century of women rulers."

Until now my Russian history has consisted primarily of Peter the Great before making a huge leap to the early 20th century and the ill-fated last Romanov tsar.

My memory of that day is interrupted when the woman who seems to think she's in charge of me tightens her grip. I pull away forcefully and march to the men's fire.

"They are very late," someone grumbles. I know that's what he said, though it doesn't sound like English. It cannot be French, in which I'm fluent thanks to my parents.

A few men return from the forested area behind us and toss more logs in the fire. Flames shoot upward, momentarily illuminating a church across what a frozen river. Perhaps the Neva? The church bears an uncanny resemblance to Peter and Paul Fortress and Cathedral, where my second tour took me. Even from a distance, the gilded needle-like spire appears muted, as if made of wood and painted yellow rather than sheathed in 24-karat gold.

And then the fire settles to reveal only silhouettes.

Am I dreaming? Or could I have passed out and gone into a coma? And where the heck are my phone and camera? My clothes? I feel like falling to the ground and crying out of frustration.

The woman I abandoned taps me on the shoulder. "Come, Maria. It is almost time."

"Time for what? Who is Maria?" She cannot possibly know my name.

She does not reply.

"Why can't we go inside?"

Shaking her head, she gives me an odd look.

Who or what is everyone waiting for? At least a servant emerges from the darkness to pass cups of some strong-smelling liquid, which I gulp down. Inside I feel colder than before. *What have I done to get here?* Why am I surrounded by dream-like characters on a black winter night instead of the white nights of June? And why are there more stars above than I've ever seen at one time?

I'm starting to get frustrated even more than this morning when Aunt Roberta insisted we get up at some ridiculous hour to wait for what seemed like forever to enter the famous Hermitage Museum.

"I'm going out on a limb here and presuming you don't need a complete guided tour. You will, however, need a map," Aunt Roberta said after we passed through security. She's right; I really *don't* need a guide, especially with my aunt pointing out some of the most significant pieces, not to mention navigating us through halls that often open from one into another before hitting a confusing dead-end.

"A great deal of what you're seeing grew out Catherine the Second's huge collection," she pointed out, wisely assuming I've not been reading the guidebooks. I've visited Catherine Square twice, plopping on a bench to breathe in the lilacs' blossoms. A huge statue of a magnificent old woman—Empress Catherine the Great—dominates the center, pigeons settling placidly on her head. I'm uncertain what she accomplished to make her so "great," but perhaps she earned the moniker for her art collection.

My aunt's favorite section is the second floor, with its seventeenth- to twentieth-century Russian cultural and historical artifacts. This is just one of the residences of the tsars, so it's informally still called the Winter Palace. Although I cannot keep centuries or palaces straight, I had to admit this is fantastic.

"It does make you understand why they had a revolution." I waved expansively at all the gold, silk and satin furniture, cases of gems and jewelry, and other elaborate furnishings and accessories.

"Indeed. Now it belongs to the people of Russia. Succeeding tsars kept adding to Catherine's collection, and now this is one of the most magnificent art museums in the world—perhaps even *the* most."

I was hungry by early afternoon, so we made our way to a chaotic cafeteria on an upper floor. My aunt sipped a weak coffee, while I picked at boiled eggs, dark bread, and pickles.

"I can find my way back into the exhibits," I reassured Aunt Roberta, who'd started shaking her left foot—a motion I recognized as her impatience to be off. "Can we just meet somewhere later?"

"Let's say four o'clock by the cloak rooms."

"Done." We hugged before parting, and I watched her enthusiastically dodge around diners.

It took several attempts and various staircases to get where I was going: the lowest level open to the public. The Antiquities section was almost empty of tourists, perhaps due to dozens of huge wooden crates in assorted sizes that half blocked the corridors.

The wooden crates are what jar my memory.

No, I'm not in a coma; *This is how I got here*!

Recalling that initially I ignored the crates, opting to explore glass cases filled with prehistoric artifacts, I remember that when the mummies started to depress me, I moved into the ancient exhibits. I've not studied much about early Greece, Rome, or Egypt, but enjoy imagining those times.

The wooden crates also fascinated me. A few had packing slips laid loosely atop them—often in English: *Painting: Rembrandt* and then the size, or *Brass Basin: India, 8th century*. Since the corridor contained only one Chinese tour group, I continued to sneak peeks. The hinges and other metal parts were shiny, the birch or linden wood pristine. I recognized only one name besides *Fragile:* "Tsarskoe Selo." I knew it means "Tsar's Village," and it was on our itinerary for the last day.

"We have to see at least a couple other restored palaces," Aunt Roberta insisted yesterday. "I absolutely want you to see Catherine Palace at Tsarskoe Selo, although unfortunately the recreated Amber Room won't be unveiled to the public for a few years." She tapped a photo of a breathtaking robins-egg blue palace with golden cupolas and gold trim, and another of a room that sparkled with orange and gold hues from floor to ceiling.

After covering the antiquities section, I decided to head for the Hermitage's cloak room early and wait for my aunt.

Noticing a few large boxes pried open, revealing straw-like packing material, I leaned over one curiously. This crate had something partially sticking out, and after a hasty peripheral check to ensure none of the ubiquitous women who served as museum police were around, I recognized the top half of a statue.

Only the woman's head and shoulders were visible when I impulsively pushed aside a bit more straw. Based on the length of the box, she must've been nearly as tall as I am. Above her wide marble eyes something resembling a helmet perched atop short curls.

Closing my own eyes, I tentatively reached out and touched her, wondering how many hundreds—or thousands—of years ago—she'd graced someone's palace or park.

I allowed myself to run fingers gently over the carved marble curls, then the helmet's edge.

When I opened my eyes and attempted to remove my hand from the statue's smooth and cold marble whiteness, something started to quiver. *As if it were alive!*

Suddenly my whole hand—even my body—trembled.

Frigid air swirled in a silver gossamer haze. I blinked rapidly several times, but the statue, the crate, the exhibits . . . it had all dissolved!

Instead, behind me hovers the identical semi-circle of young women, each dressed in a similar ankle-length gown and cape with matching fur trim that gave them an old-fashioned appearance. In the museum, there was hardly anyone downstairs except the Chinese group wearing modern street clothes.

"It should be soon!" one of the women—more of a girl, actually— calls excitedly.

"I don't hear horses yet," another responds.

After a moment I realize that although I can understand them both, they're speaking another language. Unable to figure that out, I look around fruitlessly for the hallway I entered.

What in the hell has happened? I've been *here*—wherever that is— at least an hour. Where is that damn statue? I pull my "new" cloak tighter around me against the cold.

Again I notice the young women around me are well dressed and cheerful. Beyond them, tethered horses huddle in the courtyard of a long building. They neigh and sometimes prance in place. Except for a tiny house perched atop sleigh runners resting beside the horses, no cars or other vehicles are visible.

The girls, however, flutter back and forth between the soldiers and their fire like colorful moths alternately drawn to and away from the flames.

I think I am going to faint. From the cold. From the shock. From the fear.

CHAPTER 3

(SOPHIE) 1743-1744

At last Sophie grew taller, with gleaming chestnut hair and sparkling eyes that flashed from silver-grey to a penetrating blue, almost violet. Twice she was ordered to pose for formal portraits. Most renowned artists had mastered the art of flattering their subjects, and both canvases portrayed this adolescent as a budding beauty. Even if her nose showed up a bit too long or wide, her mouth rather narrow, and that pointed chin too prominent, each painting featured Sophie's penetrating eyes.

The portraits were shipped to the Russian empress, since suitable marital candidates for Grand Duke Peter were being sought from all the European royal houses.

Sophie had other matters on her mind: a potential romance, although at first she hardly considered it as such.

At twenty-four, Prince Georg Ludwig of Holstein-Gottorp, Johanna's youngest brother, was a dashing and outgoing cavalry officer.

Uncle and niece became re-acquainted first in Zerbst and then Hamburg at ceremonies to honor another of Johanna's brothers, Adolf, who'd assumed the Swedish throne after the orphan Karl Peter had renounced it to become the Russian heir.

It started innocently at one of many celebratory balls. "You're my absolute favorite niece," he told her. "And by far the most lovely."

When Johanna was otherwise engaged, Georg visited Sophie in her room. They talked, laughed, teased, played cards, and soon became almost inseparable.

At last Babet warned Johanna and Christian August, "Prince Georg interferes with your daughter's lessons."

"They tell me I cannot be alone with you," Georg complained bitterly. "If only you weren't my niece! We could marry!"

"But you *are* my uncle!"

"We could get a special dispensation from the Church!" he said earnestly. "I will give you time to think—to realize how happy we'll be together."

"As *friends*, not as . . . not as lovers."

"We *could* be," he insisted.

She was confused. Perhaps she should've expected this, rather than assume they'd simply been having a wonderful time together.

Uncle Georg increased the pressure. "I am lovesick!"

At last Sophie tentatively indicated she *might* be willing to accept his proposal.

Encouraged, Georg became even more ardent. He began to touch her brown curls, her neck, her lips. To steal kisses, which eventually she responded to without need of theft.

There were things about her body she recently had started feeling. A certain yearning for those kisses. A tingling from her eyebrows to her toes. Of course, she realized physical things happened between men and women; exactly what those were, she didn't know for certain. Her body only gave her hints.

"Perhaps," she admitted to Babet, "there are worse possibilities for my future."

"He is not for you. Trust me. I have watched you grow up. I know your mind, your intellect, perhaps a bit of your heart. This man is not only a close relative, but he would soon bore you."

"Do men and women have to be equal in intelligence? I mean, it makes sense, but no one has ever mentioned such a thing before. Although," she added thoughtfully, "I believe that Countess von Bentinck might say the same."

Babet nodded vigorously. "She would. And I cannot help believing, *ma cherie*, that you are destined for much, much more. Please do not let your young heart be turned by what you now imagine as love!"

Sophie admitted to herself that she really knew nothing about love. When she did dwell on the concept, she could not associate it with Georg.

On New Year's, a mail packet arrived with a seal that inspired Johanna to grab the letter and tear it open.

"Go!" she waved Sophie away when she tried to read over her shoulder, but not fast enough to prevent her daughter from spying her own name.

Both parents hurriedly retired to another room.

Three days later, no one would discuss the contents of the correspondence, and a flurry of successors with royal seals followed.

The first letter seemed to hum from its all too visible hiding place. Sophie scanned the French penmanship quickly, her mouth dropping.

It contained an invitation from the Russian empress for Johanna and Sophie to present themselves at her court—the implication being that Sophie was invited to renew the acquaintance of the new grand duke. She struggled to recall the unimpressive orphan boy she'd met nearly five years ago.

Excitement surged through her. She knew Peter Ulrich had recently been pronounced sole heir to Empress Elizabeth's new crown, but the thought of him as a potential suitor all these years since their meeting had never crossed her mind.

When Sophie confronted her about the letter, Johanna proffered a litany of reasons they shouldn't go: it was too far, too dangerous, the government unstable, the roads treacherous, too many other noble girls were competing, and what about Johanna's brother's proposal?

Sophie seized on the last one. "As if I care about Uncle Georg. He means nothing to me."

Johanna dismissed all of Sophie's arguments, uncharacteristically concluding, "This is something we must discuss with your father. It will be up to him to make the decision."

For perhaps the first time in her married life, Johanna tossed a verdict to her own husband, as if it were a firecracker too hot to handle.

Christian August proved reluctant, weakly protesting the distance of the journey but never mentioning his own exclusion from the invitation. "My main concern," he at last told his daughter privately, "is your eternal salvation."

"What do you mean?"

"You know these pagans believe in Popish ideas. If you're selected, they will undoubtedly require you to abandon the Lutheran faith. I cannot bear the thought of my precious daughter damned forever."

"I will never abandon my faith," she promised.

She had other things on her mind, including her ability to impress the empress, let alone the older version of that rude little boy she barely recalled.

If news of the decision that they *would* go to Russia pleased Sophie, it positively energized Johanna, who, despite her earlier reluctance, launched into full-time preparations. Hour after hour she barked orders, dispatched letters, oversaw packing of trunks, tried on gowns, and sent everyone scurrying on errands.

Sophie quietly packed what she had: three dresses, a couple chemises, stockings, and handkerchiefs. The only indulgence permitted was a new pair of gloves. Her father's brother presented her a farewell gift of a bolt of silver and blue brocade. Sophie couldn't help imagining the impression it would create unfurling in glittering folds as she glided across an imaginary dance floor.

While her mother scurried about, Sophie sat quietly amidst the chaos, immersed in books that would have to be left behind.

On January 10, Sophie said her farewells. They'd been commanded to tell everyone they were traveling only to the Winter Carnival in Berlin. Babet suspected something, yet no matter how hard she tried to pry it out of her charge, she might as well have attempted to yank a reluctant pearl from its shell.

At the last minute, Sophie could no longer hold herself aloof. Breaking into tears, she hugged Babet as if they never would meet again.

As the carriage pulled away, the clip-clop of hooves seemed to echo her past, a period she might be forced to spend a lifetime forgetting. Still, she was eager to depart, and it was not in her nature to look back.

At King Frederick II's Berlin palace, Sophie sat beside the handsome new monarch. She wore a borrowed, oversized gown, as Johanna had spent the entire clothing allowance sent from the empress on herself.

Surprisingly, the young king recalled her well. "Do you remember what you did when my father visited you?" he asked. "You were only four!"

"What did she do?" a guest asked curiously.

"His late majesty showed up in Anhalt and met this wisp of a child. But when it came time for her to kiss his hem, she could not reach it."

"What then?"

"She turned to her parents and complained! Since she couldn't quite reach his hem, she demanded—and loudly—to know why the king was 'too poor to afford a longer coat!'"

The guests all laughed at the temerity of this poised young lady who'd had the nerve to be rude to the king no one had liked.

Throughout the remainder of the multi-course dinner, the king quizzed Sophie rigorously, as if probing her intellect. While she struggled to answer wisely and fully, his penetrating grey eyes never left her face.

When the conversation evolved into literature, the fourteen-year-old shone. She blushed at the king's gallant compliments regarding her insights. Frederick began to gesticulate with his thin white hands, their minds meeting in witty exchanges that turned his eyes to blue fire. Sophie sparkled back in the afterglow of his praise.

At the end of the meal, he referred to her as "Loves and Graces," and she left the dining room pleased with herself.

"I promise," she told her father as they parted at Schwedt, "that I will always be your humble, obedient, and faithful daughter. I will be worthy of your love and your faith in me."

"And of our religion?" he asked earnestly.

"Father, you know I will keep our Lutheran faith."

"I pray so, my daughter. There will be much pressure on you to adopt pagan ways."

He sent her off with pages and pages of notes, instructions, and exonerations to keep their faith.

Although she clung to him and wept when they parted, she dared not look back. She must proceed on her Great Adventure, as she secretly dubbed the journey, and pray only that she would eventually return safely at least to visit the nest that had been her home.

The convoy of four coaches carrying a cook, valet, chambermaids, and footmen lumbered the first couple weeks across the frozen plains, stony ditches, and bumpy ravines of East Prussia and Pomerania. Roads deteriorated to almost impassable, ruts bouncing and jolting them until their teeth rattled. Sophie discovered new bruises almost daily. Fierce winds blew ice pellets in her eyes and only woolen scarves protected her face from frostbite.

At first they encountered larger villages where they could count on a warm room, roasted fowl, and cups of chocolate. Post stations offered fresh horses and sometimes meager provisions. As distances increased between villages, smaller outposts boasted a single inn with a gigantic stove in a common parlor. The stove, usually built of hollow earthenware tiles in the shape of ordinary flowerpots, provided extra foot warmth. Sophie joined all ranks of merchants, peasants, and maids seeking shelter as they stuck dirt-covered feet into the tiles' apertures.

Curled gratefully in the heat emanating from the latest inn's stove, Sophie barely heard the screaming babies after a while. Older children sniffled and coughed from their huddles beneath straw, resembling an ever-moving bin of lumpy potatoes. No longer did she notice the sounds and smells emanating from the inn's other indoor occupants: dogs, chickens, cats, goats, even pigs. She even managed to ignore the howling wind blasting through the roof holes and the uncomfortably close sound of squeaking rats. She was always too relieved to abandon the coach and stretch out, even if it meant sleeping on the floor and scratching all night at the fleas residing in the blankets. On a good evening, a featherbed would be drawn up for her beside the stove.

By the third and fourth weeks, there were no more provincial inns. Nothing except relentless, bitter wind—teeth of the storms threatening to bite them. Sophie's toes swelled to sausage size, her feet grew nearly frostbitten, her skin developed chilblains. At every stop thereafter she needed to be carried in and out of the carriage.

At the worst ice-clogged river crossings, they loaded the coaches on ferries and poled across; Sophie tried to avoid looking below at the ice, splintered into chunks the size and shape of pancakes that hinted at cold black depths below.

When there were no ferries, they often faced hours-long delays. "What is going on?" Sophie asked the first time this happened.

"We await fishermen to cross the ice and see if it will bear the weight of the carriages," Johanna said casually.

Horrified, Sophie looked out from her side. "Why would anyone risk his life that way?"

"It's their job, daughter. Close that door before I get frostbite."

As the small convoy rattled northward along the Baltic's mist-shrouded shores, peasants wrapped in rags ventured out into the frigid air to stare, often seeming to mutter heathen prayers accompanied by indecipherable hand motions.

Sophie, enfolded in thin blankets, pulled her scarves tighter and attempted not to dwell on air whistling relentlessly through the roof and floorboards. On broken axles periodically requiring long delays to fix. On howling wolves in the distance. On Johanna's incessant whining. In the case of the latter, she frequently pretended to be asleep, wondering if this trip were too reckless, if her mother too ambitious, she herself too impulsive at making this horrible journey. Above all, she wondered what awaited her.

By February, she began to look forward even more to leaving the carriage late at night. Something spectacular had appeared to brighten the skies far above silver-gray marshes: an enormous comet glittering the ice fields with diamonds. From the comet trailed a dozen rays, then six more lights that fanned upward to form a massive peacock's tail in the pre-dawn sky.

"It's a portent of disaster," the drivers commented fearfully.

Sophie dismissed this as nonsense. For her the celestial spectacle promised not only radiance piercing darkness, but an illumination of the mind—and the promise of a starlit future.

Even heavy snow couldn't dampen their joy at being on the last leg of their journey.

Just past the city of Mitau on the Russian border, a six-man military escort materialized like knights out of the whiteness. A colonel appeared in a magical white swirl, surrounded by garrison and regiment officers bearing greetings from Empress Elizabeth. Transferred into a new carriage, Sophie and Johanna rode in much more comfort.

In Riga, it was if someone had waved a magic wand and created a fairytale. Their royal carriage was met by a procession of dignitaries, booming cannons, banging kettle drums, and ringing church bells. As the princesses swept from room to room in a sumptuous castle, trumpeters and buglers announced their movements and guardsmen snapped to attention. From comfortable chairs, they held audiences for a never-ending parade of well-wishers who kissed their hands repeatedly.

Sophie was astounded to learn they'd changed calendars. Although Prussia had long since adopted the Gregorian calendar, Russia still utilized the older Julian Calendar, now eleven days behind the one she had left. They entered Riga in early February, but didn't depart until late *January*. How fortunate, she thought, to gain nearly two free, extra weeks of her life.

As ten horses galloped away toward St. Petersburg at a fiery speed, they did so in far different circumstances than those in which the princesses had left Germany. Even in ever-thickening snow, the horses pulled a heavy scarlet imperial sledge ornamented in silver brocade and lined with fur walls. The sleigh and its accoutrements, designed by Peter the Great and now used by Empress Elizabeth, resembled a snug miniature house complete with stove and windows that raced along on runners.

Swathed in costly sable courtesy of the empress, the two princesses relaxed on quilted featherbeds covered in fur-lined chintz blankets. They snuggled against satin and silk cushions, feet blessedly warmed by heated stones. Candle lanterns swung from the roof so they could read and the Tatar whose only job was to prepare coffee could find his way.

Between their compartment and the coachman, a snug area for storing luggage served as an area occupied by chattering gentlemen by day and giggling maids by night. The rest of the great entourage and its array of sleighs carried a squadron from the grand duke's regiment, a detachment of the Livonian regiment, city and military officials from Riga, and dozens of noble, magisterial, business, and military representatives. Officers galloped alongside. Close to the end of the trip, they were joined by a detachment of foot soldiers and a squadron of cavalry.

Traveling at three times their previous speed, they could barely hear the tinkling of the the sleigh bells or cracking of ice, making the trip in three days. They stopped only to take meals or change horses. The "house" was so high they had to take lessons in how to crawl in and out of both the sledge and the beds, usually feet first.

"Princess Sophia . . ."

"It is Sophie!" Johanna leaned over to correct the maid. "Not Sophia."

"Ah, yes. In German, of course," one gentleman clarified. "But in Russian Sophie is pronounced Sophia, as it is in the Orthodox religion. Expect, Your Highness, to be called that from now on, or at least throughout your visit."

"*So-fee-a*. I like it!" It was her given name, but no one ever used it. "It is a lovely Russian name. I shall like to have a new name." *Not only a new calendar, but a new name for my new life.*

She believed she was ready for what she fervently hoped would be a fresh beginning. As much as she loved and already missed her father, baby sister, surviving brother, and especially Babet, she couldn't imagine returning as a failure if she were rejected by the empress, the grand duke, or the Russians themselves. She resolved to become one of *them*. To become Sophia, not Sophie.

CHAPTER 4

(MARIA)

The women beside me resemble costumed animators who hang around key spots in St. Petersburg, posing for photographs in centuries-ago finery for rubles, euros, or dollars. Yet these are, I suspect, not impostors. The cold air isn't the only thing causing me to shiver uncontrollably.

In the distance bells ring louder, blending with the unmistakable noise of dozens of horses' hooves pounding the snowpack.

"Quickly, ladies. We must greet the princesses inside the palace," the oldest of my three mysterious companions urges in what I *think* is Russian. Disoriented, I hesitate until the woman again nudges me: "You, too, Maria."

In dreams I am always *me*—not someone totally different but with my name. Did I fall? Pass out at the Hermitage? I've never been unconscious, let alone in a coma. Which is it? Once more I run through possibilities. I *know* it has something to do with the statue I touched in the Hermitage. Not that that makes more sense.

I feel frozen to the packed snow. Then, as I start to pull away for the second time despite having no idea where to run, an arm snatches me back.

"*Davai*! Let's go!" another lady insists.

Deciding to play along, as if I'm an improvisational actress, I yield to the hands reached out to me and follow everyone around the corner. At least I've stopped shivering.

We scurry inside the palace, which appears to be located on the Neva River in the same spot I remember, yet looks much different than the Hermitage I thought I was visiting. A wide staircase also lacks the gold and white grandeur of the one I climbed in the former Winter Palace barely an hour ago.

The four of us decoratively arrange ourselves like flowers at the foot of this staircase. A steward or gentleman-in-waiting hastily takes our cloaks and fur hats. Beneath outer garments, we each wear an elegant gown, my own, I realize, of burgundy silk.

Gentlemen in all manner of uniforms jostle with us for position at the foot of this enormous, albeit somewhat plain staircase.

The noise grows deafening as a convoy of horse-drawn sleds, sleighs, and carriages approaches. Suddenly the sound of sleigh bells slows, replaced by salvoes of cannon fire from across the river that reverberate through the palace foyer.

The first sleigh, a huge scarlet and silver brocaded contraption pulled by ten sweating horses, stops at the door. One would have to leap to get down, but two handsomely gowned women alight almost gracefully. The older one wears an air of self-satisfaction. Perfectly coiffed blonde hair wreathes her face beneath a fur hat, and she smiles graciously but coldly as she reaches the wooden planks paving the entrance. She sweeps through the crowd, immediately surrounded by gentlemen hastening to greet her.

The second passenger—a slip of a girl—descends more carefully and appears slightly overwhelmed by the chaos. Yet she bears herself proudly, standing tall in a silver gown and fur wrap and taking everything in with sharp eyes.

My companions nudge me forward, and I follow their lead as we curtsy dramatically to this younger arrival. She makes a quick motion with her right hand as if to dismiss us, and we rise in harmony. Amidst a flurry of hand-kissing from scores of gentlemen and many more curtsies from other ladies, the girl makes her way up the staircase, surrounded by the maids or ladies in waiting I deduce we are supposed to be.

As the women introduce themselves to the girl they address as Princess Sophia, I learn our retinue consists of Irina, by appearances the oldest; Natasha, the youngest, with sparkling eyes and hair the shade of corn silk; Katrina, who wears a violet gown to match her eyes and seems to fight a frown, and me.

In a high-ceiling room with a massive bed and two marble fireplaces, the four of us apparently are entrusted with waiting on the princess. Irina produces a fur blanket and settles Sophia in a velvet-covered chair, Katrina begins to fuss with the princess's long brown curls, and Natasha scurries off only to return with a pot of what appears to be coffee or tea. I merely twist my hands and wish for the muff back to hide my nervousness.

"You must be exhausted," Irina croons in French.

The princess shakes her curls emphatically. "No, I am exhilarated to be here. Yet it has been a long journey, and I'd like time to sleep. They tell me we might be off again within a day or two—all of us."

"To the empress's court, Your Highness?" Irina asks.

"Yes. That is where Her Gracious Majesty currently resides." She has, I realize, been speaking in French, too, but with a trace of an unfamiliar accent. Maybe Polish? German?

After a few sips of what smells like coffee, she asks casually, "Tell me what the grand duke is like. I've met him once when we were ten and eleven. Just children."

"He is fun," Katrina says finally.

"He plays games all day and night," Natasha adds.

A tiny crease appears between Princess Sophia's deep-set blue eyes. "He has time for such frivolities in a busy court?"

"Oh, the empress takes care of state business. She and her ministers, of course. Grand Duke Peter has a lot of time to himself," Katrina tells her.

"He's very involved in military affairs," Irina puts in.

"How so?" Sophia leans forward, eyes brightening and the crease gone.

"Well," Irina says slowly, "He has an entire regiment of his own!"

"Does he go into battle with them? I'm not as well-informed as I should be on the war strategies of what I hope will be my new country."

"Oh, they don't fight. They just practice. Every day they drill," Katrina says. She glances sideways at the others, and I sense an uncomfortable undercurrent passing between the women.

The crease reappears. "They drill to go to war?"

"Who can say, Your Highness. Russia is a mighty country, but the empress would like it even mightier. The situation with Sweden goes on. Perhaps she will order the grand duke to battle, although he is still young," Natasha suggests brightly.

For a half hour Sophia grills us, yet not in a way we notice as being unusual or even particularly nosy. I understand now that she has arrived in Russia potentially to marry the grand duke, who is apparently the nephew of the empress—whose name I still do not know. I am a little befuddled, as no mention has been made of the four Romanov sisters and I am quite certain no would-be fiancée arrived in Russia to marry the hemophiliac heir, Alexei.

I'm certain I fainted, perhaps even slipped on the glossy museum floor after touching the statue and then hit my head. Of course, things do not need to make perfect sense, historically or otherwise, if I'm unconscious. This is the only possible explanation. I resolve not to panic, to at least live with all this until I awaken.

After tucking Princess Sophia into bed for a nap, the four of us reach our own room—smaller and hung with brocades and tapestries only slightly less attractive than those in the princess's quarters. A few resemble those I saw in the Hermitage, but these are bright, with much richer threads.

Giggling, my companions slip out of their gowns down to some sort of bloomers, which Natasha refers to as her chemise. I follow slowly, glancing all the time at my body to ensure it's the same one I've always had. I half expect to see it changed, but sure enough, there is the scar I received during my brief stint with fencing lessons—and the tiny mole on my wrist.

The only one who looks at me oddly is Irina. "Your French is much more fluent than it used to be."

"*Spasibo*," I murmur. "*Merci*." I cannot explain to anyone that my parents, the Meekhofs, raised me almost bilingual. Of course, not *this* Maria's parents, whoever or wherever they are or were.

As we climb into two four-poster beds, I presume I'll fall asleep and awaken in some Russian hospital—or my hotel room. Or perhaps still passed out on the floor in the Hermitage's lower level.

Lying beside Natasha for our "pre-dinner rest," I try to recall everything I've absorbed, albeit unwillingly, from years of half listening to Aunt Roberta's conversations and lectures. I vividly recall her commenting our first week here on the irony that Peter, a thoroughly masculine giant who had his own son murdered and his first wife and later his own sister locked in a convent, ended up leaving the country to a series of women who ruled for nearly a century. First his second wife, then . . . I don't know. All I can remember is Catherine the Great, and maybe that is, indeed, who we are going to Moscow to see. And if so, I am half thrilled, half afraid. Because that would put me all the way back to an earlier century—the seventeenth? Eighteenth? At least I will have an interested listener when I awaken and recount all of this to Aunt Roberta.

Irina awakens me, standing over the bed bearing a plate with sausage, a hunk of cheese, and bread. "Sleeping Lovely, it is time to rise for the princess's retinue. You've slept through mealtime already."

I eat hungrily, unable to recall eating in a dream before, let alone tasting it.

Whistling through flimsy walls and floorboards confirms it is indeed still winter, not the lovely June of the White Nights where I belong.

Slipping into yet a different gown with the assistance of a servant, I follow Irina, Natasha, and Katrina through high-ceiling corridors arranged in circles. They apparently know their way; I make a half-hearted attempt to memorize our route. Within minutes we arrive at the door of the room we left a few hours earlier.

Sophia is dressed in yellow and black satin that sets off her almost ivory skin. I've seen women in magazines with skin that pale, but hers appears to be without benefit of powders or other makeup. Two seamstresses carry armfuls of gowns in and out of the room, occasionally pausing to take measurements or fuss with Princess Sophia's gown. Another woman fastens those shiny brown curls into a pile atop her head. The princess appears invigorated.

"Come in, ladies, and cheer me. I am somewhat nervous, as we are to be summoned soon. To dinner, I believe, and then to the palace grounds for this evening's entertainment."

So we "cheer" her up, our sole function seemingly to entertain and cater to Sophia's needs. "Do you play cards?" Irina asks her.

Without answering, Sophia commands a footman outside the door to bring another table into the apartment.

We spend the next hour playing an unfamiliar game with giant paper cards decorated on one side with lovely paintings. I toss out the thin cards more confidently each time my turn comes. Sophia seems to delight in the fact that all of us are losing, so I don't struggle too hard to figure out the rules, just how not to break them.

A knock announces the arrival of a heaping platter of pastries and an elegantly designed silver pot.

"Does Her Highness drink tea?" I ask.

Sophia smiles at me. "Ah, the tall and beautiful maid of honor does speak. Tea? When one can get such delicious coffee from the New World and British colonies?"

"Of course," I stammer, feeling flushed. The New World? Isn't that what they once called the Americas? Why not just say so? I know the answer even as I formulate the question: this dream is taking place *before* the American Revolution, which means I am unconsciously in the seventeenth or perhaps the eighteenth century.

During a lengthy, elegant banquet consisting of some dishes I prefer not to identify, I watch Sophia carefully. She seems as awed as I am with golden spoons and plates edged with precious gems until her mother mutters something to her in German. I've seen the younger princess exhibit the same wonder when she fingered her satin bed-sheets. She appears enchanted with everything around her, and her genuine delight makes us all smile.

The evening's entertainment turns out to be a courtyard full of elephants—a gift several years ago from the Shah of Persia. Fourteen of the magnificent animals pirouette and lumber gracefully from stool to stool, performing circus-like acts. One, draped in a silk tent, elicits oohs and aahs from the elegantly dressed audience.

An enthralled Sophia loudly applauds each time an elephant sweeps a performer up into its massive trunk or nudges a colorful ball. I sympathize with the elephants who've been captured from hot jungles to be reluctant entertainers on stage in a frozen country. We're all stranded where we don't belong. Unlike the elephants, who appear destined to live out their lives in captivity, I at least expect to awaken or come to and return to my own life.

The elephant parade is followed by a show of dancing bears in ballerina-like tutus who do not appear quite as miserable as the elephants must be. Perhaps I should try to be more like the bears and adapt to this situation. Whatever it may be.

Bundled in furs, we walk along the Neva River, gazing in wonder at giant ice hills fashioned in a variety of shapes and apparently constructed for the carnival season. I sense Sophia's excitement as people stand up and, wearing something resembling skates strapped to boots, descend the ice hills at such breakneck speed. Others slide swiftly down the precipitous slopes seated on some sort of trays.

No one protests when Sophia pleads to take a ride on the ice toboggan, and her squeals and giggles make us all laugh.

"I would very much like one of those trays," the princess mutters after she reaches the bottom.

And most likely you will have one, I think. Whoever this short, determined girl—barely above five feet by my estimate when she stands beside me—wants, I have a feeling she will get.

There's no point in dwelling on my past—or future, to be more precise. Life goes on at a speedy pace despite my discomfort. Before I can adjust to where I am, let alone accustom myself to the inconveniences of centuries old clothing plus drafty floors and walls, the ladies and I are packing—and helping Sophia gather what she brought with her plus the new gowns gifted by the empress.

Preparations for our trip to Moscow create a flurry of activity. Servants and nobles alike scurry throughout the palace and load things into a formation of at least twenty-five sleighs and carriages rivaling the parade in which Sophia and her mother Princess Johanna arrived.

Amid the chaos, Sophia obtains permission for the five of us and a contingent of guards and nobility to take short carriage rides around St. Petersburg in the days before we depart. Excited at this potential opportunity to discover exactly where—and when—I might be, I hope the city will provide clues.

To Princess Sophia's and our delight, what appears to be a winter carnival is still going on. Booths selling everything from hats to candies line the streets of what I recognize as a more subdued version of St. Petersburg's main avenue: Nevsky Prospekt. One of the guards, however, points it out to the visitors as Great Perspective Road. Beyond the wooden booths, ladies gowned in a rainbow of colors laugh and shriek on giant swing sets. Bears wearing silly hats prance on leashes.

More ice slides do a booming business in daredevil rides.

On one tour, our carriage pulls up at what a hefty countess pronounces a military barracks, although the inside boasts only tiers of wooden bunks. I hold my muff over my nose to mute the odors of sweat and stale beer. In rapid-fire French, the countess recounts the activities that took place here when "our great empress took her rightful place on the throne."

Sophia seems beside herself with excitement. "Tell me, can we retrace the route the empress took to claim the palace?"

This prompts a running commentary by three noblemen who constantly interrupt one another with murmurs of "Long live our Little Mother Elizabeth Petrovna!"

Engrossed in listening to the countess's tale of how Elizabeth and the grenadiers of the Preobrazhensky regiment assumed control of the country (apparently only three years earlier), I don't realize at first that this is indeed the eighteenth century. Wasn't Elizabeth Peter the Great's granddaughter? Or perhaps daughter or niece? But there is no Aunt Roberta to consult. No books in which to look up dates. No possibility of a Google search.

The mud streets stink of the putrefying corpses of dead horses no one apparently has been ordered to move. As we skirt the edges of what *should be* Palace Square, I note what I suspected on my initial "arrival": it is merely an empty field framed by a forest. And most of the pastel wooden and stucco buildings resemble painted, wooden facsimiles of their future forms.

Other buildings—most notably the massive St. Isaac's Cathedral with its impossible-to-miss copper dome—are missing entirely. And as we conclude our little expedition, I know beyond a shadow of a doubt I'm looking at an older wooden version of the Winter Palace. Stonemasons fill the air with noise; only piles of timber and stones mark the riverbank spot where the Hermitage stood before I fell into this dream. This alternate place. This very different time.

I'm somewhat nervous to discover we will travel in a contraption like the one in which the princesses arrived. It resembles a flimsy six-windowed mobile home perched on runners that will be pulled over snow and ice by ten horses.

The enormous interior, however, is heaped with feather beds, furs, rugs, and damask or velvet pillows. Since we're expected to lie down for the journey, Sophia obligingly demonstrates how to climb into the feather beds feet first. Servants supply a charcoal brazier and heated stones, as well as replenish supplies filling cupboards built into the sleigh's sides. A candle-lit lantern hangs suspended from the top so "we can play cards at night," according to Sophia.

At first it's difficult to get accustomed to the slight swaying and even jostling of the sleigh house—which everyone calls a *sledge*—making me yearn for the invention of trains. Then the motion smooths out with a pace almost as exhilarating as a roller coaster. We're told we must travel the equivalent of nearly four hundred miles, stopping every dozen or so for fresh horses to replace those slick with sweat, froth bubbling from their lips.

Sometimes all thirty sleighs in our retinue reach an alarming pace over roads illuminated by peasants tending bonfires. At one post-station half buried in snow drifts where they offer tea and steaming fish soup, I discover that the road we're sliding on was built from giant tree trunks!

Natasha, whose youth belies her knowledge of everything going on behind the scenes, whispers it is at Princess Johanna's insistence that we proceed with such haste so we can arrive in time for Grand Duke Peter's sixteenth birthday. She points to the man tasked with serving tea, who has mere minutes to dash in and out of our sledge to serve us at each stop.

Ahead lies only glittering white, a world seemingly coated with diamonds, interrupted occasionally by a pack of wolves staring at us through gem-like eyes. Seeing them, I'm relieved that royal guards gallop alongside.

Despite heavy veils to protect our faces from frostbite, Princess Johanna frets loudly that her eyes are freezing shut. "There are even icicles in my nose!" she nearly screams soon after, and a lady assigned to her hurries to cover the princess's face with furs already pulled up to her neck.

"I cannot imagine how she survived the journey from Prussia," Natasha giggles. "She must have driven everyone in their entourage crazy!"

When we stop to change horses, we also partake of tasteless dinners at roadside manor houses or, while the tiny chamber pots in the sledge get emptied, we're permitted to climb out to squat behind a tree. As I discovered days ago, no one seems to know about toilet paper. For that matter, I was never given anything resembling underpants!

At times small groups of people often wrapped in rags surround us, cross themselves, and sometimes reach out to touch Sophia's fur coat.

Dismayed to find three coachmen unfastening one of our horses and pushing it onto the side of the road, I realize the poor animal has dropped dead in its harness, undoubtedly from our breakneck speed and/or the extreme cold. Remembering a few seemingly unscheduled and brief stops in which we stayed inside the sleigh, I wonder how many other horses have been—and will be—sacrificed to our journey.

On the second night, our sledge careens around a corner too

tightly, clipping a small house in a dark village minus the usual bonfires. Several cries, a shaky stop, and the appearance of two lanterns illuminate the scene. The accident appears to have been caused by a heavy iron bar that supports the roof being knocked off the sleigh, seriously wounding two grenadiers.

For two hours we huddle around shivering while Princess Johanna insists she, too, is injured and even dying. Her ladies laboriously remove each layer of clothing and then hasten to rub brandy on her unbruised neck and arm.

Sophia's mother, who, as Natasha correctly pegged her, is a haughty royal pain, does not appear to be hurt, yet makes angry protests to the contrary. "Perhaps the furs protected me," she finally concedes after being thoroughly examined.

She seems angry when the attention aimed at her ebbs, making a face as though she drank curdled cream.

We reboard the repaired sledge, and the convoy moves on. One of the injured men does not reappear.

At our final stop before Moscow, the drivers hook up sixteen fresh horses to speed up our lead sledge. Each horse wears a glittering harness and tack, as well as a feather plume on its head.

Sophia professes herself too nervous to eat. There is little time for it anyway. Instead, a contingent of courtiers urges us to dress in our best dinner clothes, as "Her Majesty is eagerly awaiting your arrival."

Directed to a sledge not far behind us, we obediently rummage through shelves and struggle to change gowns. Sophia, emerging with the help of several maids from another sledge, appears in the twilight gowned in floor-length rose and silver; a single ruby adorns her neck. "The dress was selected personally by Her Majesty," she says in wonder. To protect her from the freezing sleet and wind, attendants bundle the princess in a heavy sable coat decorated with gold brocade and a fur collar; we ladies also receive furs to cover our court gowns.

For this final dash, the empress's envoy perches on the box and urges the driver to utmost speed. Even so, for some reason we've been instructed not to enter Moscow until after dark. Nearly three days have passed, and I've only caught snatches of sleep and picked at the picnic-like lunches provided for us when there was no place to stop. Although my younger self did see Moscow once, I'm curious as to what it looks like now. I risk holding on to one of the cupboards to peer out our windows.

Flaming torches and Chinese lanterns swing from the city gates and steeples of what seem to be hundreds of churches. "There are a thousand churches in Moscow," Natasha comments behind me.

"Forty times forty," Irina corrects her.

"Everything is illuminated for the grand duke's birthday tomorrow," Natasha continues.

"You've been here before?" I ask without thinking.

"Of course, silly girl. The empress has dragged us here multiple times on her pilgrimages. You may have been at court since you were a little girl, but you cannot have forgotten so soon how miserable our lives have been with her. What is wrong with you?" Natasha whispers, so the mother and daughter princesses cannot hear us, although they are speaking urgently to one another in incomprehensible German.

"Our lives have taken a turn for the better, dear Maria, don't you agree?" Irina rejoins the conversation.

"Absolutely," Natasha jumps back in. "The empress still terrifies me, and I fear she may order us back to *her* service if she does not find favor with Sophia. And just remember all the work! This little princess arrived here with barely three gowns of her own. The empress has nearly fifteen thousand, not to mention five thousand pairs of shoes. Don't you recall the time she ordered Katrina and Irina to count them all?"

"Fifteen thousand dresses?" I must have misheard her.

"Nothing is too good for our beloved Peter the Great's daughter, although she is a very vain woman," Katrina nearly hisses quietly. "Let us pray to the mother of God that we do please Princess Sophia Augustus of Anhalt-Zerbst, this girl of only fourteen. I could use some relaxation, if you know what I mean."

I don't know.

Despite the gleam from torchlights and lanterns, it is difficult to judge an older Moscow at night. We race past opulent stone mansions interspersed with flimsy shacks leaning like paper doll sets. I don't see the magnificent Kremlin towers and churches I recall.

We stop in front the ornate, timbered Annenhof Palace, which is, as Irina comments absentmindedly, also called the Golovin Palace and located along the Yauza River. None of this means anything to me; however, if I had a pen I could write it all down for my aunt, who I miss.

By now I've mastered a method of slithering off and then half leaping, half dropping, to land on my feet. Before completely recovering our balance, we're led up a white and gold staircase illuminated by a massive chandelier. An entire court has lined up to greet the princesses. After a dizzying array of salutes and introductions, we're escorted down glaringly lit halls so warm I want to remove both fur and cloak. Only Princess Sophia seems nonplussed by the sudden change from frigid temperature to stultifying heat as we're whisked into her prepared apartments.

Walls gleam in various shades of green, blue, and yellow. A giant tiled stove gives off almost oppressive heat. Before we get completely wrested out of our furs, one of the doors bursts open. Princess Johanna, still unpinning her traveling headdress, nearly pricks herself trying to rise and then curtsy.

A lanky, slightly unkempt boy with a lock of sandy hair across his face strides inside in what is clearly a breach of court etiquette. He is almost ugly, with heavy lips, pimpled skin, and pale, sallow complexion.

Both princesses curtsy nearly to the floor, and after the briefest pause, we all follow suit.

"I would've harnessed myself to your sledge if it would have made you arrive faster!" the newcomer exclaims in a breathless, high-pitched voice.

Two uniformed gentlemen accompany the boy I now realize is Grand Duke Peter, who again introduces the Prince of Hesse-Homburg—the empress's aide-de-camp who ushered us to our apartments. The shorter, jolly one is Count Lestocq: Elizabeth's advisor and physician, who steps forward and with a grin announces, "Her Majesty is beside herself waiting for your arrival. She will see you immediately."

After a bit of hesitation, Irina motions us to trail behind her, and we barely keep up as we bustle through one after another low-ceiling rooms. Within seconds, it seems, we're stopped at a small antechamber opening into another room into which the princesses proceed without us. As we peer curiously inside, we see the two of them bow from the waist and curtsy deeply to one of the most remarkable women I've ever seen.

The empress, impressively tall so any extra weight flatters her, stands in her chambers. Even at this distance, I can detect her lapis lazuli eyes, slightly upturned nose, and haughty yet benevolent smile. She must be in her thirties at least, but heavy makeup covers a still youthful face and nearly flawless bosom. Wearing a wide pannier or hoop beneath her silver taffeta and gold lace dress, she has enhanced the goddess-like effect with a heavy sprinkling of diamonds in almost black hair. A tall black feather rises upright from her head.

After kissing the princesses on both cheeks, she steps back and eyes them speculatively yet fondly. It is the first time I've seen Johanna anything but dismissive or frivolous. She removes her gloves and fervently kisses the empress's hand, gushing in French, "I have come to lay at Your Majesty's feet feelings of the greatest gratitude for the benefactions which your bounty has heaped upon my family."

"It is little compared to what I should like to do," the empress, obviously pleased, replies. "Your blood is as dear to me as my own." She scrutinizes Johanna's features once more, raising her etched-on black eyebrows, before reaching out instead to hug Sophia. Then she leads them deeper into her bedchamber while we wait but cannot see or hear.

Several minutes later, the empress rushes out, sweeping past us as we hastily and awkwardly attempt to curtsy.

"Her Majesty is overcome," the count announces after a long wait. "She must be alone for a few moments after witnessing the remarkable resemblance of Princess Johanna to her brother, the empress's fated fiancé."

"He died of the pox during their betrothal, you know," Katrina whispers.

We hear Sophia tell her mother, "She is much more beautiful and magnificent than the portrait I have of her on my snuffbox!"

Shortly thereafter the teary-eyed but breathtaking empress sweeps back into the room and chatters gaily, promising the princesses they shall have their own courts, and that while she would love to join them for dinner, the grand duke will do the honors.

"I realize you are not yet Orthodox," the empress says kindly, "but my court cannot partake of any meat or anything made from warm-blooded animals during Lent. My ladies and I are accustomed to dining modestly at this holy time, although I want you to rest and get plenty to eat after what is always an unpleasant journey. Thus I am going to instruct the chefs to prepare meat and cheese dishes specifically and only for you."

And just like that they are dismissed. It as if the sun has retreated behind clouds.

Throughout dinner I'm distracted by history—or attempts to recall it. The grand duke is foolish and childish, that much is immediately clear. Princess Sophia, by contrast, acts far more mature and intelligent for her age. Are these two to rule Russia someday? And if so, how can the princess even stand the sight of him? Since we sat at dinner, except for kissing Sophia's hand and consulting her on wine preference, Peter's done nothing except complain about Russia: its customs, church, weather, language (which apparently neither of them speak), and lack of decent German food. Sophia stifles a yawn, either due to three days of little sleep in a bouncing sleigh or her potential fiancé's boring conversation.

The only time Peter acts animated—more in the manner of a ten-year-old than a teenager—is when he discusses his vast collection of soldiers, which turn out to be mostly made of tin! I find myself nodding off over something resembling beef, and can hardly wait to get to our room. As he chatters on and on about regiments and artillery, Sophia alone appears interested. I suspect she finds it all as tedious as we do but is much too polite or well-bred to show it. If being an empress or a tsaritsa one day will require the ability to interact with any number of bores and show-offs, she will indeed make a fine consort.

I suspect Grand Duke Peter seldom gets so much attention from those not paid to listen to him, and certainly cannot imagine the majestic empress putting up with his prattling. But then, it is this poor fourteen-year-old girl who is apparently destined to marry the disgusting little boy, and I find myself praying for her sake that he grows up quickly.

Again we ladies share beds almost next to the princesses' rooms, and we squabble briefly for the position nearest the stove. Irina, of course, wins. I'm so exhausted after days of traveling that I fall asleep next to Natasha almost instantly—and without caring that I feel filthier than I ever have in my life. I resolve to seek out whatever passes for a bath the very next day.

I should be too weary and aching to think about whether I'll awaken in the eighteenth century again, but by now I must face the alternative: somehow, inexplicably I have become a time traveler. Too many days and nights have passed, all in "real" time. An hour feels like an hour, a day like a day, and worst of all, a night like a night. I eat, urinate, and sleep like a normal person, not a comatose or sleeping one. It is *this* reality that has started to terrify me. Somehow, some way, I have slipped into another time. How did it happen? How will I get back? *Will* I ever get back to 1999—and if so, when? And how?

The latter question troubles me most, since we're far from St. Petersburg and the as yet un-built Hermitage. Logic—if that plays a role here—suggests if the marble goddess statue somehow brought me here, my chances of getting back to where I "came through" have lessened considerably now that I'm so far from it.

I toss and turn until Natasha pokes me with her bony elbow, and it is near dawn before I fall asleep. It is a dream-filled sleep, and in the morning I acknowledge the obvious: people in a dream state probably do not in turn have dreams about dreaming!

That day we find ourselves once more in front of Elizabeth, who wants to present the Anhalt-Zerbst princesses with special ribbons and stars: the Order of Saint Catherine. "It is a great honor," the count assures them. "The insignia is named after Her Majesty's mother and established by Peter the Great himself for her in celebration of a military victory. Only a select few people have been thus endowed. The Order will mark you as 'princesses of the blood' and put you under the empress's royal patronage." Newly beribboned with the over-the-shoulder sash decorated with diamonds and a star, Sophia smiles proudly. Apparently the patronage comes complete with more benefits, as Sophia's and Johanna's rooms soon fill with lavish gifts: imported lace, fabulous jewels, bolts of brocades and velvets, and all manner of trinkets.

At night we celebrate the grand duke's sixteenth birthday. It seems to take hours to get dressed, although probably not nearly as long as the empress. She arrives in a brown silk robe embroidered with silver, her bosom, head, neck and waist bedecked with jewels.

Trying to sound casual, I ask Katrina about the grand duke's exact date of birth. Although this probably only confirms her assessment of my slow intellect, she gives me a polite response.

I do the calculations almost instantly. My grudging adjustment to my new life is now muted by the sobering knowledge I may in fact have ended up in the year 1744! Two hundred fifty years before my own time.

Once more I strive not to panic.

Elizabeth departs early to attend late evening church services, although not before Natasha points out to me that she has lingered behind one of the doorways to spy on the first impressions the young couple makes on the guests.

It is difficult for me to concentrate, so I pay little attention. I press myself near a wall, forcing myself to focus on Grand Duke Peter's nervous energy, his long white face, and stringy figure with a thin chest. Of course, he is still young and perhaps not unattractive to some women.

Glancing at the ball crowd, I realize it is a night of a thousand eyes for the imported princess and even her ladies. Somewhat nervously, I shrink back farther. The last thing *I* want is to be discovered as an imposter, let alone some kind of science fiction freak from the future.

◌◌

Nothing short of a whirlwind month begins; we ladies are expected to trail behind Sophia from morning to evening—struggling to keep up with a skinny adolescent with boundless energy even though she only picks at her food.

Although Sophia seems to be losing weight from pure nervousness, the rest of us are gaining. Part of the pleasure of this life—if there indeed is any—would be eating, although it takes only a few days for the interminable time spent "at table" to begin to annoy me. I come from a fast-food time, not one in which hours go by and ten-course lunches evolve within a short span of time to their extravagant dinner counterparts. My waistline grows ever larger from the procession of soups, sauces, relishes, vegetable pies, tortes, and elaborate sugar confections that obviously require an entire pastry staff. Gradually, however, the chef eliminates the roasts, meat pies, and cheeses, thus indicating that the empress must have changed her mind about permitting us not to observe Lent.

We change clothes frequently—sometimes three times per day—for an endless parade of receptions, church services, audiences with the empress or her ministers, interminable card games, and even elegant balls. I'm surprised when Katrina complains, "This is all so subdued. I cannot wait until Lent is over." She hastily crosses herself.

The evening of my first official ball, I'm awed by my own new teal silk gown. It seems the ladies of honor get not only their own servants, but seamstresses—a blessing in the case of the latter if I'm to continue swelling in size. As if to make us look even fatter, the dressing attendants fit us with huge whale bone *panniers* like the one the empress always wears. They add a full foot to each hip, making it impossible to get through some doorways without sliding sideways.

I'm star-struck by the glitz, at the same time concerned for my safety. Because the gentlemen all wear full regalia, jeweled swords swing at their thighs. It is only a matter of time, I estimate, before one of the hoop skirts falls victim to the sword, leaving some embarrassed woman *sans* gown—or gravely wounded. Perhaps aware of the dangers of these maneuvers, many ladies climb up on chairs to observe the festivities and, early on, to get a good look at Princess Sophia.

Fortunately, no one pays much attention to her ladies, although Sophia is looked at as closely as if the nobility and even the servants are examining a prospective livestock purchase rather than a potential grand duchess.

No one, however, gets inspected more closely than I examine myself. Every day I continue to check my body for changes, and for those familiar aspects that reassure me I am still myself. I still have the black and blue mark on the back of my thigh from my carry-on suitcase banging against it throughout our trip to Russia. In addition to the fencing scar, I still have one on the bottom of my foot from when I stepped on a razor blade in sixth grade.

Whoever or wherever the true Maria is, I wonder if she really looks as much like me as I do her. Is she living my life with Aunt Roberta?

Does she know the girl is an imposter? Or is she worried sick about me? I return to the same thoughts again and again, although continuing to push them aside as relentlessly as I slap at the fleas that all too often share our beds.

CHAPTER 5

(SOPHIA) 1744

"The Church had no objection to the marriage; that the couple were cousins did not count since they were related on the maternal side only. Their relationship was therefore merely 'the shadow of a relationship.'"
— Katharine Anthony

The first time Peter laughed aloud and told a joke in the middle of church service, Sophia was mortified. As she surreptitiously looked side to side, she could almost divide the other attendees into those who apparently had grown accustomed to such antics and those convinced he would burn in hell.

This was not the only example of her potential fiancé's inappropriate behavior, merely one of many that would require getting accustomed to if she were to be accepted. Like it or not, it was not up to Sophia to decide whether she wanted him, but up to Peter and Elizabeth to decide whether they wanted Sophia. Painfully aware of this, she tried her best to listen politely and attentively to Peter without interrupting. At times he made her blush, not only when he lapsed into one of his self-absorbed discourses on everything he hated (which included pretty much all things Russian), but when he referred loftily to his admiration for other women.

"Alas, I am to marry you instead," he shrugged a few times, although they were nonchalant shrugs that at least gave her some comfort that thus far she hadn't been rejected.

If she dared write in a journal, she at least would've had someone in whom to confide. So many nights during and after meals she feared she could not continue feigning interest in things that interested only him. He tended to carry on a consistent magpie-like chatter about drills, uniforms, soldiers, and other military topics.

The only thing he'd done to charm her had been to haul out a map he'd used to chart her trip from Prussia to Russia. He had created a miniature carriage that he rolled along each day, marking what he estimated would've been her progress. She laughed in delight.

Although during Lent the court was expected to curb all culinary and other indulgences and attend church repeatedly, Peter had been granted a special dispensation to dine with Sophia, Johanna, and their ladies. As eagerly as a boy with a new toy, Peter devoted each meal to boasting about his supposed exploits in battle—exploits impossible for him to have achieved at his young age even if he had served.

"I have a headache," Sophia pleaded often as an excuse to return to her rooms early. Sometimes she really did suffer from headaches, perhaps caused by the strain of pretending to listen to and care about Peter's conversations. Unfortunately, sometimes he took the late meal with them in Sophia's or Johanna's apartments, and then escape was more difficult.

It was the empress who made the entire situation palatable. She seemed as enraptured with her choice for her nephew's dynastic help-mate as Sophia was captivated by this ruler of a sprawling nation: a woman who ruled millions of men but was possessed by none. She began to think of Elizabeth as more of a mother to her than Johanna ever had been. Although rumors abounded of Elizabeth's savage and unpredictable moods, Sophia thus far had been the recipient of only kindness and love. Elizabeth seemed to be nothing short of a radiant, bejeweled goddess, both beautiful and benevolent. *She is my ideal,* Sophia thought several times in those early months. *My fairy god-mother at last.* She fervently hoped that this perception didn't seem easier to maintain because she saw little of the pious empress during Lent.

One afternoon, sipping tea in order to adapt to the favorite Russian beverage, Sophia confided in one of her ladies. They spoke in French, since she still knew only a few phrases in Russian, and Maria, the quietest, was fluent in both. "Don't you think the empress is perfect?" she asked the girl, who she knew was roughly her own age.

"She *is* beautiful."

"I think that never was a head more perfect," Sophia said enthusiastically. "And her mouth is unique, all graces, smiles, and sweetness. It could never look sour, could never take any but a gracious shape; reproaches from it would be adorable, if it could ever proffer reproaches."

Maria simply nodded.

"If I were a poet," Sophia continued, "I would say two rows of pearls show through the coral of two lips that must be seen to be imagined. The eyes are full of sensibility; yes, that is the effect they make upon me."

Now slightly embarrassed, she abruptly changed the subject. "How long have you been at court?" she asked.

Maria did not answer immediately, then seemed to stammer. "Since I was a young girl, I believe."

"And how old are you now?"

The girl, almost a head taller than she and a rare beauty, again hesitated. "Seventeen, Your Highness," she finally said.

"And your parents?"

"They are both dead."

"I'm sorry. So the empress took you in?" Although scarcely aware of it, Sophia possessed a manner of listening avidly, and was genuinely interested in people.

She was a little taken aback, then, when Maria picked up the empty teacups and asked to be excused.

It must have been something tragic, Sophia thought, and resolved to be even kinder to Maria in the future. Her ladies were gradually becoming her friends; having come from noble or at least reputable families, they all seemed to be her best chance of having interesting conversation.

In the meantime, the empress showered Sophia with gifts. Her favorite was a toilet kit covered in a rare dyed green shark skin. The interior contained porcelain jars filled with multiple shades of rouge, elaborate perfume bottles and other glass bottles her maids filled with sweet almond milk or barley water for her skin and violet scent to sprinkle on her hair. A silver box contained an array of facial spots cut from black taffeta into round, square, and crescent shapes. These black stick-on marks, considered a beauty symbol when worn by both women and men, had long been popular in the western courts of France and England. Elizabeth was especially passionate about all things French, from fashions to food to culture.

Sophia also adored the cameos often used to decorate bottles or sometimes worn. These carvings with raised relief images of everything from mythological figures to scenes from nature fascinated her, and she resolved to someday possess more of them.

Wishing she could communicate in the empress's native language, Sophia nonetheless wrote careful thank you notes in French. Elizabeth had promised her a Russian tutor, and she could not wait to learn the language of what she prayed would be her permanent country.

Not since meeting the Countess von Bentinck a few years earlier had Sophia been so impressed with a woman. If only she could find a way to please the empress as much as she pleased Sophia. She'd attempted to copy Elizabeth's preference for Russian food, ordering with her breakfast an awful beverage called *kvass* made from fermented rye. In the afternoon, meals often included sauerkraut soup just as she'd drunk back home (unfortunately thickened with oatmeal here), dark rye bread, *kasha* or porridge with stewed mushrooms, and too many pickles, and herring. One of her servers promised to introduce her to a thin pancake-like treat called *blini* as soon as Lent ended.

Fortunately, she knew at least she could make the empress happy by learning her native language plus her religion.

Within weeks of her arrival, the eager pupil welcomed a new language instructor at the same time as she went under the tutelage of Father Semyon Todorsky, Abbot of the Ipatiev Monastery; the latter was appointed to prepare Sophia to be received into the Russian Orthodox Church.

Simultaneously she gained a new dance teacher, though tolerating his lessons with nothing close to the same fervor.

She admitted reluctantly to herself that not only Babet's tutelage but Herr Wagner's insistence on rote memorization had prepared her well for this immersion in something she considered more important than anything she'd learned in her entire educational life. She resolved to write more often to Babet to thank her.

She also found herself craving knowledge of the country's history, and borrowed book after book from Peter I's massive Imperial Library. In this way she began to piece together the complex succession that had followed Peter I's untimely death at age 52. However, it was the older servants and chamberlains who'd been in court service for decades who revealed interesting tidbits about Peter the Great and ensuing years. She learned that as a boy he had shared the throne with his less capable brother, Ivan V. That so many mourners paid their respects when he died the black rug in front of the bier had to be replaced multiple times. That his second wife Catherine (a former peasant laundry woman), who died a mere two years later, had reigned in his place but seemed incapable of ruling, entrusting that to others. That fewer than three years later, Peter's ineffectual grandson, Peter II, succumbed to smallpox and died at age fourteen without naming an heir. That Ivan V's widowed daughter and Peter I's niece, Anna Ioannovna, had started her autocratic ten-year reign the same day the northern lights illuminated the skies of Moscow with fiery scarlet pillars, said to be an omen.

"One of Her Royal Majesty Anna Ioannovna's favorite past-times," an old babushka who tended the samovar told her, "was to order the creation of magnificent ice cities and even a life-size castle made entirely of ice!"

"It sounds marvelous!" Sophia exclaimed.

"Not always, Your Highness. Some awful things went on there." She noticed another woman, slowly dusting the paintings, shiver as if she were inside a palace of ice herself.

"Such as?"

"Newlyweds were often dropped inside from a cage," the woman polishing the samovar confided. "Mattresses, pillows, blankets—everything was made of ice. And in the morning . . ."

"They were ill?"

"Worse," the other woman muttered, and hastily went back to her dusting before backing out of the room.

"Empress Anna was a cruel woman," Sophia heard over and over. Stories abounded of vindictive and cruel punishments, even burnings at the stake: for suspected witches, for Jews, for Muslims, for criminals, for those who displeased Her Majesty.

In the meantime, no matter how much knowledge she acquired, she was careful not to discuss it. She remained painfully aware that her every word, facial expression, action, and garment remained on trial. She might escape with some missteps in dance, but in nothing else would an error be deemed acceptable.

CHAPTER 6

(MARIA) 1744

Only when the princess has lessons are we not expected to be in attendance. However, since her frantic social schedule makes finding studying time difficult, she often dismisses us early so she can work. We usually sink gratefully into our beds or sit up and play a card game called *faro*.

Sophia's language lessons have become the source of the first friction between her and Peter, who speaks primarily in German and calls Russian "the language of savage beasts." Normally she caters to him in all things, but a stubborn streak occasionally asserts itself.

"It is the language of the country!" Sophia's clear and perfect French rings out. Even when she is upset, her voice comes across as calm albeit firm.

Down the hall we can hear Peter's squeaky, high-pitch yell, this time in broken French: "*This* is not my country. It is a boorish place! I wish my aunt had never chosen me for her heir. I would have been far happier as Duke of Holstein!"

Since Sophia and Peter's engagement is soon to be formally announced—hence the rush for this round of tutoring in language and religion—the argument does not bode well. My roommates can speak of little else.

"He is a boar!" Natasha says dismissively.

"A boar who dares wear a Prussian uniform in the Russian court!" Irina adds with disapproval. "If it were anyone else, he would be exiled to Siberia."

"And I heard," Natasha leans forward, "that he has told Sophia all about his former girlfriend and how he preferred to marry her instead of Catherine."

"Imagine! If I were the princess, I'd want to go right back to Prussia," Katrina chimes in.

"Well," Natalie observes, "I think the empress might be more than willing to send Princess Johanna back soon. I've caught some disturbing looks on her face—and you know how suspicious of everyone the empress is."

"Why?" I ask.

"Because plots against her are everywhere. It's probably why she doesn't sleep at night. Don't you pay attention, Maria?"

I *do* pay attention, but court intrigues confuse me. Occasionally I see someone surreptitiously slip a letter to someone else. Whispers and murmured conversations echo through palace corners, and the word "spy" seems to be on everyone's lips. Rumor has it that Princess Johanna, in particular, holds secret meetings in her chambers around the clock. Exactly what she is plotting I have no idea, but I distrust *my* princess's mother.

Katrina, definitely the pessimist among us, tries to sort through the weeds in the garden of intrigues. "Count Lestocq, the Prussian ambassador, and the Marquis de La Chétardie favor an alliance with Prussia and France. But Vice Chancellor Bestuzhev and his assistants prefer Russia ally itself with England, Austria, and Saxony. The vice chancellor has everything to gain if Sophia dies and a Saxon princess is brought here to marry the grand duke."

I also learn the details of the empress's love life from, of course, Natasha. "They call him the Emperor of the Night," she giggles, referring to Count Alexis Razumovsky, who assisted the empress in awarding the Orders of St. Catherine. "Officially he is Master of the Hunt, but he is also her lover." I remember the gentleman in question: amazingly tall and strikingly good-looking even beneath his ubiquitous powdered wig.

"At Peterhof, she cooks his favorite Ukrainian dishes for him. They even say she secretly married him, though I cannot imagine why. My Alexander says—." Natasha has the grace to blush before continuing. "Well, my sources tell me that she did so only because she cannot bear to share the crown with anyone else."

That much has become clear in my infrequent interactions with the empress. She is a proud woman who wields her power capriciously yet firmly. Her subjects tremble before this imposing royal autocrat, and with good reason. I've seen her throw two temper tantrums since our arrival, including boxing the ears of one of her ladies who turned up late for church. A woman like this would not want to share a kingdom with a man—and, from what Natasha tells me—a Ukrainian peasant.

During rare moments alone, I marvel at my circumstances. I have grown up in a democracy, not an autocracy; the fact that I am basically a high-class servant with no rights and virtually no freedom is disturbing. Yet without access to the Hermitage or the touch of the mysterious statue that purportedly brought me here, what choice do

I have? I am a prisoner in another time. All I can do for now is live the life into which I've been thrust, for however long that may be.

Sometimes, curled up next to Natasha in the middle of an eighteenth-century Russian winter, I cry for what I have lost.

One night just a few weeks since my—and Sophia's—arrival here, I sneak out of our room to look for something to drink in the antechamber where we played cards until almost dawn. I don't expect to bump into anyone, although palace servants must work around the clock.

In the uncarpeted corridor, a sconce balancing a torch lights the way. I'm surprised upon reaching the imperial suite to see Sophia hunched over a table with a lone candle.

"Your Highness!" I startle her. When she sees me, Sophia relaxes. Wearing only a dressing gown and no slippers, she has wrapped a rug around her shoulders as her only concession to the cold.

"It is freezing in here!" I announce the obvious, observing, too, that at night in particular icy drafts penetrate right through damask-covered walls.

"I did not want to awaken anyone to relight the brazier." She smiles guiltily, and I don't have to ask what she is doing. Books and papers litter the table, indicating she's been tackling the complexities of Russian syntax.

"Are you making progress?" I ask hesitantly. "With language lessons?"

"Slowly, yes." She rubs her eyes and taps one finger on a book. "Sometimes I fear it is hopeless." Yet she is speaking in Russian right now, and it seems to me she is imbibing the language as thirstily and greedily as her fiancé inhales wine.

"You need your sleep," I dare suggest. Since her arrival, she's been expected to undergo a grueling procession of receptions and audiences, not to mention endless nights at table where soups, sauces, and sugared treat courses are interspersed with lengthy entertainment.

"You are right, Maria, but I need to learn this more than I need sleep. If I am going to be Russian like you, I must be able to speak the language. I believe the people of this great country should expect nothing less. Yet it is a grammatical nightmare. German has cases, too, of course, but these are too much for my simple mind."

I cannot help a small laugh, because there is nothing simple about this young woman—or her mind. "It is true that each Russian word has more cases and forms than . . . well, than there are—"

"Saints in the Orthodox Church?" she finishes for me.

"Exactly." I admire her dedication, at the same time comparing her to Peter, who growls at anyone who speaks Russian.

As she returns to her studies, I feel guilty about being thrust into this world with the inexplicable ability to speak a language I probably never could've mastered in my own time. Discovering a leftover glass of juice and a pastry, I head quietly back to bed, but not before nudging the rug back up over the future grand duchess's bony shoulders.

Unexpectedly, the four of us have gained plenty of free time. Princess Sophia is very ill and has no need of our attendance. Speculation runs wild. Some servants murmur she was poisoned so another girl could take her place as Peter's prospective bride. Frightened courtiers whisper that she has contracted the dreaded smallpox. From the corridors we hear Johanna vigorously debating the empress's Dutch physician, who insists she has inflamed blood and must be bled while Johanna argues that bleeding will kill her.

The one time I enter the room, I find a physician applying ointment to Sophia's chest.

"She caught cold from all that studying," Irina dismisses the expert's opinion. "The other morning her stove was out and I found her hunched over her Russian vocabulary. She was wearing no shoes and barely wrapped up. No wonder she is sick."

Feeling guilty that I had the same experience but that neither of us thought to report it to anyone, I wonder what will happen now. To me it appears as though she has contracted pneumonia—something easily curable if she had the benefit of antibiotics. I'm frightened then, thinking how easily a minor illness can take a life in these times. I hope the vaccinations and flu shots my late parents and then my aunt faithfully insisted upon have provided some immunity. But I also fear for Sophia, of whom I have become fond. And if she dies, what will become of the Russian dynasty? Of my position, for that matter. I reassure myself that history has already been written, and whatever this girl's role is, I cannot and should not interfere.

Natasha takes full advantage of our freedom, slipping back into the room in the middle of the night or early morning. She obviously has a gentleman friend, perhaps this mysterious Alexander whose name she lets slip too often, but I relish having the bed to myself. We have linen sheets and wool blankets topped with furs, and even though my nose gets cold at night, I am snug and warm.

Katrina, it turns out, is married, but secretly, since maids of honor are forbidden to do so without the empress's permission—and risk losing their positions. "The empress would never grant me leave to go home," she complains. "But now I will visit my husband for a few days if no one here objects."

"We can cover for you," I try to explain in French and then in Russian, although neither language translates this phrasing well.

"Thank you, Maria," she says gratefully, and packs a small travel satchel.

We do not see her again for nearly a week.

Empress Elizabeth, when told of the princess's illness, rushes back on the fifth day from the monastery where she was doing one of her frequent lengthy devotions. Within hours of her arrival, Irina and I are summoned to Sophia's bedside for some reason.

The empress has swooped in and taken charge immediately, ordering doctors out, snapping directions to servants, pushing the hand-wringing Johanna aside, and ensuring that Count Lestocq assumes charge of the patient. Taking the frail girl in her arms, the empress watches as another surgeon pricks a vein in Sophia's foot and begins to drain blood into a basin.

I've heard about bloodletting, but never expected to see it. I want to scream at the surgeon to stop. As if sensing how upset I am, Irina tightens her hand on my arm.

For a moment it seems that something has worked. Sophia opens her eyes, now appearing larger than ever in her deathly pale face, and looks up into Elizabeth's concerned features. It suddenly seems as though she is aware of all of us, but then she lapses once again into sleep or unconsciousness.

Six hours later the surgeon tries again, and approximately every six hours thereafter. I cannot believe he won't drain all her blood. However, at least if she survives, she'll have plenty of jewels, which the empress sends after each bloodletting. The first is a diamond-encrusted snuffbox and matching diamond earrings, followed over the next weeks by enough jewels to fill a silver box that resides on Sophia's dresser.

Yet nothing seems to be working, and the patient continues to lie in a stupor. Irina and I are rarely called anymore, and I begin exploring the palace more thoroughly. Once, bundled in my furs, I stroll the grounds, but all I can see are snow-covered statues and a few lonely crocuses. How I long to gaze upon all of Moscow, but Irina tells me we dare not go out into the center of the city in case we are summoned by the empress.

"She will box your ears if you are not there when she calls," she warns. "And Her Imperial Majesty never forgets a slight or a misbehavior. She seems to have eyes everywhere—and fists to match!"

Indeed, she does call for us one morning shortly thereafter. Natasha is fortunately back, looking happy but exhausted for a somewhat flighty girl of sixteen, and Katrina has just returned from her husband and home appearing well rested and without her usual sour face. The four of us report to the empress's state bedchamber, where we find her selecting jewelry for herself and Princess Sophia. Surprisingly, she wants our opinion on her choices.

The young jeweler's apprentice, one of the most handsome men I've ever seen except for perhaps the empress's Count Razumovsky, stands politely and quietly while Elizabeth fingers each of his wares in turn.

For herself she selects a pair of ruby earrings and a few tourmalines in her favorite pink. Calling us—surprisingly—by name, she then consults each in turn on what the princess might like.

"Perhaps Her Highness would like the emerald broach," I suggest when my turn comes, and am rewarded by an approving nod from the dreamy-looking jeweler.

"Monsieur Blukhov, we shall take the broach, as well as the sapphire necklace that Natasha recommended. These ladies know the princess's taste in jewelry and color better than I. For now, that is."

Monsieur Blukhov bows. "I will notify my uncle," he says as he gathers up the precious gemstones the empress discarded on the table. He carefully but efficiently scoops them into his velvet-lined cases.

"And Monsieur," the empress says before dismissing him. "We hope that you and your uncle will be in Petersburg next winter. We shall need to coordinate my jewels with the new gowns arriving from Paris. We can count on your presence there?"

It is obvious to all that this is a command rather than a request, and the man—probably not much more than twenty—bows slightly and nods. "Yes, your Majesty. We will be there when you need us."

I imagine his dark eyes gaze at me just after he says this, but perhaps it is only wishful thinking.

Day after day Princess Johanna rushes in and out of Sophia's chamber, arguing constantly with this or that doctor. Since I've never seen her show any real affection toward her daughter, I suspect the prestige of being the mother of a future member of the imperial family is what drives her, rather than any real concern. Eventually an impatient Empress Elizabeth bans her from the sickroom, sending the fuming Johanna back to her own salon where she can rail at the injustice of it all and presumably continue to plot on behalf of the Prussian king.

In the meantime, Johanna has demanded a Lutheran minister attend her daughter. During one of her conscious moments when ladies are allowed in the bedchamber, Sophia turns her sunken eyes to the empress. "Better to send for Father Todorsky," she utters. "I wish to speak with him."

News of her request for an Orthodox priest spreads throughout the palace and into the city rapidly as the news she had fallen ill purportedly while studying the Russian language. It is not unusual to hear conversations in the halls in which Princess Sophia is referred to as "one of us" or "as Russian a princess as we can hope to get." If they took surveys or polls in this century, her approval rating surely must have soared. In each retelling, Sophia becomes more and more marvelous, to the point that I hear servants whisper how she has already gained fluency in Russian. The empress showers her with affection and gifts and refers to her as "my dear child," a title never given to the conspicuously absent Peter (who at least has the decency to send his fiancé a watch set with diamonds and rubies).

Gradually, after all the bleeding and the questionable "cures," the princess's fever breaks, and almost immediately she coughs up quantities of pus. This is preceded by the bursting of an abscess on her right side, and more likely it is the removal of this source of infection that causes her recovery. Once more we're allowed in the bedchamber, and we sit on chairs surrounding the sickbed, embroidering pillows and chatting while Sophia periodically dozes off.

I am amazed at how indiscreet my companions can be while we stitch. As if Sophia cannot hear us, they gossip incessantly in French and then Russian about this or that court personage. Often Sophia's mother and her apparent political indiscretions are the subject.

I'm not certain if I imagine it or really do sense a change in the princess's breathing patterns that indicates she may be awake. Small wonder, if she is to be thrust into this court resembling a den of gossips and plotters. Perhaps every little bit of information she gleans can someday, somehow be of use.

In the meantime, spring has started its slow unfolding. Even the mountain-size piles of snow—not to mention the equally high ones consisting of snow-covered trash pushed up against the palace gates—start to dissipate. The four of us finally can stroll the palace grounds in lighter cloaks, breathing in the scent of crocuses and tulips and pausing occasionally while Natasha flirts with a guard. Servants tote blankets so we can sit on wet benches and let the sun warm our faces, and my mood lightens.

Occasionally the empress orders us to accompany her to a church other than the elaborate chapel at "our" own palace. It is a delight to be able to gaze from carriage windows upon eighteenth-century Moscow, despite peasants throwing themselves face down into the dirty snow or prostrating themselves in one of the filthy gutters as the imperial carriage passes.

We end up at a different cathedral each time, and I'm always humbled and overwhelmed by the beauty of the liturgies and interiors. Bearded priests in richly embroidered vestments chant prayers and give readings in a form of Russian I barely understand, but no one seems to mind. Instead, the empress and her ladies duly bow, cross themselves endless times, light candles, press their lips to jeweled icons, and chant. On April 5, Easter turns out to be an elaborate ceremony that begins the night before and finally releases us from our dietary restrictions with sweet cakes and other desserts.

Twenty-seven days after the onset of her illness, Princess Sophia sits up in bed, orders a hearty meal, and within hours has called for her books.

The doctors apparently agreed to credit the bursting of one inflamed lung to her sudden recovery and rapid regaining of her strength.

After that we often enter the patient's room to discover her with books and quills spread out on the bed, a new determination in both her eyes and voice.

"It appears there is much contagion in this court," she comments to me one morning when we're alone.

"Oh, no, Your Highness. I don't think anyone else has been ill."

Her eyes, managing to look serious and mischievous at the same time, sparkle. "There are many kinds of illness and many versions of contagion."

I feel myself blush. There is no doubt in my mind that over the past week—if not earlier—she in fact has been privy to the endless disputes, slights, petty squabbles, and animosities infecting court like an insidious miasma of viruses.

"Yes, Your Highness," I murmur. I would like to tell her this is even worse than high school—and the stakes much higher—but realize this would not seem funny to her. In fact, I spend more time thinking about what I *will* say than speaking in this new or old world. How I long for someone to confide in, or more impossibly, someone who can relate to the world into which I was born.

❦

On April 21, Sophia's fifteenth birthday, she re-emerges in public for the first time. She appears taller, thinner, and pale. The empress attempts to counter her cadaverous appearance by sending pots of bright red rouge to her room, commanding the future grand duchess color her cheeks.

"This is the best rouge," Natasha comments admiringly. "They make it with vermilion and red lead."

"Lead?" I am incredulous, and vow never to let this stuff touch my skin.

Sophia has lost nearly all her lovely brown waves, which, although the hair will grow back, must be covered with a wig and a headdress to hide the fact that now she is as bald as a fledgling bird.

"I am ugly as a scarecrow," she muses as she examines herself in the full-length mirror.

"You are not," Irina counters. "And only a few guests will have a good view of your face tonight." This is only partially true, since while the dinner party will be for a small group of forty, it will be followed by a ball.

Yet to me it seems that this girl will never be ugly, and I help her don the diamond earrings Elizabeth gifted her after the first bloodletting. Even the diamonds do not outshine her bright blue-violet eyes.

CHAPTER 7

(SOPHIA) 1744

"Having personal relations with the empress was harder than walking over ice in high-heeled dance shoes."
— Evgenii Anisimov

D ear Father," Sophia wrote to Christian August early in May. "As I have mentioned previously, it seems that the Lutheran and the Orthodox faiths differ in little but minor rituals: not in doctrine. Therefore, I am resolved to convert . . ."

Privately Sophia not only put aside her guilt at breaking her promise to her father, but any doubts she might have had about this very different religion, with its pageantry, rituals, and saints. Each chapel and cathedral boasted jewel-encrusted icons, royal doors penetrated only by bearded priests attired in rich vestments, floor-to-ceiling frescoes, thousands of candles, and the ubiquitous shaking of incense-filled silver and gold censers. Everyone repeatedly made the sign of the cross, kissed icons, chanted prayers, sang an *a capella* rendition of the archaic Old Church Slavonic, prostrated themselves routinely, and as for the women, constantly adjusted and readjusted their headscarves. No one ever sat down, and even Sophia's teenage knees and feet found the hours-long ceremonies and liturgical performances uncomfortable.

In the meantime, she secretly concluded that the Russian Orthodox Church existed and thrived to satisfy and even control the people. The setting and rituals seemed overly lavish and dazzling, enough to satisfy the peasants and the nobility that Someone higher up looked out for them even as they endured the brutality and poverty of their lives, and perhaps encouraged them to forgive the sins and excesses of the wealthy who ruled them.

Sophia was learning fast, but the Church's excessive holidays, saints' days, and fasts required mental juggling. The empress herself fasted thirty weeks of the year, all during that time denying herself and her court meat, eggs, butter, and milk—instead subsisting primarily on mushrooms, fish, vegetable oil, and pickled cucumbers.

For the other twenty-two weeks everyone gorged themselves. Elizabeth, perhaps due to her frequent fasts interspersed with dining on excess luxuries, remained voluptuous as ever. Rumors also had reached Sophia that the empress had a fondness for strong liquor, cherry vodka being her favorite. It sometimes happened, she was told, that the empress would be so indisposed that she would fall in a swoon.

"They say her ladies often must cut off her dress and her corsets to get her into bed at night," Katrina whispered one evening.

"And yet she still beats them," one maid added.

A moment later, Katrina and the other ladies concentrated fiercely on their cards, and it was as if no one had spoken. Sophia preferred to think she'd imagined the comments, and blamed her delusions on her recent illness.

For her, such rumors did not coincide with the pious yet adventurous woman she now interacted with regularly. The empress, as if relieved her chosen future grand duchess had faced down almost certain death, seemed to want Sophia beside her daily. Over the next weeks they took meals together, attended plays and concerts, prayed in church, and turned heads wherever they went.

She is a divinity, Sophia thought. *She warms me with kindness, showers me with gowns and jewels, and in every way has become the mother I never truly had.* Elizabeth, for her part, acted pleased with her candidate for wife of the future emperor.

Elizabeth dyed her light auburn hair and matching eyebrows blacker yet, apparently to emphasize her Russianness, and swept through the palace as a noble and graceful empress.

As for Sophia's own Russianness, she continued to cultivate it with almost a vengeance—an enthusiastic one. With Semyon Todorsky, who had written an astounding eight hundred books in the Ukrainian language, Sophia quickly excelled due not only to motivation, but her excellent memory. Within weeks of her convalescence, she'd surpassed the Grand Duke Peter's paltry knowledge of Russian.

In addition to Todorsky's lessons on Eastern Orthodoxy and the Cyrillic alphabet, she worked with Vasilii Adodurov, a writer who quickly made valuable suggestions. Because Todorsky was Ukrainian, he spoke with a thick accent; Adodurov advised his pupil to practice the Creed in a parrot fashion that would mimic his own diction so people wouldn't laugh at her Ukrainian accent when she stood for her conversion.

It didn't take long for Sophia to master both, and privately she rejoiced at this new, rich language that provided so many opportunities to manipulate all its facets.

Her progress with Peter was less satisfactory. Although warming weather took him out into the forests with his entourage to walk and shoot, he apparently had sought marital advice from his lackeys, which left him with a new and swaggering antagonism toward his fiancée.

His German valet Roumberg, in particular, advised him the proper way to treat wives: "with a firm hand and even a whip." The ensuing conversations between the affianced couple left Sophia, normally strong-willed and intelligent, quaking and even slightly terrified.

"Roumberg says a wife must be in constant fear of her husband, scarcely breathing without his permission," he told her in German over supper. "A husband should demand complete obedience; the wife is his to use, to mold, and to chastise!"

This was perhaps the first inkling Sophia had that the childlike friendship the two of them tentatively had reached might be fraying.

"But we will be partners, as well, will we not? We—I mean you—will eventually have an empire to govern, and if it pleases Your Highness, as your consort I believe I could be of some usefulness."

"Nonsense. Your views will be forbidden," Peter argued.

"Thus far we have been able to share our views quite amicably," she said quietly, knowing in her heart this was far from true.

"My gentlemen tell me it is best to beat one's wife from time to time, particularly on the head. I will do this to you, too, Sophia, as this is the conventional way to handle a disobedient wife."

Sophia protested in vain, trying not to think about some of the tales she'd heard about punishments doled out from husband to wife—not only in the countryside, but even amongst the court. Stories abounded about wives hanged by their hair, stripped naked, then beaten until bones broke and flesh turned raw.

She could not help but shudder, vowing she'd return to Prussia and even marry her Uncle Georg before allowing Peter to do such a thing to her. Yet she wanted to please this callow youth, and she loved her new country. She was, however, much more afraid he might follow some of his predecessors' and contemporaries' punishments of unwanted wives: locking them up in a convent. Even her new hero, Empress Elizabeth's father Peter I, had done this both to his sister and his first wife. For Sophia, this would be nothing less than entombment, and she wondered if she could more willingly endure a beating than that.

For weeks after such conversations, Peter would seem more distant—and even menacing. Sophia prayed she could win him back over with kindness and sympathy. Of any infidelities he might embark upon, she worried less, as his already visible infatuations with various court ladies left her hurt but only mildly jealous. This was often the way things were in a royal marriage, and she had no expectations her own might be any different.

"I am reading Russian history," she announced to Maria shortly thereafter, when the girl was polishing her jewelry.

"In Russian?"

"Well, sometimes, although I am not fluent enough yet. I was able to secure some books in French."

Maria's butterscotch eyes glowed. "Would Your Highness like me to read some of it to you so that you can rest your eyes?"

This seemed a satisfactory solution, since Sophia spent so much time reading now that she had to have cold compresses on her eyes at night.

"Excellent!" She handed a hefty book to her maid of honor. "I am reading about previous decades in Russia, when the tsar would send out throughout the kingdom for marriageable girls to assemble at the Kremlin palace so he could choose one."

"'They flocked from all corners of the kingdom,'" Maria began reading. "'Before entering the tsar's chambers or attending the balls, many knelt for hours in the chapel to pray to the Holy Mother that they would be chosen.'" She continued reading about the process, as well as the misfortunes that seemed to befall so many.

"Hmm," Sophia mused. "Perhaps some of the women prayed *not* to be chosen. After all, it sounds as if it were a stakes game, with all those families interfering and plotting. Do you think," she asked, "that Tsar Michael Romanov's first choice really became mad—or was she poisoned?"

"The historian seems to imply she was indeed drugged."

"And I read that it happened again years later when Tsar Alexei fell in love with his first choice, Euphemia, but that her jealous ladies twisted her golden hair so tightly she fainted."

"That is in here." Maria moved her fingers along the page. "The chronicler also says that the court physicians pronounced it epilepsy, and she was exiled to Siberia. That is when he selected his second choice, but she died young after giving him only baby girls."

Sophia sighed heavily. "Her Majesty detests reading, claiming it hurts her eyes. Perhaps it does, since it makes mine grow weary, especially when the alphabet is so challenging. But it is strange, of course, since this part pertains to the empress."

"Her mother was the tsaritsa with all the girls?"

"No, but you see, after she died, he married Natalya, and *she* gave birth to Tsar Peter, who was, of course, Her Majesty's father. And so the deaths of the first wives led to the empress's ascension—admittedly not immediately, but eventually."

"It does not seem fair, Your Highness. I mean, unless these women wanted to marry the tsar or the heir . . ." She stopped, as if realizing to whom she was speaking.

"You are perceptive, my dear Maria Sergeievna. I, too, am here as a potential chosen bride. But," she added resolutely. "I *want* to be here. So let us pray no one decides to drug me lest they believe I am crazier than I am!"

They both laughed, perhaps out of nervousness, perhaps out of relief, perhaps out of fear.

During those times Peter seemed to forget about wife-beating, he and Sophia got along well. On one such occasion in early June, after being summoned to Troitsky Monastery where Elizabeth had secluded herself, the two teens were startled while playing games in the cloister to hear Princess Johanna rudely called into the room where the empress and her ministers had gathered.

For over an hour, both attempted to ignore the angry but indecipherable yells and recriminations echoing through the vaulted cells.

Although Peter continued to tell jokes to drown out the noise, he stopped abruptly when Johanna emerged, tears streaming down those usually carefully powdered features.

Before either could react, she had swept by them, replaced by Doctor Lestocq.

Although Sophia and Peter had been dangling their legs from a ledge on which they had perched themselves, the advisor's presence caused them to jump down.

"This is no place for games!" he said brusquely.

Peter started to respond, but the count interrupted, focusing his attention on Sophia. "You will soon be back in Prussia, anyway!" he told her loudly, and whirled on his heel before she could respond.

"What does he mean?" she whispered.

Peter shrugged. "I think it is your mother. She is a spy, you know."

Although she started to protest, Sophia realized this was probably all too true. "But I cannot go back there!" she nearly wailed, tears seeping into her eyes.

If she had expected Peter to defend or reassure her, his indifferent shrug told her as clearly as if he had spoken exactly where she stood.

Fortunately, when the empress emerged at last, she smiled and kissed them both. Perhaps the crisis had passed, although later they learned that Count Bestuzhev had intercepted several incriminating letters from Johanna to various foreign leaders, particularly King Frederick of Prussia.

Sophia began to realize that no matter the cost, she must start distancing herself from her own mother, even if it meant their paths diverged. Although her duty might be to follow her mother, her own plans and ambitions did *not* lie back in Prussia.

Chapter 8

(Maria)

The young imperial couple seem subdued when they return from the monastery. Earlier Princess Johanna had slammed the door of her chamber, appearing to be half crying, half raving.

"She has fallen out of favor with the empress for certain," Katrina observed.

"And no wonder. All that plotting," Natasha added. "You would think she was here as the emissary of Frederick of Prussia instead of at the Empress of Russia's behest."

"She called the empress all kinds of awful names. She made fun of her weight—and even her morals—in the correspondence," Irina told us smugly. "They have intercepted all her letters."

"And then there is Count Betsky," Natasha added in a whisper. "Everyone knows that Princess Johanna and he are having an af--"

"Hush!" Irina warned. "We have no idea how true, let alone how serious, any of this may be, and certainly our own futures are in jeopardy if Princess Sophia is sent back to Prussia."

I shuddered, recalling stories about Elizabeth's famous temper. *And what will happen to me then?*

But days go by quietly, and Princess Sophia, while looking somewhat worried, appears calm. Johanna has been banished to her chambers, and her sharp German rebukes to her daughter are not missed.

Some mornings we're enlisted to help the princess with her dance lessons—taking turns as her partner while her instructor, a famous French ballet master, puts her through the paces of minuets, waltzes, quadrilles, and even Russian folk dances. We've all observed the empress's impressive dancing skills, and there seems no way out of these compulsory lessons.

Sophia bears the instructions well, although it's obvious she'd prefer to be studying language or theology. But the empress has priorities. We ladies are secretly glad dancing is one of them—rather than one of the Elizabeth's other passions: riding and hunting.

In addition, we help Sophia prepare for her official conversion to Orthodoxy. We drill her on the Creed, which she struggles to recite in passable Russian. She spends most days studying, which often means skipping a dance lesson, and we help as much as we can. Since Natasha tries to cover her own near illiteracy, she pouts in the corner on tutoring days. Irina and Katrina seem well educated, however, but where and how *I* learned all these Biblical and even Orthodox creed passages, I have no idea. Yet I'm proud to be of some assistance in quizzing her, as it seems certain the princess will be on perpetual display and judged harshly for any mistakes.

Four days before the official conversion ceremony, to be followed a day later by an engagement ceremony—a relief for all of us who take it as a confirmation that Sophia will not be sent back to Prussia—the empress summons the four of us again.

I nearly forget to bow when I notice Monsieur Blukhov in her chamber with his jewelry cases spread out. Our eyes meet for a moment, and I note how his appear to be a dark, almost chocolate shade that matches his wig-free brown hair. From that moment I am too disconcerted to concentrate on Her Majesty's words.

Gradually I realize we're once again here to voice our opinions on selecting a special piece of jewelry to mark Sophia's conversion ceremony.

"Ladies, do you think she might prefer a necklace, a ring, a watch, or a broach?" the empress demands. "I have gifted her many such trifles, but I scarcely recall which I sent. I do not wish to duplicate my gifts, and I want her to have something to match her gowns. Although," she adds thoughtfully, "she could always have gowns made to fit the jewelry, as I do myself sometimes."

Monsieur Blukhov gives us plenty of space to examine the pieces spread out on trays balanced atop a velvet cloth.

I cannot stop from exclaiming, "The pieces are breathtaking!"

"And obviously meticulously crafted," Irina adds calmly, almost as if trying to make up for my outburst.

"My Uncle Giuseppe, my late mother's brother, does most of the work, although I do some designs myself," he ventures, glancing at the empress, who appears too engrossed in fingering one piece and then another before scattering each on the table to care what he is saying. "But my uncle, while he delights in the honor of serving Her Imperial Majesty, has been ill and too weak to travel back and forth to the palace. He's fine now," he hastens to add.

"You're amazing," I mutter under my breath, but sense he somehow knows what I said. Then more loudly I ask, "Are you Italian or Russian then, Monsieur?"

"Both," he says simply. "My father was Russian, but my mother, as

I mentioned, was Italian."

"The Blukhov and Campani families have served us well," the empress comments. "First Giuseppe Campani, and now his nephew Igor Blukhov, have provided us with jewelry fit for a royal." She adds something rapidly in apparently fluent Italian.

Igor appears embarrassed by the praise, which even I realize is rarely bestowed by the empress. As if feeling so herself, she briskly turns to us and, returning to Russian, demands our opinions.

"Perhaps the ruby and diamond ring," Irina suggests, rather timidly for her.

"Perhaps," the empress responds, but the look on her face announces she is not all that interested in the ruby with a circlet of diamonds.

I fear for my turn, and then, without thinking, turn to Igor. Having noticed that he clutches a velvet pouch in his other hand, I gamble. "Monsieur, I see no sapphires here. Might you have some additional pieces we've not seen?"

Igor smiles at me. "Of course, I always save something special for the empress herself." As he reaches into the pouch, I can sense Elizabeth's excitement. This is a woman who takes her jewels very, very seriously.

The jeweler spreads four pieces on the table, and we all gasp. A sapphire necklace framed by pink rhodochrosite captures the empress's attention immediately. "I will take that one myself," she announces.

We turn to the other three pieces: a sapphire and diamond ring mounted in a nest of gold, a sapphire pendant, and a spectacular pin clustered with diamonds and sapphires.

The empress must have heard my intake of breath. "Maria? Do you have a clear preference? A sense of what our darling princess might like?"

"The broach, Your Imperial Majesty. I believe she would adore the broach. And it matches her eyes!"

For a moment I'm uncertain whether the empress is pleased, jealous, or angry at my impertinence. Then a smile washes over those beautiful features. "My sentiments exactly. Wrap it up for me, Monsieur Blukhov, along with my new necklace. And please allow Sophia's maid Maria here to select something small from your wares. Perhaps an emerald necklace to set off the auburn highlights in her hair."

"Your Majesty, I couldn't—"

"You will."

I'm not sure if I'm more nervous about being forced to choose a priceless gem in the face of the envy I can already sense from Natasha, Irina, and Katrina, from the closeness of Igor as I move toward the table where he is picking up pieces to show me, or from the fact that the empress has just issued me a command.

Throughout the next two days, Sophia intensifies her lessons and cancels all public appearances. On the last day she fasts, imbibing only fish fried in oil, and one look at her face would reveal to anyone her dislike of it. In the morning she attends confession, and then returns to the empress's apartments to be dressed by Elizabeth herself. We are there to help, but so are a virtual army of maids and ladies in waiting.

Each of us previously has been appointed specific tasks, from managing Sophia's collection of ribbons and hair ornaments (Natasha's job) to serving tea (Irina) to fiddling with her shoes (Katrina). My job delightedly has evolved into taking care of and assisting her in selecting jewels to wear. I suspect the empress had a hand in this, and am honored at the trust placed in me. Although I've never been a fanatic about jewelry, handling the "crown jewels" and ornamenting Sophia in them is a job in which I take pleasure. I know by now that of course there is a real Royal Treasury established by Peter I, yet still this is a tremendous honor.

With my assistance, Sophia chooses to wear a limited number of jewels today, and those primarily selected from the array sent by Elizabeth during the princess's illness.

Sophia has opted to leave her hair loose and unpowdered, adorning it with a single white ribbon. The empress has selected Sophia's dress—crimson and silver, with a modest hoop and train—to match her own rose silk with silver braids and seams.

As we arrive at the chapel—actually a slightly garish cathedral on the castle grounds—we assemble in some kind of order: her Imperial Majesty leads, surrounded by a flank of gentlemen of the bedchamber and chamberlains; she is followed by Johanna and Peter with his own contingent of gentlemen; Sophia walks with one of her gentlemen of the bedchamber, and the rear is brought up by a bevy of princesses, portrait ladies (those noblewomen permitted to wear a miniature portrait of the empress), maids of honor, various private guests, and at last the ladies and gentlemen in waiting.

My fears of not being able to see or hear are allayed when we form a circle behind the array of archbishops and priests and Sophia kneels on a velvet cushion near the iconostasis. Relief, however, turns to regret as hours drift by, and I would give anything to sit down or escape the cloying odors of perfumes and incense for some fresh air. My entire body aches.

In her role—way more demanding than just standing at attention for four hours—Sophia performs beautifully. Her reading of the Confession of Faith, which runs nearly fifty pages, sounds flawless, as does her later recitation of the Russian creed. The empress weeps, inspiring courtiers to follow suit.

After placing salt on Sophia's tongue, the archbishop dabs holy oil on her eyes, neck, throat, forehead, and front and back of her hands. More songs, litanies, prayers, and Sophia's communion and baptism into the Orthodox Church drag the ceremony into the afternoon. Without understanding much of the significance, I do know that it is meaningful and spiritual, and that our young princess has acquitted herself with grace and nobility.

The biggest moment comes for me when Sophia is christened with a new Russian name: henceforth she is to be known as Ekaterina Alex-eievna. Catherine in English. As in, I presume with sudden surprise and pleasure, Catherine the Great.

Is this really possible?

As the interminable ceremony draws to a close and the priests retreat behind the male only golden doors of the iconostasis, Elizabeth reaches out and pins the sapphire and diamond broach on Sophia/Catherine's left shoulder. She hugs her and calls her "my Katinka" repeatedly.

In the empress's apartments, Elizabeth presents the newly christened Catherine with even more gifts, which she hands off to me to store. The first two, a diamond clasp designed to be worn on the bodice and a girdle covered with jewels, are mesmerizing. But it is the third—a "necklace" of sorts consisting of framed holy pictures and portraits of saints all joined together—that delights the princess.

For two more hours, a procession of court ladies and other nobility parades past the two princesses, kissing their hands. When we start to follow her back to her own apartments after the long ordeal, Sophia, aka Catherine, waves us away.

"I must beg off dinner and have a rest. Someone will attend me. Go dine and rest yourselves." It is just like Sophia/Catherine to think of her maids and ladies as well as herself.

After securing the new Catherine's gifts in the growing number of jewelry pouches, I cannot wait to select my dresses for tomorrow before climbing into one of the heavy gold ornate carriages that will whisk us to the Kremlin for the engagement ceremony. Hours later we are summoned to accompany Catherine (it will take all of us awhile to get accustomed to her new name) to the grand duke's apartments. As she and others congratulate him on the eve of his Name Day, Catherine presents him with the gifts the empress has provided: a hunting knife and a diamond- and emerald-ornamented gold cane head.

It is still light outside after our late supper with the grand duke and duchess, and we all travel the fewer than three miles to the Kremlin. At precisely midnight, the bells of the magnificent golden cupolaed churches within its white walls begin to ring to announce a feast day for the morrow, and continue ringing and clanging in response to thousands of other city bells. At first the noise aggravates me, but eventually I imagine I can pick out a hymn. I sneak a glance at Catherine, who, as always, appears perfectly composed. For a moment I catch a glimpse of a pleased half smile on those earnest, regal features.

It is the heat of summer, and once upon a time, I was the kind of girl who would have planned for a day of air-conditioned shopping malls, the beach, or swimming pools. Now I debate which linen chemise to wear beneath my elaborate gowns and listen carefully throughout the night for the rope bell that could summon me to Catherine's side. It might seem too frivolous or, conversely, too stern and regulated a life for an almost twenty-first century seventeen-year-old, yet sometimes—other than missing Aunt Roberta—I feel inexplicably happy.

Everyone who is anyone is waiting inside the cathedral: the highest dignitaries of the Senate, the Synod, the State, the Army, etc. Our large contingent, led by the empress in her imperial mantle and crown and protected by a huge silver canopy that requires eight major-generals to hoist, makes our way down a staircase to cross Cathedral Square. There we are received by clergy and the archbishop at the doors of the Cathedral of the Assumption.

Catherine, wearing a portrait of the empress and a diamond bracelet inset with the grand duke's portrait presented to her that morning, is trailed by a large group in roughly the same order as the previous day.

After being blessed on the altar and on the Bible, the engagement rings are placed on Peter and Catherine's fingers by Elizabeth herself. During this exchange and the subsequent singing of Psalm 100, the city's church bells ring incessantly, quieting only as the archbishop reads the formal engagement decree, which also declares that henceforth Catherine will be known as Her Imperial Highness and Grand Duchess of All the Russias.

For the first hour, my attention is captured by not only the patriarchal throne and the events taking place on the velvet dais, but by the magnificence of the interior of the fifteenth-century Cathedral of the Assumption, or Uspensky Sobor in Russian.

I had no idea this would turn out to be yet another four-hour ordeal, and once again flash back to my old life, in which a ten-minute cafeteria line made me crazy. And after the betrothal ceremony there is a lengthy mass, followed by the metropolitan's sermon!

Eventually we move along to endless kissing and bowing in the empress's apartments, as well as more gift exchanges. Even Johanna receives a long strand of pearls from Catherine and a snuffbox and ruby watch from Peter. While hastening to insert the diamond-encrusted watch and fan sprinkled with tiny diamonds presented to Catherine by Peter into special pouches I've been given for this purpose, I overhear Princess Johanna whining to anyone who will listen that she bears a mark "the size of a German florin" on her right hand from all the kissing.

In the evening, after yet another change of clothes and dinner in the Faceted Palace, Catherine must attend a ball in the Throne Room. This time we're excused to allow space for all the diplomatic guests, and the four of us gratefully escape for a nap. Sleep, however, is nearly impossible, as cannons fire periodically.

"Just another toast," Irina, noting my nervousness, assures me from her place in bed. "Each time something significant happens or one of the imperial family makes a toast, you will hear it. Have you never noticed this?" she asks curiously.

I shrug in the darkness. "I suppose I never paid attention."

"A friend of mine has the job of rushing back and forth between the soldiers and the ballroom to let them know when to fire. Anyway, I think it's marvelous that this is the date selected for the betrothal."

"Why?"

"Maria," she chides. "Why do you act so silly and empty-headed sometimes, when you really are not?"

"I'm sorry."

"Well," she pauses and, as if to humor me, adds, "Of course it has to be today, on the feast day of saints Peter and Paul."

Saint Peter. Yes, now I recall that this is Grand Duke Peter's Name Day, as important as a birthday in Russia. "I'm sorry, Irina. I'm just exhausted after these past two days." Idly I wonder if I have missed the Name Day for Maria's, but dare not reveal my ignorance.

However, I really do not want to sleep, as explosions of fireworks replace the cannon fire. Slipping out of bed, I peer out the windows in wonder to see giant wheels and cascades of falling silver stars lighting the skies.

Many card games later, the imperial party adjourns for a two a.m. meal at which we join them. I'm jumpy but finally as exhausted as I pretended to be earlier.

Only Natasha, who as usual slipped away for a few hours, is excited. "You would not believe what is going on in the streets of Moscow," she tells us. "Beer flows from the fountains, oxen roast on spits, and everyone seems to have abandoned themselves to pleasure!" She goes on to describe fire-eaters, dancing bears, and a parrot with a hurdy-gurdy man. I would've loved to go with her, although she never invites me, and I resolve to get up the courage to ask when she again sneaks into the city.

It occurs to me not for the first time that I should be keeping some sort of journal or at least take notes in case I ever get to return to my own world and time. In case. I try to fight past the alternating nausea and tightness in my chest that I have kept at bay for so long.

Eventually I fall asleep to the sounds of pre-dawn fireworks popping in the skies outside the window, my mind now fully focused on the summer's activities in the court of the future Catherine the Great.

CHAPTER 9

(SOPHIA / CATHERINE)

Awakening late, she remembered immediately: *As of today, I am Ekaterina Alexeievna.* Since Sophia's father was August, not Alexei, the empress's choice of Catherine's new patronymic seemed odd. Yet she realized with pleasure that her baptismal first name had been chosen in honor of Elizabeth's own mother and Peter the Great's second wife: Empress Catherine the First.

As if signaling her awakening, a lengthy serenade commenced outside. Military bands pounded out tunes on oboes, timpani, trumpets, and side drums. Church singers performed Italian music. Instrumentalists played what sounded like secular music to her untrained ear. On the grounds, Elizabeth's own Italian choirmaster busily directed a musical drama he'd composed for the occasion.

Before her headache powders could take effect, the music blessedly quieted—only to be replaced by an incessant buzz of voices in the hallways. Here a crowd of merchants had congregated to tempt the new grand duchess and gain her patronage. This provided her first inkling that everyone had an opinion on how—and on whom—she should spend her newly acquired allowance of 30,000 rubles. Since learning her remaining brother was ill, she had already determined to set aside some money to send back home; today it would become obvious that saving much would provide a challenge.

It's as if wise men have shown up at my new "birth" to offer gifts, she thought as she sifted through hundreds of complimentary samples. She owed so many ladies, servants, and other court members the small gifts that served as currency in court, where all services seemed to be bought. Only her own maids of honor did not ask for anything outright, although she selected a pair of gloves and a fan for each of the four who'd assisted her preparations for both ceremonies.

At tea, she finally had an opportunity to reflect upon the past two days—not just their significance but all the details. She knew, for example, that although she had been weak and somewhat dizzy from fasting, she would never forget her Confirmation Day. There was no doubt in her mind it had been a success, no matter the concentration it had required to speak confidently and with conviction. Since she'd studied a German translation of the Creed, she'd known exactly when to enunciate and vary the pitch of her voice, which she sensed carried strongly throughout the sanctuary.

Nor would she ever forget the chapel's womb-like dimness, with the flickering of thousands of candles and dozens of golden chandeliers casting light on a kaleidoscope of vivid colors and flickering hues created by icons and mosaics.

That evening she had leaned out of the window in her room in the Terem Palace, savoring the panoramic view of the Kremlin fortress, its illuminated golden-domed churches, and the city stretching away to distant hills. Like worker ants, columns of people wound their way to the Kremlin.

The following day's setting had, if anything, been even more spectacular. Inside the five-domed Uspensky Sobor, which, like most Orthodox cathedrals, rivaled anything in the Protestant world of her childhood, tier after tier of icons reached toward the ceiling. Corinthian columns and walls swirled with paintings and glowing frescoes added to the lavish display, and the newly named Catherine had felt as if she were inside an illuminated manuscript.

It seemed that she had only been aware of Peter's presence dimly, as if it were all for her alone. Yet she could easily envision the empress here just a few years ago, in this magnificent holy place that served as the traditional coronation site for Russian rulers. Did Elizabeth think back fondly and proudly to that day? Of course, she would have, but Catherine realized as the ceremony droned on that Elizabeth must have been forced to attend other coronations here long before her own day arrived. And someday, God willing, she and Peter would stand here to assume the throne!

Her thoughts were interrupted by another fitting by the head seamstress. Catherine would've preferred to celebrate with a gown made of the fabulous blue and silver bolt of brocade given to her by her uncle as a going away gift, but somehow Johanna had managed to maneuver it into her own possession while her daughter was convalescing around Easter. The girl then known as Sophia had been much too weak to wage a battle over the precious Prussian cloth. When someone reported to Elizabeth what Johanna had done, an incensed empress ordered two lengths of even more expensive fabric in the same color and sent it to the future grand duchess to replace her loss, adding to the mountain of brocades she'd already accumulated. *So the empress does love me*, she thought again with a suffusion of happiness.

On the other hand, it was no secret that the empress detested Johanna, who entered the apartments close on the seamstress's heels. Her mother stood awkwardly, a sour face marring those usually pretty and delicate features.

"You may sit," Catherine said, equally awkward.

Both had been told in no uncertain terms that henceforth the Imperial Grand Duchess Catherine Alexeievna would outrank her mother. This meant Johanna was forbidden from entering a room ahead of her daughter; nor must she never sit without Catherine's permission. Based on the expression on Johanna's face, this new court decorum would never be forgiven.

"Yes, yes," Johanna said rudely as she settled her gown into an elaborate chair. "I neglected to kneel and kiss your hand this time. It will take some getting accustomed to. I'm sure you understand, daughter."

Catherine turned away to hide the smile that threatened to insult Johanna even more.

"We must make plans," Johanna said without additional preamble.

"About?"

"The succession."

"There are no plans to make," Catherine dismissed this line of conversation with some embarrassment. She knew better than anyone that her new political significance was solely as the chosen vessel to continue the Romanov dynasty.

Johanna waited a moment for the seamstress to leave. "Of course there are. You are now in line for the throne—as amazing as that seems," Johanna muttered the last phrase.

"Peter is in line for the throne, and I as his consort," Catherine said sharply. "And this is a conversation we should not be having."

"Of course," Johanna added smoothly. "The empress will make

the final choice. She could even bypass the grand duke if she deems it necessary."

"She would not. And you forget, my dear mother, that the empress is still young. She could marry and even bear children herself."

"Rather than bastards!"

For several moments neither said a word. Rumors that Elizabeth had already born children to Alexei and then had them spirited away regularly made the rounds of the palace nobility and servants.

"Enough! You are dismissed!" Catherine said, rising and turning her back.

When she was certain Johanna had left, she sank back onto her daybed and finished her tea. Such talk was dangerous. Such conversations must never take place again. She knew only one thing: that her duty was first to the grand duke, then to the empress, and then to the Russian people.

Anything else would be considered treason.

CHAPTER 10

(MARIA)

It strikes me I'll need to design some system besides special pouches and odd-sized boxes for storing all Catherine's jewels and gem-covered gifts. Perhaps I can consult Monsieur Igor, I think, and smile at my own transparency. After all, who wouldn't love a handsome man in breeches, a waistcoat, and knee-high stockings? And such nice legs! I admit to being disappointed at not spotting him at the confirmation or engagement festivities, although perhaps he does not rank high enough as apprentice to one of the royal jewelers to rate an invitation. Or maybe, through the teeming crowds of gentlemen, I just did not notice him.

That, however, is unlikely.

After enduring another seemingly endless concert ordered by the empress, Catherine flounces back into her chamber and flings off her headdress and jewels, sending me flying around to retrieve them. "Why is it music, music, all the time?" she frets.

"Her Majesty favors it, particularly opera," Irina comments on the obvious.

"It resembles the sound of dogs barking, which I actually find much more pleasant!"

Catherine's lack of interest in music is something we have all accepted, but then Her Imperial Highness surprises us. "I shall take up an instrument," she announces. "We shall have a tutor teach us to play something or other."

The empress, of course, is delighted, and within days a music instructor and a harpsichord appear in Catherine's chambers. We ladies disappear, assuming she will attack this new challenge with the enthusiasm and dedication she shows for all her lessons.

We are wrong. One night she summons us to her chambers purportedly to play us a concert. Instead, we find her bed pillows piled on the sofa, and the harpsichord case leaning against it.

"Help me gather more cushions," she urges, and we scatter through the apartment to do just that, heaping each one on the sofa and even upending a mattress.

"Our new sledding hill!" she proclaims, climbing atop the pillow mountain. Astonished, we watch her take a leap and then slide gracefully down the lid of the harpsichord. Encouraged to try out her new "toboggan," we find it immensely fun to romp around Catherine's rooms indulging in her latest amusement.

"Imagine if the empress could see us now," Natasha giggles, and all of us burst into peals of laughter.

After that, the harpsichord disappears from her room, although the wooden case remains, since Peter and his retinue of gentlemen often join us to go "sledding." They also love to play blind man's buff (apparently an older name for blind man's bluff), in which we all participate. I never realized how much fun it could be to play these games at my age, wondering, though, how much Catherine truly wants to participate or whether she does so to indulge her fiancé's childish whims. With "my lady," who is in many ways still a child herself, it is not always easy to read beyond those mesmerizing blue eyes.

Despite her dismissal of music, Catherine rededicates herself to dancing lessons. "Court dances don't require a sense of rhythm," she comments, and no one can argue with that. Dancing well is also one of the very few things Peter and Catherine have in common.

Most Tuesday evenings the palace ball requires guests to follow one rule perhaps every court member except Elizabeth, Catherine and I find uncomfortable: dressing in clothing of the opposite sex. The empress's love of outfitting herself as a man shows no sign of abating, and we all struggle to get seamstresses to sew us breeches and tunics faster than they produce the gowns we otherwise wear. They must also race to finish dresses for the men.

Irina, who manages to get "ill" most of the time rather than endure this affront to her dignity, complains most. "Everyone hates it! Just watching those old soldiers wearing hoops and corsets is too much to bear. They are miserable. Last time I watched a glum cavalry officer waving his fan like a sword while dancing the minuet. He was almost crying."

"And most of us do not have the figures to endure this kind of apparel!" Natasha adds indignantly.

Sometimes the overweight, short-legged court ladies do look decidedly silly in men's breeches, although the empress cuts a fine figure as she revels in the masquerade. With her tall stature and long, slim legs, Elizabeth looks as fantastic in breeches with a sword swinging at her side as she does in her immense hoop skirts. Catherine, too, slender as a twig and always graceful, seems to enjoy dressing up for what she calls the Metamorphoses.

One evening the forced elegance of a court that prides itself on emulating its French counterpart in Versailles becomes chaotic and even dangerous. During a waltz, Catherine becomes entangled with her dance partner, a gigantic major general wearing arms' width hoops. Falling flat on the floor and beneath his skirts, she at first cannot get up. We fear her arm is broken until the speedily summoned doctor reassures everyone it is only a sprain. Catherine is too busy laughing to mind.

But the masquerades and what I think of as crossdressing balls persist. If there are those who enjoy them, they dare not admit that—at least not in the eighteenth century.

We have a new "boss." Countess Maria Rumyantseva has been appointed head mistress of the grand duchess's household, and it's unclear who spends more time staying out of her way: Catherine or her ladies. Fortunately, this formidable woman and stickler for rules has one weakness she shares with other court members: gambling. High stakes faro games might last until dawn, and the countess never fails to turn up wherever and whenever the game is underway. Although she's known for losing large sums and even borrowing from Catherine (who has recently been given a "card allowance"), we forgive everything because it keeps the countess occupied all night and asleep all morning. Natasha, who persists in her mysterious nocturnal disappearances, has become especially fond of a lady too busy to monitor late night departures and early morning arrivals.

"This is so much better than serving the empress," she mentions, crawling into bed as I am just awakening. "Remember how she kept us up all night? She still has ladies to sit with her until dawn and rub her feet all night. It was so disgusting!"

Of course, I do not remember, but gradually am getting the impression that being a maid of honor to Catherine is infinitely preferable to being one to Elizabeth. And when I look around the palace, it appears I'm fortunate indeed not to have arrived in the past as one of what appear to be a few thousand servants! Their lives and those of the peasants or serfs appear indeed pitiful, and a few times when I absentmindedly reach out to help someone move a chair or set down a heavy silver platter heaped with tea or pastries, I'm reprimanded with disapproving looks and shakes of the head from Irina or Katrina.

The countess is not the only new member assigned to Catherine's household. Elizabeth has also appointed three Russian gentlemen of the chamber and three young Russian officers of the chamber. The latter—Prince Alexander Golitsyn, Count Peter Bestuzhev-Riumin, and Count Zakar Chernyshev—speak French and German. Also handpicked for the new court are three new maids of honor, including two princesses.

This swelling of our ranks doesn't impact the lives or duties of Natasha, Irina, Katrina, and me; on the contrary, it gives us a bit more freedom from the countess's watchful eye. Yet our days of sledding down the clavichord case and playing blind man's buff seem all but over, since Catherine almost immediately supplants us with her two new best friends: Praskovia and Anna, the countess's daughters, who are fourteen and fifteen. Together the three sometimes treat life like a pajama party, staying up all night and playing games and pranks. I admit to being a little jealous, but don't begrudge Catherine her fun. After all, she has her entire life ahead of her to run a kingdom, although she does not know that.

At least I think she doesn't, but who can say how much she suspects. At times this spunky fifteen-year-old appears to juggle her duties and relationships as delicately and politically as if she knows the succession is at risk. Her fiancé is a sickly-looking juvenile, a patently spoiled child whom she goes out of her way to pacify. Her mother is a scheming court flirt, dangerously close to—if not embroiled in— treason and consequently out of favor with the empress, yet Catherine also goes out of her way to be kind and sometimes even to defer to her. Her future mother-in-law apparently feels spurts of maternal love toward Catherine; she also complains about her spending and wields the power to send her back to Prussia on a whim. And absolutely everyone—all the courtiers and generals and ambassadors and royals and attendants and servants—wants something from her.

In all the fairytales my parents and aunt once read me, life as a princess sounded romantic. Now I realize it is not. If I had to be sent here to live, I'm quite content to do it as an attendant. Maybe there really is no such thing as "happily ever after." Just happily today.

Although a frenzy of operas, comedies, masquerades, fireworks, and balls in midsummer mark peace with Sweden, the whirl of celebrations often occurs without Her Majesty. Instead, I've learned that the otherwise extravagant, elegant empress is never happier than when traipsing around the countryside living a nomadic existence.

"She will camp until autumn and play at being a peasant," Irina complains when word reaches us Elizabeth has ordered the court to start packing. "I detest sleeping in those tents!"

"Please, please don't make us go with her this time," Katrina begs, crossing herself. "I cannot live that way another summer."

That way is something that we are all about to experience, however. Natasha breaks the news, flying into the room and flopping on our bed in tears. She has just bid farewell to her latest paramour, who has told her we are all to accompany the empress on a pilgrimage to Kiev.   A similarly dismayed Katrina flounces around for the next few hours muttering about the empress's complete disregard for families. No one points out to her that Elizabeth could hardly be expected to acknowledge a husband she does not realize exists.

Irina heaves a series of long sighs.

Peter and his men simply shrug.

Only Catherine and I—and the empress and her lover Alexei Razumovsky—can barely wait to depart. I'm getting restless trapped in the palace, let alone in this life. Surely a long trip will get my mind off my past, really the future.

We set off with over two hundred courtiers, government and church officials, diplomats, and essential craftsmen and householders from hairdressers and performers to huntsmen and grooms. It appears absolutely nothing will be left behind: the empress travels with the palace furniture, linens, wall hangings, nearly one thousand gowns, livestock, hunting dogs, chapel furnishings, and hundreds more carts piled high with provisions, trunks, and boxes. What is even odder is that the hundreds of us are trailed by *thousands* of weary servants who must cling to the carts or walk behind for what Irina tells us is more than five hundred miles!

Initially I relish the massive sleeping coach covered in mattresses in which we ride, since it seems much more comfortable without the snow and cold of the trip to Moscow. But it takes only a couple days for me to begin hating the pilgrimage. If we sweat inside, it is no better each time we stop, as apparently thick black clouds of gnats have been lusting for our visit. Each time we halt, they invade the hot, dusty roads, intent on annoying the swarm of locusts our own migration must resemble.

Indeed, just like locusts, the mass migration devours everything in sight. When we do overnight, it is at the homes of nobles who, from what Irina tells us and I can see, are forced to take on enormous expenses not only to entice the entire entourage with all manner of delicacies, but to redecorate rooms, lay out special gardens, and even hire opera companies for one night's entertainment. In some cases, she reminds us, the palaces were thrown up hastily in honor of this pilgrimage.

Fortunately, Catherine and Peter's route eventually diverges from that of Elizabeth, and although we're stuck with Johanna and all of Peter's tutors in our entourage, we no longer must wait whenever Elizabeth decides to walk beside her comfortable carriage or Aleksei Razumovsky's to issue commands or greet haggard-looking subjects who line roads to greet her.

Elizabeth also rises early to hunt, prays at every wayside shrine, makes impromptu visits to cottages to chat with people, and enjoys evening entertainments imported hundreds of miles across the treeless, sparsely populated southern provinces and steppe lands of alternating plains of wheat and fields of dust. When we do reach the cooler forests, Natasha points out how much else has been done to honor the empress: roads and bridges have been specially built or repaired, buildings constructed or renewed, signposts and fences freshly painted.

I continue to be amazed at the apparently enormous expense, but not as much as I am to learn every person in every village pays a price. I eavesdrop on provisioners who routinely ride and up and down the entourage reporting on what they've secured—or stripped— from granaries, barns, and households: thousands of chickens, sheep, and horses, not to mention uncountable cartloads loaded with grains, vegetables, eggs, cheeses, cured meats, and honey. There is no way to calculate the gallons of beer, wine, and spirits. We are a ravenous bunch, even stopping alongside the road to strip fields of unripe crops or fruit from orchards. It seems nothing or no one is safe from the entourage's appetite, and I marvel the people remain loyal to a system in which the Crown takes whatever it wants regardless of cost to the people. I suppose I've been too involved in my own situation within the privileged court to think about all the sacrifices made to enable this way of life to thrive. I'm even more grateful I ended up living in a palace, not as a farmer or laborer, yet feel somehow guilty. Above all, I have a much better understanding of exactly why there was, or would be, a revolution in fewer than two hundred years!

These are things I did *not* ponder while growing up. I'm uncertain whether I'm maturing or just being forced into a situation in which I cannot help notice such inequities.

I forget my guilt the moment we arrive at a palatial home of one of Alexei's brothers. I have no problem abandoning my ridiculously tight corset, whalebone stays, and a hot and dusty gown—not to mention the absence of private places to relieve my bladder. I revel in cool basins of water, splashing fountains, clean clothes, porcelain "toilets," and frivolous days. God help me, but I just want to survive here in something that resembles comfort.

CHAPTER 11

(CATHERINE)

*". . . the journey was destined to never be effaced from her memory,
but to have visible influence on her mind and even on the
character of her future government."*
—K. Waliszewski

*"[Catherine and Peter] were both lost in a country they hardly knew;
they both must serve their apprenticeship to power in
the shadow of the Empress."*
—Henri Troyat

Absolutely unacceptable!" the empress raged in the palace where Catherine and Peter's entourage had waited for weeks. It was nearly the end of a fruitful summer, Elizabeth had finally broken her mushroom and berry religious fast for the culinary delights stocked en route, Russia still celebrated its triumph over Sweden, her subjects had greeted her with adulation as she made her royal pilgrimage toward

Kiev, and she had every right to be in a generous mood. Instead, every little thing seemed to incite her fury.

"Why is Her Imperial Majesty so upset?" Catherine asked Irina, who could always be counted upon to supply answers, albeit sometimes diplomatic ones.

"It is the signposts, Your Imperial Highness. They are all new and freshly painted, but some are slightly inaccurate."

"I see." Yet Catherine did *not* see, especially after some of the awful problems she'd witnessed on this royal pilgrimage.

Initially she'd reveled in the trip, her first opportunity to observe her new country's provinces without a snow blanket. And although heat and dryness marked the initial part of their journey, the farther they traveled into Ukrainian lands, the more the countryside gave way to wheat and rye fields alternating with birch, sycamore, and willow forests. An occasional village appeared, marked by rows of crazily tilting wooden cottages.

She had admired the empress's rapport with her subjects, as Elizabeth often strode in breeches or a loose caftan and boots from cottage to cottage, stopping at a whim to settle down for a drink of kvass, a sampling of cabbage soup with fresh mushrooms, or a plate of *blini* made by local women. The empress posed knowledgeable questions about breeding stock, fruit farming, or hunting techniques. Catherine envied how her heroine so ably transformed herself from an elegant and pampered stateswoman into a woman of the people.

Yet gradually other things began to make Catherine feel inexplicably uncomfortable. Thus far in Russia she'd been surrounded by members of the nobility, the military, the clergy, the merchants, and even the relatively well-fed palace servants. The common people—serfs whose hard work and production made all this possible—had been absent from her surroundings, apart from a few beggars stationed in front of cathedrals. But out here, beyond the almost pic-turesque cottages surrounded by vegetable gardens, daisies, cornflow-ers, and picketed fences to secure the pigs, she was at last observing another reality. Other villagers lived in wretched ramshackle shacks with muddy yards minus wildflowers and fences. Thousands of ema-ciated people and stunted, haggard children lined the route with lean, hungry faces. They dressed in grimy rags, most without shoes, and all with holes in what clothing they possessed.

Her compassionate sensibilities made her sometimes turn away to avoid looking at the dulled eyes, the faces pitted with scars, the with-ered or missing limbs of those she knew would someday be Peter's and her subjects.

Those who possessed Sunday clothing donned it to line the roads and prostrate themselves in the dust or mud, perhaps forgetting for a time their toils and hardships as they offered bread and salt and repeatedly crossed themselves to honor their Little Mother and the imperial heirs. This is how it was, and there was no reason for a fif-teen-year-old grand duchess to question the system.

At the Razumovsky estate in Kozolets, Elizabeth's voice rever-berated through the palace. "And I want that pitiful new huntsman replaced. He had the audacity to miss the most obvious shot. This morning we had three—no less than three—grouse right in front of his feet! He missed them all!"

The tirade went on, as the empress ordered everything from sta-tion houses to fences demolished, not to mention servants fired and horses traded.

"If this damn wedding hadn't been postponed, we'd be making plans instead of dealing with this ineptitude! Those idiot doctors don't know a thing. Imagine telling me I *must* wait a year, Alexei. Can you explain to me why I should be denied grandchildren for another year, let alone two?"

Postponed? This was the first hint of such a thing Catherine had heard, let alone that it was due to doctors' orders. Was her spring illness to blame? Or was it Peter, although he had been no more sickly than usual since leaving Moscow. They'd celebrated their betrothal only two months earlier. Why the rush? But the empress's words provided one important clue: Elizabeth was desperate for grandchildren, and this, of course, was the whole purpose of bringing Catherine to Russia.

"Perhaps we should play cards," Irina interrupted softly, as if trying to protect Catherine from hearing all this.

It worked, although inwardly the grand duchess groaned. Madame Rumyantseva had already borrowed Catherine's entire monthly card allowance, and while all of them had waited impatiently for weeks for the empress to catch up with them, the number of high stakes games were having serious consequences on her allowance. With a deep sigh, she retreated to the rooms set up for her, reluctantly rejoining the gentlemen and ladies of her court.

Johanna, too, had been unusually cross—even for her—the entire trip. One day she had her first argument with Peter. "You imbecile!" she yelled when, while chasing around Johanna's room, he'd jumped in the air to impress Catherine. When he bumped into the stool that held the reticule in which Johanna kept many of her cosmetics, fans, and jewels, everything had fallen to the floor, scattering letters, bracelets, bon bons, and pots of rouge and powders.

"Get out, you uneducated lout!" she screamed, forgetting whom she addressed.

When Peter shouted back in broken Russian, Catherine was surprised and pleased to discover he had at least a rudimental knowledge of the language.

"It was an accident," Catherine defended her betrothed.

"Nonsense! He did it on purpose!"

When Catherine persisted in calling it an accident and failed to help her mother pick up her things, Johanna snapped.

"Take this!" she screamed, then cuffed her daughter on the ears.

"This you will not do! You are not permitted to strike the grand duchess. No one but I has that right!" a furious Peter yelled, interceding for the first time on Catherine's behalf.

Although both stalked out of the room in anger, later they laughed at the incident and poked fun at Johanna. The event seemed to draw them closer together.

Johanna, however, had made a new enemy. The grand duke would never forgive her.

On the final leg to Kiev, an impatient Elizabeth had set out first. The grand duke, fed up with his future mother-in-law and committed to dodging his tutors, rode in his fiancée's carriage.

The court halted several times at convents or estates to be entertained by ballets, comedies, and dramatic performances. A fireworks display had been arranged to follow one of the performances, but as it began, one rocket misfired. It flew straight into the main marquee and showered sparks atop the imperial tent. The empress was unharmed, although the ensuing pandemonium and stampede of horses threatened to accomplish what the golden rocket had not.

After crossing a river, they finally arrived. Almost immediately a huge body of clergymen met the Imperial party. After that they walked, the entire group heading for the monastery led by a priest carrying a processional cross.

Catherine marveled at the magnificent clusters of cupolas in the distance, rising from a bluff overlooking the Dnieper River's western bank. They resembled golden bubbles rising toward heaven, and she was instantly enthralled at this holiest of all holy cities in Russia.

Long before she could explore the cathedral interiors, they were swept up in a massive welcome. "You would think Jesus had just ridden into Jerusalem on a donkey," she murmured to herself, watching the empress, now also carrying a cross, engulfed by immense crowds.

For most of the weeks they spent here, Elizabeth exuberantly visited every single shrine, church, convent, and monastery. She also attended each festivity. Nightly a new historical drama or religious allegory was performed, which Catherine and her ladies endured out of necessity. Fortunately, at times when the performances lasted too long, Elizabeth would rise with a yawn, order the performance to cease, and sweep out of the theatre.

Then it was time to visit the place that would impress Catherine most: the eleventh-century Cathedral of the Dormition, where the most important Russian saints were venerated.

"Look at this," she whispered to her ladies, equally in awe. Indeed, the splendid Byzantine exterior and Gothic-style interior ranked as the most magnificent cathedral she'd ever seen. "I've never been more struck by anything in my life." The cathedral could've served as a ballroom for all its size and grandeur, including tiers of gold and silver icons coated with pearls and glittering with diamonds, rubies, and emeralds.

No less impressive was St. Sophia's Cathedral, the previous site of coronations and other royal ceremonies, and Pechersky Convent, with its solid gold shrines and gem-encrusted icons. If the settings were astounding, they were no less so than the history. It was in Kiev that Prince Vladimir had accepted the Christian faith in 988. And here the head of that same prince had been returned to the monastery. And here St. Andrew had preached the first gospel of Christianity. Here, too, the most sacred of all Russian relics was preserved: the miracle-working icon alleged to be painted by Saint Luke.

Except for these mandated events arranged for the imperial pilgrims, Catherine remained in the shadow of the empress—one that served her well as she and Peter now had unprecedented freedom. The only site to which they were forbidden access was the famous catacombs, filled with mummied martyrs and saints contained within and beneath the special type of monastery known as a lavra.

"They might catch a cold underground," the doctors warned, and thus the grand duke and duchess were somewhat at liberty to explore the city with their respective retinues.

What amazed Catherine even more than the extravagant churches and the city's history as the birthplace of Russia was the pageant of people. Everywhere she looked, Turks, Jews, Greeks, Armenians, Cossacks and Poles hawked wares. The richer delegations arrived to pay homage to the empress. Their prancing horses, unusual weapons, and diamond-studded scabbards contrasted with half naked anchorites with manacled wrists and tangled beards. She found this medley of peoples enthralling and felt disappointed when it was time to return to Moscow.

"I would like to return here someday," she confessed to Natasha, Irina, Maria, Katrina, and the princesses as they settled into their mattress-lined coach for the return.

"Certainly Your Imperial Highness will have such an opportunity," Maria ventured.

"Perhaps," Catherine answered softly. She dreaded the rural rambles that would eventually return them to Moscow. She also dreaded the sights of the serfs working the fields, overseen by whip-wielding foremen. Most of all she dreaded her marriage, which fortunately would not take place until they returned to Petersburg. At least the long journey would delay the inevitable, and in the meantime, she determined to bury herself in amusements, card-playing, and mindless chatter with her ladies.

Back in Moscow, Catherine was drawn into a whirl of celebrations and religious holidays, culminating with her own Name Day on November 24. The following day, the most important on the court calendar, marked the anniversary of Elizabeth's accession to the throne. Unfortunately, the grand duke missed nearly all the festivities, confined to his bed most of that autumn due first to a chest infection and then a lengthy bout of chickenpox.

Catherine, assured it was nothing for her to concern herself with, threw herself wholeheartedly into theatrical performances, balls, and masquerades. She danced each evening in an even more magnificent dress. At times she revealed her dazzling white skin in a low-cut gown, which provided an opportunity to show off the jewels of which she was so fond.

Changing her dress three times a day, as was the court custom, soon took a toll on her finances. Resisting the need and desire to assemble a suitable wardrobe and toilette was nearly impossible with Moscow tradesmen and their attendants persistently lined up outside her bedroom. They coaxed her to look inside bundles and crates containing lovely fabric samples, lustrous pearls, delicate laces, Parisian millinery, wooden dolls dressed in the latest French fashions, glittering rubies, pomades, and perfumes guaranteed to entice men, moisturizers or concealing ointments, and the essences of narcissus, orange blossom, and rose petals. Unable to resist, she often selected what she wanted for herself, at the same time aware that her own servants' loyalty must often be bought and that a reputation for generosity rather than stinginess must be fostered. Thus she continued helplessly mired in the court habit of sweetening tempers with gifts.

Often her ladies attended this parade of merchants, convincing her to purchase items that appealed to them, from powder puffs and beauty spots to white gloves and needlework bags. Fortunately, most of the merchants who sold to the Imperial Court were accustomed to lengthy waits for their money, and Catherine carelessly took advantage of the lavish credit extended. It was all too easy to borrow from one creditor to pay another.

In the meantime, she and her ladies, including her new friends the princesses Anna and Praskovia, made the most of the autumn festivities. Under ballet master Lande, who brought a pocket violin twice a day, she practiced the latest dance steps, as well as the more traditional minuet and polonaise. She became so proficient that Lande himself dared whisper, "You are almost as good as Her Imperial Majesty!"

Long after the music ceased, Catherine and her court retired to her rooms to laugh and discuss the latest mishaps at the balls. "Did you see Count Vavilov blush?" Anna giggled. "I swear his face resembled a tomato! He kept trying to hide behind his fan, but he dropped it so many times I thought he would drown beneath his hoop skirt."

"I love to watch them stagger in petticoats," Katrina added. "Especially when they collide with their partners. Truly, how difficult is it to do the minuet in hoop skirts? We manage it all the time!"

All hilarity and late-night sessions ended abruptly one night at the theater when Count Lestocq entered Catherine's box during intermission. "Her Majesty is greatly displeased," he said without preamble. "She has sent me to chastise you." His face was angry.

"Why?" Catherine demanded.

"You are overspending, and word of your debts has reached Her Imperial Majesty. She demands you get yourself under control and your finances in order!"

Catherine, now trembling and pale, could barely find the words to dispute what she suspected to be true. To have Elizabeth angry with her—to be at the receiving end of her now famous temper tantrums—was more than the grand duchess could bear.

Count Lestocq ranted for several more minutes, listing examples of how many rubles Catherine owed to which merchant.

As if she weren't already close to tears, she heard Peter chime his agreement.

"Everyone knows," Johanna leaned over to add, "that giving this type of financial freedom to a mere girl is unwise."

Catherine stared straight ahead at the rest of the performance without seeing or hearing it. She felt frustrated, hurt, angry, and betrayed by everyone.

The next day she reviewed her accounts, only to discover her debts were all too real, not to mention approaching exorbitant. She was at a loss as to how to remedy this, except not to spend another ruble. More importantly, she absolutely had to find a way to ingratiate herself once again with the empress.

Yet Catherine was learning. She'd seen plenty of Elizabeth's capricious whims over the past few months, although she also noticed Her Majesty forgave quickly. Even knowing that this incident, too, would pass, for the first time Catherine seriously worried about her relationship with a woman who changed her mind as easily as she changed her gown.

And that, indeed, was the problem: if the empress tired so quickly of a dress, how long before she might tire of the fifteen-year-old girl she had summoned here from Prussia?

Peter rejoined the court festivities at the end of November. As Catherine danced at a masquerade with him once again, she felt full of charm and vitality. The empress seemed to have forgotten about the debt crisis, and Peter acted as if he admired the girl he'd soon be forced to marry.

Basking in court events, in Peter's recovery and attention, and in Elizabeth's forgiveness, Catherine glowed. And she knew that, despite being forced to disguise the fact she occasionally wore variants of the same gown more than once, she had never looked better. Her waist was so narrow that she could almost encircle it with her hands. She wondered what it would feel like if someone else did that.

As for Peter, she desperately wanted to believe he felt some love for her, even—dare she hope it—with enough passion that someday they would create the grandchild that the empress wanted and needed. In the meantime, she could enjoy herself, even imagine a hopeful, happy future with a loving husband and children.

CHAPTER 12

(MARIA) 1744-1745

To my relief, the court is to migrate back to Petersburg for the winter holidays. I'm convinced any chance of returning to the future lies there, whether via the statue I touched nearly a year ago, or at least at the site of what will be the new Winter Palace—eventually to be called the Hermitage.

I presume my *real* eighteenth birthday passed a month ago. No one asks when Maria's birthday is, but I feel panicked I might spend many more of them here. Jostling along in the sledge, I have too much time to think. By now Aunt Roberta must have returned to the States. She undoubtedly considers me dead or kidnapped. On the other hand, I fret about whether the real Maria has taken my place. Yet how could an eighteenth-century teenager adapt to a life of cell phones, computers, televisions, autos, airplanes, ATMs, jeans, Y2K . . . well, the list goes on. Most likely it is much easier for *me* to adapt than for *her*. That is, of course, presuming we somehow switched.

Sometimes, looking out at ships docked along the Neva, I wonder if I could or should book passage for the Colonies. I'd at least dock in the right country, although I'm certain nothing much yet existed in East Lansing, Michigan. My god, I realize when I consider the date: the American Revolution would occur in fewer than twenty years. Then what? Should I be there instead of here? What if I'm going to be stuck in the past until I grow old and die here? But then how could I or would I still be born in 1982? At such times, I am at least grateful for the headache powders that seem every bit as effective as aspirin.

My other concern is not having any idea how much time has passed—or not passed—in the future. It seems that in time travel novels and films, the character imagines he or she is gone for months or years, but upon returning to the present discovers only minutes have passed. In that case, Aunt Roberta is still wandering around the Hermitage looking for her niece! I miss her. I especially miss the opportunity to recount my experiences to her, although there is a low probability that she would—or will—believe me about all of this. And what happened on December 31, 2000? Did all the computers crash and were my friends' parents hoarding food and toilet paper for good reason?

"Did you know my parents?" I ask Irina tentatively as she shuffles a deck of cards on one of the mattresses in our sledge.

"Of course not, Maria. Exactly how old do you think I am?'

"But *I* don't remember them, that's all. I was hoping someone else did."

"Her Majesty could tell you. After all, it was she who took you into her court when you were a girl. I do know you were in service to the crown long before Elizabeth actually became empress."

"They were sculptors, were they not?" Katrina asks. "Or at least your father was. Surely you at least know that?"

Sculptors? Surely that is too much of a coincidence!

When Katrina is forced to repeat the question, I manage to say airily, "Of course, I did know *that.*"

The conversation devolves into stories of their own parents, all members of noble families who apparently live far from court. Only Natasha, like me, is an orphan taken into service as a child first by Elizabeth's sister, Empress Anna, and later by Elizabeth herself. Presumably there is some type of hierarchy amongst the maids and the married ladies in waiting that roughly corresponds to Peter the Great's Table of Ranks, although I cannot figure it out. All I know is that Irina gets an allowance of six hundred rubles per year and I get nothing. On the other hand, what is there to buy? Everything is provided.

We make it barely halfway on our return, somewhere past Tver, when the cortege is halted, and Dr. Boerhave gets summoned to the grand duke's carriage to hover over Peter. We're told to rest overnight in Khotilovo, where we settle in without concern. Peter is sick frequently, and reported stomach pains, dizziness, and fever seem no more serious than his other frequent bouts of illness.

"Oh my God!" Katrina screams as she rushes back into our room in the morning. "They say he has erupted in spots!"

My companions recoil, but I'm confused. He just recovered from chickenpox, so why are we worried? Can you even get them twice? Again I remind myself that I was vaccinated for chickenpox, measles, and mumps as a child, so thus far have not felt overly worried about my own health. I fear I'm more likely to contract food poisoning or die from an overabundance of flea bites!

"What kind of spots?" I ask.

"It is the pox, you idiot!" Katrina gasps. "Smallpox!"

"We are all at risk," Irina says soberly.

All of us? Of course, that includes me. I had thought smallpox was eradicated and am nearly certain I never received a vaccine for it.

One of Johanna's ladies enters. "Princess Johanna insists we leave this morning!"

"She would, of course," Irina agrees, already moving to gather up gowns, stays, and chemises. "Her brother—Her Majesty's betrothed—died of smallpox."

"And in her condition . . ." Natasha adds, although Irina puts one gloved hand over her mouth to hush her. We all know that it is a secret—or at least a rumor of one—that Johanna is pregnant. It is just one of the two reasons she has been a holy terror to be around on this trip. The second is that her presumed lover, some count or other, was forbidden to accompany the rest of the court on the Kiev pilgrimage.

"Does the empress know about the grand duke?" Katrina asks, nervously running pale fingers over her smooth complexion.

"I don't believe so," the lady answers. "She is far ahead of us, perhaps nearly back to Petersburg."

By the time we've packed and dressed, Catherine's sledge, overseen by a clearly terrified Johanna, is at the front of the convoy prepared to leave.

Irina practically yanks all of us into a sledge behind Johanna's, and within moments we are hurling across the snow toward Petersburg.

Someone must have galloped ahead to notify Her Majesty, as close to Novgorod we encounter her sledge racing in the other direction. Everyone halts, while a grim-looking Elizabeth leans out to speak with Catherine and Johanna. She issues orders we can barely hear, sounding crisp as the fresh-falling snow.

Minutes later we're enroute once more, Catherine's sleigh sending her to the capital and out of harm's way, and Elizabeth's flying in reverse toward her ailing nephew and heir.

As dark falls and barrels of lit pitch illuminate the way, we are all lost in our own thoughts. Each of us has witnessed faces ravaged by the effects of smallpox, the least damaged ones strategically covered with the popular beauty strips. The other victims are hideous, and even servants risk their jobs if they survive but appear so repulsive that they are considered unfit for court. Everyone except me has known someone who died from the disease, which is apparently highly contagious, and we're all mentally retracing our steps over the past days in the hope we did not get too close to the grand duke.

Could his death right now be the reason Catherine will end up ruling alone? At the moment I am unsure whose future looks blacker: Peter's, Catherine's, Elizabeth's, the dynasty's, or even my own.

What happens in the future if I die in the past?

CHAPTER 18

(CATHERINE) 1745

"Absence, distance and anxiety had softened Catherine's mental image of Peter. True, he was puny, bony and heavy-lidded, with a smile that was sometimes crafty, sometimes foolish, but such as he was, she liked him and was impatient to see him again."
—Henri Troyat

Secluded in Petersburg lest she contract the dreaded pox, Catherine had too much time alone with her thoughts. Yet sometimes she longed for even more solitude. At the empress's command, she and her mother settled into separate apartments in a house beside the overcrowded Winter Palace. This meant her primary companion was Johanna, who complained bitterly that Catherine had much nicer rooms. They were virtually identical, but this did not prevent Johanna from hurling insults at her daughter. Nor did it prevent her endless squabbles over precedence that were as annoying to Catherine as the biting insects that had plagued them on the trip to Kiev.

Throughout the damp winter Catherine steadfastly avoided court balls and festivities that persisted even in the empress's absence. Those few times she did venture to the palace, the temperatures were no less frosty inside, as certain courtiers already turned away when the grand duchess passed. It was as if her position at court had become nearly as tenuous as her mother's in the months since the empress had ordered that Johanna be ignored.

Fortunately, her Russian lessons and a procession of faithful visitors provided some relief, as did the giant staircase separating the two apartments. In her rooms huge stoves smoked and crackled as Catherine scribbled letter after letter in French, although her teacher not only edited them as he translated, but added the required overblown sentiments in perfect Russian. She then carefully copied each one, so that the empress would receive multiple heartfelt inquires about the grand duke's health.

There were no responses.

For six agonizing weeks the empress refused to leave her nephew's side, trapping herself in a dingy farmhouse, rarely changing her clothing. The woman rumored to possess thousands of gowns neglected not only her hygiene and appearance but risked her own health.

"They say she hovers over his bed the way she once did over mine," Catherine mused to Katrina. "Do you think this means she really does love us both?"

"She must. Why else would Her Majesty dismiss the threats to her own health and life?"

Why else indeed? Yet Catherine shivered at the idea of potential disfigurement that accompanied the smallpox's ravaging effects.

It was not only the knowledge that the empress, that proud beauty who ruled a massive empire, would depart this earth that frightened Catherine. *Peter might die.* And aside from the grief that would accompany such a loss, she knew that without him she'd no longer be a grand duke's fiancée, the potential wife of a future tsar. The chilly reception she already received at court made it all too clear that her *raison d'être* was in jeopardy.

She would be nobody. Nothing. Any credit, monetarily or socially, advanced to her—not to mention any power she might now possess based on her future position—would be yanked away as suddenly as it had been bestowed upon her a short year earlier. Most certainly she would be sent back to Prussia, away from this place in which she had immersed myself. This place she now called home.

Ashamed of her thoughts, she dared not share them with anyone. She wrote often to her childhood governess, Babet, but inevitably tore up the letters and tossed the pieces in the stoves. She could not trust anyone, and the letters expressing her doubts might be considered treasonous. In the meantime, she could only wait, worry, wonder.

Finally the long-awaited message from Elizabeth arrived: *My dear niece, I am infinitely obliged to Your Highness for your agreeable messages. I have delayed replying to them because I could not reassure you with regard to the health of His Highness, the Grand Duke. Now this day, I can assure you that, to our joy, God be praised, we may hope for his recovery. He has come back to us.*

Waves of relief washed through her. That night—and every night thereafter for some time—Catherine fled her apartments to attend a masquerade, a ball, or some other new triumph, as if she had regained her confidence with the quieting of her fears.

Suddenly she found delight in everything. Entering the ballroom trailed each night by her own and the empress's ladies, she thought of herself as leading a flotilla of beautiful boats festooned with paper and jeweled flowers. In fact, due to the enormous width of their hooped skirts, it made Catherine laugh to realize they resembled huge ships all trying to navigate the tiny canals that wound their way through Petersburg.

It took awhile for her to slow this pace, and when she did, it was to move in an entirely different direction.

It began when Count von Gyllenborg, the Swedish envoy, took the opportunity while dancing with Catherine to chastise her for frivolity.

"You must read," he scolded.

"But I do." She proceeded to respond to his penetrating queries by reciting the titles of all the popular novels she'd recently completed.

"I mean that you should educate yourself on something beyond lurid romances," he chided, and when in a fit of levity she began to quote from a salacious scene in one of the novels, he bowed and excused himself.

Yet the count's words had by no means fallen on deaf ears. Catherine responded immediately to his criticisms, locking herself away for several nights until she had completed what she titled, "Self-Portrait of a Fifteen-Year-Old Philosopher."

Impressed with the grand duchess's skill, intellectual bent, and loquaciousness, Count Gyllenborg replied in a twelve-page letter that included an entire reading list. The philosophers and writers he recommended included Plutarch, Cicero, Montesquieu, and Voltaire.

In response, Catherine enthusiastically ordered a servant to procure works by these writers so she could immerse herself in their work. Although it didn't happen immediately, the count had planted seeds in the soil of her mind. In this fertile place, they would germinate at an even riper time. A time when she would be ready to cultivate them.

In the meantime, she awaited not only the books but her fiancé, and fell asleep dreaming of Peter's return.

In the palace's reception hall, it was late afternoon, still shadowed in the semi-dark of a Petersburg winter.

Not dark enough, however, to shield her from the terror that had once been her betrothed: this monster, this swollen being with a ravaged, pitted face. Catherine was speechless. Barely able to look at the unhealed pockmarks, she focused instead on the horrifying, enormous wig that so obviously hid what must be a shaved head.

Only months earlier she, too, had found herself looking like a bald scarecrow, but she did not think of this now.

"Do you recognize me?" He gave her a twisted, obviously forced smile.

It took her several moments to respond. Too many moments.

And it was this hesitation, this failure to smile warmly and quickly, that she realized only much later he would never forgive.

Eventually she managed to get control of the involuntary shudder, to summon up every ounce of her courage. "Congratulations on your recovery," she stammered.

This first encounter lasted a brief but agonizing few minutes, until Catherine mumbled her apologies, gathered up her pastel satin skirt, and fled to her apartments.

There she collapsed in tears.

A full day later she sat up, ordered tea and fruitcake, attempted to tend to her own hair, and stopped berating herself for the way she had handled the meeting with Peter.

I did not come to Russia to marry a face, she chided herself, *but an heir, even an empire.*

But she knew—and would always blame herself for it—that when she saw that distorted face, her blood had run cold.

"May I read to you?" a soft voice intruded on her thoughts from the antechamber.

It was Maria, who may or may not have seen Peter yet. Catherine would not ask. She could never share her thoughts on this, just as she could never openly reveal her feelings on so many things that had happened since her arrival.

She wordlessly handed Maria one of her favorite novellas, one Babet had read her so many years ago: Madame de Villeneuve's *La Belle et la Bête*. And as Maria's melodious voice filled the room, Catherine closed her eyes and listened. If Beauty could face the horrifying prospect of marrying a monster, if she could live in a palace with him with some happiness, if she could find a loving future with her prince, then she, Her Imperial Grand Duchess Catherine Alexeievna of Russia, could do so, too.

That night, swallowing her revulsion, she dined with Peter. She had had time to recover from the first shock, to put on a normal face, to assure him that his scars would fade.

In the coming months she would have to overcome the fact that his appearance sickened her. She would have to find a way to love him.

Time, however, did not dim Peter's agony over what he had become. Rather he seemed to retreat even further than before into his childhood, like a turtle afraid to abandon his shell. He invented elaborate excuses to stay in his apartment, avoiding the limelight at all costs.

He apparently found solace in his toys, particularly dolls and the soldiers that he could order about. Although Catherine could deal with the toy soldiers, one day she arrived to find his apartment crowded with servants costumed as soldiers.

"March!" Peter roared, and led them in military drills that involved parading through his rooms. He had conjured up his own army and laughed as he struck at servants who failed to stay in line.

He has found a new remedy for his former illness, she thought, and left with a sense of foreboding.

During Lent, news arrived that her baby sister, Elizabeth's namesake, had died. She was only three years old. Although when Catherine and Johanna had left Prussia Elizabeth had been just a toddler, Catherine vividly recalled the little girl's soft, sweet smell. Her cornflower blue eyes. Now in her grief, Catherine was unsure whether to mourn or feel relief for this child, who would never need be a pawn in the marriage game.

In part to assuage her mourning, Catherine finally got her wish to take formal horseback riding lessons. Only in the countryside, trotting and then eventually learning to gallop, could she feel free, as if she were her own self, not a cog in the imperial wheel.

Riding also served to hold at bay the inevitable, since she had a great repugnance about hearing the day named for her nuptials. Irina and Katrina told her the truth, however: the empress was growing increasingly impatient for the grand duchess to produce an heir.

"The physicians have warned her to wait," Irina confessed over needlepoint. "One of her ladies told me that the doctor objects to the marriage because His Imperial Highness is not ready physically—and perhaps not emotionally." She allowed her voice to drop on the last word.

"She is afraid some sort of illness will recur before the wedding can take place," Catherine stated matter-of-factly.

"And after the assailant was captured . . ." Katrina shuddered.

No one was supposed to know what had happened the previous night, but since ladies and gentlemen of all three imperial courts mingled frequently, nothing remained secret. The way Catherine heard it, the empress's bodyguard had discovered a would-be assassin wielding a knife and hiding in the empress's wardrobe.

"He always protects her," Irina assured them. "He sleeps at the foot of her bed, and with those massive arms and fierce scowl I cannot imagine anyone would have dared attempt to kill Her Majesty. Years ago, I made the mistake of entering her bedchamber to check on her, but I didn't seek permission first. He leaped off that thin little mattress and nearly strangled me!"

"They say his arms are so powerful because he is a former stove-stoker," Natasha volunteered. "Imagine the strength it must take to do that all day and night!"

Now, the morning after the assassination attempt, Elizabeth had promptly issued a Royal Decree naming July 1 as the date for the joining of the two young people. For the next three days, drum rolls and hollering heralds would announce the joyful news to the public.

Catherine forced a smile at her ladies, as if relieved that the date had been set. She hoped that the way she jabbed her needle at the center of the embroidery hoop did not betray her, for beyond the facade, she knew the tears would fall freely once she was alone.

Only in the nearby forests and pastures could she literally give rein to her true feelings. She increased her riding lessons as if to build her self-confidence, feeling herself gradually grow strong enough to embrace court life. While on horseback she saw herself as a beautiful, gay, and spontaneous girl—almost a woman.

As Peter flirted daily with this or that one of the empress's maids of honor, as he scorned his fiancée with callous disregard—or worse yet purely filial treatment—she also realized that the wedding could not be coming at a worse time. Was it even possible that the two of them would become even more isolated from one another despite their shared destiny?

No matter how much Catherine tried to engage him in meaningful conversation, Peter insisted on happily extolling the virtues of his favorite women. And unlike the budding beauty the grand duchess was becoming, each of his parade of favorites seemed coarse, vulgar, and specially selected to inflict the most bruises on Catherine's pride. In fact, Peter professed to love most those who had some kind of physical defect, so that he surrounded himself with women who suffered from a squint, a harelip, a hunchback, or homely features. It seemed as if his penchant for other women, even though he purportedly never consummated any of those relationships, would be a potential recipe for Catherine's and their marriage's demise.

Too many nights now she dreamed about reversing her journey from Prussia, about being a snow maiden flying back across the tundra to a life she had before.

Sometimes she almost believed this was what she wanted.

CHAPTER 14

(MARIA) 1745

In early summer the court moves to Elizabeth's favorite place, Peterhof, built by Peter the Great for his wife on the Gulf of Finland's shores. For me, there are perks besides the spacious grounds and delightful palace. I've exhausted possibilities searching for that one critical sculpture at the palace and summer gardens in Petersburg; now, however, I recall from my visit with Aunt Roberta that cascades of gilded fountains and dozens of mythological statues embellish the upper and lower gardens.

Indeed, we spend nearly every day and evening strolling Peterhof's manicured gardens, savoring suppers in special giant tents, taking carriage rides around the grounds, and sailing the canals in elaborate barges. Since it is White Nights season once again—another painful reminder that I have been in the past for well over a year—we seldom retire before dawn.

Even with all these chances at inspecting Peter's statues, none looks familiar. No helmeted marble goddess with wide open eyes. No more chances here than anywhere else to make what I continue to presume will be the physical connection that takes me home. From time to time I reach out to touch a different goddess—just in case—but to no avail.

"Ah, a goddess meets another goddess," a familiar male voice catches me in the act one afternoon.

I whirl around, afraid I've been caught by someone in Peter's retinue, since his gentlemen love to flirt shamelessly and almost insolently with the ladies.

But there is a warm and almost humorous touch in the voice, and I'm surprised to discover it is Igor Igorevich Blukhov who has caught me fingering the arm of the statue. We are far from the palace, almost to the sea, and it appears he has just arrived by boat.

Realizing I've strayed from Catherine's entourage, I know the odds of us meeting this way were slim, and am pleased at last to have the chance to speak with Igor about something besides broken clasps and carat weights.

"Good evening, Monsieur."

"You are an admirer of Aphrodite, I see," he smiles.

"Who?"

He waves toward the statue. "Venus, according to the Romans, who simply changed her name."

"Oh yes, the goddess of love."

"It is fitting, I believe."

At that, I feel myself blush, something I know I never did in the past/future, where such banter would simply be lighthearted, even meaningless flirting. "I don't know about that."

"You are not in love with anyone, Mademoiselle?"

"*Nyet*. I'm not."

"In that case, perhaps we could sit on this bench and rest a bit. It has been a long walk from the pier, and I'm afraid there are no horses free."

The "old" me spreads her skirts and settles immediately onto the bench with pleasure, at the same time as my eighteenth-century persona realizes this is far from proper without an escort.

As if reading my mind, Igor sets his parcel down and settles at the opposite end of the bench. "No disrespect intended, Mademoiselle Maria. I am sorry, but I do not believe I know your surname."

Sometimes I don't recall what it is supposed to be either, but I make an effort. "Kurchov. Maria Sergeievna Kurchova."

"Ah yes. I do recall now hearing that one of the Imperial Highness's ladies was the daughter of the sculptor Sergei Kurchov. That would explain your interest in our Venus."

"Did you know him? My father?" I ask eagerly. Ever since learning my parents were sculptors, I have been grilling everyone I can find about their work and lives.

"I'm afraid not, as I, too, was young when he died, but I believe my uncle might have. I shall ask him. He will be back in Petersburg today. So many preparations for the royal wedding, as you know."

"Her Imperial Highness is somewhat relieved, I suspect, that it has been postponed yet again until late August."

"We are all relieved, Mademoiselle."

"Please, call me Maria."

"Maria. Such a lovely name for a lovely lady."

"You are embarrassing me," I confess, waving my fan rapidly not to shield my face, but because the heat outside is mirrored inside me.

"I didn't mean to do that. Again, please forgive me."

"You are forgiven," I smile, and the answering grin he flashes makes me want to laugh with glee. At last. At last I get to speak with this Adonis.

As if to relieve my embarrassment, he returns to the subject of the wedding. "I'm afraid we shall all be in debt for years to come from this wedding."

"I understand that Her Imperial Majesty has given precise orders to nearly everyone in the kingdom about what to wear, what to buy, and how much of each."

Igor laughs. "I suspect she is determined to make this an event to eclipse anything previously done in the empire. Each nobleman must secure elegant new livery for their servants, new carriages, and sumptuous finery. In fact, she has dictated to the top fourteen ranks that each must hire no fewer than twenty footmen, not to mention a cotillion of pages and runners. And each has been assigned specific velvet breeches and coats, matching silk stockings, lace cuffs, and metallic trims."

"I do know that court officials have been given a year's advance on their salaries to update their fashions."

"Ah, if only the same were true of the merchants. We can only pray that someday we will get paid, although I am grateful there are no such mandates about our wardrobes," he chuckles.

I cannot help laughing with him. "I understand the ports are clogged with ships?"

"I'm surprised they don't sink one another."

"Tell me about it. We are so insulated here. Well, except for that." I wave across the pathway to the main one where Igor most likely was walking when he saw me. The broad area that sweeps from the sea bustles with pedestrians, carriages, and horses bringing servants, merchants, artisans, workmen, and officials back and forth up to the top of the hill where the palace sprawls.

"Well, you must realize that such an event—the likes of which neither of us has seen in our relatively short lifetimes—is unprecedented. Ever since Her Majesty's ambassadors have returned to report on all the details of the recent wedding of the French *dauphin* to the Spanish *infanta*, activity has grown more frantic. The ambassadors studied the western courts' protocol and rules of precedence. Versailles is, I believe, Her Majesty's Mecca, and she has enticed French carpenters, pastry chefs, artists, decorators, and seamstresses to come to Russia by offering them exorbitant salaries. They bring drawings and descriptions in minute detail of what has been done at other weddings, and what must be surpassed. Special fountains being erected at the Admiralty will spurt with wine, tables will be laden with food, and workmen are even erecting scaffolding with velvet and cloth hangings to seat spectators."

"Go on."

"Well, the harbors are clogged, as you pointed out, with shipments to fulfill the empress's requisitions for fine fabrics, golden saddles, Italian stirrups, delicate porcelains, cases of pineapples and other tropical fruits, herds of cattle, crates of poultry, and casks of wine and mead. Ships from Italy, Germany, France, and England dock bow to stern, their hulls laden with liveries, draperies, tableware, and spices. A friend tells me he recently observed one with an entire cargo of just buttons and braiding, and another carrying nothing but soaps, scents, and cosmetics!"

"Just imagine! However, I do not believe there are enough seamstresses in all the land to keep up with the demand for creating so many elaborate gowns, stitching on embroideries, and sewing on what must be thousands and thousands of beads, seed pearls, and jewels."

At this last, he suddenly rises. "Speaking of jewels, I am afraid I should be at the palace now."

"Oh, dear. I hope I didn't detain you from your business."

"Absolutely not," he smiles. "The pleasure was more than worth being a bit late."

"Ah, then you do not know Your Imperial Majesty the way you should!" I laugh.

"Fortunately, I am here today on business for the grand duke's gentlemen. Especially now that diamond shoe buckles have become fashionable, we cannot keep up with the demand. I am grateful there are so many jewelers arriving in the city to help."

"You don't mind the competition?"

"Not a bit. But do not let my uncle hear that I said such a thing." Once again, his smile lights up his face. And my heart.

"Might I see you again, Maria Sergeievna? I mean," he nearly stammers, "in a less than official capacity. Perhaps it is not proper to ask, but I find I enjoy your company."

"I think . . ."

"Of course, forgive me for asking. It would not be proper."

"But Monsieur . . ."

"Igor. Igor Igorevich."

"Igor, perhaps there might be a way," I suggest boldly.

"Perhaps." He bows then, and when I decline his offer to escort me back to the palace, I feel inexplicably sad. I want to sit here awhile, savor our conversation, and wallow in my regret that things here are so incredibly structured and riddled with protocols. I already know it would not be considered appropriate for me to be seen socializing with a man alone, let alone someone of the merchant class, and this frustrates me nearly to tears.

As the Big Day approaches and wagons from the empire's remotest corners arrive in an endless procession into Petersburg, we return to the city. The post-nuptial celebration is to last for ten days, and there are still a myriad of preparations. Although all of us in Catherine's retinue are kept busier than ever, it is also easier to be overlooked and have a bit of breathing room.

Part of this occurred when the empress unexpectedly added eight new maids to Catherine's entourage in May. They speak only Russian, and so Catherine has become even more fluent. They are as delighted as the rest of us to play tag and slide down the harpsichord case when invited; other times I hear them all chattering and laughing as they experiment with the latest French hairstyles.

Catherine has assigned them tasks that for a time give the original four of us, as well as Anna and Praskovia, more flexibility. One takes charge of her lace, one oversees her ribbons, one keeps her supplied with slices of fruitcake and plum preserves, etc. She has also assigned her new dwarves to specific tasks: one manages her combs and hair powders, one oversees her rouge and patches, and one is supposed to take charge of the key to her jewels. Thus far I have taken care of getting broken things fixed, sorting matching necklaces with earrings, and choosing which gems go best with her various gowns. Now it seems that I am to be replaced and reassigned to do who knows what! I realize not only how much I loved the responsibility, but how much overseeing the jewels gave me extra opportunities to be close to and even speak with Igor.

Fortunately, before I lose the key to the dwarf's keeping, word of Catherine's initiative reaches the ear of the empress. Within days she and Catherine's "jailer," the countess, have vetoed all the grand duchess's arrangements. It seems she is never to get her way in anything small or large. For me it is a tiny triumph.

In the meantime, I'm frequently free to roam the Summer Gardens and the labyrinthian palace. By now I've discovered that the crumbling walls behind the tapestries are so thin you can hear things those on the other side might wish to keep private. Wooden panels also offer enough knotholes to make spying almost a presumed activity.

Because of this, the weeks and then days leading up to the wedding provide several surprises. "Nothing is getting accomplished," I overhear a minister complain to another official one afternoon. "Affairs of state have been all but suspended. Not one damned decision has been made, not one paper read."

"That is not the worst of it for the people," comes the reply. "Civil Service wages remain unpaid, as do those of the Army. Even the extra taxes she has raised and all the new export levies cannot make up for that. She is using it all for this abominable wedding."

"Agreed. She has even asked the monasteries to contribute! Let us get this thing over and marry those children off so the government can once again operate!"

It doesn't surprise me that the empress is accomplishing none of the business she was anointed to oversee. Even Catherine is getting little reading or studying done—despite the fact that the empress refuses to allow her to make major or even minor decisions about her own wedding. Johanna, feeling perhaps more left out, scolds anyone who crosses her path. Only Peter seems unaffected, working endlessly on the puppet theatre he built, and to which we must all pay homage when he issues occasional invitations—or commands—to gather and watch the latest doll show he wrote.

The most embarrassing moment—had anyone else known I overheard it—comes when I accidentally and then on purpose eavesdrop on Peter's lackeys responding to his questions about what happens in the marriage bed. At least I think that is what is going on, since the responses are not only crude, but sometimes nonsensical. As they attempt to describe the physical union to him, I stifle a giggle, because I have a strong suspicion most fabricate details to cover up their own lack of experience. When I hear Peter snigger, I have the sense he might be more afraid than aroused. But who am I to judge— an eighteen-year-old virgin whose sole knowledge of sex comes from television, movies, and my former friends?

Once, leaving the rooms I share with the other maids of honor, I spy Catherine standing rigidly in the hallway between hers and Peter's apartments. She is dressed in a Holstein uniform identical to the ones Peter makes his "men" wear. She does not see me, instead remaining motionless while the sound of her fiancé barking orders reverberates through nearby rooms. Like the best-drilled grenadier in his toy sol- dier collection, she has apparently been commanded to stand there at arms, wielding a heavy musket that dents her shoulder.

An hour later she is still stationed there, her face expressionless, and not one feature betraying what surely must be discomfort. She is an incredibly patient person, this girl who will someday transform an empire.

I don't believe for one moment I could put up with her fiancé, regardless of the power rewarded at the end. I think about Igor, and wish I had someone like him—and preferably him—to share my thoughts with. The other ladies are friends in a sense, yet mostly I see them more as colleagues. The enormous secret I carry around must remain mine alone, and I do not think I can trust anyone with it.

With any luck, I will not be here long enough to have to worry about it.

Chapter 15

(Catherine) 1745

*"All the attention the grand duke had previously showed me ceased . . . I was well
aware of his lack of eagerness and affection; my pride and vanity suffered, but
I would not have dreamed of complaining . . . when I was alone, I shed
many tears, then wiped them away and went to romp with my maids."*
—Catherine II

*"A gradual mental deterioration dates from this time. The vicious cruelty and
addiction to drink which characterized [Peter's] later years can all be
traced to that fatal illness the winter of 1745."*
—Joan Haslip

As the last of her temporary reprieves expired and the steamy
August days marched toward what she sometimes considered
her inevitable doom, the only thing uniting Catherine with Peter
was their common enemy: Johanna. Her mother scolded her over

everything and nothing in those final weeks, perhaps a result of her resentment at being left out of the wedding plans.

If anyone deserved to be upset, it should have been her own father: Christian August seemed to be the only thing or person omitted from the empress's astounding list of imports. Perhaps Elizabeth feared his reaction to the sumptuousness of the Orthodox ceremony. Perhaps she wanted to take revenge on Johanna, who had pled for months for her husband's inclusion. Whatever the empress's reason, it was intentional. In all matters related to the nuptials, Elizabeth carefully and deliberately weighed, schemed, reckoned, evaluated, calculated, compared, estimated, judged, imitated, innovated, and assessed. No detail was too small to overlook. Even the orangerie gardeners at Oranienbaum had been ordered to raise lemon trees as quickly as possible; these would sweeten the scent in the halls and chambers of the Winter Palace.

The only detail overlooked seemed to be the bride, as if Catherine were merely a puppet placed like a cake decoration—a puppet that, like Peter's wooden ones, could have its strings manipulated at will. Other than standing for hours-long gown fittings, she had little to do except curl up with a hefty book.

It was nearly time for the nuptials when at last she summoned the courage to seek answers from her ladies about the actual wedding night—the mystery that had been bothering her for months.

Catherine tried to push aside her doubts about this boy who would share her bed for the rest of her life. She must unwrap herself from suspicions he might be as stupid as he was ugly. She must listen carefully and attempt to please him in this one crucial area.

To her surprise, her ladies seemed as clueless as she.

"My sister says that there is a physical act that comes in tandem with some kind of spiritual exaltation," Irina started out.

"Humph! I doubt that," Katrina interrupted. The other ladies looked at her strangely, as if they knew something Catherine did not, but then everyone stared at the floor or the mattresses where they'd arranged themselves. Although Katrina was married, she apparently did not wish to voice that fact in front of the others.

Others advanced some suspicious hypotheses about what happened when a man and woman climbed between the sheets together, although none seemed logical.

"But we do undress, correct?" Catherine pressed.

"Of course," Natasha giggled. "Not that I would know for certain," she hastened to add.

"I grew up on a farming estate," one of the Russian ladies who had recently been appointed to Catherine's court volunteered. "I can tell you exactly how cows get with calf, but I have no idea what happens with people."

"Tell us about the cows," another asked, but the farm girl refused to continue, other than to mumble, "it is very different, I believe."

Irina had tried her best, and since she was in her early twenties, the others looked to her for definitive answers. "My mother always tells me I will discover such things—what happens at night—after I am married."

"That hardly seems fair," Maria observed.

"My aunt says it is terrible," another of the new ladies contributes. "She said all women who marry must learn to endure much pain due to Eve's sin in the Garden of Eden."

A collective shudder seemed to go about the room, and somehow the subject was dropped. And if anyone were not as innocent as the court expected her to be, that person did not share any experiences with the nervous, naive Grand Duchess.

Catherine, no more enlightened than before, could barely sleep that night.

In the morning she broached the subject with Johanna, who'd obviously birthed many children and surely had an obligation to impart her knowledge with her own daughter.

To her surprise, however, Johanna refused to reply. "You are impertinent," she said simply.

Resigned to waiting for the night she and Peter would share a bed, Catherine attended her final gown fitting. The dress *was* breathtaking, made of imported silver silk patterned with leaves and roses. Thick metallic embroidery embellished every seam, and an extra hem of gold tinsel reached halfway up the skirt.

No one had consulted her about the wedding gown, although she had to admit it seemed designed to accentuate her seventeen-inch waist. Already she could hardly breathe in it, however, and feared what would happen when they tightened her corset and stays.

The night before the wedding, she dined alone with the empress, who proffered plenty of advice but no specifics. When Catherine dared to hint of her unpreparedness for events after the ceremony, Elizabeth forced a laugh. "You will have a wonderful time, my dear. After all, my nephew *is* a Romanov!" After two more sips of cherry vodka, she added, "You might be pleased to know I have dismissed Peter's so-called marital advisers. I do not believe they have served him well. In fact, you should disregard much of what you have undoubtedly heard."

"Such as, Your Imperial Majesty?"

"Such as all this nonsense about knocks on the head and beatings with an iron rod. I do not for one moment believe you will be a woman he can control that easily. Nor should you be. He may be the future emperor, but you need not always hold no opinions save those of your husband."

At this point, Catherine began to suspect that the empress might be getting a little drunk. Only a few days ago, one of her maids had whispered to Catherine that Her Majesty viewed Peter's treatment of Catherine as harmless and temporary. "He will be good to her if she deserves it, although of course she must remember to defer to His Imperial Highness in all ways," Elizabeth had been overheard to say.

That was the real empress, albeit, Catherine thought, a hypocritical one. There were no circumstances under which she could imagine Elizabeth herself deferring to *anyone*.

Surprisingly, Johanna showed up shortly before midnight, and the two talked longer than they ever had. For once Johanna had checked her crabbed temper and withdrew her claws. She even ventured a few answers about the dreaded Wedding Night, primarily in subtly worded ways, then finishing with dark hints: "You must be prepared to carry out your future duties without complaint. And after that, you must remember that we women are born to overcome more burdens than a man could realize." Any attempts to identify these unspecified burdens failed, and the comments did little to overcome her daughter's nervousness.

Before leaving, Johanna raised the subject of baby Elizabeth, and the two broke down weeping and holding one another in their shared grief. Just this once in their relationship, they could share tears of sorrow, tears of affection, even tears of worry.

After Johanna departed, church bells for miles around started ringing, accompanied by two straight hours of cannon fire. Covering her ears with pillows, Catherine tried to stop thinking but could not. She recalled especially how recently Peter—always discreet as a cannon ball—had told her, "You should not expect love from me; you should expect fear."

At long last the soon-to-be wife of the heir to the Russian throne fell asleep. Half angry, half trembling.

At 5 a.m., cannons resumed roaring from the Admiralty, Peter & Paul Fortress, and every warship anchored on the Neva.

Catherine tried to ignore the noise as she rose to take her bath. She was shocked when her "other" mother, the empress, showed up unannounced while she was still naked. "Stand up and turn around," she commanded somewhat genially, although it was an order with which the still shy grand duchess knew she must comply.

"You'll do. I expect you will soon be able to bear a child splendidly, but meanwhile I advise you to eat more," the voluptuous empress suggested before returning to her own rooms.

The first thing her ladies and maids did after Catherine's bath was dress her in a sheer knee-length bed gown of gold and silver—what the French called a simple *déshabillé*—before inserting a small hoop beneath it and then layering that with additional undergarments and petticoats. Before the formal dressing began in the state bedroom, both Johanna and Catherine made short speeches of thanks to the empress.

Things deteriorated from there, however, as the hairdresser and Elizabeth tussled over the latest Parisian curls Catherine's maids had recently cut for her.

"She will not wear her hair in that manner!" the empress, her own hair already dressed but her eyes slightly red from rising so much earlier than her custom, shouted for several minutes before wheeling and stomping out.

"Please tell Your Imperial Majesty that it must be so," the hairdresser, reluctant to tamper with the cherished new curls without a fight, begged Countess Rumyantseva.

The countess promptly left the room, presumably to convey the hairdresser's words, and returned several minutes later.

"Her Majesty insists 'no curls,'" she shrugged. "I do not believe she will change her mind."

The empress herself soon reappeared, scolding the hairdresser for several minutes, but fortunately not hitting her. "I want that hair flat! How else can we affix the jewels securely?"

"They will not fall off, I assure you," the hairdresser said bravely. "Here, allow me to demonstrate, Your Imperial Majesty."

Catherine, secretly rooting for the hairdresser, knew better than to jump into the fray.

At last the countess's surprising diplomatic skills bore fruit, as the empress threw up her bejeweled hands and yelled, "Go ahead! Do what you want. I wash my hands of all of this. Call me when she is dressed," she added more calmly.

In the end Catherine got her nut-brown curls, their glossy texture unmarred by powders.

The next step was to attach a wooden form to her bodice, which would serve to control and weight the three-yard train. Already Catherine felt as if she would tip over, and matters got worse when it took three ladies-in-waiting to lift the heavy formal dress, embroidered in silver roses, over her head. A lace cloak floated over this spun silver gown, the entire ensemble weighing nearly as much as Catherine herself. A bright pinkish-red sash, lace cuffed collar, and puffy lace sleeves were the only items that did not contribute to the burdensome heft she would carry around for the next sixteen or so hours.

Another contingent of ladies outlined her strong chin and longish features with rouge until at last it was time to call the empress back.

Elizabeth reappeared to touch up the rouge and then place the grand ducal crown on Catherine's head. She waved her arms expansively: "Choose any jewels you want. My own are at your disposal."

Maria and Natasha helped her choose diamonds that glittered across her hair, throat, earlobes, wrists, and fingers.

I feel like a sixteen-year-old knight weighted down in silver armor, Catherine thought as she viewed herself dispassionately in the full mirror. While everyone else clapped, Her Imperial Highness Ekaterina Alexeievna turned and took the first slow, heavy steps toward what she secretly saw as the new war front—and a battle she was determined to win at all costs.

Peter awaited, dressed in matching silk and handsome in his formal Russian military attire accessorized with diamonds. Together they moved outside toward the massive carriage surrounded by mounted and unmounted guard regiments.

They settled into an enormous, gilded carriage pulled by eight white horses attired as elaborately as their passengers. Jewel-studded harnesses glistened, and tall feathers danced from their manes. Catherine wondered if they felt as weighted down as she did.

For just a moment she had an overwhelming urge to alight, then swiftly commandeer one of the horses before galloping away, lost in the crowds, riding toward the eastern horizon.

The thought passed immediately, and at exactly ten a.m., accompanied by the sound of trumpets and kettledrums and led by one hundred horse guards, the great procession began to move. One hundred twenty-four intricately carved carriages in the baroque style the empress favored—each containing ladies and gentlemen nearly as resplendent as the imperial party and each accompanied by its own cavalcade of detachments from every military service—inched along the great avenue.

It would require three hours to progress the half mile route. For that entire time the Imperial Grand Duchess Catherine, a vision sparkling in silver and diamonds, waved until her arms hurt, smiled until her cheeks ached, and wondered if she were truly riding toward her triumph. Or her doom. Certainly toward an unknown fate.

CHAPTER 16

(MARIA)

She reminds me of Cinderella," I observe.

"Who?" Irina asks.

"*Cendrillon*, I mean" I correct myself, having learned that here they refer to the Perrault collection of fairytales; presumably the Brothers Grimm have not yet been born. "Her Imperial Highness, of course, complete with prince."

"Ah. And is Her Majesty really the fairy godmother?" Katrina asks skeptically.

"More like the evil stepmother," Natasha whispers, a gem-sprinkled fan blocking her lips.

"Perhaps neither, but look at that carriage!" Indeed, only magic could've created such a gigantic carriage of gold that resembles a miniature castle. Each panel glows with mythological scenes. Gilded cherubs are affixed to nearly every part of the doors and roof. Wheels glitter with foil and mirrors.

"*Oui*," Irina laughs. "Surely the wheels must be transformed pumpkins to pull something so massive." The whole contraption must weigh at least a ton, with each wheel tall as a man.

Once Catherine, Peter, and Elizabeth have been assisted into their carriage, we ladies climb inside one some distance behind the royal coach and those carrying dignitaries. All morning we've had ample opportunity to be with our mistress and to see her gowned, coiffed, and prepared for what the people consider the most important day of her life. But it will be the second crucial day, I realize, wishing for an instant I could see her coronation that inevitably will take place in the future. *I won't be here, though*, I resolve, before giving myself over to the celebration.

I, too, look gorgeous, thanks to my own lady's ministrations, although Countess Rumyantseva has ordered us to use rice powder to turn our upswept hairstyles white. My gown, a lavish teal brocade sprinkled with sewn-on pearls and what Igor taught me might be either fluorite or dioptase gems, is low cut and fashionable. If only, I hope, scanning the crowds, Igor Igorevich could see me. Surely he must be somewhere in this mass of people.

Kazan Cathedral is huge and awesome, and Natasha and I clutch each other as we find standing room in the nave. Overlooking the fabulous, jeweled iconostasis, we strain to listen amidst occasional murmurs and sweet choral voices. Burning incense and thousands of candles force me to hold back a sneeze so I can concentrate on the ceremony.

It is to last for three hours, which I should have suspected based on experience, although by now I've learned to shift weight from one leg to another, to wiggle toes and feet from time to time, and to hang on to Natasha for support.

Archbishop Todorsky officiates, his strong and clear voice exhorting the couple to love and cherish one another. He then blesses the two filigreed wedding crowns held above the couple's heads throughout the ceremony. Eventually he and the empress bless the gold rings Catherine and Peter exchange, after which the couple prostrate themselves before the empress raises them and gathers the two in an embrace.

When it is over, when the *Te Deum*—the traditional concluding Latin hymn of praise—has been played, when triple cannons have discharged in the distance, and when every church bell has chimed its pleasure, the rest of us are allowed to slowly make our way out.

Breathing in the fresh air before returning to the carriage line, Natasha and I chat for the first time in hours. "Have you seen Lieutenant Varkov?" she asks, her lovely brown eyes scanning the crowds, and when I shake my head, she gives me a five-minute description of his merits. "I can just imagine myself standing with him at the altar," she says wistfully.

"But you are only seventeen," I protest, knowing both of us are considered of marriageable age already. The bride herself is all of sixteen.

"The empress might let me have my way," she says confidently. "If not this autumn, perhaps next year. It is better, do you not think, Maria Sergeievna, to choose for oneself than to let her choose as she usually does?"

This piece of information is something that somehow has escaped me. Even though I have heard of several ladies' engagements and attended two weddings for the empress's maids, it never occurred to me these were arranged marriages. Oh, my God. What if this happens to me? I am probably now eighteen, and have absolutely no desire to marry, let alone be railroaded into such a thing. It is a horrifying thought!

When Catherine and Peter move toward their carriage, I remind myself that although only sixteen, she seems to be taking this wedding in stride. Of course, I know that this is how it is done for royalty and members of the nobility, who marry for alliances and produce heirs regardless of personal feelings, yet never have I included myself in that category.

Lost in these thoughts, I barely notice the painstakingly long trip back, surrounded by crowds fervently crossing themselves and trying to touch the splendid carriages.

The reception brings my thoughts back to my search for Igor and his uncle, whom I have still not seen, and as Catherine's ladies must sit together, I have little hope of catching a glimpse of him. I do spot a nobleman wearing a jacket with its back decorated with a tree of diamonds, complete with spreading branches and leaves, and I wonder if Igor was involved or supplied the diamonds. Perhaps he will be at the ball later, I comfort myself. In view of my fears of marriage, I cannot believe I am even *thinking* of a man.

"There are fifty courses," Irina explains matter-of-factly when we settle at the banquet. I am warm in the heavy gown and cannot imagine how all this hot food will add to my comfort.

At the imperial table, Catherine glows, though she must be sweating in that dress. I wish I could speak with her a few moments to alleviate the fears I know she has. Katrina should've enlightened her about the marriage bed, of course, but I know she lives in fear of being discovered.

It's been over a week since Catherine asked us about sex, and on that occasion I dared not say anything that might be misconstrued. I do remember distinctly how I felt in sixth grade when a classmate explained things. I did not believe her at first, and I suppose Catherine might not believe it either. Still, she should know *something* rather than enter her bridal bed like a sacrificial lamb!

The meal is lavish, yet interminable. Rather than permit us to excuse ourselves when nature calls, Elizabeth has ordered barrels installed beneath the tables. Just like our counterparts in the English and French courts, we must slide down to inconspicuously relieve ourselves as the need arises rather than search for the nearest privy. Unwilling to do so, I resolve to limit my intake of fluids—not an easy matter considering all the toasts raised in the long gallery.

When the ball begins, I at last have an opportunity to get close to Catherine on the pretext of checking the placement of her jewels. Sweat drops betray her discomfort. "This crown," she whispers as I check the diamonds on the magnificent dress. "I think it is cutting grooves in my forehead!"

"Ask the empress if you may remove it for a while."

"I've made my request twice to the countess, who seemed offended. She claims it is a bad omen to remove it."

Yet a few minutes later, Countess Rumyantseva approaches Catherine to announce that Her Majesty reluctantly has consented for her to remove the crown, albeit for merely a few moments—and out of sight of the hundreds of guests.

I trail behind her, helping a maid lift the ponderous train, and in an alcove find myself alone with Catherine for only a minute.

"Your Imperial Highness," my voice drops to a whisper.

"Yes, Maria Sergeievna?" She seems understandably distracted, albeit relieved to have the poundage of the crown temporarily removed.

"There is something I must tell you . . . something I heard from one of the married ladies."

"Is it about tonight?" she asks anxiously.

"*Da*, it is. She told me that the act of consent is very short—and that it hurts, but only for a few moments. After that, she assures me, it will be something pleasurable for both of you."

"Is this possible?" she demands.

I nod before she is summoned back to the ballroom, where I watch from the sidelines as she engages in one of her favorite dances: a set of polonaises.

She glitters like a constellation that outshines all the stars in the ballroom, every eye upon her.

I, too, have opportunities to dance and even flirt, doing so with little enthusiasm. I yearn to speak further with the new bride, chastising myself for letting this important information get postponed until the final hour. Yet it is not as if I have any personal experience to impart, having managed to remain a virgin thus far.

As if reading my thoughts, Her Majesty abruptly and impatiently announces, "It is bedtime for the bride and groom!"

Within minutes she whisks them away, trailed by Johanna, the countess, ladies and maids, and a handful of servants. The empress has turned the entire process into a triumphant ceremonial procession winding through the ballroom and toward the prepared bedroom.

We are followed by knowing looks, muttered jokes, lewd comments, and amused but curious glances. I was not even aware I knew so many French and Russian slang words for sex, but unfortunately, understand them all. Only a few of us, I suspect, feel any compassion.

CHAPTER 17

(CATHERINE) 1745-1746

"In the first days of our marriage . . . I said to myself: 'If you allow yourself to love that man, you will be the unhappiest creature on this earth.'"
—Catherine II

Catherine scarcely knew what to think as the procession ending in the bedroom prepared the bridal pair. At first she was much more interested in having someone removing the weighty crown than many someones removing her garments.

Her eye fell on the nails above the bed where the wedding crowns now hung, forcing herself to concentrate on them while her ladies reversed the elaborate dressing ceremony conducted hours ago. As each item came off, she felt freer and barely noticed when her Mistress of the Robes redressed her in a lace-trimmed pink chemise, part of a French trousseau gathered for her.

The weight on her head remained until she was reunited with

Peter, who entered in his dressing gown. Only then did Her Imperial Majesty carefully remove both crowns, confer a bedtime blessing, and embrace the couple who waited on bended knees.

Within minutes the maids of honor had retreated after making three curtsies to the boy standing there in bows and lace.

"The bed is remarkable, is it not?" Catherine said nervously.

Peter grunted, oblivious to the enormous bed with its poppy-hued coverlet decorated with silver wreaths and nosegays. The room's scarlet velvet walls added to its majesty.

His swollen features barely looked at his wife, and without saying a word, he slipped out the other door.

Assuming he must take care of his toilette, she waited.

An hour passed.

Then two.

Surely something must happen, she thought. But it did not. It took self-control not to chew on her fingernails, a habit she'd tried to break for months.

What was expected of her, she wondered. Should she remain in bed? Or should she get up?

At last Madame Krause, her newest head maid, cheerfully entered the room.

"Where is His Highness, do you know?"

"Awaiting his supper, Your Imperial Highness. It should be served shortly."

"But —" *How could he possibly eat again after that enormous banquet?*

"I'm sure he will be here when he finishes," Madame Krause said primly, and disappeared.

More hours dragged by, and Catherine tried to check her tears. Was this Peter's way of getting even with her for not being the bride he desired? Was he still angry about some perceived slight? Was it because she'd been unable to hide her revulsion that afternoon she first saw him after his smallpox?

When at last he stumbled into the bridal suite, it was obvious he'd spent the past hours drinking. This habit Catherine had become somewhat accustomed to, although not that he would lurch toward the bed in a tipsy state, reeking of spirits and tobacco.

It required all her effort to smile, not to mention put up with his feeble joke: "Ah, it surely would amuse my valets to discover us in bed together."

After this misguided attempt at humor—or perhaps pure ignorance—His Imperial Highness rolled on the bed. Within seconds, he was snoring.

Not only was the sound unfamiliar and annoying, Catherine found herself having to swallow her anger at Peter's neglect of her. Whatever was *supposed* to happen in this bed, this certainly could not be it!

Eventually she, too, rolled over on her own side. The distance between them seemed wide as the Neva River. Nearly as wide as the distance from Prussia to Russia.

For the moment, at least, she would have to acknowledge that she could not cross that divide.

When Catherine awoke after her marriage night, she felt as ignorant as she imagined a nun might.

Peter was gone, and were it not for a sense of yearning for someone to touch her, she would assume her senses still slumbered. Yet she could not help touching her own nipples, running her fingers down her belly. Yes, something should have happened. She did not yet have specific fantasies, knowing only that she longed for a man's touch.

As maids and ladies entered with breakfast for two, they each slyly offered congratulations.

Since she'd done nothing to deserve or earn those as far as she could determine, she responded to each with a murmured, "*Merci*" or "*Spasibo.*"

Peter did not appear for the entire day.

Elizabeth's renowned architect Rastrelli had designed that evening's banquet hall, and Catherine resolved to enjoy herself and act as if nothing had happened, which of course it had not.

Ornately filled with sculptures and musical fountains, the hall was an accomplishment the likes of which no one had ever seen. She and Peter presided over one hundred thirty honorary guests at a series of tables arranged with marble statues and dozens of pyramids of flowers.

Her favorite of Rastrelli's innovations was a collection of crystal lamps illuminated with, according to rumor, no fewer than eight thousand flames! She could not stop staring at one nearest her, hoping to feel a reciprocal glow. Here was the illumination she had expected to feel today; instead, she felt only fragile and very cold, as though someone had neglected to light the candles in one of the crystal holders.

Smug looks directed at the royal couple persisted throughout the banquet, as Catherine forced herself to laugh and pretended to revel in the festivities.

For the next ten days, she and Peter dutifully attended parties, comedies, operas, banquets, balls, regattas, and concerts, culminating each evening with virtually a repeat of the wedding night: Peter either came to bed drunk or else hauled out his dolls to play soldiers. He spread them on the bed, often insisting they play together with them.

All the honorary events served only as an anticlimax to the non-existent bridal nuptials: absolutely nothing had changed between them.

Johanna exited Russia a month after the wedding, and to her surprise, Catherine discovered she missed her mother. No one else grieved her departure, and Her Majesty seemed almost giddy at being rid of the tainted spy. Catherine was in tears, not only because her mother had left in a cloud of suspicion and, on the pretext of not wanting to swell her daughter's grief, with barely a goodbye, but because Johanna also had left all her bills behind: an exorbitant debt Catherine must pay.

On the other hand, she barely had time to wonder about her parents, Babet, and her old life. Her married existence continued to frustrate her, especially when a mere two weeks afterward. Peter confessed he was again in love with one of the courtiers.

Desperately trying to cover her jealousy—which, had she admitted it, consisted more of hurt pride at being ignored in favor of another—Catherine struggled to keep up with Peter's other demands. These consisted primarily of her playing billiards with his tutor Bergholz to occupy him while Peter whiled away the hours with his gentlemen. She also had to pretend to admire Peter's prowess with the sword during his fencing lessons and attend each of his ear-splitting violin concerts.

When they climbed in bed together, Peter inevitably pulled out his dolls and toy soldiers. To humor him, she played along with the games and role-playing he devised.

After the toys had been put away—usually hidden under the bed—the two remained on separate sides. It was a situation apparently unlikely to change soon.

Soon there were new worries. Angry the new bride had not yet conceived, Elizabeth initiated an arbitrary dismissal of members of Catherine's court. It started with one of her favorite maids-of-honor, the Estonian Maria Zhukhova, followed almost immediately by a gentleman of her bedchamber. From then on it seemed whichever of her ladies or gentlemen Catherine favored, that person would be removed from the grand duchess's court.

In a desperate attempt to stop this thinning of her staff, Catherine began to go out of her way to ignore those she liked the best, realizing that if she *did* want to get someone removed, she had only to make friendly overtures.

In the meantime, new accusations—even about Catherine—seemed to spring up in tandem with those about her ladies.

"They flirt dangerously," the empress insisted. "All of them! And I know of at least two secret rendezvous that the grand duchess's maids have had. I will not tolerate such improprieties!" And a day later, this or that maid would be snatched away on Elizabeth's orders.

"There is no cause for this!" Catherine wailed one evening to her faithful valet, Timofei, the only one she felt she could still trust and one of her few original servants remaining.

"You still have Irina and the other Maria," he tried to comfort her.

"Indeed, since Irina is above all others blameless. She is perhaps more pious than Her Majesty herself."

"And Maria Sergeievna?" Timofei asked.

"Maria remains because I ignore her, even pretend to resent her at times. I no longer permit her to read to me when anyone might encounter us. She still takes care of my jewels, but furtively. However, I do miss Katrina and Natasha, not to mention four of my newest ladies."

"It is sometimes the best thing for them, you know," Timofei assured her. "Everyone knows, Your Highness, that Katrina wanted nothing so much as to return home to her secret husband before she was discovered."

"And Natasha?" Yet she smiled in relief, having worried for a long time that the bubbly and stunning young girl's eye for gentlemen would eventually lead her into trouble.

Timofei grinned back. "Mademoiselle Natasha will take care of herself, I believe."

"At least I'm free from billiards for some time," she said wryly, since Peter's most stalwart tutor, too, had been dismissed for no apparent reason. "I must admit, I was beginning to enjoy the game. And I was getting very, very good at it."

"Madame, you certainly were." He chuckled at the amounts of money his mistress had won.

That winter, Peter once again took ill. Although Catherine installed herself faithfully at his bedside, occupying herself with prayers, a book, or her embroidery hoop, weeks dragged on with little improvement.

This time there was no specific illness to blame. His ailments seemed to include an alternating range of fever, headaches, and general aches and pains.

One afternoon Catherine received a brief note in Elizabeth's handwriting: "No matter what happens, you will not be abandoned." One of the empress's special prayer books, printed in extra large type the way Elizabeth ordered them to ease her eyes, accompanied the note.

If she could find a way to get Peter—when he recovered—to do his duty and help her conceive, she would have fulfilled her expected function of ensuring the dynastic succession.

More insipid performances must be on the way, she thought one evening, nursing a raging headache and unable to ignore the constant hammering from Grand Duke Peter's apartments. Ever since his recovery, he had immersed himself in construction of his latest marionette theatre.

"You do love the puppets, Your Highness," one of her new maids reminded her.

"It's the shows themselves that leave much to be desired."

"Here, let me put this cool towel on your forehead," the maid offered.

After she left, the knocking on the wall mercifully stopped, and Catherine began to relax. Blessedly alone, she nevertheless was happy to hear a hesitant half knock on her door. That would be Maria Sergeievna, who she'd warned to be as inconspicuous as possible lest Elizabeth notice that she hadn't yet been dismissed.

"I am sorry to interrupt, Your Highness, but you should know what the grand duke is doing."

"Must I, Masha?"

Maria smiled ruefully as she knelt by the couch. She was so much taller than the other ladies that Catherine was amazed the empress seemed to have forgotten her existence.

"You will want to know," Maria insisted.

"What is it this time?"

Peter, hearing voices behind a door walled over for privacy, apparently had decided to satisfy his curiosity by boring holes into that same wall with one of his carpenter's tools. "I don't know exactly what is in there, but I could hear Her Majesty's voice."

"Oh, no! That would be the empress's private dining room! No one is permitted to enter without a special invitation—not even servants may cross the threshold!"

"But then who tends to her and her guests?" Maria asked.

"Ah, you have not seen her famous mechanical dinner table?"

"No, Your Highness."

"The table and its settings are raised and lowered from beneath the floor so that the servants may clear dishes and send up new ones. It's a marvelous invention. There is a much larger and more elaborate one at Catherine Palace. Someday you will get to see it."

"I hope so, but now you really must come with me, Your Highness," Maria begged. "His Highness has already started asking for you!"

"Damn him." She slowly rose and reached for the dressing gown Maria presented her. "I will go, if only to put a stop to this latest nonsense."

"Excellent, Your Imperial Highness, but I believe I will retreat to my room."

"A good idea, Mademoiselle. I do not wish anyone to know you have spied for me."

By the time Catherine arrived at Peter's apartments, he'd gathered all his friends and most of Catherine's ladies, demanding that they witness the scene behind the extra peepholes he'd made. Through them, Catherine glimpsed Elizabeth's lover Alexei in a dressing gown, as well as a half dozen guests clinking champagne glasses. Had they not been under the influence of alcohol, perhaps they would have noticed that their activities were under scrutiny.

To make matters worse, a delighted Peter had pulled up additional benches and chairs to form his own amphitheatre of voyeurs who peeked with him through the perforations.

Horrified, Catherine hissed, "Enough!" In addition to prudently refusing to take part, she whispered a loud warning to him about the potential consequences if he were to get discovered.

Shortly after returning angrily and nervously to her own rooms, she heard the scampering footsteps of ladies and gentlemen fleeing through the hallways. They, at least, had heeded her warning, scurrying away like mice being chased from the Swiss cheese wall.

In the end, the empress did find out, storming into Catherine's apartments immediately after Sunday mass to upbraid her nephew, who'd just wandered in carrying his nightcap.

Catherine cringed. Peter stammered words of defense for spying on his aunt, which enraged her further.

Like one of the Furies, Elizabeth screamed even louder. "My father disinherited his own son, remember that. Even murdered him! And my sister Anna punished those who were disrespectful by locking them up in a fortress. Is that where you want to be, nephew? Disinherited and locked in a cell across the Neva? Or dead?"

"No, Your Majesty, please. I didn't realize what I was doing."

"Oh yes, you did! You are ungrateful and impertinent!" Elizabeth stormed.

Catherine, unsure how to respond since she knew she, at least, was innocent of any involvement in the Peephole Incident, stood quietly in the corner.

At last Elizabeth's typhoon of rage toward Peter trickled to a stream. Slightly calmer, she turned to the grand duchess. "I know you had no part in this, Catherine Alexeievna. I have been advised of the details, and my informants tell me you refused to participate. You, therefore, are absolved."

Moments later, the empress whirled and marched out of the room, leaving the grand duke and duchess relieved to be, for now, out of the eye of this most recent storm.

Madame Krause entered from the antechamber with some advice: "Had you called Your Majesty 'Little Mother' and begged her forgiveness, you would have received it. You will accomplish everything by saying the simple phrase: 'We beg your pardon, Little Mother.'"

Catherine listened, learned, and filed the phrase away for future reference.

For the next several days, Peter continued to tremble, as if he had survived an earthquake.

The aftershocks continued to reverberate through the Young Court, which Elizabeth had now determined once and for all to reorganize. Something must be done about this pampered couple who had failed to conceive a child after nine months of marriage. They must be more closely supervised, she decided.

There were other reasons for this. It had come to Elizabeth's attention, according to Timofei, that Catherine's relationship with three of Peter's gentlemen—two brothers and a cousin named Chernyshev— had become too familiar.

Andrei Chernyshev was a consummate flirt, although for Catherine it was all harmless and light-hearted. Peter encouraged his friend to call Catherine *Little Mother*, and she then jokingly called him *son*. Sometimes she wondered if by getting Peter jealous, she might make him see her differently. Although this ploy failed, the five of them always had fun together, especially when Andrei would get Madame Krause so drunk she stumbled to bed early.

One day Timofei pulled the grand duchess aside and warned, "The entire household is gossiping about Andrei and you. What you call loyalty and affection because this man is faithful to you, your entourage believes is *love*."

Catherine was stunned, as if hit by a thunderbolt. This was something that had never occurred to her.

"I have warned Andrei that he is in a dangerous situation," Timofei went on, "and sent him away from court with a fake illness."

A month later Andrei returned. One evening when Catherine

had fled to her apartments to escape another of Peter's awful violin concerts, she could barely make her way through the usual array of scaffolding and construction racket that marked renovations to the summer palace. Pausing with her door half open, she was surprised to see Andrei waiting outside the room.

"It is too loud out here to speak in the hall, Your Imperial Highness. Might I come into your room to talk?"

"That is something I cannot do." Barely had the words escaped her mouth when she turned her head to observe Peter's chamberlain, Count Devier. He insisted that the grand duke wanted her to return with him to the wretched concert, which she agreed to do.

In the morning, she learned the Chernyshevs had vanished from Court, supposedly reposted in distant regiments.

But the situation was far from over, as she discovered when Father Todorsky used the Confessional to question whether she'd kissed one of the Chernyshevs.

"Of course not!"

"You sound indignant, yet someone said you were observed doing exactly that," the priest said calmly.

Catherine continued to vehemently deny what she knew never happened. "This is slander!"

"Perhaps, but Her Majesty has been informed that you did indeed kiss Andrei."

Outraged, hurt, and now afraid, she could only repeat her denial.

The priest seemed to believe her, but admonished, "You must be on guard so as to avoid future suspicions, Your Imperial Highness."

She left the confessional feeling like an innocent Daniel in the den of lions. One misstep, and she could be eaten.

The repercussions did not end. Shortly thereafter, Catherine learned exactly what it must have been like for Daniel to be caged. Her jailor arrived in the form of a new chief governess, senior to Madame Krause, with the mission of ruling over Catherine and her court. Madame Maria Choglokova, five years older than Catherine, was also Elizabeth's cousin, not to mention, as Catherine soon discovered, an uneducated, malicious, and narcissistic woman. With her husband Nikolai, who served as one of Elizabeth's chamberlains, frequently absent on diplomatic missions, Maria Choglokova had plenty of time and energy to devote to her own mission. She was also close to Chancellor Count Bestuzhev, whom Catherine had always mistrusted since he made no secret of resenting her as a bridal choice and potentially a Prussian spy.

In the end it was Bestuzhev who delivered the final blow. He and the empress had drawn up harsh and specific instructions for how the Choglokovs should fulfill their supervisory roles. The lengthy instructions seemed to have twin purposes: to ensure political isolation by forbidding Catherine communication with absolutely anyone, including pages, servants, cavaliers, etc., and secondly, to make certain that she would be a fruitful baby producer.

This second goal meant henceforth the malicious Madame Choglokova would do everything in her power to give the couple time and privacy. Although that entailed everything short of standing over them in the bedroom, she would in all other ways superintend marital intimacies and ensure fidelity. As if, Catherine thought bitterly, her vigilance would have any influence over Peter's lack of interest. It was all too obvious that the Choglokovs had been placed in such proximity to the imperial couple to set an example: they seemed to be madly in love, and Madame Choglokova predictably produced one baby per year.

Perhaps due to the new rules and frequent bouts of crying, Catherine developed a serious headache. While waiting for the surgeon to bleed her, she had even more reason to cry. Her Majesty thundered into the room like a furious Juno on her chariot, raining down abuses and lashing out with accusations: that Catherine was a spy like her mother, that she was an unfit wife, that she was in love with someone else, and finally that she was deliberately refusing to get pregnant!

"None of this is true, Your Majesty!" *Maybe she thinks she* is *the goddess of childbirth,* Catherine could not help thinking.

"Don't lie to me. You knew your duty when you chose to come to Russia. I never would have forced you to marry my nephew if you had had any aversion to doing so! But now it is done, and you have a duty to me—not to mention to Russia—to love your husband."

"But I do love him," Catherine lied.

"Then stop crying and start acting like it!"

For a moment Catherine feared Elizabeth's clenched fist might strike her, and she hastened to assure the empress once again of her innocence. "Yes, Your Imperial Majesty. I am sorry if I have displeased you in any way." Then, remembering Madame Krause's advice, she added, "Please forgive me. I beg your pardon, Little Mother."

It was as if the storm had abated, and the sun emerged once again from behind the clouds. At this moment Peter arrived, and the empress greeted him graciously.

After Elizabeth's departure, the surgeon was permitted to enter. He bled Catherine two times before she crawled into bed to cry for the rest of the day.

CHAPTER 18

(MARIA) 1746

These days I'm uncertain who is the most unhappy: Catherine or me. The Great Purge of the Young Court shows little sign of abating, and I have no idea what is to become of me if I cannot return to the future. Apparently, the *real* Maria Sergeievna had no family beyond her deceased parents, and was only taken into the inner court circle as a favor to the renowned dead sculptors. Here I am housed, fed, and clothed. I can occupy myself reading to Catherine (furtively) and myself, walking the grounds, and playing cards. I've even started studying something I never would have expected to enjoy—gems and minerals.

At any time I might be dismissed. I miss Natasha, who's been married off to a member of the elite Preobrazensky Guard. Katrina has returned to live with her husband, despite being in disgrace with the empress. For me, marriage would seem the only way to survive in this society—but to whom? Is that the only way I can get a place of my own?

Last week I was congratulating myself on at last mastering the *polonaise,* with its mechanical yet precise rows of dancers coming together and then relining as neatly as the gears of a watch. Yet passing through the line that night, I realized Igor was part of the couple passing through the center, his hand casually resting on the tiny waist of one of Elizabeth's ladies. I nearly stumbled, flushed with something I later admitted was jealousy. There are no other men who attract me, and I cannot imagine being paired off with a stranger at the whim of the empress.

I feel so much of Catherine's pain, as well. She is no longer permitted to do much of anything, and the empress and Chancellor Bestuzhev have served both Peter and her with separate memorandums outlining expected behavior. For Peter, this means little more than to attend church two extra times a day with Catherine, as well as to refrain from pouring the contents of his glass over the servants' heads, using coarse expressions, and telling improper jokes—especially to important court visitors. He also has been ordered to cease and desist from publicly making grimaces and continually jerking his limbs.

This would all be laughable if Catherine hadn't been given a much stricter surveillance, amounting to house arrest. I've reread most of the new instructions to Catherine twice: "She has been elevated to her present dignity of Imperial Highness with none other but the following aims and objects: that her Imperial Highness might by her sensible behavior, her wit and virtue, inspire a sincere love in His Imperial Highness and win his heart, and that by so doing may bring forth the heir so much desired for the empire and a fresh sprig of our illustrious house."

Catherine also has been commanded not only to avoid state affairs, but to refrain from offending the grand duke or treating him coldly.

The real war begins shortly after the Choglokovs assume their posts. Madame Choglokova empties every cabinet, desk, and coffer of all correspondence and notes.

"Where are you going with all that?" Catherine nearly wails when the dreadful woman orders Catherine's precious inkstand, quills, and stationery sheets removed.

"Her Imperial Majesty's orders," the woman says simply. Later we will learn that this is to be her standard response to every complaint from anyone.

"I am not allowed to write to my parents—or to my former governess Babet—anymore, anyway," Catherine tells me sadly, then brightens somewhat. "At least Madame left me all my books, although I've been ordered not to discuss serious topics with anyone!"

Nor is she permitted to leave the bedroom at night. She and Peter are literally locked in and ordered to "couple."

"You wouldn't believe what—well, no, no one would believe," she admits to me one afternoon. "The grand duke stands in the middle of the bedroom cracking this huge military whip. I would fear for my safety, but thus far he is the only one who has been injured with it."

There is more, a lot more, and some I hear from Irina, who is permitted to see the grand duchess a few times a day to attend church. "He has come up with a new contraption for playing with the toy soldiers," Irina tells me. "He nailed strips of wire across a table and then attached those with strings so if he pulls the string, the wires make an ungodly noise. His Imperial Highness insists that that is what the rolling of guns sounds like."

"Oh, dear. When I was in her apartment the other day, she had a list of all the regiments of Peter's soldiers. He has ordered her to memorize it." I can only hope he hasn't given each individual names, as well, since his collection includes hundreds of toy soldiers made from lead, starch, wax, wood, and tin. Who knows how many of them crowd the large four-post bed?

"They will be caught one day," Irina fears. "Right now, Madame Krause helps them hide the toys at night because they lavish her with gifts and gambling money, but the Argus is a different story."

"*She* is the one who should be caged in," I mutter, and we both know who the Argus is. Madame Choglokova misses nothing, although I suspect that Catherine will just get more creative given time.

"Exactly. Catherine is the one who calls her Argus because her eyes are everywhere, but to me she is more like Cerberus, the three-headed dog. She certainly growls and bars her teeth as if she has three sets!"

We share a rare laugh at this, and I am grateful that the level-headed, discreet Irina is still with me. But for how long?

Now that the imperial couple takes most of their meals together in their rooms and goes virtually nowhere, I rarely see Catherine, who is the subject of endless court speculation—as is the topic of her fertility.

"Well, of course she is not yet with child," one of the older ladies in waiting mutters. "It's all that reading she does."

Galina, the most senior maid, confirms this: "Books make one barren, and the grand duchess spends half a day peering at papers and such. She should pray to saints instead. Maybe Saint Paraskeva."

"Who is she?" I venture to ask curiously.

"Patroness of marriage, I think. Not sure," someone murmurs.

Galina ignores us, simply pointing toward one of the dozens of icons on the wall.

One afternoon I am permitted to seek permission from Madame Choglokova to enter Catherine's rooms and collect jewelry that needs repair. Since the evil woman is absent from her usual post—undoubtedly due to one of the frequent naps necessitated by her latest pregnancy—I slip in unobserved.

Anticipating the potential to see Igor after obtaining the jewelry, I'm not really concentrating. First, I don't register what I am seeing: Catherine is bent over a couch, part of one breast bare due to her stays being cut. This is not unusual when a woman in this time can barely stand another moment of the tortuous corsets, but they appear to have been cut rather than loosened or untied. Then I notice something else.

On the table beside the couch lies a knife!

In a few short strides, I grab the weapon, take the grand duchess in my arms, and begin to stroke her hair. "No, no, you must not," I murmur again and again.

"I'm sorry," she gasps, tears streaming down her reddened face.

"But why?" I ask, as if I cannot figure out all the possible answers.

It takes awhile for Catherine to get control of herself, and I realize I've never seen her at a loss for words.

"It is just all too much! Nothing I do is right. All my efforts to please everyone only bring more scoldings. One day I dress 'too elegantly,' and the next day 'too slovenly.' I rise too late or too early. I spend too much time at the mirror, or do not take enough care with my appearance. I am told I am bad-tempered. Supposedly I am presumptuous and do not know my place."

The knife now rests beside me, and she stares at it but not, I hope, with the intention of using it. Instead, the flat-bladed knife seems to mock all her efforts, her concessions, her sufferings, and undoubtedly her longings. It is no secret to her ladies that she is still a virgin regardless of all the empress's efforts to force a conception.

"You must not tell a soul what I tried," she begs.

"I will never tell, Your Imperial Highness. I promise, no matter what happens in the future, you may always trust me."

"Oh, Maria Sergeievna," she says, letting me brush out her hair and wipe her eyes. "There is almost no one I can trust. Is it possible you might be the only one?"

"I believe there are—and will be—others, but you must be patient."

"Perhaps you are correct," she sighs, and then sits up and resumes some semblance of herself. "You'd better leave now. I treasure your friendship and your service, but *she* might return any time."

"Are you certain you will be all right?" We both know what I'm really asking.

"Absolutely, my dear friend. In fact, I have been reading most of the day and night since the wardens arrived. It has become my great diversion. Recently I have discovered some new French writers who have fascinating theories and philosophies. I promise to share them with you when we can."

I slip out of her apartments with the broken jewelry and the knife, and back to my own. Catherine didn't die, but I cannot presume it is because I was there. After all, she will pass into history as one of the greatest leaders and statesmen of all time. I realize that I possess a very dangerous power: the ability—or at least the potential—to alter the future.

CHAPTER 19

(CATHERINE) 1747-1748

"She was a thousand times more dependent, more restricted in her actions,
than the wife of the poorest citizen. Elizabeth had her every movement
watched by a hundred, indiscreet, prying eyes; she subjected the young
wife to the interrogation, censure, and admonition of a hundred
tongues—ladies of the Court, waiting-women, even lackeys . . .
In a thousand humiliating, hurtful, and offensive ways
Elizabeth gave Catherine to understand that she was
falling daily into even deeper disgrace."
—Gina Kaus

Time dragged, interrupted only, it seemed, by tragedies. The previous year her dancing instructor, ballet master Monsieur Landé, had died. Now, when Catherine had been looking forward to permission to attend the upcoming wedding of one of her favorite maids of honor, that princess unexpectedly contracted a severe fever. Within days she had died.

Coupled with the departure of so many others from her retinue and Peter's, this was a terrible loss. She grieved over the princess's death for weeks, until even more devastating news reached her from Zerbst: her father, Prince Christian August, had died suddenly of a second stroke.

Catherine was inconsolable. For the first couple years she'd written to him regularly, but now that her correspondence was closely monitored if not forbidden, she'd heard nothing from him in at least a year. Because in many ways her father had been the bulwark of her childhood, she'd been disappointed and then deeply hurt that he'd been forbidden not only to travel to Russia with her and his wife initially, but also denied an invitation to her betrothal and then wedding. Knowing she'd never see him again, she crawled in bed and wept until the doctor arrived to bleed her.

She cried for eight more days.

The empress sent her a firm and heartless warning to stop: "Remind her that her father was not even a king!"

"He was not a king, no, but he was my *father!*" she protested to Madame Choglokova, who had delivered the message.

After that, she was ordered to leave her room and permitted to wear black silk mourning gowns for only six weeks.

Weighted with sorrow, she barely noticed when a vicious rumor spread that she'd been insulted at the paucity of condolence cards, particularly from ambassadors. Even though the source of the offensive rumor—Elizabeth's Grand Master of Ceremonies—apologized, she could feel the accusation in people's looks as they watched her resume court activities.

"She is so pretentious!" she heard one courtier say and bit her lip to keep from confronting the gentleman. He had not said it to her directly, since virtually no one was permitted to speak to her. Even her ladies, maids of honor, and servants had been forbidden to inter-act with her other than in the affirmative or negative. Since everyone feared the empress's wrath for breaking the prohibition, Catherine lived life in near silence.

"I might as well be a prisoner confined to Peter and Paul Fortress," she dared complain to her personal warden.

"You are an obstinate young lady!" Madame Choglokova responded.

"In what way?"

"This is what Her Majesty says of you."

"But why? Why does she say such things? In what way am I obsti-nate? Because I do not conceive a child?"

"She has ordered me to call you that."

Catherine jabbed the needle she was threading into a piece of embroidery. She'd grown accustomed to this kind of senseless con-versation with the dull, thick-witted chaperone who for now, at least, controlled her fate and daily life. Occasionally she glanced up and stared rudely at Madame Choglokova's thickening waistline, as if will-ing it to expand faster. Only when her jailer went into confinement for her pregnancy would Catherine cease to be under round-the-clock scrutiny.

With a heavy sigh, she set aside the needlework and picked up a volume by her favorite author: a Frenchman named Voltaire whose writings so excited Catherine that she often risked sneaking out her hidden quill and purloined vellum, furiously scribbling notes beneath her bed sheets. Someday she would love to meet this great philoso-pher, and when she did, she would assure him he'd saved her from certain insanity in her time of isolation and tedium.

In the meantime, if she looked for relief from her husband, it was a waste of time. Rather than break up the monotony, he only added to it.

At first she had been thrilled when he smuggled six dogs into their apartments. She adored dogs, expecting to play and cuddle with the spaniels.

Peter disabused her of her plans almost immediately. "They are hunting dogs, meant to work for their supper."

"But you do not have to treat them so cruelly!"

"Not your business!"

"Well, the stench is my business. You should have someone clean up after them when they defecate all over the floor."

"And risk Her Majesty knowing?"

"How could she not know? They bark half the day." *More like whine and yelp in fear*, she added silently.

Nor, according to His Imperial Highness, was it any of her business when night after night Madame Krause, who detested the Choglokovs, double-locked their door before smuggling in Peter's toys. Sometimes Madame would join them for a while, playing with the model fortresses, tiny cannons, and miniature soldiers, many of which she procured for him. As small as the war toys were, they took up most of the bed and weighted down the blankets. Woe be to Catherine if she accidentally knocked one off, let alone had the audacity to ask for some space in which to sleep.

"It is like a battlefield on the mattress. Toys and toy corpses are strewn everywhere," she dared complain once.

Peter considered that a compliment: "Isn't it splendid? Someday I will have this many soldiers of my own. Human ones! And look how many my regiment has destroyed!" He swept his arm toward the foot of the bed, where the "dead" sprawled facedown or face-up, but no longer on their teensy fake legs.

During the day, the toys vanished along with the dogs, although at least the war menagerie remained silent. Instead, Peter divided his time between practicing his violin and pacing the room, his giant strides requiring Catherine to attempt to keep up as he talked about himself and his grandiose plans for hours on end. Oblivious to his wife's weariness brought on by his nocturnal escapades, he outlined his aims: "I will establish a monastery where all of us—the entire court—will live! We'll all ride donkeys and get our own food from the farm we will start. And our clothing, of course, will be simple: everyone will wear brown robes!"

Excited, he commanded Catherine to draw up the diagrams immediately. This she did, over and over, day after day, making sketches that he demanded be redone. *I think I must have done this a thousand times,* she thought, *but nothing I do will ever please my husband.*

Catherine at last had some good luck when a letter from Johanna arrived via an unexpected source. It happened at one of the rare receptions she was permitted to attend. When a Knight of Malta bent to kiss her hand, she felt him slip a tiny roll of paper into it. Claiming to smell smoke and thus diverting everyone's attention to the phantom fire, she deftly transferred the note from her glove to her bodice.

In her room, she scanned the note eagerly, relieved that word of her situation had reached someone in the outside world. "They say you are virtually a prisoner," Johanna wrote. "In Zerbst we even hear that you might be in an *actual* prison. Please reassure me that there is no truth to the rumor, but as you well remember, I have never trusted that crone the empress . . ." In cramped writing, the letter went on to provide brief directions for getting a reply out of the palace via a musician in the grand duke's orchestra who would leave a vest pocket open whenever she passed him.

Catherine watched as the fireplace flames erased all evidence. She could only hope the usually indiscreet Johanna would do the same with her daughter's eventual reply.

The problem was that she had no method of writing back, other than tearing pages out of her books. Within days one of her hairdressers solved the first obstacle, although at great risk. "Look in the dressing room cupboard," she managed to whisper while fussing with Catherine's chestnut curls. "Press on the center of the bottom."

A delighted Catherine discovered paper, quills, and ink—a secret stash of treasure. After that, she smuggled supplies into the commode to do her writing. If anyone noticed she spent an inordinate amount of time tending to nature's call, no remarks were made about it.

Other secret correspondence made its way out of the palace via her wardrobe girl, Katarina, whose fiancé was a court servant with access to the outside. Katarina also kept everyone amused by prancing around with a large pillow beneath her skirt to poke fun of the ever-pregnant Madame Choglokova.

By this time Maria Sergeievna, her favorite maid of honor, had also disappeared from the Young Court, but fortunately only to be transferred back to the empress's contingent of ladies. They saw one another only at matins, mass, and vespers—daily opportunities enabling them to pass close enough to one another to exchange notes and even an occasional book. Since most of her maids were semi-illiterate or exhibited zero literary inclinations, Catherine especially valued Maria's friendship and her intellect.

Catherine continued to find such tiny rays of sunshine to pierce her otherwise shadowed world. If Madame Choglokova was driving her to distraction or Catherine yearned to stroll on the usually forbidden balcony, her servant Lizaveta would offer Madame a cup of coffee. "It is very strong," she whispered to Catherine the first time this happened. Minutes later, the horrible dragon lady would repair to her own room, pleading heart palpitations.

"Perhaps it's time for you to offer some gifts," Lizaveta murmured mysteriously on another occasion. "Would you like me to call your jeweler? Maria Sergeievna assures me Monsieur Igor Blukhov has some fine new trinkets."

Suspecting immediately there must be more significance to this than a casual comment, Catherine wasted no time sending a message to Igor. She had always trusted Maria, and if her name was involved, her former maid of honor must have a plan.

The prize came in the form of an ingenious hollowed out pen— ideal for rolling up and hiding secret notes—that Igor slipped her while she ostensibly examined his wares.

Except for a few such random acts of kindness and access to her favorite books, no amusements, no lively conversation, no nurturing, and no attention sweetened the tedium of Catherine's life.

By autumn, restrictions on the couple intensified for some unknown reason. In addition to being forbidden access to the apartment without permission and forced to communicate in one-word answers, staff were ordered—on pain of dismissal—to always wait outside in the antechambers even when summoned. If the Choglokovs gave the requisite permission for a rare visitor or merchant to enter, Peter and Catherine were told to speak loudly enough so everyone in the halls could hear.

When the court moved temporarily back to Moscow, Catherine began to wonder if she should've opted for a sharper knife the day she'd halfheartedly tried to take her own life. The contrast between her optimistic expectations upon reaching Moscow four and a half years ago and the reality of the present were highlighted when she and Peter were allocated the same apartments she and her mother had shared on their long-ago arrival. The rooms were adjoining, and she vehemently opposed a proximity even closer than what they had had in Petersburg. Whether barking at his toy regiments or thrashing his dogs until they howled, his awful yells repeatedly brought her to tears. The scraping and squealing from his violin shattered her nerves. Moscow's endlessly clanging bells, a thousand-fold louder than those that had once annoyed her as a child in Stettin, seemed to make fun of her predicament, to mock her ambitions and her hopes of being loved.

A fever, sore throat, and pains throughout her body in January did not seriously concern her, and as a bonus she and Peter were excused from attending the traditional ceremony and the blessing of the waters on the Feast of the Epiphany. When she awoke later, however, she discovered small spots on her hands and chest that indicated she must have contracted the dreaded smallpox. She should have panicked, or at least felt a great sense of relief when the doctors diagnosed her with the measles. Instead, by this time she cared little about her life.

During her long convalescence, Peter gained permission to host a series of masquerades in her bedroom with his newly regained freedoms. Catherine was forced to lie on the couch night after night as he ordered gentlemen and ladies to dance around the room in costume while he accompanied them on the violin. Her only relief was donning a literal mask rather than the forced one of tranquility she wore on her face every day.

The noose of her life had tightened until she feared choking to death on her anger and humiliation. On her pain and boredom. Above all, on her loneliness. *After the dogs*, she reflected, *I am surely the most miserable creature in the world.*

CHAPTER 20

(MARIA) 1748

Being ordered to rejoin the empress's ladies turns out to be fortunate. Despite some drawbacks, including losing the protection and companionship of the grand duchess, there is one marvelous benefit: Igor has come into my life more frequently and prominently.

Everything has happened so quickly—and joyously—since the day Her Imperial Majesty summoned me to her stateroom and insisted it was time for me to "return" to her service, not to mention the opportunity to assume the duties she had determined for me: coordinating all her jewels.

"You have an eye for gems," she commented, and I strive not to disappoint her.

My first opportunity came when all of us were playing with her huge collection of cats and the empress accidentally broke the clasp on one of her favorite necklaces. "Maria!" she immediately turned to me. "Have this fixed immediately. I have no time to await worthless merchants. Have your driver locate one fast."

"Which jeweler?"

"It matters not," she waved dismissively. "I want it back by the ball tonight."

Taking this as an unexpected and fortuitous opportunity, I commanded the groomsman to take me to the House of Gems.

The delighted look on Igor's face reassured me my feelings perhaps were not unrequited.

"Mademoiselle Kurchova, this is an unexpected honor!"

We chatted about nothing—or at least I was too suffused with happiness to remember the subjects—until he asked exactly to what he owed this visit.

I'd almost forgotten my errand but waited quietly while he fixed the clasp in minutes before offering me a tour. "After all, you have seen most of our merchandise. Perhaps you would like to know more about what goes into creating such glorious items."

"I would!" Time flew as we examined bins of gems and minerals, not to mention a large polisher and an array of cutting and buffing tools. At last I looked up in surprise to see that the driver who'd taken me to the location near Gostiny Dvor market had come inside, snow-covered hat in hand, to check on my progress—or perhaps my safety.

"I would like to learn so much more," I told Igor while gathering the wrapped necklace and my fur hat.

"Then you shall, whatever and whenever you want." His smile assured me of his enthusiasm. "In fact," he added. "I have another book for you if you are interested. It is the most recently published overview of gems and minerals."

"I couldn't," I protested weakly.

"It's not a problem, really. If anyone questions why you have this, simply tell them it is part of your duties to Her Imperial Majesty to stay informed on the latest jewels and mineral discoveries." He surreptitiously slipped the slim volume to me.

Elated, I climbed back in the carriage for the return. Not only did I look forward to reading it, but to sharing my new knowledge with Igor Igorevich. I vowed to be back here soon, even if I had to break every single piece of the empress's jewelry.

Since that afternoon, I have educated myself systematically on more than Catherine's books on philosophy.

I have been to India, where the Burmese weave wicker baskets to pan river shingle for sparkling strawberry-colored rubies.

I have imagined Polynesian divers emerging from aquamarine water with precious black Tahitian pearls resting on shell beds of rainbows.

I have watched as miners extract Inca Rose, the nickname for the pink beauty streaked with bands of white and black that is the semi-precious rhodochrosite.

My opportunities to discuss these things with Igor have been rare as the gems he handles, yet even more precious. "The creation process for amber," he explains when I visit his shop to have the empress's jade beads restrung, "is incredibly complex."

"It is formed by sticky resins given off by trees, is it not?"

"Excellent. Yes, and sometimes they capture bits of flora and fauna, as you know."

"And insects?"

"Yes, but only one piece of amber out of roughly a thousand yields those, and most of them are some type of fly."

"I did read that the pieces get tossed around the Baltic Sea for millions of years."

"They do indeed," he smiled, and I can tell he is impressed by my growing knowledge of his field of expertise. "I like to imagine them there," he adds, "their soft flickering gold making it appear as if the sun has lit candles beneath the sea."

Yes, this is the man I am falling in love with. How could I not?

"Fascinating," I murmur, feeling his large yet delicate hands take mine in his. I cannot help compare myself, though, to one of those insects, trapped for a prolonged period of time in a warm, honey-colored nugget of amber with no hope of extrication. A tiny time capsule, I suppose. For just a moment I yearn to tell Igor this, then imagine the shock and disgust on his face when he disbelieves me, as surely he will.

Perhaps, I fear later, the empress would learn who I claimed to be and order me locked in her private Mad Room, where she keeps a menagerie of people who apparently have lost their minds. I've been dragged there once, to this asylum containing a semi-circle platform against the back wall where we're supposed to sit and enjoy the sights or, in my case, struggle not to vomit.

"Be silent!" she scolded us. "God speaks to us through strange channels."

One by one, the residents were led in through a paneled door. They included a monk who had sliced off his genitals with a razor to purify himself from unclean desires; a valet who foamed at the mouth and claimed a demon woman with snakes in her hair had tried to lure him into a state of undress, and a sailor insisting he was the real Ivan VI—the boy tsar who disappeared seven years ago when Elizabeth had him locked up so he couldn't claim his rightful throne. The inmates all thrashed around in this giant room made of cedar to ensure it could be washed down repeatedly.

Although I worry about ending up there, it seems to me more and more likely it is the grand duke who will find himself locked up. As months and years drift by, it becomes more apparent that this man-boy who jerks and twitches his arms and legs like a marionette, who wears a perpetual scowl giving his face the illusion of a grotesque mask, this foul-speaking, hot-tempered young husband, is indeed slightly mad. Or perhaps he will go mad, some whisper. Many ladies and courtiers avert their eyes from his own slightly wild ones when he enters a room. In my own time he might be prescribed anti-depressants or anxiety medications, but now there is nothing. Nothing and no one to stop his lunacy, except occasionally his aunt.

Irina is the only one I dare discuss such things with, and she, too, shares my fears for Catherine's safety. "It is not just that he initiates fights with her and taunts her with other women—even those old enough to be his mother," Irina sighs. "I've actually heard him threaten Her Highness and even strike her. Especially when he is drinking."

"Can you narrow that down?" Irina laughs. "He drinks at balls, at table, at concerts" she ticks them off on her fingers.

"In private, in public, behind screens, in front of screens . . ." I add.

"Don't forget on horseback!" We burst into nearly hysterical giggles, recalling a recent glimpse of Peter swaying side to side in his Prussian general's uniform as his horse galloped away.

Sometimes I wonder whether his physical disfigurement from smallpox is at least partially to blame for his drinking and his obvious psychological imbalance. It is becoming more and more difficult to recall aspects of my own early—and confused—days at court. I even catch myself forgetting who I am—who I really am—for days.

I've made great progress with my geology studies, not to mention many of Catherine's philosophy books, yet my learning curve in Her Imperial Majesty's court has been steep.

For one, no matter how exhausted we are at night, we ladies are not permitted to sleep until first light, when Her Majesty herself at last sleeps or passes out from cherry vodka or cherry brandy. Perhaps because she herself overthrew her predecessor, the regent Anna Leopoldovna, and ordered the infant Emperor Ivan VI carried away one night while they slept, Elizabeth seems to fear the same kind of treatment.

It was one thing to *hear* she rotated her bedrooms nearly nightly, but another to be responsible for keeping up with her and tiptoeing behind the servants ordered to move her favorite canopy bed from place to place. She counts on this nocturnal unpredictability to foil possible assassins or usurpers who might hide in a closet or beneath her bed. Only her dozens of cats—all shapes, sizes, breeds, and ages— seem to find her with no problem.

Throughout the night we're charged with keeping her awake, not only using feathers to tickle her feet and playing cards but recounting the daily minutiae of court life. We're expected to function as much as a network of spies as ladies in waiting and maids of honor. This is how I learn how the ladies and court gentlemen weave a sticky web of tales and intrigues perfectly capable of entrapping both innocent and guilty.

Even Irina comes in for her share of gossip, mainly in the form of mimicry of her pious walk. Elizabeth's ladies all refer to her now as the Nun.

Catherine walks the tightest rope. Although she is still forbidden to attend many court activities (the empress believes in that way she can ensure the grand duke and duchess are copulating all day in a wild attempt to conceive), tongues wag anyway. After Catherine smiles at her hairdresser, a maid tells Elizabeth that "she is too familiar with her servants." She neglected to smile at the coffee server the previous day, so "the grand duchess is too haughty."

"It is all nonsense," Igor comments one early spring morning when

I confide my fears to him. We are at Peterhof, walking together at dawn below the wide dark pink facade, painted at Elizabeth's orders in her favorite color.

Before I can reply, I have another sneezing fit. I seem to be allergic to Her Majesty's cat collection, which continues to grow. And although Elizabeth is terrified of mice and claims the cats keep them away, the cat army seems to exhibit no interest in assuming their feline duties.

"The cats again?" Igor asks, sympathetically handing me a handkerchief.

"They're everywhere," I confirm. "They lounge on each night's chosen bed, on the furniture, and all over the floor. She's much more patient with them than with us."

"At least your hair has escaped her eye," Igor smiles, reaching out to smooth a few tendrils from my face. I've been wearing it swept in a chignon, mostly to prevent it from falling victim to the empress's scissors. It is not unusual for Her Majesty to grab the scissors before we all leave for a ball and chop off someone's front curls, ribbons, and even on occasion cutting some skin if she dislikes—or envies—a lady's hair style.

"Is it true," he asks, "that she once had a lady's tongue cut out for wearing her own favorite color?"

"Yes," I sigh. "The lady made the mistake of wearing pink, which the rest of us are supposed to avoid." It occurs to me not for the first time that this incident alone should warn me that pursing a friendship—let alone a romance—with Igor could be dangerous.

As if reading my mind, he puts an arm around me. "Everything will be all right, my precious opal. At least we have some time together this summer."

It is true that we can meet more frequently at both summer palaces, first Peterhof and then Oranienbaum, each offering hundreds of acres of foliage, paths, and an occasional maze. Although Catherine and her ladies remain prisoners, Elizabeth's ladies are free most of the day due to Her Majesty's lengthy daytime slumbers. If they themselves are not asleep, that is.

We've made our way into a sheltered labyrinth of hedges, where we've kissed so many times. My body yearns for much more. I suspect that if I—or the two of us—were living in the twenty-first century, our affair would have long since become just that.

Igor's eyes, which today remind me of swirls of brown flecked with green jasper, miss nothing. "And what, my sweet Maria, are you smiling at?"

"Nothing important." I wave my fan at an early morning mosquito. "I was thinking how important some things seem when you are young that matter little as you age."

"Speaking of age . . ."

"Yes?" Igor knows I am now twenty-one. Not that I am twenty-one *plus* about two hundred and fifty.

"Won't Her Majesty be searching for a husband for you soon?" He looks closely at me as he asks, the way I imagine he might examine an indecipherable rock mixture, or even a diamond glittering from a kimberlite matrix.

"I pray not."

"And why is that?" he asks carefully. "Her Majesty does not usually like to have her maids reach your age without being married."

"She has had much older maids of honor," I murmur helplessly.

"Yet it is my understanding that she loves nothing so much as to plan and attend her ladies' weddings."

He strokes both of my bare forearms, and it is challenging to concentrate even though we are having the conversation I've dreaded and yet anticipated so long.

"She does," I reply finally. "But thus far I have been spared."

"Then you do not wish to marry?"

"Perhaps. Yes, someday. Yet I would prefer to choose for myself," I say boldly.

"You do not trust Her Majesty's matchmaking skills?

"Igor," I whisper.

"Yes, my sweet?" He pauses for a long time, and surely must feel me trembling. "Do you need me to say it?"

Staring at my lap, I reflect that I really know little about this man. Little besides that I have fallen in love with him and have been in that state for a long time.

I feel him take a deep breath. "I am merely a poor merchant, not an officer or a nobleman. We both know what that means. Or cannot mean."

Reaching out to place a finger over his lips, I tell him, "You are not poor, you are not ignoble. Say what you want to say."

He enfolds me in his arms, holding me as if I were fragile as coral the shade of my dress. But when he begins to kiss my neck and then my breasts, we both discover the truth: I'm actually sulphur or quartz—minerals that when squeezed give off something like an electrical charge.

He stops too soon, and looks deeply into my eyes, my head cradled between his hands. "I would give everything I own—everything in the world—if I could have you for my wife!"

Fortunately, the towering hedges hide everything when I reach up and throw myself back into his arms. He kisses me deeply, and despite tears filling my eyes, I am ready for him to throw me down on the grass and take me.

Suddenly he stops, pushing me gently away while kissing my tears.

"I love you, Maria Sergeievna. Surely you must know that."

My mind whirls. How can I have him? Beyond the empress's wishes and the obvious class barrier of this period, there remains the overwhelming question: would he want a freak from the future? Would he believe me? And even if he does believe it, what will happen when I return to where I belong, as could happen eventually? How could I leave him then? Worst yet, how could I abandon any children we might have?

Reluctantly, I pull away and hand back the second handkerchief he proffered. I don't have to look up to see Igor's presumably puzzled and hurt expression at my failure to respond to his declaration of love.

No matter what he must think, I must flee.

He does not call after me.

Her Majesty does not seem capable of staying in one place more than a few weeks, and all the packing and traveling has become exhausting. In late May, we visit one of Andrei Razumovsky's estates west of Petersburg. Gostilitsa's buildings include a small wooden palace perched on a hill, so the empress lodges nearby. Most of us stay up all night reveling, as the servants like to call our parties, and by dawn I yearn for nothing more than to crawl into the closest bed.

Everyone seems in a good mood, especially Catherine, who just spent eleven days in Tsarskoe Selo with little supervision. She dined with the empress several times, and I'm pleased to see her face has regained its pinkness.

Just before dawn, we discover there is insufficient space in the empress's quarters for all her ladies, so three of us join Catherine's maids in the wooden house occupied by Peter and Catherine's retinue. We slip into the second-floor rooms where the Choglokovs and Catherine's ladies are asleep. Beneath us, weary servants, workers, and groomsmen slumber.

Despite the weariness, I toss and turn. Perhaps because I'm surrounded by so many unfamiliar snores of people who are virtual strangers. Perhaps because I keep playing Igor's and my last meeting over in my head. Perhaps because the wooden house creaks incessantly even when no one walks its floors.

When the sun has long since risen, someone—presumably a guard—shouts while dashing upstairs. Monsieur Choglokov's voice joins his, followed by the sound of breaking glass. At the same time, something suspiciously like an earthquake shakes the room.

Slipping out of the bed I share with a screaming girl, I'm thrown against the wall amidst a group of scrambling ladies as the entire house begins to rock, walls begin to collapse, and the floors heave violently.

"The staircase is gone!" someone screams.

Half-dressed women push each other out of the way in a frantic attempt to leap down the space moments ago occupied by a staircase, and suddenly, just ahead of me, one of Catherine's maids is instantly crushed by a collapsing stove. A tumble of bricks knocks two others out.

Eventually the rest of us escape. Only safely outside can we turn back and assess what has happened: the wooden palace has slipped off its foundation.

I try to help, even with some painful bruises, but it appears too dangerous to reenter. Only a few servants brave what remains of the staircase, and it is then that I realize Catherine is missing. The rest, bloodied and limping, exit the house as if in a daze.

Peter stands outside in his night clothes shaking, making no attempt to assist or check on anyone.

We're all struggling to pull bodies from the wreckage when I turn to Peter and scream, "Where is the grand duchess?"

He hears me, yet only shrugs. For this alone, I realize at that moment, I will never forgive Peter.

At last I spot Catherine in the arms of a soldier straddling a mountain of rubble. He passes her off to another man, and in a relay the servants get her safely to the ground.

"Are you all right?" I ask when a sergeant of the guards finally brings her and Madame Choglokova to safety.

Trembling, Catherine looks back at the collapsed house. She does not ask about Peter, as if knowing he fled early and is safe. "I'm fine," she gasps, while Irina and I examine her wounds. Bruises cover her arms, legs, and right side.

"It is nothing. I will heal." Then, her eyes sweeping the fields around the palace, she adds, "Some never will."

In fact, dozens of courtiers, servants, and maids were maimed or killed. Bodies lie at the bottom of the hill, covered with hastily rescued blankets.

"The fireplace fell on the servants below," Irina whispers, repeatedly crossing herself with her uninjured hand.

We learn later that sixteen workers assigned to build a sleigh run at the mansion had been asleep below when dozens of beams and limestone blocks had collapsed, crushing them all to death.

A doctor insists on bleeding Catherine to calm her nerves. She does not object, and I begin to search for friends. Fortunately, most of those I know are safe, albeit black and blue and shaken.

The empress arrives to survey the damage, trailed by a weeping, apologetic Alexei. Even if the shoddy construction were his fault, he begs his lover and his empress to forgive him. "If you cannot, I am afraid I must end my own life," he sobs until Her Majesty puts her arms around him, seemingly more concerned about him than all the dead and injured.

If this is eighteenth-century architecture, I reflect later, catching smallpox or dying in childbirth would appear less risky than being killed in my own bed.

Only Catherine, even after narrowly missing being crushed, seems to want to tell the story over and over. She always describes the awful sound as "an entire ship being launched from the shipyard" before throwing all of them to the floor.

For me, the only positive consequence turns out to be a letter from Igor, which reaches me almost immediately after we return to Petersburg:

> *My dearest, I have been beside myself with worry and grief that you might have been seriously injured or even killed. This I could never live with. Promise me—if this reaches you and you have survived—that you will forgive my forwardness at Peterhof. Although I meant every word, I would happily sacrifice my yearning to be with you as long as you are alive and healthy, even though it might not be with me.*

Then and there, I vow that no matter how many obstacles might be in my way, no matter what I might have to sacrifice, if Igor once again raises the subject of love or marriage, I will do what I must. I *will* be with him!

CHAPTER 21

(CATHERINE) 1748

"Peter & Catherine continued . . . estranged by a thousand mutual misunderstandings and mortifications . . . a desert of unspoken animosity stretched between them."
— Robert Massie

"Elizabeth's court concealed dirty intrigues, envy, and hatred . . . that divinely beautiful empress could transform at will into a very real witch who was capable of releasing her fury at the drop of a hat, abusing and harassing the people around her with trivial carpings, although they had done nothing wrong . . . there was no limit to her whims and suspicions."
— Evgeni Anisimov

Everyone around her seemed to be having affairs: everyone, that is, except Catherine herself. Even Her Imperial Majesty was rumored to be seeking a replacement for Alexei, and court was rife with speculation and wagers as to whom he would be. At Peterhof,

Madame Krause discovered a scarcely veiled secret: that Monsieur Choglokov, the upstanding model of respectability who along with his virtuous wife was charged with overseeing Peter's and Catherine's marital integrity, had impregnated one of Catherine's maids.

When a furious Empress Elizabeth confronted him, Monsieur Choglokov (now a count, although Catherine steadfastly refused to refer to the couple by their new titles), was generously rescued by the oblivious Madame/Countess Choglokova. After the overly fertile lady denied the possibility of her husband having an affair, the empress presented her incontrovertible truth in the form of the pregnant maid herself. Still, Madame pleaded her husband's case, largely based on her brood of children in need of a father. Elizabeth appeared to relent, permitting Monsieur Choglokov to stay on. When everyone departed for Oranienbaum that summer, the young woman disappeared from court forever.

Although Maria Sergeievna seemed to be an upstanding member in Elizabeth's service, Catherine also suspected her former maid of honor of having developed a love interest. She dared raise the subject only with Irina, whom she knew she could trust and who remained best friends with Maria.

"I don't know," Irina stammered. "She is no longer young, although still younger than I."

"It seems I encounter her too often when I go for my morning rides," Catherine smiled gently. What she did not add was that at both Peterhof and at Oranienbaum that summer, on several occasions she'd witnessed Maria emerge from different sections of the grounds, often disheveled, sometimes with a stray oak or chestnut leaf caught in her auburn hair. Catherine would never reprimand, let alone report, her. She could see for herself the new shine in Maria's demeanor, and she wished only happiness for the orphaned maid—something she herself had despaired of ever knowing.

That summer numerous weddings took place, most organized by Her Imperial Majesty, while in Catherine and Peter's bedroom, the idea of being fruitful and multiplying seemed as distant as the planets. Instead they played cards incessantly, including a new game called ombre at which Peter imagined he excelled. "You cheated!" he accused her when she won. When he did win, he demanded, "Give me my money this instant!" Completely broke, Catherine gratefully yielded when he wanted to switch to playing hazard. Even then, without the financial stakes, he would fume when he lost—often for days.

As the watchdog Choglokovs withdrew to their own quarters to recover from their marital disgrace, they forgot to impose the usual rigid restrictions on conversations and activities. For Catherine, this meant the card games slowed to a trickle, and it was as if all the orange and lemon blossoms at Oranienbaum had bloomed at once.

Since Her Imperial Majesty had given Oranienbaum to Peter and thus the young couple as a summer residence, this became where they both felt most at home, albeit for different reasons.

Early that summer, Catherine found an outlet for some of her excess energy: the solitude of the grounds. Here she developed a habit of rising at three in the morning, donning a man's outfit from head to toe, and slipping out to meet a huntsman whose help she enlisted. Accompanied by the man's pointer dog, they worked their way into the tall canal reeds, where a small fishing skiff and an armful of rifles awaited.

Elizabeth, an avid hunter, might have forbidden her nephew's wife to join the frequent royal hunting parties, but Catherine was determined to master the sport on her own. Already an excellent shot, she seldom missed. Stealthily sneaking through the brush and reeds, she, the pointer, and the huntsman spent hours bringing down ducks. If occasionally the skiff drifted beyond the canal and out into the open sea, it was even more exciting.

Sometimes Peter joined them after his breakfast. They returned mid-morning, when everyone was just rising and too bleary eyed to notice where the couple had been. No one ever reported or even saw them, except Maria Sergeievna, who turned a blind eye when *they* didn't appear to see *her*.

Catherine continued to wonder idly about Elizabeth's maid of honor's mysterious early morning rendezvous, hoping only that it was someone worthy and that no unexpected pregnancy would get her exiled from the palace.

Only once did they speak after Maria inexplicably emerged right in front of them and curtsied to the grand duke and duchess. "Perhaps, Mademoiselle," Catherine said lightly, "You might like to join us sometime on our fowling expeditions, since you enjoy our morning peacefulness."

"Yes, of course, Your Imperial Highnesses. I mean yes, I do enjoy the dawn, especially at this time of year when it is virtually always light outside. But I'm afraid I've never fired a gun."

"Nonsense. The grand duke can barely hit the broad side of the palace," she whispered, "but he takes great pleasure in it." Seeing Peter draw farther ahead with his long strides, Catherine added with a twinkle in her watchful blue eyes, "Unless, of course, you already have a hunting companion."

"No, no. I do not hunt at all."

"Not for ducks, anyway," Peter, who had turned back around in his impatience and overheard them, interrupted slyly.

"I prefer fishing, Your Imperial Highnesses," Maria responded smoothly. "If you might excuse me, I must attend to errands for Her Majesty."

For Peter, tiring of hunting as summer wore on, the spacious private grounds of Oranienbaum offered the opportunity to bring his fantasies to life on a grandiose scale. He had decided every single gardener, maid, cook, sweeper, groom, huntsman, turnspit, valet, page, and chamberlain assigned to the palace should be issued some kind of uniform plus a musket or other weapon before being assembled into regiments. All day, rain or shine, he drilled them in his high-pitched voice, pausing only to change his own Holstein uniform multiple times a day. Any disobedient mock soldiers were threatened with punishment. They also discovered a new life on the lower floor of the mansion—now transformed into a guardhouse—when not on parade. Midday found them eating in the "mess" wearing their makeshift uniforms, and at night they were given the honor of attending balls with orders to dance with Catherine's ladies.

Nonetheless, many recruits grew bored or restless, and not a few fumed with irritation and resentment—especially at being forced to wear Prussian uniforms. As for Peter, he was in his element, and it made not the slightest difference to him that he had co-opted most of the palace servants, leaving a skeleton crew to perform regular duties.

At first, Catherine felt mostly relief, since she found that she could get away not only with morning hunts but afternoon rides through birch and larch forests. By now she was beyond passionate about riding, preferring to ride astride rather than in the English side saddle manner mandated for ladies. When somehow the empress got wind of this, she became convinced it was the cause of Catherine's failure to conceive.

In response, Catherine managed to procure a special saddle arranged so that she could mount it as if doing so side saddle, and then swing into her favorite position as soon as she was out of everyone's view. Best of all, her German groom modified the saddle with a moveable pommel to further her ability to gallop the countryside astride. A trusted maid sewed her a specially designed divided skirt that resembled the real thing but converted into breeches. At times she spent up to thirteen hours a day in the saddle, returning only to take supper with her ladies and later attend one of Peter's plays.

Two unsettling events marred those relatively happy days. The first was the arrival of a new head mistress to oversee Madame Krause. The empress's appointee, Madame Praskovia Vladislavova, was well over fifty, thoroughly Russian, and possessed of a prodigious knowledge of generations of gossip about each noble family going back at least as far as Peter the First's time.

Although Madame Vladislavova was less strict than Madame Krause, or maybe because of it, the overseers did not get along. Thus it shouldn't have surprised Catherine when Madame Krause was suddenly sent into retirement.

As much as Catherine loved to get Madame Vladislavova talking so she could gain an overview of everything that had happened in the Russian court for the past century, she resolved not to put her trust in her.

"Be very careful," Timofei warned. "She has been seen slipping away too often to visit Her Imperial Majesty."

That wasn't the only valuable warning Timofei gave. Although everyone was excited about the upcoming wedding of Count Lestocq to one of the empress's maids of honor, Timofei insisted Catherine be careful what she said around the newlyweds; he also advised her to make it a point not to visit them in their new home. He offered no explanation, and Catherine soon forgot about it. A month or so after the wedding, while playing cards in the empress's apartments, Catherine approached the count to ask him about married life. To her surprise, he nervously pulled away from her, and said in a low tone,

"Do not come near me, Your Imperial Highness. I am a man under great suspicion."

She laughed, dismissing his fears because she knew how valuable his medical and other services had always been to the empress.

Two days later, while working on her hair, Timofei told her, "Count Lestocq and his wife have been arrested and escorted to the fortress as state criminals."

As details and rumors emerged over the following days and weeks, Catherine hardly knew what to believe. She did know Elizabeth had taken a vow never to exercise capital punishment during her reign, resulting in the French calling her "Elizabeth the Merciful." However, the title and the vow were often at odds with the gruesome punishments meted out or at least sanctioned: backs turned to meaty strips of flesh by the knout; ears, hands, and tongues cut off; and prisoners nailed to a board and thrown into frozen rivers as a form of torture.

The rumors hit too close to home when a prince who served as one of Elizabeth's gentlemen of the bedchamber told Catherine one day, "Count Lestocq has been tortured."

"In what way?"

"They say he was hung by his arms in the fortress before being sentenced to exile in Siberia."

"But what did he do?" she whispered.

The prince shrugged, but then leaned over her in the giant sleigh en route to Moscow. "Apparently he was carrying on secret correspondence with the courts of several of our enemies—and," he paused dramatically, "he spoke disrespectfully to Her Imperial Majesty."

Catherine shivered, and not just from the cold. "But surely . . ."

"Do not worry, Your Imperial Highness, he did not implicate you."

"But . . ."

"I only meant," he hastened to add, "that anytime there are suspicions about spies for Prussia, your name automatically comes up."

Shaking and pale even though her skin had been purple as a plum a few minutes ago, Catherine turned back to her ladies and pretended all was well.

A month later Count Lestocq was accused of using his medical knowledge to poison a potential key witness against him. At news of this charge, the count tried to starve himself to death, only to be force fed before having all his lands confiscated. Sentenced to exile, he was to remain in the fortress indefinitely. Catherine feared the man who had been kind to her and taken care of her during so many illnesses would not survive.

In many ways it was a wake-up call to Elizabeth's power and paranoia. Catherine had no idea whether Count Lestocq was, in fact, treasonous and blameworthy; yet it seemed as if it would take little in this imperial court to prove even an innocent person guilty. A chill much deeper than the one outside passed across her skinny shoulders.

CHAPTER 22

(MARIA) 1749-1751

Back in Moscow, I have even more freedom to wander the palace grounds, yet I'm lonely. Neither Igor nor his Uncle Giuseppe has been summoned, since Her Majesty has plenty of jewelers here, so I find myself writing long letters that may or may not reach the man I love.

I am especially petrified because the empress has just mandated the wedding of Catherine's Finnish wardrobe girl. "You must be careful," Catherine warns when I contrive to stand next to her at mass. "I believe Her Majesty is marrying the poor girl off against her will very soon, and solely because I have shown some predilection for her."

"What can I do?" I murmur, crossing myself three times to divert attention from us.

"We will talk again," she whispers during the chanting.

The problem seems temporarily postponed when Her Majesty falls ill during Carnival, just before Lent. She has been stricken by some mysterious stomach illness accompanied by severe constipation. All of us are sworn to secrecy, ordered by her not to tell anyone, including the grand duke and duchess.

Despite the sickness turning out to be no more serious than a bad case of colic, suddenly we hear murmurs everywhere about the succession. Since the empress hasn't appeared in public for some time, all types of possible scenarios get bandied about. The question of the transfer of power if she were to become more ill or even die should be obvious: Peter would become Peter III, and Catherine his consort. But since Her Majesty has no children of her own, the young Ivan VI remains sequestered in solitude in a prison, and no shortage of ministers oppose Peter assuming the throne, plenty of clandestine meetings and rumors of a possible coup permeate the palace.

Ten days later, the empress is well enough to leave her bed, immediately complaining: "Those wretched children did not show the least bit of concern over my indisposition! They never even sent word to see how I was. It seems they are too eager to take over the throne and were probably hoping I would die!"

"But Your Imperial Majesty, we were told not to inform—" one of her ladies tries to protest.

"Enough! They are ungrateful and show little interest in providing me with a child to carry on the dynasty."

Although she upbraids them for their perceived lack of concern, I am told that Catherine finally appeases her by telling the truth: the Choglokovs had kept the knowledge from them for some inexplicable reason. I suspect someone, however, had confided in the couple, and Irina nods when I tell her my thoughts.

"It would explain why the grand duke has been so agitated," she says. "And of course, the grand duchess cannot report on her own tongues." The slang word for spies makes perfect sense. I wonder, too, if I am a "tongue," since my loyalty has always been to the grand duchess rather than the empress I'm assigned to serve.

"The grand duchess is extremely bored," Irina, who I suppose is my tongue, tells me on more than one occasion. "She is still permitted to do so little that she buries her head in those books all day and night."

"I wonder what she is reading now."

"She is working her way through someone named Plato, and another book that is in ten volumes! I *think* it's the entire *History of Germany*!"

"Amazing she can even concentrate."

"You mean because she has been assigned reading observers?" Irina smiles, although we both agree having a chambermaid assigned to watch her read is the ultimate insult.

For a good part of the year we spend in Moscow, Catherine's problems and Elizabeth's eccentricities keep my mind occupied. It also seems that the more temperamental the grand duke grows, the more of a parallel situation develops with his aunt. Although Elizabeth treats her cats and other animals kindly—even to the extreme—she often treats humans unreasonably, not to mention violently.

Sometimes my nerves get on edge, since the empress persists at repeatedly summoning her maids-in-waiting and servants wearing matching caps and aprons to scurry to her every time she tinkles a silver bell. When she gets angry, the bell rings faster and louder. At times she hurls it across her bedchamber.

"I wonder how many of those bells she goes through in a year," Tatiana whispers one day.

"Has she ever hit anyone?"

"Occasionally. Don't forget to watch her hand," Tatiana advises. "When she taps it on her lap, get out if you can."

Sure enough, a week later I notice one of the empress's beauty spots quivering at the same time as her heavily beringed fingers restlessly tap her lap. This is moments after the French ambassador has been to see her, and just before she overturns the tea leftovers. Silverware, porcelain vases and teacups, gold plate, crystal glasses, and platters of food crash to the parquet floor.

We're in her presence for even more hours when Her Majesty decides to spend nearly the entire summer camping and roaming from one monastery or estate to the next.

One afternoon at an estate about forty miles from Moscow, she starts screaming in her tent at a meek little man who trembles and turns pale as his cows' milk. "You are in control of this land, I tell you!" she yells. "Not only have others apparently been hunting on my grounds, but I also cannot find one single hare! How is this possible?"

The empress continues to spew insults, pausing only to kiss Catherine and Peter, who have arrived to ascertain the meaning of all the noise.

"I assure you," she continues, "Your Imperial Majesty is quite familiar with land management. We know how to avoid expenditures, how to avoid debts, how to dress simply and cheaply when traveling."

This last seemingly irrelevant comment is clearly aimed at Catherine, who has shown up in a silver and lilac gown.

For an hour the diatribe continues, until the poor estate administrator appears ready to topple. Although she has been known to hit her maids and servants frequently, this time she contents herself with a harangue of words.

To me, it is obvious aunt and nephew are related. Not only do both adore music and detest reading, but they share tendencies toward violence, yelling, irrationality, and drinking. Both are also paranoid and superstitious.

Elizabeth also relies heavily on her own secret police, known and feared as the Secret Chancery, who devote their efforts to listening at keyholes, investing heavily in paid informants, and in poring over every scrap of paper or law that might provide an excuse to bring anyone and everyone up on charges of treason.

As for superstitions, I can only watch in disbelief when Her Imperial Majesty balks at the signing of a document because one of her favorite relics—Saint Veronica—somehow has indicated that the paper is a mistake.

"You should see her when a fly lands on a document," Lady Tatiana, who has become somewhat of a tentative friend to me in Elizabeth's court, whispers to me once when we've been dismissed so her councilors can have a private audience.

Stealing a glance at Catherine at vespers, I wonder idly if she regrets having come to Russia, having married Peter, having become the pawn of an unreasonable empress, having given up on love. I can only pray that both of us find the love we crave.

One person who, temper tantrums or not, *is* getting love—of a sort—is the empress. Salons all over the city remain rife with speculation as to who will replace the Emperor of the Night. Ever since affectionately sending Alexei away, Elizabeth clearly has been auditioning potential replacements in her bed. The battle between various gentlemen goes on for months, with the empress sampling various possibilities.

By autumn, she has cast her eye on Ivan Shuvalov, with his sensuous lips, soft curls, engaging grin, and boyish charm. Regardless of being eighteen years younger, Ivan wins the role as the new Gentleman of the Bedchamber.

I am soon grateful for even more free time, although I wish I didn't know how I have gained it: even though she has chosen Ivan,

Elizabeth has taken no fewer than four different lovers at one time.

As Tatiana puts it so bluntly, "Her Imperial Majesty is fortunate that a man still wants to take her to bed, let alone four!"

I've been thinking along the same lines lately, since the empress's once marvelous looks dissipate monthly. She wears more and more rouge, which scarcely conceals the shadowy, poached egg pouches beneath her eyes. It takes longer and longer for her maids to handle her toilette, and although she is still relatively young, it requires heavy powders to cover lines that crease her mouth and forehead like chicken tracks.

"The poor seamstresses," I mumble to myself. Despite frequent religious fasting, Her Majesty has acquired a bulk requiring the hundreds of gowns she has on order at any given time to be altered and re-altered to accommodate bloating, corpulence, and rolls of flab encircling her waist, belly, and hips.

Catherine, too, seems unhealthy during the autumn months, but Irina tells me it is due to an awful toothache that has become so serious she has come down with a series of fevers, and once even slips into a delirious state.

"Now she has a sore throat and fever," Irina informs me soon thereafter.

By the time we finally pack to return to St. Petersburg, I pay little attention. Although I have seen Igor's Uncle Giuseppe several times at his Moscow shop, nearly a year—and a handful of letters—have passed since Igor played a face-to-face role in my life.

Unlike me, most courtiers and nobility have no great desire to return to the marshes of Petersburg. Antechambers fill with those pleading for leaves of absence. Favorite excuses seem to be personal or family illnesses, not to mention a torrent of supposed lawsuits and business affairs that require courtiers' presence in Moscow from "just a few months" to a year.

By late December, we are a smaller but determined group. I catch a glimpse of Catherine in her sleigh, and she looks the most determined of all. It must be the tooth, I think, noticing her clenched jaw and muffed hands held up to her temples.

Irina complains bitterly. "The grand duke absolutely refused to allow the sleigh to be closed, only reluctantly permitting her to pull a tiny green taffeta curtain to block the icy wind. Fortunately, the moment we arrived, the grand duchess sent for Dr. Boerhave."

"And this helped?"

"Yes and no. She begged him to pull the offending tooth until he relented and called for the surgeon to yank it out with tongs."

"So she is well now?"

"Not exactly. The surgery did not go smoothly. It was so awful, Maria Sergeievna. Her entire face ran with blood! There were even fountains of it flowing from her mouth. The idiot surgeon yanked out a piece of her lower jaw!"

Tatiana, who somehow managed to be at the surgery, adds, "I'm not certain whose face was redder—hers or his. There is apparently not only a missing jaw piece, but he left *in* part of the tooth *and* the actual root."

"Like a half-pulled tree after a vicious storm," Irina observes.

In the meantime, servants enter and exit Catherine's room carrying poultices, hot cloths, basins of water, and other more suspect remedies to help her recover from the gruesome operation.

"She won't leave the room anyway," Irina reports. "Nor would I if I were her."

"Why not?"

"Because the damn doctor . . ." She pauses to cross herself before continuing, "left an imprint of all five of his fingers on her face! You can see them perfectly. Her face is totally blue and yellow."

We all shudder, especially me. I consciously move my tongue around the inside of my mouth in a tooth inventory. Ever since arriving, I've struggled to find ways to take care of my teeth, but this so-called dentistry is frightening. While it isn't unusual to see even the wealthiest nobles with missing, rotted, or blackened teeth, it has never occurred to me that here was yet another risk of eighteenth-century life: dying of poor dental hygiene or from careless physicians.

"Of course, the empress's father knew exactly how to do this," Madame Vladislavova mentions matter-of-factly when the subject comes up.

"What do you mean?"

"He had a collection of teeth. They're at the Kunstkammer, that scientific museum he established across the Neva. He pulled teeth from his lackeys, friends, ministers. He did it for fun, though, and to build his collection."

Ah, Peter the Great. I can barely hear a mention of everyone's idol without thinking of Aunt Roberta—and now, not only her research, but all the times I fussed when she made me get semi-annual dental checkups.

At nearly the same time, another risk occurs. Catherine's young hairdresser had barely begun to comb her hair when he complained of being hot and having a headache. "Perhaps you, too, have a bad tooth," she joked.

By evening he was diagnosed with smallpox. Only luck and God's will protected the rest of the court.

How I long to discuss all this with Catherine, to tell her what possible cures and advances would be made in the future, both in dentistry and smallpox. Better yet, I yearn to speak with Igor, who has become a best friend as well as the man I love.

Finally in March I have an opportunity, and it seems as if the carriage I am riding in has never moved so slowly, snow or no snow.

Uncle Giuseppe is in the shop, and since we have gotten acquainted in the past, we spend time in idle chitchat while I wait for him to polish some of Her Majesty's gems.

"I am surprised to see you back in Petersburg so soon," I venture.

"Of course, I would have preferred to stay in Moscow even longer," he smiles, "but I've run out of illnesses to use for an excuse."

We laugh before I ask shyly, "And your nephew? Is he still working with you?"

"*Si, si, signorina*. He should have his own business, however. I do not need to maintain two workshops myself. I tell him this daily, but I do not know what he waits for." I imagine he winks at me as he says, "He should return in a few hours. Business is too good right now. Too many scabbards and jeweled buckles and diamond tiaras. Ah, that I should complain. But we have taken on two new apprentices, and perhaps this will help."

"Would it be possible to specialize?" I ask curiously, trying to quell my disappointment at knowing I will miss seeing Igor today after such a long wait.

"Yes, yes, indeed. That is my plan. My nephew—my sister's son— is the genius with gemstones, and I would like to see him branch out on his own alone. And his designs! *Mama mia*," he intones. "Spectacular, *si*?"

"*Si*, spectacular," I smile. "Please do tell him I said hello, *Signor*.

This time the wink is unmistakable, yet playful. "Igor Igorevich will be broken-hearted to have missed you, my dear. I will give him your best regards, and perhaps arrange that he may need to make a visit to the palace now that the entire court is here."

It is later that spring, however, before Igor's and my paths cross.

The opportunity comes during Lent, when Her Majesty leaves for Count Razumovsky's estate to celebrate his birthday—and all her maids of honor and the usual court contingent are sent to Catherine Palace at Tsarskoe Selo. By now Igor and I have resumed our previous foolproof method of exchanging notes and messages, since he, his coachman, or his uncle make frequent trips to wherever the empress is in residence.

Like Peterhof and Oranienbaum, Catherine Palace seems under perpetual restoration. All three also offer endless gardens and wooded areas where a couple can meet discreetly. Although neither the trees have leafed out nor the gardens planted, the more permanent hedges and bushes afford us chances to be together.

We embrace tightly, and I am breathless pulling away, and not yet ready to discuss what must be on both our minds.

Instead, we catch up on the past sixteen months, and he finds my stories of life in Moscow as amusing as I do his from St. Petersburg.

"Although nothing much happened here, as you can see." He points to the paths where grass has grown in the streets in the absence of the missing court's horses and carriages.

"I have noted since your return that the grand duke has a new crush," he grins, and I cannot help admiring his straight white teeth.

"Indeed, the Princess of Courland. He follows her around like Her Majesty's cats do her, although usually drunk on something stronger than milk."

"It is not easy to comprehend our future emperor. He has a fine, beautiful wife he all but ignores or makes fun of, yet he becomes infatuated with a truly ugly hunchback." He whispers the last three words, although my grimace evolves into a rueful laugh.

"Anything or anyone German . . . well, you know the man."

"Indeed." He tries his best German accent to imitate Peter by carrying on about Prussian superiority, which sends me into such a fit of giggles he covers my mouth gently with his hand.

"But, my dear," I offer when I recover, "Her Imperial Highness is also Prussian, although she never speaks of it. Nor does she use the German language unless it is necessary."

"The entire court and population consider her Russian, though, and that is one of our great mysteries—and fortunes."

"Catherine admires the new mistress very much. The Princess of Courland does have beautiful eyes and great intelligence, which is unusual for Peter's choices. She even plays cards with Their Imperial Highnesses and the Choglokovs. And as of now, she is our chief maid of honor."

At last our conversation drifts to where it must inevitably go, and I remember the promise I made to myself after the house collapse last autumn.

Igor appears to be thinking in the same direction. "Speaking of court romances,' he says softly. "Anything new on your own nuptials?"

"No. And you?" I ask cautiously, struggling to keep my tone light. "*You* do not need permission from anyone to marry." I lean closer to hear his reply, thankful I've taken time not only to chew a sprig of parsley to sweeten my breath but gargled that morning with vodka.

Igor does not answer immediately, and my heart races in fear of what he might say.

"No, I don't need permission," he replies as last. "And haven't we had this conversation previously? Or a version of it?" He squeezes my hand.

"No, I mean yes, we have, but that was a very tricky way of dodging the subject, Monsieur."

"What?" he cups his other hand to his ear and turns it toward me.

I cannot help laughing, knowing full well he heard me. Yet there is no ignoring the incessant noise behind us. Her Majesty's architect, Bartolomeo Rastrelli, is working his crews round the clock to add onto the already extraordinary length of the yellowish-gold palace, which I recall from the photo Aunt Roberta once showed me will someday be robin's egg blue.

Today, however, the noise proves to be a particular hindrance.

"You were saying?" I repeat. "About your romantic possibilities? Or is it possibility?" I hold my breath.

Igor does not answer quickly, and my heart races for fear of what he might say.

"There *is* someone, isn't there?" I say at last, and almost immediately feel a horrible sense of sorrow and loss.

"No, no, of course not. Well, not exactly."

"I must go," I turn and gather my skirts to leave before breaking down.

"Wait!" Igor grips my arm.

"I mean not exactly because she hasn't accepted me yet."

"So if she does . . ."

"If she does, I will be the happiest man in the world."

"Don't . . . don't do this to me!"

"Maria, *she* is *you*. I mean *you* are . . . Can you not understand?" His earnest look stops me emotionally and physically from fleeing.

"I don't understand."

"How can I say this? I've said it once before, and you rejected me! I cannot live without knowing how you feel!"

"Try again," I say, so softly I'm uncertain he hears over the construction racket.

He extricates his hands and throws them in the air. "I give up! I love you, Maria Sergeievna Kurchova!" he shouts over the hammering.

Within minutes I'm in his arms, this time without restraint. I've no idea whether it is due to my overwhelming joy or the physical need I've had for him for ages, but by the time a group of gardeners rounds the hedges nearby, we are wrapped together. They quickly avert their eyes.

As his lips brush my breasts, I am grateful I still wear the low-cut fuchsia gown from last night. Vainly, I suppose, I wanted Igor to see it, but this works out even better! It is his only chance to admire it—and mine to wear it—since Elizabeth forbids all court ladies to wear the same gown more than once. Even now, when she is out of town, she has a man assigned to mark the back of all gowns as we exit, using a type of permanent ink that will expose the truth if we ever attempt to wear the same one again.

"We need more time, and we shall have it," Igor assures me as we move apart and stand. Just in case the gardeners are still in sight, he bows and kisses my hand.

Disregarding his lead on etiquette, I reach for his hands and kiss them both. "Well," I tease, "you did promise I could watch you work at the shop again."

"Tonight," he replies automatically, as if waiting for just that question. "I will send my coachman—and my aunt—to pick you up at the north entrance by the church."

"Your aunt?"

"Aunt Gina, remember? She is my mother's and Uncle Giuseppe's sister. I have told her all about you, and she not only wants to meet you, but has volunteered to act as chaperone. Can you get away?"

"I will," I vow.

Meanwhile, Catherine's relationship with her husband declines to the point of outright hostility. When I point this out, Tatiana agrees. "And who could blame the grand duchess anyway?" She pinches her nostrils together, and we laugh, recalling instances when Peter flat out refused to take a steam bath, even for religious occasions.

"They say he insists no one sees him totally naked."

"I have heard the same," Tatiana confirms, "although that would make it pretty difficult to take care of bedroom business."

"But how can she bear to be with him anywhere, let alone *there*?"

Tatiana gazes at me from beneath nearly lowered eyelids. "Not everyone can know the pleasure of true love, you know."

"Well, he did get her the puppy," I concede at last, trying to focus on the conversation and not my own apparently not-so-secret love life.

Tatiana rarely stays focused on any topic very long, except for her infatuation with gowns. "Ah, yes, little Ivan Ivanovich is so sweet! Have you seen him walk on his hind legs and dance around her room?"

The always wriggling black poodle has become a court favorite, with the servants vying with each other to spoil him, even dressing him in skirts and shawls. "Last week I saw him sitting at table with a napkin tied around his neck!" I add.

It is no secret that Catherine adores dogs, and I wonder not for the first time how she can bear to see the abuse Peter heaps on his own.

One of Catherine's new maids told us last year she found Catherine wailing in her rooms. Her Imperial Highness had heard awful noises and walked in on Peter while he was dangling one of his English Spaniels by the collar, and having a servant pull as hard as possible on the dog's tail while Peter flogged the poor animal with a whip handle.

"When I tried to intercede," Catherine cried to her lady, "he only struck the dog harder! I can take no more of this!"

Indeed, I do not know how she can. I know only that she must—and presumably will.

Meanwhile, my own "love life," as sly Tatiana put it, is indeed a success. Igor and I are passionately in love—albeit without the full physical culmination of that passion.

"We must marry soon," he pleads monthly. "Before the empress captures you as if you were a rabbit too near her marriage snare." Indeed, the risk grows greater day by day, as one by one Her Imperial Majesty seems to delight in making what she considers brilliant matches for her own and Catherine's ladies.

"I dare not ask," I say. We've repeated a version of this conversation multiple times. "If she refuses—which we have every reason to believe she will—then all is lost. You will be sent away."

"And you will flee with me."

I sigh heavily and move away from him on the sofa in an alcove of Aunt Gina's sitting room behind the shop, where we meet in the winter. "And I will be caught and punished."

"Not if we go far enough away. I have relatives in Italy, you know that."

My heart flutters nervously at this, as usual. I cannot tell him the truth—that I still cling to a tiny hope that someday I will be able to return to my own time, and that any possibility of this happening must surely reside in St. Petersburg—or at least in Russia.

"I do love you, my sweet," I murmur, turning into his frock coat to avoid letting him see the tears threatening to overflow my eyes.

"Maria, I have respected your desire to wait to consummate our relationship. I realize the risks of pregnancy are great and would mean disaster for both of us. Yet I am a man with needs, just as I know you are a woman who feels the same. And someday I would hope we could have our own children, not to mention work side by side in the jewelry business."

This last is now a given, as I've learned to polish, wrap, and glue gems, even creating my own designs. I don't expect to ever be as talented as Igor and Uncle Giuseppe, but enjoy myself immensely. And unlike most men of this time, Igor does not believe women should remain at home or confine themselves to the traditional feminine pursuits. As for children, I am still terrified of bringing someone I might have to abandon into this world—not to mention adding someone to the annals of history who would not otherwise exist.

Yet I cannot lose Igor. I admit to wanting it all.

"Very well," I agree at last. "I will try to get an audience with Her Imperial Highness Catherine Alexeievna and see what she thinks I can do."

We hug tightly then, showering each other with kisses, both painfully aware that once I confide in Catherine, there is no turning back.

It is as if something has at last been settled. Perhaps because of this, the kisses become more desperate. I do not stop Igor when he bends his head and licks, then tugs at my nipples with his hot tongue. Nor do I resist when he hikes up my skirts and strokes my calves and then thighs.

The bulge beneath his tight breeches has teased me long enough, and I reach out my own bejeweled hands to stroke the satiny cloth at which it strains.

This, then, is what it is all about. After the first few seconds, there is no pain. Only pleasure. Again and again, as if I have at long last found the sword that fills me with diamonds.

CHAPTER 23

(CATHERINE) 1752

*"When he desired a woman, he was totally obsessed . . . and devoted all his
time and energies to winning her; the determination of a field marshal,
the cunning of a diplomat, the valor of a Cossack, the endurance of an
explorer, became his; he moved heaven and earth; difficulties
served only to redouble his determination, opposition trebled
his passion—in short, he was the perfect seducer."*
—Gina Kaus

"I held out all of the spring and part of the summer."
—Catherine II

There had been seven masked balls since New Year's alone, and
Catherine drew admirers like moths to a lighted window.

"You are so incredibly beautiful," one besotted army courtier
repeated whenever given a chance to approach her. Although Catherine had never heard these words before, the mirror confirmed he was

correct: the ugly duckling had evolved into a something much more lovely. Perhaps a swan or a peacock.

Her ladies slipped her messages from other admirers, some containing elegiac verses written by candy makers, and eventually one suitor's love poems.

"I have a thousand more poems in my head," he announced mid dance one evening.

"Do still your quill," she laughed.

"Please, Your Imperial Highness, do not make fun of me in couplets—unless they are centered around love." He begged, "It is imperative that we have some time alone, perhaps even in your chambers."

"I am flattered, Colonel, but as I said . . ." She fluttered her swan-feathered fan in front of her bosom as if to hide it. Within weeks the colonel was to report back for duty, and in the meantime, she felt herself too susceptible to not only his compliments, but those of other court gentlemen.

Each night her attention was diverted by attractive courtiers who suddenly claimed to love her. As if lit from within, she burned with a glow that lured all the wolves of the night. Knowing she could never acquiesce to the pleadings the same way she could not summon a wolf out of the woods and risk losing herself, she struggled to remain steadfast in her polite yet often flirtatious manner.

On such evenings she transformed into the belle of the ball, and the Choglokovs seemed to have at last opened the gates—whether it was their own idea or the empress's—to permit their captured bird to fly where she would.

After the colonel departed, she was disappointed, although quickly recovered as she remained the constant recipient of whispered confidences, compliments, and romantic notes. Her life up to this point had been a series of shattering blows to her self-confidence, and she found herself susceptible to even the most trite, insipid flattery and the clumsiest praise.

This attention, which she'd craved all these years in seclusion, came with a price: each night shortly after midnight she fled the court balls alone, leaving the gentleman as frustrated by her denials and rebuffs as the object of his admiration felt. It was then that the dream world evaporated, and given that she had no tiny slipper to drop on the stairs and no fairy godmother as Cendrillon did, all seemed destined to remain in this sensuous stalemate.

Alone in her bed, which she and Peter rarely now shared, she would imagine someone beside her, touching her breasts and then the mound between her legs that ached for attention no one could give. She had lived in celibacy for so long in a court filled with sexual liaisons that she could not help occasionally crying frustrated tears. For years she'd known it wasn't Peter she wanted, but someone eager to touch her, hold her, do what men did to women's bodies, and, above all, to love her.

That spring one gentleman newly assigned to her court made himself much more persistent and alluring than other contenders. Sergei Saltykov, with his ebony hair, dark skin and eyes, and muscular yet graceful body, refused to be ignored. He approached seducing Catherine as if he sought a glittering prize, and indeed he possessed the honeyed tongue, the polished manner, and the compelling arguments to win what he now wanted above all.

"You are married," Catherine reminded him on more than one occasion. Just two years ago he had made an impulsive match with Matriona, one of Elizabeth's ladies.

Sergei waved his hand dismissively. "It is a sham. Not to mention a huge mistake. I think only of you." His walnut eyes melted her sapphire ones.

She might have been able to resist this obsessed twenty-six-year-old seducer had it not been for their constant proximity. Not only did Peter delight in these new chamberlains and repeatedly seek out their company, but the Choglokovs continued to relax their guard almost, it seemed to her sometimes, as if they had been ordered to do so. Catherine was even more suspicious when Madame Choglokova, pregnant once again and mostly confined, often summoned the Imperial Grand Duchess to her room. There Catherine would find not only her husband, but three newcomers: Sergei, his brother, and Lev Naryshkin. She was equally suspicious, since the Choglokovs were incredible bores and less than intelligent, about the way Sergei and his companions had ingratiated themselves into their favor.

Why? she longed to ask Timofei, who sadly had been terminated by the empress over some flimsy dispute with a coffee-bearer. *Why would Sergei spend all day talking nonsense with this egotistical and dull couple if he didn't have an ulterior motive?*

She had to admit the men knew how not only to earn the caretakers' approval, but to handle them. Sergei and Lev's ingenious method of getting rid of Monsieur Choglokov was to heap lavish praise on the poetic lyrics he had started writing. "We need to hear more from you," Sergei would suggest following another insipid reading, getting the others to clap enthusiastically and yell, "Bravo!"

Flattered, Monsieur retreated to a faraway corner of the room. There, immersed in his writing, he became too absorbed to look up or even rise from his seat for the remainder of the evening.

Catherine could barely keep from laughing, forced to hide her mirth behind a fan each time Lev or Sergei prevailed. "Ingenious!" she told the men. "I must admit I do not understand, however, how you can devote so much time to speaking nonsense all day and night."

Sergei's eyes twinkled. "It is, after all, the only way I can find time to speak with the woman I love."

"Ah, you speak of love as if it were such a simple thing, something that can be conjured up with a few tricks."

"Of course not, Your Most Gracious and Beautiful Imperial Highness. I speak of what we must have to feed the soul."

"The soul?" she repeated, half grinning, half thoughtful. "Perhaps I should clarify this for the priest at tomorrow's mass. He will be delighted that you are looking out for my religious future."

"You tease, Madame. I do not believe we need to share such things with the men of the church, who, after all, do not deny themselves love." It was true that Orthodox priests, unlike their Catholic counterparts that Catherine had met in Prussia, married and had children.

She knew only that she was once again fighting her feelings, not realizing how her unavailability—and by now commonly rumored virginity—added to her glittering appeal, and in fact led Sergei to launch an even faster and surer campaign to win her heart and presumably her body.

In this charming, hilarious atmosphere of camaraderie, she found herself relaxed and amused at the same time she felt her defenses weakening. Whenever Sergei wanted to spend more time with her on the divan at the opposite side of the room from Monsieur Choglokov, he would rise, refill their glasses of wine, and stroll over to the man to propose yet another theme or topic. "You must compose something for us on the subject of the moon and stars," he'd say to the grateful versifier, who then busied himself for several nights brooding over quill and parchment.

Occasionally Monsieur would complete something unimpressive, and the prankster Lev would step in, offering to set the verse to music if only the writer would honor them by returning to his composition process for yet a while longer. Lev hastily strummed a tune on the clavichord, singing the verses to the room crowded with Catherine and Peter's ladies and gentlemen. Although no one listened, preferring to utilize this free time to carry on uninterrupted conversations, each praised the poetry after the song's conclusion: "Profound!" "Charming!" "Wonderful!" "Your best work yet!" they gushed.

"A poet extraordinaire!" Sergei praised him loudest, and after that the evening was theirs.

While Lev strummed noisily on the clavichord and sang at the top of his lungs, Peter delighted in his new friends and the freedom from observation occasioned by their pranks, which also enabled him to carry on yet another obsessive courtship, this time of Mademoiselle Shafirov. Even the empress, pleased that her nephew had found Russian rather than German friends for once, did not interfere with these evenings.

Under cover of all this noise and activity, Sergei continued to press his suit. The young philosopher Catherine, as hungry for love as for learning, did little to stop this minuet of seduction. She found herself willingly drawn into the silken snare he had set for her in the atmosphere of courtly love. Repeated hand-kissing and occasional hand-holding had to suffice, but at night she still lay in bed dreaming of more.

When she did have moments of pure rationality, she pressed him about his wife, who was one of the ladies who sewed puppy costumes for the little Ivan Ivanovich. In fact, Matriona had been so enamored of the dog and he of her, that eventually Catherine had gifted him to her.

Sergei usually shrugged, adding to her part alarm, part delight by insisting that in his marriage he had paid "a high price for a moment of weakness and infatuation. Be assured, Your Highness, that all that glitters is not gold."

"Are you telling me that your gilded marriage has turned to lead?"

He grasped her hand more tightly. "My feelings for you are much, much deeper than anything I have ever known. For you, they are cast in an even more precious metal."

"I believe this is exactly what you told Matriona two years ago. And do look how quickly you tossed her overboard. Yet you are willing to risk all now—even Siberia—for the sake of coming to my bed?" she pressed.

The reply was an adamant yes, followed by more protestations of love.

"And how do you know I haven't given my heart elsewhere?" she asked another day.

"Because you and I are like the sun and moon," he replied urgently. "Neither can rule the skies alone. We must complement one another; we must live in the heavens in that state of perpetual bliss for the world to have any meaning."

To her he was a god of perfection, particularly in the physical sense. Had Timofei still been there, she reflected, he might have done some investigating of his own, or at least offered her a different and perhaps more rational perspective.

But this was truly her first love, and as he followed her with even more devotion than her dogs did, she could not turn away. It would have taken a saint to do so, she often reflected, and she no longer wished to remain a saint.

The logistics of such a match proved even more challenging. Catherine was never alone, with seven maids of honor often sprawled on floor mattresses or reclining in antechambers. Even with a very pregnant Madame Choglokova out of the way, the grand duchess remained under constant surveillance.

Often, unable to sleep and irritated beyond measure with the lockdown, she would find hidden exits to follow, fleeing before dawn along marble staircases that led to the sea or the gardens, turning over and over in her head her options. She'd long since ceased deluding herself that she and Peter would grow to love one another, let alone fulfill their conjugal duties. It had been eight years since her wedding night. Eight frustrating, celibate, unutterably lonely years.

In mid spring she turned twenty-three years old. It was enough.

That summer she continued her indefatigable riding, often hunting at a full gallop on her interchangeable saddle. She had ordered her tailor to design azure silk riding habits with silver braid and crystal buttons, and kept him busy stitching replacement after replacement, since the silk on each habit wilted when it rained and faded in sunshine. She had, perhaps, never looked finer, her glossy brown hair curling out from beneath a three-cornered black hat, or tricorne, trimmed with diamonds. Even her complexion shone, prevented from getting weathered and sunburned by another concoction from the empress: lemon, egg white, and French brandy.

Meanwhile, Sergei interpreted every *no* as having an inflection of *yes.* "You must accept us," he begged, and although she tried to silence him with a hand that eluded his grasp, eventually he captured it and put it to his lips.

Finally, late that enchanted summer, he came to her, his mouth a sugared raspberry. His hands played her neck, her bosom, her nipples. By now she had a fairly clear idea of what to expect, or so she presumed, although she could not have been prepared for the flaming of her body.

The actual act was beyond what she had imagined. As he slid his fingers down her gown, simultaneously removing her chemise and touching the spot she had touched so often herself, she could feel her own moisture. She arched her back, thrusting up to his fingers, then crying out as he probed inside.

When he moved atop her, it was as if all her life she had been awaiting this, this tide of feeling deep inside that swept her up into a series of waves of pleasure. There was no pain that first time, and she felt only her entire body on fire with want.

Once he had taken her so expertly, he let her meet him and then take him in return. She believed she could never get enough, that this magnificent hardness between her legs and then filling her inside was rewarding her for all the years of waiting by granting her a deep pleasure for which she had no name.

The empress knew. Not about Sergei and their liaison, but at last she'd been informed by Madame Choglokova the reason for Catherine's failure to conceive.

"You should have heard the screaming," Maria Sergeievna told Catherine. She had requested a private audience with her former mistress and the two had agreed to meet after each declared the need for a walk in the gardens.

"How could she not have known?" Catherine hissed but with some consternation. "Everyone else in court seems to know that her nephew is incapable of bedding a woman, not to mention unwilling."

"Perhaps all his so-called 'mistresses' threw them all off," Maria offered. "I mean, they give the appearance that he is a very virile man. And surely such neglect is unusual in any marriage, let alone an imperial one."

"True, and of course I did nothing to disavow Her Majesty of the assumption that we were a normal couple." She half snorted. "And now? What might she do now, since she has already tried locking us in a bedchamber together for years?"

Hesitantly, Maria repeated what she had heard. "The empress has hired someone. I believe her function is to initiate His Imperial Highness into the joys of love. Or sex."

"Humph." Her eyes calculating and her sapphire ring tapping out a note on the stone bench, Catherine finally looked up and smiled. "Perhaps this will solve many problems."

"They say," Maria offered even more hesitantly. "That the lady, Madame Groot, is a very pretty widow, and Peter's French valet has selected this experienced woman to initiate your husband into the mysteries of sexual love. I do not know if she has yet come to him, only that she has been selected. As for any of his other problems . . ."

Catherine looked at her former maid with a sparkle in her eye. "Ah, yes. You are afraid to tell me what the rumors say about his physical readiness. I cannot give you an answer, my dear Maria, since I myself have never seen the offending member. Several gentlemen have hinted that there is a certain biological problem that can be readily cured if they can simply get my husband drunk enough to succumb to a moment of pain."

Maria's cheeks nearly matching the redness of the maple leaves heralding the season. Catherine laughed again. Love had transformed her, she knew, into someone who laughed and meant it. Laughed and played and loved with abandon for the first time in her life.

It was the time of year known as Women's Summer, when the days shortened and the trees and bushes transformed into ruby, topaz, and gold. This year it had swept in as fashionably late as a bejeweled courtier at her fiftieth ball. The leaves, too, seemed to delight in nothing so much as a flirtatious swish of scarlet petticoats, a satin rustle, crackle of silk, swirl of hems that float above the ballroom floor as if each waltz will never end. Catherine savored every moment, realizing never had she felt so attuned with nature. So alive. So infatuated with everything and everyone.

"We have discussed my problem," she said suddenly, "although I sense we are here to discuss yours, as well?"

"My deepest apologies, Your Imperial Highness. I know not where to turn."

"Let us begin with love. That is, I surmise, the problem, if one can call it that."

"It is. I have fallen in love, and now Her Majesty has suggested—insisted, really—that I marry a military lieutenant, but I cannot. He is not the one I live for."

"If I were to make an estimate," Catherine said slyly, "I would guess your young man is not of the military or of the nobility."

"No, no he is not."

"A merchant and craftsman?" Catherine's eyes gleamed, and Maria returned the gleam, although her eyes were tinged with sadness.

"You are, as usual, perceptive, Your Highness. Yes, it is Igor Igorevich Blukhov, and I suspect this type of match would not meet with Her Imperial Majesty's approval. In fact, I fear what she might do to him. To us. I am here to ask your advice, as I can only think of one solution: to flee."

"Flee the court? Nonsense, you are too valuable here. Both of you." She tapped her fingers thoughtfully on the lap desk she had brought with her desk, a magnificent one with oriental doors and mother-of-pearl decorations. "Have you considered," she said finally. "A secret marriage?"

Maria gasped. "Is that possible? Wouldn't Her Imperial Majesty find out? And wouldn't we be in even more trouble for flaunting her?"

"Perhaps not. Her Majesty is a glutton for love, and if we presented the marriage as a *fait accompli*, well, she might soften at the idea of two young people so in love they couldn't wait."

"That would be perfect, Your Highness. Indeed, I think Igor would raise no objections to this."

"It would be better yet if the two of you were expecting a child. Is that a possibility?" Seeing the stunned look on Maria's face, Catherine laughed again. "Of course, I can see from your face the idea is premature, so to speak. Then again, by the time the empress discovers the subterfuge, you may indeed be carrying a child."

Maria nodded, but to Catherine it seemed more of a nod of misery than one of anticipation.

"Which reminds me," Maria offered hesitantly. "To whom could I turn to find out how to prevent such a happy event?"

"Pregnancy? Ah, but there are any number of such recipes and tonics. I have no personal experience, but we can ask someone."

"Someone I can trust?"

"Yes, of course, but *you* must be the one to inquire about this. It would not be fitting for me to do so, since the entire court awaits the blessed news that I am with child."

"I understand, Your Imperial Highness. Perhaps I will approach Tatiana."

"Go along then, Maria Sergeievna. And talk to your merchant before you let me know what you want to do about this secret wedding. I believe it may not be that difficult to arrange!"

As Maria scooped up her stitching, Catherine smiled to herself. After all, if she weren't mistaken, she had other things—related things—to concern herself with today, including the very real possibility that she was carrying Sergei's child!

By the time the snow fell the following month, Catherine was certain. Not only had she missed her monthly courses, which necessitated dribbling bits of pig blood on the cloths she kept for this purpose to fool the servants, but each morning she wanted to vomit. Fearful and yet happy, she debated day after day what to do. She still had not had physical relations with her own husband, and unless she could accomplish this or convince him that pregnancy could result in some other strange way, she could not make her condition public.

Meanwhile, the court prepared to move to Moscow, and Sergei was one of those ordered to stay behind with the ever-pregnant Madame Choglokova. Unsure why she had not confessed her condition to the man she loved and perhaps the only one who might be able to solve this dangerous dilemma, Catherine prepared to leave without him in mid December.

Deep snow filled the rutted road, and jutting rocks alternating with craters created a journey that violently jostled the passengers. In keeping with Elizabeth's insistence on speed and reaching their winter home in record time, the sturdy horses had been fed nothing but oats for the previous four weeks so they would run faster and last longer. They even wore special harnesses that could be changed in a flash. The weeklong journey took only days, with the horses spurred on and whipped by the drivers to gallop day and night.

It might have been the rough roads, but halfway into the journey Catherine felt blood pouring from beneath her legs. She knew the cramping pains that seized her did not bode well for the baby she had carried for several months.

By the time they reached the last coaching station before Moscow, she had passed out, knowing regardless of whether she felt relief or sadness, she was no longer going to be a mother.

CHAPTER 24

(MARIA) 1753

Catherine is as good as her word, and in the spring, Igor slips unseen into Moscow to meet me in a church where everything has been prearranged. Sergei Saltykov and Lady Tatiana serve as witnesses, although I had to talk Catherine out of risking being there herself.

The wedding, otherwise attended only by Uncle Giuseppe, Aunt Gina, and Irina, occurs just in time. The empress, who had forgotten that she insisted I marry Lieutenant Simonov last year, has unfortunately recovered from her memory lapse.

"We shall throw you a grandiose wedding," she insists when she summons me to her bedchamber mere hours after I've slipped out of my honeymoon bed atop the jewelry shop.

"Your Imperial Majesty," I say calmly. "I am so grateful to you, but I must tell you that I feel no love for the lieutenant. Perhaps—"

"Perhaps what? You will seek out a better prospect? The lieutenant is not only handsome and debonair, he comes from a noble family descended directly from my grandfather, the Tsar Alexei Mikhailovich. I'm certain you will agree that this is quite a leap for a sculptor's daughter!"

"But Your Imperial Majesty—"

"Enough!" she waves me away. "We will arrange this for next month. You are a truly fortunate girl—in fact, hardly a girl anymore. You may thank us by presenting the court with many babies and be grateful that we have not chosen to marry you off to an *idiot!*" She pronounces the last word with disdain, and I cannot help wonder to whom she alludes. It would not be the first time she's been heard to use this word when referring to her own nephew.

I consider appealing to Sergei Saltykov, but he has fled court for a few weeks on the pretext of family illness. Catherine, however, does not believe his story. It is no secret to those of us observing that in recent weeks he has shown signs of waning interest.

"He is inattentive, conceited, arrogant, and dissipated!" Catherine confides to Tatiana, Irina, and me in a fit of anger.

"He will return soon," Irina assures her. "He is in love, after all."

Neither Tatiana nor I chimes in to agree; if the deeply religious Irina prefers to believe this is strictly a love relationship rather than to accept that physical love is involved, the two of us will not disillusion her.

"Supposedly in love," Catherine says bitterly.

No one could blame Catherine for being upset, since weeks later when Sergei does return he appears too busy to see her. The real problem is that we have returned to Moscow, a city for which Catherine makes no secret of her dislike. A city where you have only to glance outside to see three or four out-of-control fires burning in the distance. She is lodged here this winter with sixteen other ladies in a cramped room in one wing of Golovin Palace, filled with every kind of insect. At night, Irina tells me, rats scurry beneath the beds and water drips down the wainscoting. Even when she has a curtain hung between herself and a few of her maids, Catherine chafes at the lack of solitude. Since no one can leave without passing her, she eventually orders a ladder built so she can descend from the window to the ground.

She also had hoped that this innovation would help her sneak out to escape into Sergei's arms, although he is not cooperative. Eventually Sergei revives their relationship, yet there is little opportunity for her to be alone with him.

None of the women in either court has time alone, in fact, so I am surprised when one afternoon Madame Choglokova enters and dismisses all Catherine's companions. As I gather up the wretched mess that passes for my embroidery, Catherine makes a quick nod toward the unicorn tapestry next to the antechamber.

I pretend to exit and then slip behind the opening.

"We must talk about your condition," Madame Choglokova says without preamble.

Although unable to see her face, I imagine how startled Catherine must be. Although she never confided in me this past autumn, I know at least two of her ladies suspect she miscarried. Could she be pregnant yet again? I shiver at the risk this so obviously poses.

"What condition might that be?" Catherine asks at last.

"Your childless one, of course."

"Ah. Yes, I am very aware of that, Madame."

"I have been speaking with the empress."

"And? It is hardly a court secret that she wishes me to produce an heir."

"No, it is not. However, perhaps there might be another solution to . . . to the problem." Madame Choglokova is almost stammering now. Then, in a rush of words, she makes her meaning clear: she is giving Catherine permission to have an affair!

"Sergei Saltykov, for example, seems to be very interested."

"Sergei? Whatever makes you presume such a possibility?" Catherine plays her part well, sounding simultaneously shocked, indignant, and totally innocent.

"I am only suggesting you do what must be done," Madame says haughtily. "It is what everyone wants. It is what would make everyone pleased."

"Everyone?" Catherine asks incredulously. "You don't mean *everyone*, do you?"

The insinuation is not lost on Madame. "Everyone," she repeats. "Now I must go. I leave you to consider this: you are not a young woman anymore. Peter is not a young man. The kingdom . . ." I cannot hear the last part, but it sounds as if she just added something like "imperial exceptions to conjugal faithfulness are sometimes desirable in matters of great importance." Since Madame is not at all educated and seldom speaks in such lofty terms, I wonder whose words she is repeating. If I have to guess, it can only be one of two possibilities: the empress herself or Catherine's nemesis, Chancellor Bestuzhev.

The latter hardly makes sense, however, since he has been waiting for her to "fail" for the entire time she's lived in Russia. Although my thoughts lead me to miss Catherine's reply, I listen carefully to the conversation's conclusion.

"Her Majesty is also not a young woman," Madame adds.

"Do you mean not young enough to produce her own heir?"

"Precisely. Now I really must go," Madame Choglokova, clearly nervous, hurries out of the room.

I slip from behind the tapestry in time to see Catherine bent over, her shoulders shaking with laughter. "You heard?" she asks, and I cannot help join in her mirth.

"Apparently someone has ordered you to have an affair."

"Apparently! This is so amusing, Maria. I have the empress's blessing to sleep with my lover!"

"Sergei will be pleased," I smile.

"Indeed! The scoundrel! How did he manage to pull this off, I wonder?"

"He is very resourceful."

"Just think, that is what my husband calls *me*: Madame Resourceful!"

"Speaking of the grand duke . . ."

"Yes, I know. There is still that problem."

We know exactly what "that problem" is, and apparently other minds have applied themselves to solving it. "Sergei has an idea," she confides, lowering her voice. "He says that if we were to get my husband drunk and then smear the sheets with a vial of dove's blood—"

"Don't tell me. It is best if I know nothing," I say fearfully, at the same time shocked she would confide so much in me. If she and Sergei are hatching such plots and ruses, it is better that I can plead ignorance. Yet I can imagine the scenario: Catherine wearing a smug look the day after sleeping beside her perpetually drunk husband, then not so subtly letting everyone—not to mention Peter—know that the Act has finally taken place. It *might* work!

As for the other "problem," Igor tried to enlighten me before he left for St. Petersburg. "He has a physical malady. The other day I overheard the ambassadors from France and England discussing it as if it is common knowledge. The French ambassador calls it 'Le Petit Imperfection.'"

"What does that mean?"

"I'm not certain, but apparently it is a slight defect—something that he has not permitted the physicians to take care of in the past."

"I'm confused."

"So am I, but it sounds as if it might be a mere piece of skin that keeps him from, well, keeps the right part from rising."

I shook my head in disbelief. "That's not possible. Surely such a minor problem would have been corrected years ago."

"One would think so, yes. I'm only telling you what I have heard whispered. If he gets drunk enough, his gentlemen surely can summon a physician to snip it off."

"I don't believe it," I continued stubbornly. "His impotence—or unwillingness to make love to a woman, let alone his wife—would surely have been remedied if it were so simple."

"I don't know, my precious, but just in case certain of my parts grow that way, we should try to ensure that we use them—or it."

I laughed then, forgetting about both Peter's neuroses and his physical defectiveness. Igor delights in the fact I enjoy sex as much as he does, and we had very little time before he left Moscow.

Smiling now, I recall how I'd put down the pendant I was attempting to help him with, careful not to lose the tiny emeralds that must be glued around the central gem. We climbed the stairs to the bed above his shop, and did not come down until midnight, just in time for me to avoid being absent when the empress departed for the ball.

As lonely as I am for Igor, it's a busy winter, as Elizabeth continues the never-ending round of balls. These get so large it is not unusual for nearly four hundred couples to be invited. Tuesdays remain reserved for the smaller, reverse gender masquerades, with Elizabeth appearing most often in her favorite Dutch sailor suit in honor of her father's memory. For her coronation, she had a five thousand-seat opera house constructed on the Yauza's banks, and at least once a week, plus on special occasions (which occur almost biweekly) we're ordered to appear there or at a palace opera. Any member of the court who fails to attend pays a steep fifty-ruble fine, thus guaranteeing the entertainers a full audience. We also attend endless theatrical performances, in which the empress often participates behind the scenes. She even lends her jewels on occasion to the actors.

Other relief from boredom comes in the form of toboggan rides and races, as well as sledding and sleighing on Moscow's frozen lakes, ponds, and rivers. Although I missed it, I hear about the time Her Majesty ordered all the palace windows opened and water dumped on the floors so that they would freeze and thus enable everyone to ice skate in long galleries and hallways.

Absorbed in the fun even while longing for my husband, I forget about Catherine for weeks at a time. I am perfectly aware how much she resents the endless performances presided over by the empress, privately calling them "filled with *ennui.*"

"There is no amusement," she insisted to Irina and me once, "and no new cultivated guests or those well versed in literature to speak to. So," she ticked off on her fingers, "no fun, no conversation, no nurture, no kindness, no attention, simply nothing can sweeten this tedium that plagues me! Instead I must pretend, pretend, and pretend."

"I completely understand, Your Imperial Highness," I told her, realizing although Sergei might satisfy her physical needs, he cannot provide any more intellectual nourishment than Peter does.

She does attempt to turn up at most balls and salon visits outside the palace, although not always in the company of her paramour *or* her husband. If Igor were here, I would tell him what I suspect: that now that Sergei has been given *carte blanche* to bed the once forbidden fruit, it no longer seems so sweet due to its availability. Catherine may suspect the same.

On one other matter, I may also have been correct. When Sergei is at the palace, he often appears in the company of Chancellor Bestuzhev, as does Catherine. Somehow she must have achieved a detente with her sworn enemy, the most powerful man in the kingdom. Perhaps, Igor would probably say, because the man can foresee where the real power might someday reside. It is a subject Igor and I have discussed many times—Peter's apparent incompetence to rule—albeit never when any ears could tune in or tongues report us for treason.

As for His Imperial Highness's sex life, I know little except Madame Groot has been seen around the apartments at odd hours.

One day while we ladies wait for the empress to be fitted for one of her ever larger glittering gowns, Lady Svetlova comments slyly, "Maria, dear, we have not seen your lieutenant recently. Do you think you are putting on a little bit too much weight for him? Certainly your wedding gown will be too tight if he doesn't return soon."

I'd like to strangle the nosy blonde evil witch, but her words have been overheard by too many who might suddenly remind the empress I'm allegedly engaged to the nice but thankfully shy officer. Dmitri is his name, although to me he is the faceless lieutenant rather than a real person. We have danced together a few times at the empress's behest, but for some reason she seems to have forgotten me and the proposed wedding again.

"He is with his family in Petersburg, I believe," I lie, hoping for my sake that the poor man does not show up at court right away.

"I thought he was called back to duty somewhere along the Volga," another lady shrugs.

This is a surprise to me. "Hopefully he will return after he has attended to his duties," someone adds.

"Hopefully." I struggle to change the subject, which works for a short time. "Does anyone else believe that Princess Golubeva really restricts her hairdresser to her bedroom round the clock?"

"It's a fact," another lady confirms. "She locks him in a cage! Under no circumstances does she want him to betray her hair loss. My aunt told me she saw the princess's head one day when she arrived early her for a visit. Bald as a baby bird."

"I did notice that your lieutenant has such a full head of hair," Lady Svetlova neatly returns to the subject I don't want to discuss.

I nod helplessly. Truthfully, I have no idea, having never really looked at the man.

"Would anyone like another tray of sweets sent up?" Tatiana says, deflecting the conversation from my alleged love life.

This encourages the ladies to commence a debate as to which pastries we should order, and I am temporarily forgotten.

In case the missing lieutenant returns or the empress recalls her promise, I keep a small satchel beneath the mattress I share with another maid of honor. Here they refer to it as a reticule, but it is surely destined to be the forerunner of the purse. Inside, in addition to a set of Igor's clothing and some fairly sturdy boots for a disguise, I've stitched a pocket that contains money. It is my emergency escape kit, as prearranged with Igor. Should the empress get too determined to marry me off before we have time to work out how to break the news of our secret nuptials to her—or should she discover the deception before we are prepared—this is how I will be able to slip away. I will hire a horse to get to Petersburg and my husband; from there we will try to make our way out of Russia and away from the empress's long, powerful arm.

So far, so good, I decide with relief, and resolve to enjoy myself at tonight's ball even if it means fending off flirtatious soldiers, courtiers, and foreign dignitaries all night.

I suspect Catherine might be pregnant again. Each time I see her, her demeanor seems joyful with an undercurrent of tenseness. And no wonder, since I am not at all convinced she has had sex with her own husband as yet. He seems totally enamored with his latest presumably platonic relationship, not to mention *possibly* with Madame Groot.

Just days after Peter's name and feast day at which Catherine danced for hours in scorching heat, the grand duchess becomes dangerously ill. Whether this was precipitated by a miscarriage is only speculation, although Tatiana is convinced it happened. "She had all the symptoms before she became ill," she insists. "Yet now she is close to death!"

Since I am positive she will not die, I only pretend to be worried.

Irina, with more free time to go to church and play cards with us, confirms her mistress has miscarried, and that the doctors have little hope. "They cannot remove the afterbirth," she whispers to me and Tatiana. "I don't know whether Her Imperial Majesty knows the truth, but she showed up at the sickbed with holy relics. God help us," she murmurs, crossing herself repeatedly.

"If she should die . . ." Tatiana begins to speculate, but I cut her off.

"She won't. She is strong and healthy. And," I add to reassure Irina, "they say the people are lighting candles at every altar in Moscow. Everyone in the kingdom is praying earnestly for her recovery."

The crisis lasts for weeks, although to our knowledge neither Peter nor Sergei visits Catherine despite her life hanging in the balance.

She is ordered to convalesce in bed for six weeks, and I cannot imagine how she will survive the excruciating boredom. "I feel like a bear with a sore head," she has complained to Irina, who at least assures us that Catherine stays busy reading.

She summons me at last, and I try to be unobtrusive as I hurry to her bedchamber; it might look suspicious for the grand duchess to call for one of the empress's ladies. Fortunately, the empress is on pilgrimage, and brought along a smaller than usual retinue.

It seems to me throughout our conversation about literature and then court matters, that Her Imperial Highness is prone to a roller coaster of emotions. Her mood seems to shift from playfulness (teasing me about Igor) to dismay and anger (speculation about Sergei's whereabouts) to grief (over losing the baby). She is like the quicksilver Igor once showed me in the House of Gems.

"And how is His Imperial Highness?" I ask politely.

She winces at the question, which I would like to take back.

"Drunk, as usual. When he snores, which is every night, it is like sleeping next to a very loud hibernating bear," she complains. "Other than that, I seldom remember he's there. He might as well be a massive pillow."

This is more than I wanted to know, but I'm curious. "And his problem?"

"Ah, yes. I've have heard some things from Sergei that make me think all might be solved."

"That is good news."

"There was apparently a supper feast at which everyone was drunk. My husband . . ." she emphasizes the last word in a not-so-flattering tone. "My husband," she repeats, "reportedly admitted to all the men a lack of interest in certain sensations. After he passed out, presumably with the help of a little laudanum, they had a surgeon standing by with a scalpel. I know little more than that, except there was a French diplomat who witnessed it all. I've also heard Her Imperial Majesty sent Sergei a large diamond, although he denies it. And I am afraid this kind of news, from the Frenchman I mean, might reach the courts of our allies and enemies alike."

"All is well," I assure her. "No one can prove you've been pregnant."

"True," she says slowly. "But how can I be with him?"

There is no question who she means by "him."

"Because you must."

"Of course," she replies, her eyes now speculative. "Because I must."

When I depart, I'm surprised to see the Chancellor awaiting an audience. With all the misery he has brought her, it would seem they have little in common. Little, that is, except a strong affinity for and dedication to Russia. Bestuzhev has served his country faithfully for much of his life, and I know Catherine will do the same for all her remaining years.

Given that Catherine's prison doors have flung open and her health improved, I assumed she would be cheerful. Sergei appears regularly at court, and although I cannot imagine the logistics of them finding a time and place to be alone, apparently it happens. But Her Highness, I can see, is still unhappy and restless.

Part of it, I know, is her intense dislike for Moscow rather than St. Petersburg. I am not certain why, since I adore the old capital, with its thousands of cupolas that resemble golden breasts with crosses for nipples seeming to reach for the sky. And I *like* the constant round of bells, although at times their competing tunes get cacophonous. By contrast, St. Petersburg, with its order, its painted buildings, and its almost masculine appearance—complete with phallic spires—seems to appeal to Catherine. Perhaps this may be due to its founding by her hero, Peter the Great, who also detested Moscow. Nonetheless, here we must stay for the undetermined future.

One afternoon Irina slips into the room I share with two ladies from Elizabeth's court, motioning for me to come with her. She is clearly distressed.

"What is it?" I demand, as we find a place to be unheard in one of the many storage rooms that seem to be forgotten.

"It is His Imperial Highness. He is so heartless that I fear God will smite him!"

"Irina, tell me what happened."

"It is not so serious after all," she admits. "Just deeply disturbing. He is a cruel man and will someday be a cruel tsar!"

I wonder how many of her worries result from what happened a few days earlier, when lighting struck the main sanctuary of the church where Elizabeth was worshipping, and moments later the roof collapsed. Fortunately, she and her maids departed a few minutes earlier in the pouring rain for a smaller convent chapel, and everyone was unharmed. Yet the seriousness of the incident once again raised dynasty questions that reverberated through the palace.

"What did he do—this time?"

She seems embarrassed that she called me to hear of Peter's latest exploit. "He was torturing a rat," she announces more calmly.

I shudder, unsurprised. "What happened?"

"Her Imperial Highness and I entered his apartments this morning and found that he and a servant had erected gallows inside a cupboard."

"What do you mean?"

"He was hanging a huge rat! He told Her Highness that the rat was a criminal and military code demanded execution!"

This was almost—but not quite—funny. "Is it dead?"

Now it is Irina's turn to shudder. "Not yet. He told us the laws of war are harsh, and that the rat ate some of his soldiers in the fortress."

I know the miniature fortress to which she refers, and that it is full of correspondingly miniature soldiers made from starch. Just the thing for a rat to feed upon, since the lead and tin soldiers probably did not make for easy chewing. "Then what?"

"He strung it up and announced that it must stay there for three days 'to serve as an example.'"

I have no love for the rats roaming the often pathetically filthy palaces, but this seems excessive and gruesome, even for Peter.

"What did Catherine—Her Highness—do?"

"She screamed and then pleaded for him to take it down. Of course, he didn't. Then she went back to her apartment and started working on the Holstein papers."

The Holstein papers, I know, are a result of Peter's inability and unwillingness to handle the details of governing his own faraway land, and he has turned over their administration to Catherine's all too willing mind and organizational skills.

On November 1, we are in our rooms and Catherine is in the Choglokovs' salon when we hear voices, Sergei and Lev's among them, hollering, "Fire!"

Simultaneously we smell and see the smoke rapidly filling the hallways and moving through the palace from somewhere near Catherine's apartments. Assuming Catherine is safe, and with no idea in which part of the palace the empress might be, I follow others racing down the staircase just before the balustrade is consumed by the hungry fire. It is impossible not to think back to that morning when so many died due to the collapsing palace.

A wooden firetrap had been constructed outside some apartments, and it is this flimsy contraption that Catherine, Irina, the rest of the attendants, and the Choglokovs use to flee.

Outside all is chaos, and none of us can stop ourselves from staring behind us. Then, as if led by the Pied Piper, a prodigious number of gray mice and black and gray rats file unhurriedly down the staircase and outside. In the midst of them, an array of servants dodge the smoke and now flames as they try to hoist Peter's furniture out.

Everyone watches spellbound as bottle after bottle—all filled with liquor—topple out of the largest cupboard and smash on the ground. This must be Peter's private hoard, as it appears he has stuffed the massive old cupboard with brandies and wines.

The liquor was the only insignificant loss, in my opinion, and in the empress's. In the four hours it burned, the blaze consumed thousands of gowns and other finery, dozens of paintings and tapestries, entire floors of rare woods, furniture with inlaid marble, precious jewels, and countless possessions of a court that moved everything everyone owned from place to place. By some ironic miracle of planning, only Peter's Holstein uniforms were saved.

Catherine takes refuge in a carriage belonging to the Spanish singing master, and it is from that vantage point she, too, must be watching and covering her ears when cannons start firing into what remains. The soldiers are trying to dislodge the iron girders to isolate parts of the fire. The move proves fruitless, and by dinnertime nothing at all remains except the chapel (deemed a true miracle by the empress) and a few outlying summer apartments.

"I believe it started in the heating pipes," one soldier explains to the empress, who has hurried back from her sheltered position to wring her hands over the loss. Indeed, these immense but rotting pipes run beneath most of the floors.

The true miracle turns out to be that a servant has salvaged Catherine's books, and she hugs the huge copy of *Bayle's Dictionary* to her chest. I try to remember how she referred to the book when I once asked about it: "A monument to irreverence and sharply reasoned skepticism."

"We will rebuild!" Elizabeth announces loudly as the sky tinges bright orange—a fake sunset mimicking the fire's glow. Only the rats seem unperturbed, continuing to emerge slowly from the last collapsing charred timbers to crawl curiously over the wreckage's sodden goods.

The empress orders the palace reconstructed within six weeks, a seemingly impossible feat, so it would be accomplished by Elizabeth's birthday.

In the meantime, Catherine and Peter are forced to stay with one of the courtiers, whose palace is typical for Moscow; in other words, its doors and windows show signs of rot, and at this time of year, it is difficult to ignore the fact we can fit several fingers into the large floor cracks penetrated by winter air.

The aftermath of the fire does have one benefit: no one seems to be able to keep track of anyone else. When word of the conflagration reaches Igor, he hurries to Uncle Giuseppe's shop in Moscow to set up his old apprentice room, which once again becomes our love nest.

For another set of lovers, it is much easier to sneak into a carriage and head to Sergei's unobtrusive Moscow lodgings. Catherine often sends word to the empress that she is indisposed, and thus misses several late autumn balls, careful to always be back in her rooms before the festivities end. At other times, she manages to return to the temporary palace an hour or so before the ball is over, making a belated grand entrance while pressing a hand to her presumably aching forehead as if leaving her sickbed to please the empress she must surely love.

I don't know what she is thinking during these unorganized and risky times. Desperate for an heir, she will do what she must, of that I am certain. But already there are signs that the Courtly Love games she and her lover have been playing are coming to an end, that at least one member of the couple can be moody, unreliable, and uninterested.

"Do you think it is almost over between them?" I ask Igor, stroking his chest and its curly dark hairs.

"Most likely," he replies languidly. "Unlike me, Saltykov does not seem to be a man who can be content with one woman." He begins to suck on my fingers.

"Igor," I tease. "You cannot handle another woman."

"Not when I have this one, I cannot," he agrees amiably, sitting up and reaching for our glasses of wine on the nightstand.

"It's been nine years," I comment.

"Since? Oh, you mean since she arrived in Russia?"

"Yes." Since *we* arrived in Russia, I'd like to clarify.

"Your point, my dear wife?"

"Only that she must feel as if she has accomplished little. Her marriage, for one, is still a farce."

"We think," he winks. "Yet you are correct. It would appear her desire for love has been thwarted or certainly betrayed."

"Not to mention her hopes for an heir. Everyone's hopes, that is. Lately when I see her she no longer resembles a woman in love but someone who's just tired."

"Well, you would know. Since officially I am not *here*, I cannot know that."

"I'm sorry, my love. Sorry you must remain in hiding."

"It is okay, *mi amore*. I have plenty of work to accomplish in the back rooms, and I go outside only after dark. I am like a vampire," he teases, and as if to prove it, begins sucking on my neck.

I forget all about Catherine.

"If they continue to build these enormous palaces on frozen ground, they will all sink," Igor grumbles the next day. We've just received news everyone is scheduled to move into the new building the following week.

"Nothing is truly ready," he continues. "From what I hear, the workmen have stolen timber right out of the beams of other palaces. The empress herself ordered them to raid three of her courtiers' mansions to add beams and furnishings to her new suite of apartments. There may be thousands of carpenters and over one hundred wood-carvers assigned to this damn project, but none of them has time to do it right."

"The empress loves change, and so she orders the impossible." It is true that Elizabeth ordains wooden palaces be built or demolished with bewildering speed. Some fall victim to fire; others, as Igor points out, are built too rapidly or on the wrong foundation and cannot last. Most rushed builders use wood that is too green, and carelessly install stoves and kitchens. Disasters, as I well know, are all too common.

"It cannot truly be ready," Igor repeats.

But move we do, all her ladies following the empress on December 13, just in time to celebrate her birthday five days later. The new palace is much more magnificent than its predecessor, and its gilded main hall brighter with the construction of twenty-two tall windows. Even our own ladies' bedrooms are less crowded and a bit more opulent.

On New Year's Day, my new servant Liza assists me in dressing in a magenta silk gown with a matching headdress sprinkled with tiny garnets. She affixes two of the detestable black beauty marks, and I am ready for my own modest entrance. If only I could attend on Igor's arm. He has returned to Petersburg, and even if he hadn't, he would never be accepted or welcomed the way I want him to be.

Her Imperial Majesty takes her place at the banquet under a royal canopy, Catherine and Peter flanking her. Although the young couple appears happy, the empress looks much older and weary. She has an awful cough, professes to have lost or at least curtailed her appetite—meaning she must *really* be ill—and later that evening refuses to dance. The last time she danced the minuet, she grew so breathless she had to lie down.

Lately rumors of her real or imagined illnesses echo throughout the palace; seated in this commanding spot glittering in her jewels and overlooking long trestle tables of her subjects, she just looks tired. Any sickness she has must be masked, even her ever-widening girth. Already in the new palace her weakening legs and inability to climb stairs due to a seriously overweight body have necessitated special lifts constructed to hoist her from one floor to the next. Courtiers grumble that, if she visits their mansions or palaces, they, too, must have them fitted with mechanical devices to haul her upstairs, where the ballrooms are usually located.

I have no idea how close to the end my mistress might be. Her power remains unquestioned. I suspect that many foreign diplomats are drawing their own conclusions regarding the future of Russia and its next ruler. Courtiers and members of the court seem slightly on edge, as well, concern for their own futures motivating their actions. Everyone must tread gently, as no one knows how long Elizabeth's hold on the throne will remain tight.

As I try to observe Catherine unobtrusively, I ponder the future, too. Hers. Mine. That of the kingdom. Only one thing is indisputable: Her Imperial Highness's childless state must change if she is to wield any power herself.

CHAPTER 25

(CATHERINE) 1754-1755

"Catherine was to be a mere vessel through which the blessed gift would be bestowed. Her comfort or discomfort was of no significance in the light of the higher purpose she served."
— Carolly Erickson

"During that period of inhuman degradation and bitterness, the future Catherine, the real woman was born, the woman of iron resolution and indomitable will."
—Gina Kaus

No sooner had the empress held her New Year's Eve banquet than Catherine realized she was once more pregnant.

Determined not to get herself into a dangerous predicament again, she'd taken steps to ensure that should such a situation present itself, she would be prepared. She tried never to think about it, however— that disgusting evening she'd allowed her husband to fumble through the beginnings of something resembling lovemaking. He was drunk, of course, but she made certain to shake him out of it so that he knew exactly what had happened—or more accurately almost happened.

He was coarse, inept, and gross: nothing short of revolting. She resolved if she eventually gave birth to the long-awaited heir, she would never think about her duty again.

She first confided the news to Johanna, knowing the clandestine correspondence might take a lengthy and circuitous route.

Immediate accolades at home came in the form of the empress's gleeful reaction.

"We must do everything possible to protect and shelter my baby," Elizabeth vowed, and sent the Imperial Grand Duchess into seclusion in an old private house. Ordinarily this sequestering might've been welcome, but the structure itself ensured this would not happen. Huge old porcelain stoves riddled with holes required round-the-clock servants to put out the frequent fires it sparked. Even this vigilance did not keep the house from filling with smoke regularly, adding not only to Catherine's incessant morning sickness, but giving her headaches, a sore throat, and even a fever.

In some ways, the inconveniences were worth it, as not only Sergei, but her ladies and even former ladies frequently visited the weathered Moscow house. Even Madame Choglokova, who should've been delighted to be free of her jailor responsibilities, arrived often—primarily to confide in Catherine about her own affair with Prince Peter Repnin. Those friendly visits stopped abruptly, however, when her husband collapsed on Easter Sunday. Monsieur Choglokov had been ill off and on for months of some unspecified illness. Now the doctors declared him beyond hope of recovery.

Regardless of her past resentments against them, Catherine inexplicably had grown fond of the odd couple over the past couple years.

"One of my servants tells me it might be yellow jaundice," she said now.

"It is God's punishment for my sins," Madame Choglokova wailed. "Nicolai seems to have been almost at death's door ever since I fell in love with the prince."

"It is not your fault. Perhaps . . ."

"Yes, Your Imperial Highness?"

Catherine dared not finish her thought aloud. Did not want to consider the whispered word she'd overheard two maids utter when Madame had arrived the previous week: *poison*. It wasn't impossible, and potential suspects came to mind. The Shuvalov family, for one, since Sergei had confided they were concerned about Nicolai Choglokov's flirting with the empress. It would not do for anyone to supplant the power of any Shuvalov, especially the empress's gentleman of the chamber and lover, Ivan Shuvalov. Catherine shuddered, resolving to be more careful what she ate.

"I must get back to the palace," Madame said when it was obvious Catherine was not going to continue.

A few days later, the empress ordered the Choglokovs out of the palace, fearing the idea of anyone dying there. Long ago she'd forbidden funeral processions to pass the Winter Palace or adjacent streets, as well.

Monsieur Nicolai Choglokov died at home in late April, on Catherine's birthday, and almost immediately after the funeral Elizabeth suspended his wife from service. Her Majesty considered working widows a bad omen. She also believed they shouldn't appear in public, and certainly not in the presence of a pregnant woman.

Days later. Madame's recently deceased husband was replaced by Count Alexander Shuvalov, head of the Secret Chancery and cousin to the empress's own lover, Ivan Shuvalov. Madame was replaced by

Countess Shuvalova, Ivan's wife. She and Madame Vladislavova would now oversee Catherine's household. Neat as a checkmate, the pregnant grand duchess was firmly surrounded by her enemies.

This bevy of new guards made the reign of Madame and Monsieur Choglokov seem insignificant and nonchalant, and any freedoms Catherine had had were carefully sewn up. She was almost relieved when the court left for Petersburg, even though it meant enduring nearly an entire month of travel—the slow pace and lengthy stops ordered in consideration of the pregnancy—in the mean-spirited company of the rude and aggressive Countess Shuvalova.

Countess Shuvalova was not the only one to try and make Catherine's pregnancy and life miserable. The baby itself accomplished part of that, as its mother found herself a prisoner once again, not only of the empress, but of a body swelled to what seemed the size of a cask.

This time no one would leave her alone, as every lady and maid struggled to penetrate her womb's secrets. If she raised her left foot first, they insisted it would be a girl; when she reached for an object with her right hand or favored that side of her body, they determined she was carrying a boy. Catherine had a superstition of her own: Alexander Shuvalov's facial twitch, which convulsed the right side of his face from eye to chin when he became overcome with any emotion. Each time she saw him, she trembled, unable to convince herself this reaction to the twitch would not affect her unborn baby.

The empress visited daily to order Catherine to eat rhubarb and prunes. At her behest, servants smeared the huge belly with goose lard and the tailor prepared a special pregnancy girdle out of dog skin softened with butter. Exaggerated care was taken every moment to ensure the health of the unborn child.

The list of forbidden activities grew from the logical (riding, dancing, walking) to the ridiculous (hand raising, exposure to loud noises, sudden moves) to the idiotic (exposure to salt, necklaces, sadness). Resentful but resigned, Catherine did everything asked; she also stifled a laugh when she noticed any mention of the upcoming Blessed Event inspired the empress to make the sign of the cross.

Behind closed doors, Catherine knew, Elizabeth was conducting a rigorous screening of potential wet nurses. Catherine was consulted on nothing: a precursor, she feared, of the way things might be in the future.

Although the birth of a female heir might provide Catherine with more autonomy, she could only hope at least half of the predictions—those insisting it would be a boy—were correct. *If I have a daughter,* she reflected, *I will be disgraced forever, perhaps even forced to divorce.* Such thoughts haunted her as the summer dragged on slower than her unwieldy body moved.

With all the saints in the Orthodox calendar implored to guarantee her a healthy child, she tried to reassure herself nothing could go wrong. She did not even protest when, a few weeks before the due date, she caught one of her maids surreptitiously slipping two acorns beneath her mattress.

"I'm sorry, my lady," the maid stammered. "It's to help Your Imperial Grand Duchess get through the confinement."

"Perhaps it will help. Thank you," Catherine said kindly.

The pains began at midnight September 29, and she immediately was moved from a horsehair mattress surrounded by ten wax candles to a hard floor pallet. As she writhed and moaned in agony, attended by five of Elizabeth's ladies, Peter showed up briefly and ducked back out. Elizabeth, having hastily thrown on a cloak, arrived almost at the same time but then she, too, departed.

The empress returned later, gowned in blue velvet and wearing black feathers in her hair. Stationing herself in a high-backed armchair, she did not move until the baby emerged.

Dimly, Catherine was aware the minute the three-knotted cord was cut ("It means she will have three more pregnancies," one lady whispered) and the empress reached over and extracted the baby. With the bundle clutched in her arms, she whirled and, followed by a train of attendants, exited swiftly.

Catherine's temples throbbed. Thirsty and totally abandoned on the bloody wet sheets, she wondered just whom the child resembled. Alternating between anger and self-pity, she remained in isolation since apparently no maids could be spared to leave Elizabeth's and the baby's side. Her hours alone dragged. Twice she tried to stand, finding herself too dizzy to get off the birthing couch and at least replace her fluid-soaked sheets with dry ones.

Outside, she could hear distant celebratory noise, and down the hall sounds of her husband and his friends carousing. None of it was fair, she moaned, trying to ignore sore, milk-swollen breasts, as she longed to see her stolen child.

Finally, a maid showed up to retrieve Elizabeth's silk cloak. She refused to help or to answer questions, other than mutter that the empress was busy with His Imperial Highness. In this way Catherine discovered that she had given birth to the coveted boy.

A little later Peter made an appearance, announced he was pressed for time, and promised to return later. He never did.

By the next day her left side was in so much pain she could not sleep, and again, no one attended her as she lay alternating sobs with stares at the door. Booming artillery and incessant clanging church bells worsened her headache and shattered her nerves. She also feared she was getting a fever. Her usual dignity had been taken from her.

Straining her ears over all the noise, Catherine could hear nothing from the direction of Elizabeth's apartments. Was her baby even alive?

If so, did he have a name? Why wasn't she consulted? Why wasn't he brought to her? What if he had, indeed, died? Her naturally warm and affectionate nature yearned for motherhood.

Only on the third day did servants attend her.

Later she would learn that the empress's rooms were in an uproar because someone had discovered a clump of human hair and some vegetable roots hidden under Her Majesty's bed. Panic had broken out, with everyone screaming, "Witchcraft!" and the apartments erupting in fear and hysteria. Although the hateful "charm" was destroyed, the entire court would not rest until the culprit was discovered. A woman named Anna Dumacheva was arrested, along with her husband and sons, and accused of concealing the charm—as well as dosing the empress's wine—in the alleged hope of binding the two of them in friendship.

"Her husband is dead," Irina explained several days later. "He was so terrified he slit his throat with a razor. A purge has begun." Indeed, Elizabeth hastened to eradicate any suspicious item and to rid her household of all bedchamber women suspected of practicing witch-craft. To a woman often mad with superstitious terror and fear of assassination, the fact that she now guarded and mothered the heir to the throne made everything even more frightening.

"He has been christened Paul Petrovich," Irina also told her mistress.

"Is he healthy?" Catherine asked anxiously.

"He is now, although there were some problems the first two days when he couldn't nurse properly."

Any further questions, as Irina gently pointed out, would have to be stymied, lest Catherine imply she did not trust the empress to properly care for the child.

Forbidden to go to the nursery outside Elizabeth's private apartments without a summons, Catherine was left to fret alone and in silence. When the baby prince was baptized six days after his birth, Catherine was not only too ill to attend, but directed to remain, as custom dictated, in confinement for forty days. On the same day, as fireworks illuminated the sky outside her window, Elizabeth entered to present her with gifts: two rings with inferior stones, a measly necklace and earrings of shoddy workmanship, and the promise of a bank draft for one hundred thousand rubles.

The latter was retracted shortly thereafter when Peter demanded an equal sum and Catherine was ordered to give her money to her husband so as not to strain the treasury.

The grand duke eventually began to visit evenings, although his sole purpose was to see one of Catherine's ladies, Fraulein Elizabeth Vorontsova. He'd fallen in love this time with *das Fraulein*, as she was called, perhaps in part because she seemed to be his mirror image: vulgar in personality and pockmarked in appearance.

As if his visits were not trying enough as she slowly recuperated in her tiny chamber, word reached her Sergei had departed for Sweden, at Elizabeth's direction, for the purpose of making an official birth announcement. One of her closest companions was married off and sent from court. Irina had retired temporarily to a nearby convent. Even Maria and Igor seemed to be missing, although she had no idea why or where they might be. Now she had no one.

Burrowed deep in her bed, she wallowed in sorrow but at least in peace. She no longer cared if she had company. If pressed to get up, she refused, preferring isolation and thus faking leg pains if anyone insisted she rise. *I will curl up here forever with my afflictions*, she vowed.

She knew that the opposite situation held true in Elizabeth's rooms, where according to her maids, an endless parade of well-wishers visited her son and the empress.

"She takes good care of His Highness Paul Petrovich," one maid announced cheerfully. "If he even lets out a whimper, she rushes to him. She might as well be his own mother." It did not seem to occur to the maid that this was the last thing Catherine wanted to hear. Nor could Catherine totally ignore the ridiculous but persistent rumors that the child *was* Elizabeth's own baby, and since his features supposedly did not resemble Peter's in the least, this misconception was preferable to any others about paternity.

A month later, her confinement ended. The palace bustled with activity as Elizabeth held the required churching ceremony in the mother's rooms. For the first time since giving birth, Catherine was permitted to see her son. Before she could get a closer look, Elizabeth whisked him away the moment prayers ended.

Two days after that, the official congratulatory event was held, once again in Catherine's room. For the purpose, her chamber had been hastily decorated with velvet embroideries, silver coverlets, and unaccustomed splendid furnishings. For hours, Catherine held court as a procession of dignitaries, nobles, and members of the imperial household strolled by to extend congratulations and kiss her hand. Throughout it all, she presented herself as the picture of radiant motherhood, as if she were the Madonna and had birthed the Christ child.

It was all a charade. As soon as the last guest had departed, servants removed the splendid furnishings. Every table, chair, vase, and candlestick was carried out, the room stripped of its elegance and left in its former pitiful, bare condition. Even the great rose-velvet bed, fit for the mother of a future emperor, was dismantled and taken away, as if it were just a stage set, leaving its occupant to stand unsteadily on sore legs to ponder her fate.

The only pleasure Catherine had was the visit to the bathhouse permitted her forty days after giving birth. Depressed, neglected, and again abandoned, Catherine returned to her own bed and curled up. There she locked herself in, nursing her revenges instead of a child.

"The days of your bondage are over," her former enemy Chancellor Bestuzhev assured her one day when he arrived unexpectedly after bribing a maid to unlock the door. "It is time to get out of your bed and fight for what is yours."

"He is not mine, not really."

"Not the heir. You've done your duty by providing the dynasty with him. You have other responsibilities now." He leaned over and whispered, "Your kingdom needs you, Your Imperial Highness."

"Go away." She could not forget that for years he'd subjected her to a thousand humiliations, including waging campaigns against her, her mother, and her freedom. He had banned her correspondence and court activities, forced watchdogs on her, and forbidden her to get involved in politics. Now he seemed to want the opposite, and she sensed that in fact he cared more about the fate of Russia than anything else.

"I am always at your disposal," he pressed. "I've made that clear to both you and Saltykov. But he has been sent away for now, and together you and I must be wary of the Prussians and of those who would put them in power." She knew he referred to the Shuvalovs, not to mention the grand duke, whose puppet strings they pulled.

"I shall keep that in mind, Chancellor."

Neither mentioned the word "alliance"; nonetheless, its kernels sprouted from that day. Despite her caution, Catherine had enormous respect for Bestuzhev's administrative skills, intelligence, and military savvy. Her own husband knew little about anything beyond music and the outward trappings of the military, preferring to turn over the whole of Russia to his idol Frederick of Prussia.

This neither of the newly formed allies could or would tolerate.

Back in her own apartments by the end of the year, she spent the rest of fall and early winter reading and amusing herself in whatever manner she chose. No one cared with whom she carried on correspondence or to whom she gave an audience. Far from finding this neglect hurtful, she reveled in her new freedoms.

As much as she wanted to share this independence with Sergei, she recognized that the moment of his importance had passed. Knowing he'd fathered her child, she realized he would be kept from her in the future. It hurt to be this close to losing him, primarily when she remembered the things he had done to and for her body. Perhaps she and Sergei would have future rendezvous. Perhaps not. In the meantime, she could lean back in her own bed and stroke her body the way he would have.

Sergei may have been the second man who had snubbed her in her life, but she vowed he would be the very last.

She accelerated her immersion in books, devouring not only Voltaire's *Universal History*, but Montesquieu's treatise on legislative activity and governmental power, *The Spirit of Laws*. She waded through huge volumes of church history translated from the Latin, as well as Tacitus's *Annals*. The latter not only fired her imagination and deepened her understanding of ancient Rome but fed her ideas about how to protect one's own interests in an empire of strife and perfidy.

Attempting to attend Christmas services, she found herself so weakened from alternately sitting at her desk or lying in bed that she could barely return to her room. There she managed to shove a couch in front of the door, as much for warmth as seclusion. Crippled with pain, she lay reading for days, legs propped on a pillow. She vowed to get stronger physically, just as she knew she had gained in mental strength.

This strength was what she needed to extricate herself from the shadows that had bedeviled her all her life. When she emerged from her aesthetic retreat and cocoon, she had transformed on the outside from a victim into a beautiful butterfly, yet on the inside a strong and confident woman prepared to outrun and outmaneuver the petty factions and conspiracies swirling around her.

She had spun a new persona, one she suspected she would keep for life.

CHAPTER 26

(MARIA) 1754-1755

Igor has been beside himself since I became seriously ill over two months ago. "Enough!" he insists when Tatiana slips him into my sick room. "We must tell the empress we are married so I can bring you home and nurse you back to health. This is an insane ruse!"

I am just grateful to be alive, weak and with remnants of a cough, but not brought to my death by eighteenth-century germs.

The illness started just before Her Imperial Highness had her child. I developed a dreadful cough, and the empress insisted anyone ill be moved to the opposite side of the palace lest expectant mother or baby become infected. This made perfect sense to me, as did the rare seclusion it awarded. Except that I desperately missed Igor.

I'll never know what specific illness I have, although suspect bronchitis that morphed into pneumonia. I recall years ago when Aunt Roberta missed a week of teaching her university classes for the same thing, and a dose of antibiotics cured her swiftly.

"I don't want to be bled!" I insisted to anyone who'd listen, but as this is considered the premiere treatment for anything and everything from a cough or a fever to smallpox or typhoid to depression or anxiety, I have little choice.

The physician possesses an elaborate method that involves a lancet in a case, which he then releases into my flesh by cocking a spring. The puncture gets covered with a sort of bell-shaped glass cup that is heated before sucking out the blood. I watch once, and then no more.

Now, sitting up in bed and watching Igor's leaner features wreathed in concern, I feel guilty at what I must have put him through. Since fortunately I have not been feverish or delirious, I'm aware he has been here with me daily. He genuinely feared losing me, and my terror reached its own heights. The idea that I could disappear here in the past is beyond comprehension.

"The fortune-tellers forecast a precipitous year," I mention to change the subject. "It is a year of double fives, of course."

"Perhaps it will be a fortunate year, but only," he emphasizes the last word, "if we tell the empress about our marriage."

I sigh. He will not let this go, although truthfully, I'm not certain I am ready to reveal our deception. I am anxious to get out and reassume my duties, as well as to go home evenings to my loving husband on the rare occasions the empress permits time off. Yet so much is happening at court, and my position in service has become a job that I love. I admit to myself that seems odd, since I grew up in a world where, for the most part, everyone is equal and life is not structured around rigid class distinctions. But I genuinely care for Catherine, as well as for my other friends and fellow ladies, especially Tatiana and Irina. Even though I have been transferred from the grand duchess's retinue to the empress's court, I am relatively content.

Again I attempt to change the subject. "Tatiana was here yesterday, and she tells me the empress plans to spend New Year's in the Amber Room."

"Why?"

"She believes it is a place with healing powers." I'd heard of the Amber Room back in the present from Aunt Roberta, although have yet to see it.

"Maybe," he answers his own question, "she fears losing access to it when Monsieur Rastrelli has its panels moved to Tsarskoe Selo. They say it was badly damaged since His Majesty Peter the First brought it to Russia and left it in storage, but his daughter likes to have it assembled and reassembled in a different part of the palace every year, which means its gems and backing are peeling off."

"The same way she moves herself from palace to palace."

"Exactly," he grins, and opens a sack of sweets. "So you can regain your strength—and some weight," he explains, the wedding announcement temporarily forgotten.

I suck gratefully on the candies. At least I have lost some of the weight I put on before I became ill. Now, I think a bit vainly, I can have a new gown made.

On New Year's, fireworks pop and explode in astounding bursts of wheels, shooting stars, and glittering cartwheels, but mostly in shades of silver, gold, yellow, and orange. We have an entire contingent of fireworks makers, all still struggling to increase the variety of hues possible.

Igor holds my hand while we peer through the ice patterns and frost gardens formed on the windowpane, and once again I'm happier than I can ever have imagined I would be living in the eighteenth century.

For the next several weeks, a procession of balls keeps me busy. The empress acknowledges my return, failing to mention my engagement to the lieutenant she has chosen for me. Perhaps my illness has scared him off.

I don't see Her Imperial Highness Catherine until she appears at one of the reverse gender masquerades dressed as a Greek shepherd escorted by a general with silly corkscrew curls. But I do notice her edge out of the hall not long after midnight. "She thinks she is meeting Saltykov," Lady Svetlova whispers. "She may be waiting a long time. He has other interests, shall we say. Many others."

This would surprise no one, perhaps not even Her Imperial Highness. Somehow Catherine does not appear to be the helpless dove others would prefer—or that she often pretended to be before the birth of the heir. It is generally assumed—but seldom said aloud—that Saltykov, to whom she surrendered her virginity after years of marital celibacy, is the baby grand duke's real father.

I watch in admiration not long afterward when she makes her official reentry to court on Peter's birthday. She sweeps into the ball in a grand entrance that exudes boldness and assurance. Splendidly attired in a deep blue velvet gown embroidered in gold, she sparkles, appearing every inch the young wife of the heir to the throne and the confident mother of the second in line. Something definitely has changed; as if sensing this new aura, guests flock to her.

Catherine throws out a wicked joke or a pointed barb for each of her enemies, and it is humorous to note that some of the Shuvalovs, in particular, appear mortified and even a little fearful. As if secure in her newfound power, Catherine dominates the ball with bright laughter and funny stories that not only regale the courtiers but get instantly quoted and re-quoted. This "new" Catherine obviously has captured the imagination of all three courts: Elizabeth's, her own, and Peter's. For although in their past there has been a "Young Court" consisting of the retinues of the ducal couple, it has never been clearer that now they have split into His and Hers courts.

If Catherine's baby has become Elizabeth's trophy, then Catherine's persona has become her own.

"This is not the same woman I have heard about cowering in her room," Tatiana says. "I had assumed she was beaten down by all the malice and competition for attention and favors."

I look sideways at Lady Tatiana. Lately her astute observations and bold statements have surprised me, and once again I am grateful to have her as a friend, not to mention an ally.

At that moment that I am invited to dance, and to my great dismay it is *the* lieutenant who bows before me. This is terrifying, as I had supposed him far away at the front.

"I am most unhappy to hear my lady has been very ill," he stammers.

I force myself to appear bright and cheery. "I feel much recovered this evening, Lieutenant. Thank you for your concern." As a quick afterthought, I add, "In case I have a relapse, I may need to retire early."

At his obviously crestfallen look, my heart plummets. He is still interested. Nervously I glance around to confirm Her Majesty hasn't arrived yet. It will not do for her to see the two of us together, as this surely would remind her about our supposedly impending nuptials. Already her favorite, Ivan Shuvalov, is there. Judging by his scowl, he is engrossed in trying to figure out what game Catherine is playing.

With great reluctance I make my excuses and hurry to my room, simultaneously relieved to escape the lieutenant's hangdog look and nervous Her Majesty might notice my absence when she makes her own typically late grand entrance.

Tatiana keeps me updated on Catherine's emerging stronger personality. "She has definitely thrown down the gauntlet to the Shuvalovs," she laughs.

"Which makes her very brave or very reckless."

"Ah, but that makes for an interesting court. Speaking of interesting, I saw you dancing with your lieutenant. Can't you tell him you are uninterested in being his wife?"

"I would very much like to tell him that I am someone *else's* wife!"

"Perhaps," Tatiana says, "that time is nearing. The empress is in a magnanimous mood now that she oversees little Paul Petrovich—and she is relieved that you are well."

I consider the possibilities once again if I confess the marriage: exile (not so bad if Igor comes with me), prison (not survivable for either of us); disgrace (unpredictable), or a forced marriage to the lieutenant (illegal, immoral, and impossible). What else could she do to me?

"She does not have to know you have *already* married, only that you wish to be."

This makes more sense, and if I tell her that I have already "sinned" and wish to make it right, it *could* work. Last year I considered lying and telling her I was pregnant by Igor, but my illness put an end to that potential ploy. On the other hand, if I can postpone things another six weeks or so . . .

"Let us wait awhile then," Tatiana agrees when I tell her my idea.

"My fear is that Igor will lose his position as one of the court jewelers."

"He is so talented. Undoubtedly he can secure another similar position with a great person."

"Perhaps." I resolve to be more vigilant when I am in the presence of other members of the court—especially the Shuvalovs.

I am strolling near the construction site of the new Winter Palace when I again encounter Dmitri, "my" lieutenant. This is my opportunity, and, heedless of the impropriety of having such a conversation minus an escort, I decide to take it.

Although he approached on horseback, Dmitri has a blanket that he arranges carefully on the ground for me. It is a sunny spring day, albeit with a stiff breeze blowing off the Neva.

"I am already spoken for," I explain after some stilted conversation.

"Why have I not heard of this, Mademoiselle Maria Sergeievna?"

"I have kept it a secret out of necessity, but no longer believe that this is fair to you."

The beginnings of a scowl cross his features, and I am surprised that the lieutenant does, indeed, appear to have some feelings for me—or at least some pride. "I demand to know who this scoundrel might be. Is it Prince Shartenov? No, let me think. You danced the other night with Colonel Beauregard many times."

"I cannot tell you as yet, Dmitri." It is perhaps the first time I have called him by his birth name, and he flushes.

"Very well. Then you shall tell the empress!"

"Of course," I say mildly, although my heart is hammering. I did not expect this ultimatum, having hoped for several more weeks.

When he leaves, he neglects to take the blanket, and I remain there for an hour observing workers move back and forth through the construction, clearing ruins of the old palace. Already a temporary wooden one is being thrown together on a previously empty spot between Malaya Morskaya and Bolshaya Morskaya streets at the corner of what someday will be renamed Nevsky Prospekt, Petersburg's main avenue. They say the new palace will have up to fifteen hundred rooms, and not only does this astound me despite having visited the finished building in the future, but I find it daunting: just how many statues will it take to decorate all these rooms? And how soon might a certain one of a certain goddess show up?

It occurs to me also, and not for the first or even twenty-first time, that I owe Igor the truth before I commit his life to prison, exile, or at a minimum a boycott of his business. It makes no sense for me to remain in the past permanently hiding this monstrosity of a secret— my true identity—and if I cannot confide in my own husband, there is no one left who I can trust.

This is my resolve when we head for Oranienbaum Palace that summer.

No one seems to know which foot to dance with when Her Imperial Highness enters the room. Only the empress does not seem intimidated by her since she considers herself the one holding trump—even Catherine's dance cards.

Free at last from Elizabeth's ubiquitous presence because the empress prefers to keep little Paul with her at Peterhof Palace, Catherine capably assumes the role of hostess and diplomat at Oranienbaum. I cannot believe I am here, as is Igor, who increasingly, despite being an artisan and merchant, has been invited to Catherine's, if not Elizabeth's, court. Gratefully we wander, if not hand in hand, at least in close proximity, through the gardens.

Catherine has devoted herself to turning Oranienbaum into a showcase, taking on both an extensive garden project and establishing an aviary. Here she keeps Chinese pheasants, thrushes, magpies, orioles, parrots, parakeets, and canaries. She spends hours listening to them and watching the rainbow of fluttering wings, which seems to sooth her.

On the opposite side of Oranienbaum's grounds, thousands of Holsteiners camp out in full uniform under the so-called leadership of the Grand Duke Peter. This ragtag army—consisting primarily of runaway apprentices, German deserters, and drifters—has established makeshift barracks, horse stables, and even an arsenal. They march under the auspices of Russia's biggest enemy, Prussia.

"They are a disgrace," Irina, recently returned from her convent hiatus, mutters. "Just look how our own servants are ordered to wait on them hand and foot." Indeed, the palace servers and guards can barely keep up with the insatiable demands of the "army," with its incredible consumption of liquor and food. Nor can they hide their resentment at having to clean up after the hated foreigners.

"I adore the grand duke's uniform, though," I laugh, and we both watch him marching up and down drilling his new troops in an enemy Holstein uniform riddled with holes. These, we've heard, are the result of him ordering his valet to burn the cloth with hot coals so that it will appear he has been shot with a musket.

Most of the boys can barely handle a heavy musket, yet the noise of weapon fire, not to mention nightly drunken revels, persists. Much of it is instigated by Herr Brockdorff from Hamburg, who's recently joined Peter's retinue and struts around wearing a bright red colonel's uniform and a tricorne. Catherine, detesting him, calls him the Pelican in recognition of his ugliness.

The upcoming Name Day celebration for Peter—and now the little prince Paul since their name days coincide—also is to be hosted by Catherine. Based on the purposeful servants who bustle throughout the grounds, the celebration should exceed expectations.

"I must introduce you to my new friend, a diplomat from England," Igor announces early in the week. "His function at court is to facilitate a treaty, but he has invited me to his new residence to consult on jewels. I told him that one of Her Majesty's maids of honor is an expert who also speaks English fluently, unlike myself, and he would like to meet you."

Sir Charles Hanbury-Williams turns out to be a charming English-man who, while accustomed to European courts, is clearly over-whelmed by Elizabeth's Russian one. "Never have I seen such extrava-gant luxury," he gushes as we sit in his receiving room sipping claret. "Everything here sparkles," he adds excitedly. "I do not believe that even Versailles can compete!"

I smile to myself, because even after all these years, I, too, never get tired of the way everything from champagne flutes and serving plat-ters to towers and facades are thickly encrusted or gilded with gold. Throughout Elizabeth's palaces and her kingdom, light refracts off a thousand faceted and gem-studded walls, marble floors, porcelain or faceted figurines, and alabaster sculptures.

When we arrived, we passed Sir Charles's tailor departing after taking measurements and orders for a variety of finery in brocades, velvets, lace, and satin to compete. In this opulent court courtiers spend all their rubles trying to outdo one another in everything from apparel to palaces. If one orders a Parisian carriage worth four thou-sand rubles, his rivals must order carriages that cost five thousand rubles. Forty chandeliers in one palace must be upped by the addition of a forty-first at the neighbor's. Last year in Moscow I recall General Apraksin tossing handfuls of gold coins and valuable trinkets from his balcony to townspeople huddling in the cold courtyard.

"I cannot compete with all this," Sir Charles sighs now, turning to Igor. "I need your assistance. I cannot help notice that here gentlemen of the nobility array themselves in diamond shoe buckles, diamond belts, and diamond epaulets. I must assume responsibility for most of my own expenses, and thus need to find a way to blend in and keep up His Majesty King George's reputation without going into prodigious debt."

"I can help you with the brilliants and keep expenses reasonable," Igor assures him in his broken English. He speaks German, Italian, French, and Russian fluently, but as the conversation flows, he often turns to me for an English translation. Until now Igor has been one of the few people who knows I speak English, let alone that I'm trying to teach myself Latin to keep up with some of the reading Catherine recommends.

Sir Charles, a seasoned diplomat, is an astute observer of court life and the European political situation. Accustomed to Saxon, Polish, and French courts, he has indulged himself heavily, and as a result presents a stout appearance with a ruddy complexion. He also has a sharp wit, and if not always tactful, he is unusually perceptive.

"I must show you my fish," he insists. Outside the grand house he's rented, orange and red goldfish swim in chilly ponds. Inside, dozens of Russian servants keep his kitchen well provisioned, and stoves stoked.

In addition to servants he hired and those he brought with him, he has seventeen "house guests": an entire contingent of bodyguards who gobble up his provisions and, as he complains, "guard me against nobody." This security detail has been hired at the demand of the Russian court, and Sir Charles obviously resents having to pay them "sixty poods of sterling per year plus lodging for doing virtually nothing but creating a nuisance of themselves. It is unacceptable as it is I who must rent and furnish this grand house at my own expense.

"The only person I really need," he adds, "is my legitimate houseguest, a young nobleman I have brought along from Poland. Without Count Stanislaus Poniatowski, I would be lost," he freely admits. "And things have not gone well here thus far, as Her Imperial

Majesty and His Imperial Highness seem deaf and indifferent to my pleas. It is all too obvious that Frederick the Second has his eyes on Russia, but no one seems to care. I had considered," he mentions almost as an afterthought, "approaching Her Imperial Highness, as I understand that she is a level-headed lady with Russia's interests at heart."

We assure him that this is so, although I feel compelled to warn him: "The empress is not fond of the future consort getting involved in politics."

"I can at least try." He takes a sip of his claret and adds thoughtfully, "You might know something about British politics, and if so, you know that His Majesty King George of England is not known for making all of his own decisions."

"Really?"

"No, indeed. It is common knowledge that when Her Majesty Queen Caroline lived, it was she who ran England. She and their minister, Sir Robert Walpole, that is. It is not impossible," he adds slowly, "for a consort to control a nation without its ruler realizing that it is happening."

I think I understand what he is hinting, but he does not know Peter. Does not realize that the young man is too obstinate and stupid to listen to anyone with sense. Whatever influence Queen Caroline might have had over King George II, my own lady will have a much more difficult time insinuating her ideas to a man who by all appearances detests her. Yet I agree to put in a word with Catherine for Sir Charles.

We return a few days later with another assortment of fine gemstones and a set of diamond boot buckles. This turns out to be our first introduction to the much praised and witty Count Stanislaus Poniatowski. He appears to be about my age, or even younger—perhaps early twenties—with almond-shaped eyes, an aquiline nose, prominent eyebrows, a slightly tapering chin, and a heart-shaped face. It is immediately apparent he is somewhat nearsighted, which gives his hazel eyes an even more prominent look. It is also obvious he is well educated and well traveled, with six languages to his credit. It takes me only a half hour to realize that this is someone Catherine would love to meet, if she has not already.

Poniatowski, too, orders an array of diamond accessories and a pink flourite ring, before interrupting his order to sign for two shipments of Parisian port wine and Spanish Madeira.

On the day of the ball, I wish for perhaps the thousandth time for a camera. Everything gleams, to the point of being ostentatious. As ladies scatter across the lawn, I notice not only their wide gowns, but wrists and throats enriched by gems—some from Igor's shop—and hair glittering with diamond aigrettes (the name for upright plumes decorated with diamond-studded ribbons and a spray of gems). Even though the empress will not be in attendance, each court woman dreams of being included in the array of beauties whose portraits are displayed at Peterhof. Thus far three hundred ladies adorn this coveted Cabinet of Modes and Graces, and the ladies left off compete rigorously by adorning themselves in flashing jewels and plumes, as well as silver and gold laces and embroideries on their opulent gowns.

Catherine has outdone herself on the food and entertainment. Vodka and wine flow from fountains and beer in giant barrels; orchestras entertain from various corners and gardens, and footmen dodge in and out balancing platters laden with fresh seafood and roasted meats. Sideboards groan under the weight of salads, fruit and candy delicacies, and elaborate desserts. My favorites are the sweet dishes carved into ingenious shapes: parrots, swans, even entire towns or fortresses with miniature people and turrets. Pastry "trees" decorated with imported exotic fruits, including pineapples, figs, dates, melons, grapes, strawberries, and mangos, occupy other tables. Everything is served on ornate gold or silver plates rimmed with precious stones.

Amid all this opulence I watch Catherine make her way through the diplomat corps. She sits next to Sir Charles, and they appear to be observing Count Poniatowski's elegant dance steps. When he joins them at the table, Sir Charles introduces the two.

I watch idly as Catherine's and Stanislaus's heads move close together in conversation, until Igor's scowl and what sounds like an accompanying groan alert me to the presence of a Dutch diplomat's invitation for me to dance. Helplessly, I curtsy and accept. It is an agreement Igor and I have made that at times he deeply resents.

Catherine's laugh rings across the garden to where a violin quartet awaits me and my dance partner, and I smile to myself. If ever two people seem to have something in common . . .

That night, long after Igor has undressed me layer by layer, long after I have inserted into my vagina a tiny cloth soaked in tansy and rue that is supposed to keep me from getting pregnant, long after we have made love almost ferociously, I decide to at least broach the subject.

"Darling, have you ever wished you could live in another time in history?"

"I've never thought about it, though it is a fascinating idea."

"When would you prefer to have lived—past or future?"

He wraps his long arms around me. "Would you be there, too?"

"If you wanted me to I would. If it were possible," I whisper.

"All right then." He is silent for nearly a minute. I hold my breath, wondering if he will play this game.

"I think that I would have been happy in His Imperial Majesty Peter the First's court—not staying in what was then a swamp here, but traveling with him on his Great Tour across Europe. I would have liked to learn about science, the way he did, and collect samples of gems and minerals the way he also did."

"Interesting," I murmur. "You would not wish to travel back any further? Perhaps to join the heyday of the alchemists?" This is a time he has referred to previously, so I wonder if it will spark his imagination in that direction.

"No, I enjoy the conveniences of this world too much. I doubt that I would have enjoyed a time when dabbling in precious stones and metals could get you executed. And you, my sweet? Where would you like to be?"

"In the future," I say hesitantly.

"Why?" he hugs me tighter.

"So we could be together without fear of a monarch's displeasure."

He laughs. "And what else would we do in the future? Wouldn't we have to bow to the demands of yet another empress or emperor?"

"What if someday there were to be no empresses or emperors? What if the future means that the people will govern themselves?"

"Ah, a very enlightened idea. And the artisans? To whom would they sell their goods without the nobility?"

"I am wondering if it might not be fairer if everyone had access to the same goods and services."

"I admit that sounds intriguing, if not preposterous. I doubt that a nation could survive without a monarch. What else is in your future dream?"

"The ability to go anywhere and everywhere quickly. Large machines that take you up in the sky and drop you down in another country. Or faster boats to cross the oceans."

"Flying machines? Surely you jest, my love, although it is a fantastic idea. And where would you fly in this contraption of yours?"

"Perhaps to the Colonies."

"The Americas? Whatever for? There are many reports of unrest there, even rumors that they wish to have their own king rather than George of England. And it is a wilderness, not at all civilized like Russia."

"Every place begins as a wilderness, does it not?"

"Just look at what His Imperial Highness has done here at Oranienbaum by erecting barracks and starting an army," he laughs. And then, even though we are in a tiny room allotted to me by Catherine and it is doubtful anyone spies on us outside the door, he adds in a whisper, "A treasonous army."

He starts to grumble about Peter's latest exploits then, and I decide not to press the subject. It is enough for now, perhaps, that I have introduced it.

Chapter 27

(Catherine) 1755-1756

"She was at that peak of beauty most beautiful women experience . . . a vivid
coloring, with dark hair and a dazzling white complexion, large, slightly
prominent and very expressive blue eyes, very long dark eyelashes, a
Grecian nose, a mouth which seemed to invite kisses, perfect hands
and arms, and a narrow waist . . . she moved with extreme
agility yet at the same time with great nobility. She had a
pleasant voice and a laugh as merry as her disposition."
—Stanislaus Poniatowski; description of Catherine II

Catherine had seen her son only twice, the previous time under heavy supervision. She resisted crying out as she saw how tightly his nurses and the empress kept him swaddled. Wrapped in layers of flannel in a cradle lined with black fox fur, baby Paul also endured a quilted satin coverlet and another fur-lined velvet one. The toddler was bathed in perspiration, so at last she had to turn away from the sight.

As if that were not enough to try her patience, her own husband had recently threatened to raise a sword to her although she'd bravely turned it into a joke: "It would only be fair if I, too, were to have a sword." Their relationship had reached its lowest point, and if she strived to avoid him, he usually did the same.

Now none of it mattered. None of the malice or pettiness of the empress or the grand duke toward her could vex her because at last she was in love: for the first time, not the second. Soon after meeting Count Stanislaus Poniatowski she realized that what she had thought she felt for Sergei Saltykov had been little more than infatuation and perhaps gratefulness, not to mention lust. And unlike Sergei, Stanislaus worshipped and adored her.

"You were wearing a taffeta gown the shade of amethyst the first time I saw you," he said softly while they cuddled together in a bed at Sir Charles's mansion. "I am quite certain I fell in love instantly."

Catherine, while uncertain it had been love at first sight, did realize her own feelings for him had overcome her shortly thereafter. Throughout the year, they'd met countless times to converse on everything from philosophy and literature to politics and Stanislaus's travels. At first these were secret evening gatherings arranged by Prince Lev Naryshkin, who would meow like a cat outside her door late at night. This was the signal to be ready, and if the coast were clear and she was alone, she'd respond with a second meow.

It was Lev's idea for her to wear a disguise, which by her choice consisted of a uniform from the Preobrazhensky Guards. In anticipation, she laced her stays tight to flatten her breasts and covered that with a large ribbon pulled even tighter. Although occasionally assisted by a handsomely bribed maid, most of the time she donned the clothing herself: a pair of white breeches, a fitted dark green woolen tunic, and a high pair of black jackboots. With her brown curls hidden beneath a hat, she could sneak in and out of the palace at will.

Lev organized the nocturnal parties, usually at his sister-in-law Anna's home; at other times, the young invitees would be smuggled into Catherine's apartment via a secret staircase or an unguarded door. Stanislaus was always present at both locations, and the two would talk for hours, although Stanislaus insisted he was not nearly as intelligent as his darling love. Parties also presented opportunities for jovial games, and, as he had with Saltykov, Lev loved to play the jokester. Guests roared with laughter as he imitated an inebriated Peter attempting to stay upright with his violin or mimicked the empress stumbling through the palace, half drunk and too heavy to make it far without a chair.

Throughout winter, they held secret parties two or three times per week. After having just partaken of a heavy dinner, they'd dine again on quail, stewed mushrooms, honeyed cucumber, blini, caviar, grapes, and endless sweets—all washed down with plenty of wine. To add to the merriment, the partygoers devised an elaborate system of hand signs that indicated where and when to meet next. In that way they could sit in separate boxes at the theatre or opera and communicate their plans to one another. No one ever made an error, and no one ever got caught.

Catherine mastered the art of feigning fatigue, insisting on a need for quiet and rest. "I must be alone," she announced sternly to her servants before ordering them to take the evening off. She then bolted her door from the inside, rapidly slipped into her male disguise, and tiptoed down the hidden staircase whose door she could lock behind her. The remainder of the night was hers—and sometimes hers and Stanislaus's alone.

"You take many risks," Stanislaus said to her one night. They had been exchanging ideas on Voltaire's writings, but in truth Catherine had been focusing just as much on his eyes, of unparalleled beauty.

"As do you."

"Ah, but I take them for love."

"You must," she teased. "Anyone who jumps out of windows and leaps over bushes to avoid discovery *must* be in love."

"True," he agreed as he began to unfasten her stays. "Do you remember our first time as lovers?"

"Of course. It took you many months to overcome your reluctance to have me."

He smiled wryly. "Can you blame me for fearing the consequences? Peter's soldiers might not be battle trained, but those swords are genuine."

"And then you finally came to me as a virgin, or so you claimed," she continued to tease.

"It was the truth," he said earnestly. "I vowed to my own mother that I would not drink, gamble, or marry before age thirty. I took that to mean to stay out of women's beds. Were it not for you and your extraordinary beauty and mind, I might have succeeded for a while yet."

"What do you remember most about our first time?"

"That little white satin gown with lace," he replied promptly. "It was threaded with a pink ribbon, and I knew at that moment that I would devote the rest of my life to you."

That was not what she remembered most. It was the way he had come to her so shy and yet so ardent. Although it had been obvious he truly never had bedded a woman, he devoted himself to the task. She smiled to herself, recalling how that first time he had become so excited kissing her breasts and then sucking her nipples that he was finished before either of them had fully undressed. A half hour later they had tried again, and this time he'd taken her gently but enthusiastically. They'd repeated the act off and on until dawn, and by the time he'd slipped out of her bed and down the secret staircase, she had been happily satisfied, exhausted, and more than half in love herself.

Stanislaus proved himself not only a passionate and devoted lover, but a frivolous, playful child one moment and an emotional romantic the next. He never failed to be there for her, and his faithfulness and discretion provided a welcome change from Sergei's sporadic inattentiveness and indiscretions. In short, she was content. He had healed her so much that none of her previous losses or humiliations bothered her when she was with him.

The other part of that emotional and physical love was their continued intellectual connection. They could talk for hours on subjects such as abstract reasoning. Inspired as much by these conversations as her own reading, Catherine resumed making private notes, but this time without fear someone would abscond with them or forbid her to write at all as had happened in the years preceding Paul's birth.

She jotted down ideas, scribbled in margins, argued with or praised authors in a series of correspondence, and energetically continued to study not only Montesquieu, Voltaire, and Tacitus, but European history. Throughout the early morning, she would dip her quill in ever-depleted crystal ink bottles, sucking absentmindedly on cloves to mitigate her painful toothaches. Her desk held several hidden drawers, all stuffed with scraps of paper, including the beginning of her own memoirs.

After ordering piles of manuscripts from storage and from Peter the Great's library, she also set about to continue systematically learning about the history of this country she was now educating herself to govern. Exactly how that governance would play out was still an unknown, but she committed herself to playing a strong role regardless of Peter's wishes. She also paid particular attention to the errors of

Elizabeth's predecessors, as it became obvious that most of the Petrine reforms initiated by Peter I had fallen by the wayside once the kingdom fell into the hands of his successors, including his own wife, grandson, niece, and daughter.

Inspired, she composed a play about the Time of Troubles, the dark period of the early seventeenth century that had plagued Russia with a series of imposter tsars, a catastrophic famine, and a power struggle that lasted until a Romanov was invited to assume the throne in 1613.

One other aspect of her romance with Stanislaus was that it put her in constant contact with Sir Charles Hanbury-Williams, with whom a friendship ripened. Learning that the grand duchess had once again overspent her allowance, he further insinuated himself into her good graces by opening her a line of credit with an English banker. It was, after all, how the game was played: with nearly everyone in the city potentially corruptible, no one wanted to do anything without a trading of favors, gifts, or cash. Catherine needed all three, and over the next few years, she would have no hesitation in drawing out hundreds of rubles and pounds sterling.

Ignoring proprieties, she also began a lengthy epistolary exchange with Sir Charles soon after Russia agreed to renew the treaty with England that he had been sent to negotiate.

"I am elated," he wrote simply the first time. "Now our nations will be safe from the machinations of Frederick."

An alarmed King of Prussia had been quoted as saying, "I believe I fear Russia more than I fear God."

On All Saints' Day, an event occurred that captured the attention of all of Europe: a massive earthquake destroyed most of Lisbon, rocking not only the earth but the foundations of the Enlightenment movement.

"One cannot ignore that it occurred on an important church holiday," Stanislaus mused. "Theologians are speculating that it is God's punishment, a manifestation of His divine judgment on our society."

"Or perhaps on the Roman Catholic Church, to which Portugal's residents blindly adhere and whose cathedrals were all destroyed," countered Catherine, who enjoyed teasing her Polish Catholic lover as much as she savored a good debate.

Reports of tens of thousands of deaths and the devastation of nearly all of the city had people worldwide speculating on the earthquake's causes and message. Why would God allow this to happen? If it was a warning or a sign of God's wrath, then why? If He were supposed to be a Benevolent Deity, what did this mean? Were they wrong about God? Could something like this happen elsewhere, and if so, when and where?

Fortunately, the Portuguese royal family was away on vacation. The ensuing debate about the quake took place throughout Europe and even beyond. Could it mean the Second Coming was just around the corner? Or could it be, as some of the younger philosophers speculated, a warning that cities were too large and crowded and it was time for a more naturalistic way of life? Metaphors connected to the words "ground" and "tremor" and "shook" lost their innocence, no longer considered mere figures of speech.

"They say Monsieur Voltaire is writing a poem about the disaster," Catherine mused. "I shall look forward to his ruminations."

In part due to his fear of the consequences of the court Francophiles and in part due to his great admiration for the Grand Duchess Catherine, Sir Charles intensified his efforts to cultivate the Grand Ducal Court. Peter, disinterested in politics unless they involved his own Holstein duchy or the Prussian king, nevertheless enjoyed socializing with both Sir Charles and Stanislaus, ignoring sporadic rumors of his wife's involvement with the latter. He also mistakenly believed that Stanislaus was a Prussian sympathizer.

Still the world seemed to tilt toward war. Early in the new year, Sir Charles's exuberance over the treaty turned to despair. When it arrived in England King George II declared that one of the necessary signatures was not in order. In the months it took to remedy this, the courier charged with delivering the corrected treaty was delayed in his travels between Russia and England by adverse winds. In the meantime, London decided to disregard the planned Anglo-Russian agreement in favor of one with Berlin.

"All is lost," Sir Charles now wrote to Catherine. "I am desolate." He strongly believed that somehow the Shuvalovs' connection to France and their great influence over Elizabeth had played some role in the diplomatic failure.

When in the summer the Grand Duke and Duchess moved back to Oranienbaum, the subject of politics seemed closer and more critical due to one important factor: the empress was once again ill, and this time alarmingly so.

Panicked, the Shuvalovs and the Pelican, Herr Brockdorff, sought to move even closer to Peter, stirring up his already fanatical devotion to Prussia, exerting their influence even more strongly, and planting seeds of doubt in his mind about both Chancellor Bestuzhev and Sir Charles Hanbury-Williams. Gradually the Shuvalovs began to prepare for when Peter would rule—and they were not so secretly adamant that they would be the powerful puppeteers pulling the strings.

This left both Bestuzhev and Sir Charles in precarious positions, yet simultaneously strengthened their relationships with the logical—and far superior—alternative: the grand duchess. Chancellor Bestuzhev did everything he could to foster friendly relations between Catherine and General Apraksin, the new commander-in-chief of the

Russian forces now in the process of mobilizing against Frederick's army. Catherine, just as concerned about Prussia and its dangerous influences on her husband, needed little convincing. The threat of war had intensified her and Bestuzhev's rapprochement; mutual concern for the future of Russia and the potential pending transition of power had united the former enemies. Together with Apraksin, the grand duchess and the chancellor speculated on outcomes.

"We must find a way to delay any winter campaign against Frederick," Apraksin told Catherine on one of his increasingly frequent visits, then proceeded to put forth one by one his arguments. The main objection involved a serious lack of supplies, an inadequacy that fierce winter weather would only heighten. Without stating the obvious, both knew any attack on Prussia would be a waste of time if Peter were to assume the throne in the immediate future.

Sir Charles's position in the Russian court became tenuous, despite his continued close relationship with its grand duchess. She ventured so far as to write to him, "You are my Guardian Angel sent by Providence. Should I actually wear the crown one day, it will be partially due to your counsel."

Gratified, he continued to attempt to convince her to ally with England should this happy day ever come.

Catherine, no longer the naive young bride who assumed events would take care of themselves without her interference, began a prudent yet dangerous game. Since the court had divided itself into two opposing factions—Elizabeth's unpredictability but avowed hatred for Frederick versus Peter's instability yet idolization of the same Prussian ruler—any third faction had to be careful. Catherine was still officially forbidden to meddle in affairs of state, especially foreign concerns, so the imperial grand duchess must be canny as she attempted to balance precariously on the tightrope stretched between her husband and the empress. She could not afford to be seen on that rope, let alone to stumble, as there would be no net to save her no matter on which side she fell.

To keep abreast of events, Catherine gradually and carefully expanded her own network of spies and informers. Although Igor and his secret wife Maria could be trusted implicitly, she needed more allies with extensive connections and freedom of motion. She added another Italian jeweler to her list of trusted confidants: a Venetian named Bernardi. No one ever questioned the time she spent sequestered with her jewelers, as she had a genuine and well-known passion for gems. "Someday," she vowed to Igor and Maria, "I will have an entire room devoted just to my jewels."

Bernardi proved a valuable asset, and one whose profession gained him access not only to the palace, but homes of the nobility. It was he who brought her letters from Stanislaus, forced in July to return to Poland on business. Assuming he would only be away for a few weeks, Catherine did not fret too much. And besides, his constant presence had become a source of gossip, one that Count Horn of Sweden had warned both of them about before he left.

One afternoon that autumn, with Elizabeth still seriously ill, Chancellor Bestuzhev made a furtive visit to Catherine to follow up on a document he'd drawn up weeks earlier. "This is a draft of an imperial decree that must be kept secret," he nearly whispered. The ukase, as it was called, set forth plans to be effected immediately in the event of Elizabeth's death. In addition to a complete restructuring of the government, it posited that rather than Peter be crowned sole ruler, Catherine be crowned as co-ruler and in charge of affairs of the state.

She frowned at the lengthy document as she read, but when she looked up, she, too, whispered: "This is a risky document, Chancellor, and you know it."

"Are you in disagreement then?"

"Its intentions are good, although I believe it to be a fearsome plan. A suicidal one, in fact, if anyone else were to see it."

"I am not denying that, Your Imperial Highness. I want to assure you that I have only the good of the future of our beloved Russia in mind."

"Not to mention your own future," she murmured. The chancellor had included himself not only in a potential advisory role to the future empress, but proposed he be given titles that would put him in charge of the key ministries of war, the navy, and foreign affairs. He also envisioned himself as colonel of the Imperial Guards' four regiments.

"Of course, I wish to do all that is in my power to assist in building and overseeing this New Russia," he said with a forced trace of modesty. "Always I have been indispensable and completely loyal to Her Majesty."

"Who would have your head on the same platter as John the Baptist's if she were to learn of this. And my own, too, would rest beside yours." Yet she could not help being flattered and a bit elated at this potential path that, if ever followed, could see her rule the empire as an equal.

"I appreciate your efforts, Chancellor. I fear, however, that not only is this premature, but its very existence incriminates both of us to the point of treason. I cannot discuss this with you anymore. At least not at this time," she added softly but firmly.

"Then I will hide it until a more appropriate occasion, Your Imperial Highness. I must stress it is still only a draft. I must begin work on revisions and alterations."

"In the meantime, what progress have we made in bringing Count Poniatowski back?"

"I have written repeatedly to the Polish cabinet, and I believe success is in sight," he replied nervously. It was a subject they had met about many times, and Bestuzhev was getting a small taste of the indomitable will of the future empress. When she wanted something—in this case her lover back—she was determined and relentless.

"Do report back to me by tomorrow. I must have him back in Russia, and you hold much influence with the Polish foreign minister."

Recognizing his dismissal, Bestuzhev hastily pocketed the dangerous document and exited.

It was only after he left that Catherine realized she'd argued not once against the role he envisioned for her: the same role she secretly envisioned for herself.

For Grand Duke Paul's second birthday, the Empress had commissioned a grand portrait of the little boy wearing a green guards tunic as he sat astride a rocking horse waving a paper sword. The completed painting, with its gilt and diamond frame, was taken immediately to Her Majesty's bedroom and hung beside one of Elizabeth herself as a girl stretched out naked on an ermine throw. Sadly, the painting meant as little to Catherine as its young subject did. Although Elizabeth had permitted her once again to visit Paul at Catherine Palace that summer for thirty minutes, he cried when he saw the stranger they called his "mother" and toddled over to his sick aunt for comfort. Neither did Peter interfere, as he took little interest in a child too young for soldier games or marches.

As days grew frostier and Stanislaus remained in Poland, Catherine found herself compelled to attend her husband's regular Tuesday night winter concerts. Since he maintained over fifty performers on his payroll, including German sopranos, Italian instrumentalists, and an imperial choir, the concerts each lasted an interminable five hours.

"He is actually quite good," Irina leaned over to comment one night.

Catherine waved her hand in dismissal. "It all sounds virtually the same to me. And I cannot imagine my husband is that talented."

"The imperial pyrotechnician tells people that His Imperial Highness is accomplished enough now to join in Italian symphonies."

"It might be true, of course, but I suspect that when he plays a wrong note, his teachers simply exclaim, 'Bravo, Your Highness.'"

"Perhaps. Although his collection of violins is quite impressive."

"If you say so." Catherine smiled to take the edge off her comment. She had long ago given up feigning interest in Peter's activities or hobbies. "And where is Maria tonight? Have you seen her recently?"

Irina looked thoughtful. "No, I have not. However, most of the empress's ladies have been ordered out of the imperial chambers, and many have taken leaves of absence. I doubt Her Majesty knows who is and who is not in attendance at present."

"Most likely not." Catherine hoped her former lady was enjoying the happiness that she herself was—or would be again, if Stanislaus would come back where he belonged.

CHAPTER 28

(MARIA) 1756-1757

Sometimes it frightens me that I am no longer the fresh-faced teenager who arrived here so many years ago. As I approach thirty, I've noticed women here look so much older for their ages than they do in the future. I struggle to tend to my hygiene and appearance despite eighteenth-century challenges, but my skin has not reacted kindly to the drastic changes in temperatures, both inside and out, not to mention the constant wood smoke and god knows what other pollutants are in the air. Every other day I soak my skin with almond milk, which seems to work for other ladies, though every bug bite, allergic rash, or bruise takes forever to heal without bandages or pharmaceutical aids. Periodically I also check my stools in the chamber pot, thus far fortunate enough not to contract dysentery or food poisoning.

Above all, I continue to religiously soak a cloth or, when I manage it, a sponge, with the herbs rumored to prevent pregnancy. At my insistence, Igor shows up one day with something resembling a skinny leather pouch: an earlier version of a condom. I try not to laugh at it or at him fitting it, but in the end it slips off too easily, rendering it ineffective at best. It also interferes with the sensations we savor as often as we can be together.

"You do realize, my precious jewel, that this thing is vilified by the Church. You are putting my very soul at risk."

"Then we shall go down in the fires of hell together. And truly, is there a better way to go?"

"Not that I can think of, but I do wish there was some way we could have a child, my dearest."

"We will someday," I assure him; however, the thought does not enthuse me, something I reluctantly keep from my husband. "Actually, it is truly amazing that the entire population of Russia isn't dropping precipitously."

"Because?"

"Because the Church has so many Holy Days when sex is officially forbidden!"

"So true. Now, let me show you what I am working on, which will have to suffice for my 'babies' for now." He is only half joking I know, as his work does bring him a sense of satisfaction.

"Cameos have been the fashion since ancient times," he explains, pulling out a package he has recently ordered. "I've been dabbling with these for years, but I want to practice more before I present one to Her Majesty or the grand duchess." Like children opening gifts, we *ooh* and *aah* over the shipments. One contains a carefully wrapped tray of queen conch shells from the Bahamas and helmet shells from the West Indies.

"I intend to gain more experience working on these shells before I try the stones," he explains. Then in package after package, he unwraps and unveils turquoise, agate, onyx, and two precious Columbian emeralds.

Catherine has made no secret of her special love for cameos—the miniature sculptures executed in low relief on substances chosen for beauty, hardness, or rarity. Currently she possesses a small collection, but Igor and the colony of jewelers and lapidaries who continue to flock here have begun to compete for her imperial commissions.

"The emeralds will present the greatest challenge," he remarks thoughtfully. "But knowing that this is one of Her Imperial Highness's favorite gemstones, I plan to see what I can do."

"These are perfect," he says, holding each emerald to the sunlight. "Have you met Signore Bernardi yet? He is a good friend of my uncle, and tells me that the best emeralds for cameo carving should have a lot of inclusions, reduced clarity, and yet enough transparency to showcase the carving."

Over the coming weeks he spends countless hours in his workshop, and on mornings I can slip away to be there, I make every attempt to get involved in the business, from repairing necklaces to fashioning my own modest broach designs. I've also started decorating another court favorite: little snuff boxes that our neighboring goldsmith has made. I work hard to glue on mother of pearl, beads, garnets, and tiny gemstones. Catherine is one of "my" customers now, as she has developed a taste for tobacco and adores collecting the beautiful, jeweled boxes. So far I've known her to collect snuff boxes, rocks, minerals, gemstones, and books. When exactly she will develop a passion for art collecting, I don't know. I hope to be around to be part of it. Only, that is, if I can someday go home and view it as a part of the past, not of my present.

"You should show one of those to General Apraksin," a voice interrupts my thoughts.

I start guiltily. "What?"

"The snuffbox you are decorating," Igor clarifies. "The general never travels without his personal collection, even when he goes to the battlefield. I believe he owns over three hundred sixty-five of them: one for each day of the year."

"Then perhaps he needs one for each holiday," I muse. "Based on the number of saints days celebrated in the church, I could stay busy making them for the rest of my life."

Often Igor and I work companionably side by side, the way we are today, stopping occasionally for tea.

As much as I've started to believe that time is my enemy, I know that surely it is Catherine's, too. She may live in her own century, but the longer she must try to out survive Elizabeth, the greater the risk she will be removed from court. There are rumors Peter wants to divorce her and marry his latest mistress, and no one doubts he'll do so if Elizabeth dies. I alone know Catherine will succeed, though I doubt even future historians realize what she had to endure.

Above all, time races against the empress's health and vanity. It seems as if her body deteriorates monthly, despite recovering from her summer sickness. Conversely, as she ages, her lovers get younger and younger. So far that is not the case for our young future empress, but again, time will tell. Catherine ranges from meek and modest to proud and somewhat vain, so it is difficult to predict.

Tatiana brings me bad news one afternoon when I am crawling into bed at the palace. "The empress was asking about you last night," she whispers.

"Asking what?" My heart always contracts when Her Majesty calls for me, although nearly always it is to assist her in planning her evening jewelry display.

"When you left for the privy, she asked us if anyone knew if you had expressed interest in a man, since she never sees you dance with anyone more than once. And she specifically did not mention the lieutenant, which makes me think they may have had a conversation about you."

"Did she ask to see me?"

"No, something else captured her attention. Princess Shishkov appeared in a very similar gown to the one Her Majesty was wearing, and she went into a mad tirade. I thought she was going to hit her!"

Tatiana herself has been fearing an arranged marriage, but only because she has fallen in love already with a count who works with the Danish ambassador. Soon her young man will approach the empress for permission to marry her, but none of us has any idea if this will be acceptable to Elizabeth.

Sometimes I wonder if I could hide out for a while somewhere else in the palace, with its hundreds if not thousands of servants, courtiers, foreign diplomats, and entertainers. As if reading my mind, Tatiana admits, "At times I wish I were a groom. I adore the horses, and there are so many people working in the stables that no one would notice a woman."

"You would have to cut your hair," I grin, pulling on her flowing blonde locks.

"Her Imperial Highness looks gorgeous and majestic on horseback, even disguised as a man."

No one could argue that, and I watch occasionally as she gallops off in her tailored riding habit, presumably to go for another endless ride but undoubtedly to meet up with Stanislaus.

Now that we're in the city, I will miss Tsarskoe Selo and its Catherine Palace, although occasionally Elizabeth arranges excursions to ride merry-go-rounds set up for her along the Neva's banks. Others, along with swing sets, have been built for her on various islands. On the loveliest afternoons we sail in a regatta of gondolas followed by boatloads of musicians. Servants precede us so that when we disembark we will be treated to fat herring from the White Sea, platefuls of sugared plums soaked in brandy, chocolate-dipped nuts, and thick rye bread slathered with honey.

With Elizabeth recovered, she demands more and more of her maids' time, leaving less and less of mine for Igor. We must be there for her day and night, regardless whether she is having her cards read, her coiffure changed, or her salves and lotions mixed by one of the hundred apothecaries she employs. Consequently, her toilette seems to take forever as she struggles to combat the ravages of age, sickness, alcohol, and self-indulgence. This is attempted with remedies, treatments, and beauty aids concocted by specialists from France, Asia, and the Middle East. Whichever of us must serve as Lady in Attendance of the Evening Toilette inevitably ends up suppressing a silent scream.

"She is not only vain, but totally frivolous," I complain to Igor on a rare night we share. "Last night when it was so cold she summoned twenty guardsmen to warm the air with their breaths!"

"This is not a huge surprise. Soldiers grumble that although the cost of luxuries for the new palace is exorbitant, there is no money for bread in the barracks. General Apraksin knows exactly what his soldiers are doing: poking out their own eyes, crushing their fingers, cutting off their toes, even knocking out their own teeth to escape the military."

"Tatiana told me that all of the nobility in Yaroslavl have refused to serve," I add. "They have bought serfs—actually bought them the way they, well, the way they have slaves in the American colonies—just so someone can take their places in the upcoming battles." Tatiana has also learned from her new love that the supplies received do not last, that army sword belts fall apart with one washing, and that new recruits possess no more than wooden muskets to protect themselves.

"I've heard the same. The empress has no time to tend to military problems," he agrees.

"Oddly enough, she cannot seem to find *any* time for work." All month her ministers have paced back and forth, practically tripping over our skirts, as they beg for postponed decisions to get made, correspondence tended to, and bills passed.

"She has time for her icons, does she not?" Igor asks, looking up from the polisher he is wiping down.

"Of course. She can spend entire days kneeling in front of one. Twice this year she insisted an icon spoke aloud."

"What did it say?"

I half smile, seeing the gleam in his eye. "I do not know, other than she said it gave her advice. Perhaps it will advise her to give you my hand in marriage."

Any trace of humor now leaves Igor's face. He does not take our secret wedding so lightly. "We must tread carefully at Peter Shuvalov's palace this evening. Her Majesty surely will notice us together now that she has regained her health."

"She will be furious," I admit, as usual.

After fastening the blue topaz necklace that he made for me for our anniversary, he gently turns me to face him. "It is time, my love. To tell her."

It is time. The words echo in my head, not because of the empress or any real fear of her. It is the other deadline that I have set for myself: it is only fair that I confess my identity to my husband before he acknowledges our relationship to the world. Then if he does not believe me or no longer desires to be with me, no one need know we're a married couple. The priest who joined us can be bribed into a lifetime of silence or an annulment. Igor will be free to live his own life without the burden of a supposedly insane woman at his side—or at the very least one who lied to him all these years. And if he denies me, I will still have a position at court, will still have someone to feed and to support me a long as the empress does not know I have defied her.

I will also have more time to find the statue that I have always believed will take me home.

My eyes fill with tears at the thought of leaving Igor for my "old" life at the palace, let alone at the thought of leaving him forever to return to the old or new life in the past or the future, as it may be.

"Darling, what is it? What causes my precious opal to weep?"

"Tell me again why I am an opal," I sniff, needing to hear again about how much he loves me before I risk destroying all that we have together.

I've already read much in Igor's books about opals. How, coincidentally, the ancient Greeks believed that they conferred the gifts of foresight and prophecy. How the Arabs believed opals received their fiery colors when they fell from heaven in flashes of lightning. How the Romans ranked them above all other gemstones, and how much Marc Antony endured to secure one for Cleopatra. They are extolled in the oldest extant book on precious stones by the ancient Greek Theophrastus, and later by the philosopher Pliny.

Igor sits beside the polisher and pulls me into his lap. An hour previously I might have worried about the wrinkles in my royal blue satin gown. Now it means nothing. "Let me see, what stone is the most difficult to work but the most colorful?" he asks with a smile. "Which stone is delicate yet magical? And each one is unique, with perhaps a dash of blue, a swirl of purple, a sprinkling of yellow, and then a flirtatious glance of red. They could be fireworks from the earth, splashing the onlooker with a rainbow of vivid colors that seduce each man who looks. I cannot get enough of looking at you."

"You can do more than look," I say seductively.

"I must, since opals need to be worn close to the skin to retain their shine and spectacular play of color."

He then demonstrates exactly what he means.

At one of the Shuvalov palaces, I sit far down the table from the grand duke, busy picking his gums, now red with the oil he uses to polish his nails. A rare smile reveals he's lost many of his rotting teeth. The grand duchess's dazzling smile reveals teeth still white as a puppy's. On the opposite end presides the empress, struggling to decide between the array of crystal decanters containing vodkas made from beet, lemon, cherry, peach, cranberry, plum, and even horseradish. Hopefully she will sample as many as possible, as it will shorten the evening and afford me an opportunity to spend the night with Igor after she passes out.

Because Igor has become an important purveyor of luxuries for the Shuvalovs, he has been invited, and sits only one table down from me, Tatiana, and two other ladies. Occasionally we exchange secret glances and I send him fan signals. Before dinner, the guests were treated to a tour of the only private pineapple orchard in Russia, its fruit regularly fermented into the sweet, fragrant wine we now sip. I've long since become accustomed to all the drinking at court, evidenced tonight by sideboards piled with mugs, goblets, wine glasses, dippers, flutes, and buckets.

Peter Shuvalov's palace is richly appointed—to the point of ostentation. Even Elizabeth and her fondness for the baroque can barely compete. "Tasteless and ugly," Catherine murmured when we arrived and she saw me gazing at the rich gold, silver, and gem-covered furnishings, decorations, and even paintings.

"Yes, Your Imperial Highness," I murmured. *And your Russia will be more classic and more beautiful*, I think, recalling my tours on the eve of the twenty-first century.

Perhaps it is my determination to tell Igor the truth that has whisked me inexplicably back to my own past. Except for a persistent longing for a camera and toilet paper, I seldom miss my youth, my other regret reserved for the agony I must've caused Aunt Roberta. Long ago I stopped caring about the loss of television, movies, cell phones, the Internet, automobiles, fast food, and even underwear.

Nevertheless, I impatiently await the completion of the new Winter Palace—what will eventually be known as the Hermitage—hoping the statue of the goddess that brought me here will reappear.

Alas, it seems it will be several years before this happens, according to Chancellor Bestuzhev. "Endless problems," he mutters regularly. "Workers sit idle for lack of lumber, lime, and sand."

"It will be done soon enough," the usually impetuous empress scolds him.

"But Your Imperial Majesty, they are missing entire sheets of gold leaf, and the bills for what they have received appear seriously inflated. There is so much miscounting of deliveries that—"

"Enough, Chancellor! I am fully aware of the problems. Send Monsieur Rastrelli to speak to me!"

That conversation and variations of it recur weekly, with the empress riding herd on the architect and his crews despite her recent poor health.

It is time for dessert, and Tatiana grabs my arm. "You must see this! Quickly, tell Igor."

I've never seen anything like the confection carried by two footmen. It is not the mountainous shape of the cake that rivets all eyes: it is the jewels lavishly sprinkled across thick frosting.

"The jewels are from his personal mineralogical collection," Lady Gargarina comments, seeming impressed even for her.

"A cake in the shape of a mountain but studded with gemstones!" I whisper to Igor after hurrying to his table, and he turns immediately to look with a practiced eye.

Later, strolling with me amidst the pineapples before I must return to the palace, Igor observes, "When we celebrate our wedding officially, we shall order such a cake."

When I don't respond immediately, he stops and turns me to face him. "What is wrong, my sweet? Are you thinking about Her Majesty's possible response to the news? Please do not fret."

This is my chance. The opening I have awaited but dreaded.

"It is something else, my love. Something far worse."

"Worse? Are you pregnant, Maria? That would not be worse, that would be—"

"I'm not pregnant." I look around, scanning the greenery. "Did you know before today that pineapples grow on plants near the ground and not on trees?"

"A baby would be so wonderful, Maria. Please do not be afraid to tell me."

I exhale twice. Her Majesty shows no sign of wanting to depart. There is time to initiate this conversation, if not to finish it.

"I've been keeping a huge secret from you, Igor, and I'm afraid if I tell you won't believe me. In fact, you'll probably lock me up in Her Majesty's Mad Room. Yet I must."

Igor looks puzzled but wary. I reach over to kiss him, taking both his strong yet gentle and talented hands in mind. There is no going back now.

"I know this sounds preposterous, but I am not exactly who you think I am. I was born far in the future, and I have no idea how I ended up living in the eighteenth-century."

For a split second he appears relieved, as if fearing I was going to tell him I have a second husband or have been unfaithful.

"And to what century do you belong?" he says teasingly.

"The twenty-first. Well, almost. Specifically, I ended up here after living in the year of our Lord nineteen hundred ninety-nine."

As if deciding to play along, he asks lightly, "and how are things in the future? Do they have those flying contraptions you fancy?"

"Things are very, very different. I want to tell you about it—and I will eventually—but the important thing is that I touched a statue in a museum in St. Petersburg and was suddenly transported here. To a century hundreds of years before my own."

"Ah, I see." The firelight from the sconces that light the pathway reveals a tiny frown between his eyebrows, the only hint that he may now worry about my sanity.

"I cannot prove this. I'm just asking you to consider the possibility I'm telling you the truth. I am not Maria—although apparently there was a real Maria whose place I took. In my century we would have called this time travel."

"And in your century do people practice this 'time travel' regularly?"

"No, at least I don't think so. Very few people believe it is possible, either scientifically or supernaturally."

"I've heard of a book you perhaps read, since it is in English. It is called *Memoirs of the Twentieth Century*. Perhaps Sir Charles loaned it to you." He smiles hopefully, but it is a weak attempt.

"No, I have not read it. Do you know when it was published?"

"No, Maria, I do not. And I really cannot comprehend why you have spun this ridiculous story." He starts to turn back toward the palace. "I need something to drink."

"Igor, please at least listen. Perhaps I *can* prove it."

He refuses to sit down on the bench beside us, nor to ask any questions.

"Do you not want to know where I am actually from?"

"The moon perhaps?" he says bitterly. "An asylum?"

"I was born in the colonies—the Americas—and was visiting Russia with my Aunt Roberta."

"Ah, there is an aunt, too. And where is she? In the seventeenth-century?"

"No, no, it's just me. I've been terrified of telling anyone all these years for fear I would be judged insane. But I am not, my love. At least let me tell you some things, although I don't expect you to truly understand what happened any more than I do."

"No, I do *not* understand."

"I only desire that you listen, and hopefully *consider* believing me. I am like one of those pieces of leaf trapped in a capsule of amber and unable to get free."

He tugs nervously at his frock coat and reaches for the satchel he left on a nearby stone bench.

"Igor! Don't go, please! I love you."

"I love you, too, Maria Sergeievna. Or at least whomever I thought you were or are. I need to go home. This foolishness will interfere with my sleep, not to mention my own sanity and my work."

And over my protests, he is gone. I am not wearing the right shoes to run after his long strides, and collapsing in tears, I realize it will do no good.

Now I am truly alone in the past.

CHAPTER 29

(CATHERINE) 1757-1758

"Those . . . months were Catherine's baptism of fire. She emerged shaken, bruised, and exhausted. But her mental status had grown. She had faced the ultimate peril and had not flinched from it. She had bluffed, perfectly conscious that if her bluff were called all her high expectations could turn into so many dead leaves driven by the wind . . . Yet that bitter and prolonged warfare was to cost her dear. She had lost much during those battles and had no illusions left. She knew now that to stand alone meant showing consideration for none."
—E. M. Almedingen

Besides politics, philosophy, and her newly returned lover, Catherine continued to indulge another passion: gardening. She oversaw extensive new plantings and pathways started previously at Oranienbaum and executed by her brilliant chief gardener. This man was a horticulture wizard who also dabbled in fortune-telling, assuring her he'd had a vision that she would live well past eighty.

It was another of his prophecies, however, that she began to take to heart.

"I predict," he spoke quietly but firmly as they examined a newly pruned rose bush, "it is not His Imperial Highness who will be the next ruler, at least not for long. It is you who will become sole sovereign of Russia, Little Mother."

Before she could respond, the seer turned back to fertilizing the roses. As she absentmindedly snipped a few dead buds, she recalled Bestuzhev's ukase that envisioned her as co-ruler with a marionette husband. The gardener's prophecy went well beyond that. Who knows, she thought hopefully, someday it *could* be true.

As her gardens expanded and thrived, the empress seemed determined to act as a reverse gardener. When it came to Catherine's happiness, Elizabeth stirred the political soil by attempting to yank out any roots anchoring the grand duchess. Intrigues festered and thrived around Catherine, smothering the growth of friendships and relationships. Anything that would fertilize Catherine's brain once again was frowned upon and removed, so that she had to fight for each tendril of happiness.

At present, the tendril still came in the form of Stanislaus, who remained her trusted confidante and passionate lover. Yet he, too, had to go through a lot of machinations to be with her, assuming a procession of disguises from that of servant, groom, or gardener to footman, musician, or even a woman. It cost a tremendous amount of gold to seal the lips of underlings.

"It isn't fair," Stanislaus complained regularly. "You are married to a buffoon! I would match swords with him if he would only agree."

"It would be considered treason if he did not initiate it!"

"Then come to Poland with me and we can rule there together. I will devote my life to making you the happiest woman in the world."

"You have already done that," she smiled.

"There is danger here. For both of us," he said earnestly. Catherine had been discouraged from consorting with Sir Charles, as well, since now that the war had begun in earnest, England was considered the enemy.

"That's undeniable," she agreed with Stanislaus. Bitterly she repeated what she had once confessed to her lady Maria: "Elizabeth does harm gratuitously and arbitrarily, without the shadow of a reason."

These days Peter almost never visited her, a mixed blessing if not an unnerving one. Yet she feared his latest lover more. Elizabeth Vorontsova, of high birth and sent into Catherine's service when she was only eleven, had grown into a vulgar, insolent, ill-mannered young lady. A teenage bout of smallpox had marred her skin with pockmarks and clumps of scars. She was also overweight, stank like an alcoholic, refused to bathe, and had become more and more brash and disrespectful in direct proportion to the favors heaped upon her by Grand Duke Peter. Perhaps, Catherine thought, birds of a feather really do flock together, as this couple's uncanny resemblance to one another was broken in only one way: he remained scarecrow-like despite his heavy drinking, while his mistress swelled to the size of a sideboard.

Catherine suspected the mistress and her powerful uncle, not to mention the Shuvalovs, of advising Peter to put his wife aside and take Vorontsova as his consort. There was plenty of precedent for this, as the Orthodox Church permitted husbands to do so for any reason. Such wives were treated as if dead to the world. Cut off from everyone and usually placed in a convent, they were stripped of all ranks and possessions. After having their heads shaved and their bodies clothed in black, they were given nothing but one window to look out for the rest of their lives. Catherine could hardly forget that Peter the Great had dealt similarly with his sister, and later with his first wife.

As if reading her mind, Stanislaus began to fantasize about raising his sword to the strident Elizabeth Vorontsova.

"You would never penetrate those rolls of fat," Catherine chided him, as if it were a joke.

In part to take Stanislaus's mind off their problems—in part to placate her unpredictable husband and in part to impress her rivals—she decided to throw a huge fete at Oranienbaum just after her twenty-eighth birthday. It also seemed to be the right time, now that General Apraksin had at last reluctantly hoisted his corpulent body into a carriage and led his troops toward East Prussia, with both countries awaiting the invasion's results.

By now, however, she was again pregnant, and there was no question whose child she carried. Undaunted, she wore loose-fitting gowns as she flitted around Oranienbaum making plans. The empress, delighted regardless of the baby's suspected parentage, sent her baskets of delicacies from the palace kitchen and servants to massage her feet.

Catherine invested all of herself in the celebration, as well as half her annual allowance. Under the direction of the Italian architect Antonio Rinaldi, a giant cart pulled by twenty garlanded oxen was built to support a sixty-piece orchestra. Servants lined the massive garden's avenue with lamps, although the White Nights would provide semi light for twenty-four hours. They also screened off the dozens of tables with a huge curtain.

During supper, trumpets and cymbals heralded a lottery. Each guest received free gifts or trinkets ranging from fans, purses, and gloves to sword knots, porcelain vases, and snuff boxes.

Dancing lasted until dawn, Catherine staying for it all. She even danced one time with the jeweler Igor Blukhov, although when she asked about Maria Sergeievna's absence, he seemed at a loss for words.

"Is she with Her Imperial Majesty at Peterhof?" Catherine asked.

"I believe so," the jeweler mumbled, and said little more when Catherine inquired about his wife's attempts to dodge the empress's marital plans for her.

"I would not worry," she reassured Igor. "The empress is ill every other month and thus in no condition to plan weddings. Perhaps this is a 'wait and see' game."

Igor smiled wanly.

For the last hours, she and Stanislaus danced together, admiring the way the full moon shone like a gold doubloon directly over the orchestra's cart. Throughout the evening, choirs, actors, poets, and dancers performed, and guests returned repeatedly to the lottery gift booths.

"It is a triumph for you, my darling," Stanislaus repeated, and she knew it to be true. Even Peter and the detestable, drooling Elizabeth Vorontsova deigned to compliment the festivities. Guests prized their souvenirs for months, and for days no one could talk of anything but the grand duchess's generosity and good cheer.

Later that summer the court had even more to celebrate. Apraksin's troops managed to defeat the Prussian army in a battle at Gross-jagersdorf, a follow-up to their seizure of the fortress of Memel on the Baltic. Expectations soared. Soon Russia would possess Prussia, and the hated Frederick the Great would be vanquished.

Regardless of the loss to his idealized country, Peter continued to wear a large ring with Frederick's picture on it, which he nervously twirled on his finger each time someone mentioned the war. He frequently raised it to his lips.

One morning he marched into Catherine's chambers waving a letter. "I want you to look at this for errors," he demanded.

"Of course," she replied, unable to contain her surprise when she read over the scribbled note Peter had written in French to Ivan Shuvalov. There were countless grammatical and spelling errors, but she was not concerned with them.

"This says you want him to persuade the empress to permit you to leave Russia?"

"I do. Only for a few years."

"And where would you go?" she asked, knowing full well the answer.

"To someplace where I will be treated like a ruler. Someplace where I can meet with Frederick and help him with this war."

Catherine bit her lip. Did Peter not realize that this was unforgivable treason, and that in any case, the heir to the throne was forbidden to leave the country?

"It says here," she said carefully, "that you have been ill and suffer from melancholia. Is that true?"

"Of course it is true," he said haughtily.

"And have you considered me? Our child? Not to mention the one on the way?"

"You will be fine. You always are," he said dismissively.

"And your son? Perhaps two sons?"

"He is too young to be of any use. I am sending the note! I only wanted your opinion."

"My opinion," she said slowly and deliberately, "is that it would not be a good idea to aggravate the empress in this way. She may be joyful this month, but such a request could have severe consequences." *For both of us*, she added silently, realizing her husband had no feelings for her position.

"Nevertheless, I shall have the note delivered immediately."

Catherine sighed heavily when he left, unable to predict exactly what might happen if Shuvalov did indeed bring the request to the attention of the empress.

It was out of her hands. All she could do was wait, something she might have grown accustomed to, but barely tolerated.

Then something inexplicable occurred. Just when it appeared the ultimate victory had been won, Apraksin ceased marching. Only miles from taking Konigsberg, the capital of East Prussia, he dawdled.

Word of his inertia reached court simultaneously with news of his retreat. Apparently without a word of notice to the empress, the general ordered his ammunitions, wagons, supplies, and cannons torched, as well as the villages behind him burned so that the enemy could make no use of them. This might've made sense if he were losing— not on the verge of one of the greatest victories Europe had ever seen.

"Her Majesty is beyond furious," Stanislaus reported to Catherine. "I truly believed she would have an apoplexy when she received the news."

The nation's fury soon turned to shock as Stanislaus's prediction came true in September: Empress Elizabeth collapsed during a church service at Tsarskoe Selo of an apparent apoplexy.

Catherine learned about it the next day when Stanislaus sent her a note. Coming on top of the Russian withdrawal, neither she nor anyone else knew what to think.

Over the next few months, the nation held its breath. Outside every church, knots of babushkas huddled in vigils. Peasant healers read the moon and the stars as they crossed themselves fervently. Their prognostications that she was recovering usually proved to be in error, especially when the empress's confessor was summoned.

Every other day her doctors predicted she was on the way to recovery.

In the meantime, Sir Charles left Russia on earlier orders from the empress, who'd demanded George II recall him to England. Barely able to accept yet another loss at this critical time, Catherine realized she had no choice. "I love you as my father," she told him in a letter smuggled to him as he prepared to depart. She would miss the supportive and witty ambassador, and his departure saddened her deeply.

Amidst court rumors over the succession, Catherine found herself slowed somewhat by her ever-increasing girth. Unlike the previous time, Elizabeth was in no condition to manage or interfere in the pregnancy; the baby did that on its own.

The overriding problem was created when Peter denied paternity, claiming, "I have no idea how my wife becomes pregnant, but I suppose I shall have to accept the child as my own."

Catherine and Stanislaus immediately sent Lev Naryshin to see Peter. "Demand that he sign an oath that he has not slept with me in a year," she told him. "Tell him that if he refuses to swear such an oath, you will go immediately to Alexander Shuvalov and report that he has not been fulfilling his conjugal duty."

"To the devil!" Peter apparently shouted when Lev brought up the issue. Not only did he refuse to take such an oath, but he hollered at Lev, "Don't ever speak of this matter again!"

There would be no more trouble from him.

Catherine saw very little of Elizabeth that year, and on rare occasions when admitted to the ill empress's presence, she could barely keep from showing her shock. The slurred speech did not surprise her, since Catherine had seen her father suffer from the same condition. What did shock her was that the prematurely aging Elizabeth's face bore the ravages of both illness and her lifestyle. When the priest and doctor sprinkled her with water, caked-on cosmetics ran down her face in streaks, giving her skin a dappled gray look. Even sitting up fully dressed, she could not hide her glassy blue eyes, white hairs poking out from her headdress, and puckered skin around her eyes and lips.

"She is in her forties, yet appears immeasurably older," she told Stanislaus later. "In fact," she whispered, "she resembles a corpse more than a woman, let alone a monarch."

"She will recover."

"But what if she doesn't? We are not ready—I am not ready—for what is surely to come. Only yesterday Chancellor Bestuzhev was in my chambers again to hint not too discreetly that I must take a more active role in events."

"And so you should, my darling."

Catherine patted her huge stomach. "It is impossible now. And do you know what the grand duke told me just after it happened? That the day she dies he will end the war!"

Stanislaus groaned. "And he will. If only Apraksin hadn't withdrawn, it would be over by now."

"I begged the general not to waste his victories. I've written him three letters."

"Perhaps he knew that they were wasted anyway. If the empress does not last . . ."

"Then Peter will ensure that they *were* wasted by reversing them," she finished.

"It is also possible that the general realizes he would then be needed more in Petersburg if the empress gets worse," Stanislaus voiced what Catherine already thought.

Catherine was permitted to make a rare appearance during her confinement to host the celebration of Elizabeth's accession to the throne and the thirteenth year of her reign. No expense had been spared despite the empress emerging from her illness even more ornery than usual. From the servants Catherine heard that even little Paul started crying when he saw or heard her.

In the dining hall, burning perfume pills infused the room with the sweet scent of roses. A machine did the same thing with rose petals in the hallways. Footmen in felt slippers walked up and down the lengthy banquet tables to wax and buff them. Pastry chefs worked for weeks on sugared confections in the shapes of palaces and cathedrals.

Catherine did not want to attend. For the most part, her condition excused her from all court appearances—a double relief. Danger seemed to lurk in every shadow of the palace. General Apraksin had been arrested and replaced by General Fermor. The chancellor was inexplicably out of favor and being questioned. Even Catherine's spies, including the jeweler Bernardi, had been arrested. *Were I not pregnant*, she shuddered, *I, too, might be imprisoned.*

Her contractions started in the middle of the night in early December. A drunken Peter stumbled into her chambers dressed in a formal Holstein uniform and swinging an enormous sword.

"Why the costume?" she asked, trying to hide her alarm.

"I am here prepared to fulfill my duty as a Holstein officer and to defend the ducal house!"

"Fine," she snapped, still uncertain if he were joking. "Not the Russian Empire?"

When he shrugged, she tried to calm him. "Please depart quickly before Her Majesty sees you. The baby is far from ready to arrive, but the empress will be here any moment."

Fortunately, Peter heeded her advice, and when the empress arrived only to be told the sudden subsiding of labor pains meant a long wait, she, too, left.

Nearly twenty hours later, Catherine arose from her supper table and experienced sharp pains. By the time anyone knew what was happening, she had given birth to a daughter.

"She shall be named Elizabeth," Catherine declared.

But if the young grand duchess had assumed that things might be different now that she had given the kingdom a second child—and a mere girl—she was quickly disillusioned.

"She will be called Anna Petrovna, after my older sister and the grand duke's mother," Elizabeth overruled her.

Catherine looked down at the little bundle, yearning to reach out and touch her, to stroke her tiny toes and fingers, her fine hair. Yet within moments, little Anna was whisked away to the nursery in the empress's apartment where she would join her three-year-old brother. No one worried about the afterbirth, which much later had to be removed by hand. No one worried about the mother, either, who'd had a breech birth that might have killed both her and the child.

"I am so alone," she moaned when anyone was around to listen.

The truth was an entirely different matter. Having learned hard lessons from her last birthing, this time she ordered elaborate preparations to ensure there would be no repeat of her discomfort, abandonment, and neglect. Behind her bed stretched an enormous yellow silk screen that blocked off an adjoining anteroom. Ostensibly containing a commode, in fact this anteroom, newly furnished with tables, chairs, mirrors, and a sofa, was also accessible from the other end via an unused storeroom.

On any given evening during post-natal confinement, the hidden alcove hosted supper parties for Catherine, her friends, many of her ladies, and her lover. It was often all the small group could do to muffle their laughter when night after night, Catherine would order her attendants to bring no fewer than six dishes for her supper.

On New Year's Day, Madame Vladislavova knocked on Catherine's door to announce an unwelcome visitor: Count Peter Shuvalov. His visit seemed to stretch forever, even though Catherine rubbed her eyes when he arrived and claimed to have been sleeping. By the time he rose and announced he must leave to join the empress to view the gala fireworks arranged for the New Year, Catherine's friends were famished.

"Have no fear," she reassured them, promptly ordering chicken, four kinds of fishes, duckling with plum sauce, and two trays of appetizers and sweetmeats.

As servants bustled to serve the grand duchess while mumbling about her enormous appetite, the group behind the curtain could barely contain themselves. Later, when the same baffled servants arrived to clear dozens of empty plates and bowls, once again the partiers barely succeeded in smothering nearly hysterical laughter. Only Catherine managed to keep a straight face throughout. She may have lived surrounded by a noose of conspiracy, but she knew how to keep a poker face regardless of what mischief or mayhem went on around her.

It was a talent, she suspected, that she'd have much need for in the months and years to come.

In fact, she was to require them much sooner than she thought. Although early in the year the new General Fermor had seized Konigsberg, the capital of Prussia, the empress did not seem as overjoyed as one might have expected—instead seeming bent on revenge.

One of the most difficult days and nights of Catherine's life occurred when she received word that her enemy-turned-mentor, Chancellor Bestuzhev, had been arrested. Even knowing he'd been falling out of favor for at least a year and his schemes for altering the succession were bound to fail, she was shocked at his downfall.

This was the night she'd been required by the empress to open the ball celebrating Lev's long-awaited wedding, and the message of Bestuzhev's arrest came from Stanislaus only an hour before the festivities, when the ladies already were working on her toilette.

There was no time to act. She realized immediately that the secret police could find the succession manifesto he had worked on for so long, as well as any other secret papers. Her horror mounted, and she could barely concentrate.

When the ball began, she showed up in regal fashion to open it. Dressed in rose brocade and draped in sapphires, she smiled radiantly at each guest. All her newly acquired acting skills were needed as she admired the bride's gown and toasted the newlyweds' happiness.

That night she did not sleep.

Just before dawn, she tiptoed around her sleeping servants to rummage through her desk and its hidden drawers. The fire had nearly died during the night, but now flared to life as she fed it paper after paper, letter after letter. Nothing must survive, and everything was potentially compromising in some way, even the philosophy of a fifteen-year-old that she had written so many years ago.

On Monday, no one showed up with the Holstein portfolio she normally handled, a sure signal that her work on the administration of the tiny duchy had ceased, most likely on orders from the empress.

Word soon came that the jeweler Bernardi had been exiled to Kazan, and that Bestuzhev would be exiled to his own estate. Before he departed, however, Bestuzhev apparently had had time to take his own action.

"All is well," his smuggled note to Catherine read. "Everything has been destroyed."

Her relief was immense, and she did not blink when one afternoon she returned to her apartments to discover someone had rummaged through everything, leaving books, maps, and even her needlework strewn carelessly around the room and on the floor.

As days passed, her faithful woman of the bedchamber, Madame Vladislavova, as well as several others, were arrested and replaced by strangers. Countess Bruce—formerly her companion Praskovia, who had delivered countless messages for Catherine—remained, but no longer dared play her postal go between. Even Peter stayed away. When Catherine attempted to order a carriage or go out to the stables, the groomsmen refused.

Nobody wrote her, and she dared not write anything herself or invite anyone to visit, including Stanislaus, for fear of getting her friends and lover in trouble. When her own husband indicated fear of speaking to her, she understood that something incriminating must have been found.

Carnival came and she was required to appear at multiple functions, although everyone she encountered seemed aloof and afraid to speak with her. Courtiers' reactions to her ranged from embarrassed to openly hostile. Then Lent arrived, with its paucity of amusements, meager meals, and increased church services. Still alone with only her dog and parrot, Catherine restlessly paced the rooms until she wore out a pair of her tiny slippers.

Unable to bear it any longer, she at last decided to write to the empress. "I beg you," she wrote in Russian, "to allow me to return to my own country and people."

No reply came.

At the beginning of Holy Week, Catherine took to her bed, refused to see a doctor, and instead asked to see her confessor. "My soul is sick onto death," she told him. "My conscience is clear, yet it is apparent that I am accused of something no one will disclose. Her Imperial Majesty will not respond to my letters and will not permit me an audience. I beg for your assistance."

Since both she and Elizabeth had the same confessor, her plan to get him to speak to the empress on her behalf seemed like her last opportunity.

It worked. A message came a week before her birthday that Her Imperial Majesty Empress Elizabeth Petrovna would receive the grand duchess at midnight.

She sat on her sofa from eleven in the evening until nearly two a.m. waiting for Alexander Shuvalov to arrive. By the time he did, she was trembling so hard she did not know if she could face the empress and her accusations of some perceived crime.

The empress received her in a sapphire velvet bed gown, and Catherine barely had time to register once again Elizabeth's ghastly face. Throwing herself at the empress's feet, she begged, "Please allow me to go home."

"This is your home," Elizabeth replied. "How would I explain such a thing to the world? And exactly where would you go? Certainly no one in your family is left to receive you. And of course, you would be without funds." She was clearly irritated.

"I am not afraid of poverty."

"You should be."

"Then please tell me what I have done wrong. Of what am I accused?"

It did not take long to discover her crime.

"How many letters did you send to General Apraksin?" the empress demanded.

Catherine thought quickly, deciding to err on the side of truth. "Three," she replied.

"Not true. There were more," Shuvalov interrupted.

"I swear that is untrue. There were only three."

"We plan to torture Apraksin soon, and he will admit the truth—that there were many more."

"Torture him if you must—or torture me for that matter—but there were only three."

"You are clever," the empress said. "Too clever, perhaps, but you know you have no right or authority to meddle in politics, let alone military affairs. How dare you!"

"Forgive me, Your Imperial Majesty. I had only the glory and future of Russia on my mind."

Catherine glimpsed some papers on Elizabeth's dressing table. They sat on a porcelain platter next to the Empress's golden toilet set, and there was no doubt that they were in Catherine's own handwriting.

"How dare you write to my generals!" Elizabeth's voice grew louder and more furious as she paced the room. "I already possess three of your letters, and I demand to know how many more you have written and to whom?"

Peter emerged from behind a curtain. "Send her back to Prussia!" he insisted. "You are a harlot and a snake!" As he continued to hurl insults and accusations, Catherine forced herself not to respond but to remain calm and reasonable.

When Peter insisted on continuing his tirade, the empress ordered, "Be silent!"

She dismissed Catherine, who returned to her rooms shaken and afraid.

It was after three in the morning, and before Catherine could undress, Alexander Shuvalov was ushered in to deliver a private message. "Her Imperial Majesty bids me tell you not to have a heavy heart, and she will speak with you again soon. However, she also asked me to be sure you do not share this message with the grand duke."

Relieved, Catherine slept soundly. In the morning, any type of pardon seemed to be a dream. Two more of her maids were dismissed, a lackey showed up with an order to carry away some of her most treasured books, and news came that Michael Vorontzov would assume the duties of chancellor. And now that Peter's mistress, Elizabeth Vorontsova, had such high connections, the grand duke publicly announced to anyone who would listen that he planned to divorce his wife and marry Elizabeth.

Let him have the gross, uncouth drunkard, she thought bitterly. The two of them deserved one another.

This was a time to withdraw even further. She would spend the next weeks and months reading and thinking, pleading ill health and refusing to see anyone.

Alone in her bedroom on her birthday, she received a message from the empress; "I am drinking to your health on this auspicious day."

All was not lost. Catherine would persevere.

CHAPTER 30

(MARIA) 1758-1759

In order to locate forty-seven pearls to make a perfectly matched sixteen-inch necklace, a pearl processor must cull through over ten thousand of them!" Igor once told me. Now I think of myself as a sorter, sampling and then rejecting countless options for myself each week, not to mention potential portals back to my future. However, I despair of finding the right solution: the one that will work and buy me some happiness, preferably with Igor.

If he does not want me, then at least I might have a chance of finding a new life in the future.

My husband and I have barely spoken in over a year. Especially with the palace and court in constant turmoil, I yearn to confide in him. To share my thoughts and hopes and dreams. To have him love me and make love to him.

Our rare conversations have been curt. After Catherine gave birth to baby Anna, he and some friends called on the grand duchess frequently; for some reason I was not invited. On one occasion, after the jeweler Bernardi was arrested, Igor visited the empress with his wares when I was attending her. I never met Signore Bernardi, but he and Igor had at the very least a professional relationship. Although Igor appeared calm and collected as the empress groused about wanting someone to handle her jewels who wasn't a spy, I could see his hands shake and one corner of his mouth twitch nervously. How I longed to kiss that mouth and reassure him that neither he nor his uncle was in any danger.

I wonder what Uncle Giuseppe and Aunt Gina think about our sudden parting of ways, since surely Igor would not tell them about me. Or perhaps he did, and they think I am a witch or at the very least a mad woman.

"You should write to Igor Igorevich," Tatiana urges me. It is just after Catherine has gone into semi-seclusion as rumors swirl about her possible arrest for some unknown crime, and I yearn to talk to someone. Only Tatiana knows Igor and I married and now separated, although I have been very vague as to the reason.

"It is difficult to get letters out now," I protest weakly.

"Fa! An excuse, to be sure. Maria Sergeievna, do you or do you not still love him?"

"Just because *you* are now happily engaged to be married to your Danish count is no reason you must match up everyone else," I try to tease her.

I doubt Tatiana will be deterred.

I'm tending Her Majesty's swollen feet when Catherine is admitted to the imperial stateroom. Although she acknowledges me with a brief nod and smile, I can detect her terror at this personal audience. There is no one else here, and the empress immediately dismisses me. Remarkably, I can overhear bits and pieces of the conversation as I linger in the antechamber.

"Do you," the empress demands loudly, "swear on the Holy Bible you have never plotted against my life?"

Catherine answers nearly as forcefully. "Your Imperial Majesty, I swear by my own soul's salvation that I have done no such thing and never would."

"Did you write only three letters to General Apraksin?" the empress fires back immediately.

"Yes, I confess I did write to him, but only the letters Your Majesty has in her possession. There are no more to discover, as I did not write or send any additional letters or messages."

The empress's voice softens, and I can hear no more until she says, "Tell me about the grand duke. How is your life together?"

"Everything is as it should be, Your Majesty, although . . ."

A servant enters the antechamber with a tray of tea and pastries, and I bend to adjust my stockings. The voices inside are now muted. Although I nod at the woman to leave everything outside the door, she takes her time, arranging and then rearranging sugar cubes and pots of jams on the silver tray. Afraid to be overheard by the empress, I say nothing, but as soon as the servant finally departs, I follow her. Eavesdropping, let alone spying, is much too dangerous, and at this time in my life I am at the empress's mercy. Where else would I go?

Presumably Catherine and Elizabeth have reconciled. A few days later Catherine is brought to see her two children. It happens to be one of the rare times she has been admitted into the sanctity of the nursery. I am playing a version of patty cake with Paul, as Anna is asleep. Catherine reaches over to touch the little girl, whose long lashes stand out against skin as white and fragile as my childhood porcelain doll. Anna is a frail, rather sickly child, although the doctors are mystified as to the cause. I imagine a touch of sadness on Catherine's face, and her eyes water before she leaves. Young Paul, afraid of strangers, huddles against me and refuses to go to this strange woman.

I can sense the grand duchess's pain as she murmurs her thanks to the empress and then hurries from the nursery.

A few weeks later, all of Elizabeth's ladies accompany her to tour construction of the Winter Palace, which has just been repaired after the newly laid ceiling stucco started to crumble, delaying our move there indefinitely. Elizabeth apparently has forgiven Rastrelli, who has invited her and Ivan Shuvalov to check the progress of repairs in person. We ladies follow, flitting around her like butterflies in our pastel afternoon gowns.

All around us the incessant hammering of carpenters and masons drowns out the empress's conversation with Rastrelli. She appears happy, even when she stops to remove a piece of plaster stuck to her shoe. Behind her we trip over pieces of tile, discarded moldings, and layers of plaster dust, but no one minds. We are all anxious to move into this massive building that spans the Neva's bank and resembles nothing short of a gigantic flat wedding cake frosted with sculptures.

I should be overjoyed, too, since for me the construction has gone on too long. I retain the conviction that once the Winter Palace is finished, I will be able to estimate where I was standing when it was or will be known as the Hermitage and thus where I need to be to return to the future. Alternatively, I will find the statue elsewhere, although as years go by, I find myself growing more and more uncertain that I will recognize it immediately.

Early that summer Catherine and Peter depart for Oranienbaum, although I am to accompany the empress to Peterhof, as is Stanislaus

Poniatowski. I am pleased about the latter, since Igor often attends Stanislaus, who has a fondness for gemstones, and I am anxious to see Igor.

These days my duties only infrequently call for the dreaded reverse gender parties or any balls, but when they do, I can barely stand to watch any more. The courtiers have started to remind me of oddly dressed clowns covered in makeup and colliding in a circus ring. I think too, of the lumbering elephants we watched my first night in the past, most of whom are dead.

Thanks to her preoccupation with little Paul and her own ailments, Elizabeth appears rarely, although she still struggles to stay awake all night with candles blazing. Mornings after she does finally fall asleep, I continue to stroll the widespread grounds of the great pink palace of Peterhof. It is nearly impossible to forget all the wonderful meetings, talks, and kisses Igor and I once shared here at this hour, and too often I find myself imagining I see him riding along the paths or walking briskly beside one of the fabulous gilded fountains that pump water themselves all summer.

And then one day it is really him!

He is alone, on foot and strolling slower than usual toward the grand staircase leading up to the palace.

I step boldly out from a parallel path and stand in front of him, willing him to stop.

"Maria," he says calmly, as if he had expected to see me today.

"How are you?" I ask, for my part totally unprepared even though I've silently practiced possible speeches over the past year. "Do you have time to sit awhile?"

Without hesitation, he does so, and we settle on one of the same stone benches where we sat when he courted me. "I have a meeting with Poniatowski," he explains, "but we have no set time."

"That's good. I mean, I've wanted to talk to you for so long."

"And I you. I have of course had much time to think. About what you claimed—or said. And about us."

I wait quietly for him to continue, holding my breath and praying he is not going to ask me to dissolve the marriage.

He takes a deep breath, as if willing himself to recall what he has planned to say. "I'm not certain. I cannot understand an occurrence such as you described, but I *am* quite certain that you are not mad. For lack of a better word, I will suggest other possibilities: disillusioned, confused, overly imaginative, or perhaps, well, perhaps you have suffered a blow to the head. Are any of these things possible?"

I stare into those beautiful eyes and want to agree. Instead, I whisper, "No. None of them."

He heaves a long sigh. "You still insist that you come from the future?"

Looking down at my fingers, which I am twisting nervously, I know that no matter how much it costs me, I cannot lie. "I do."

For a moment it appears as if he will stand and leave. Then he reaches for my fingers to quiet their motions. "Tell me about it then. How it happened."

Instinctively I survey the area around us. Not even the grounds staff is in sight. So I tell him. Everything.

"My parents died in a plane crash—a flying machine—when I was still a little girl. But they taught me French, and of course you know I speak English. That is why. Because that is the language of my people. I was adopted by my Aunt Roberta, who teaches Russian history at a nearby university in the Colonies—which someday very, very soon will be an independent nation."

"Please continue."

At times he interrupts to ask a question or for clarification. The idea of the Winter Palace eventually being a museum open to the public and the facts that Catherine will reign for a very long time and amass a huge collection of art seem to astound him the most.

"But what would then happen to the grand duke? He is the heir."

"I don't know, Igor. Most of my knowledge comes from my aunt, who specialized in studying Peter the Great, plus the two trips I took to visit Russia."

He shakes his head and then sits silently. At last, however, he releases my hands and rises. "I must go, Maria. However, I would like very much to talk more. Could you possibly come to the shop one morning next week?"

"Yes, my darling," I say happily before I can stop myself. "I am also anxious to see Uncle Giuseppe and your aunt, of course."

"I'm afraid neither of them is well, especially Aunt Gina. It will do her much good to see you."

We part awkwardly, and at the last minute he tucks a stray hair behind my ear. "I want you to know that I am not necessarily accepting what you say. I am, however, willing to listen."

And with that he is gone. It is enough.

It is almost hysterically funny to watch Count Stanislaus Poniatowski leaving Peterhof each night. How he expects to fool anyone in his ridiculous blonde wig, I cannot imagine.

Tonight I stop him as he prepares to climb into his carriage to depart on his nocturnal visit to Oranienbaum. It is midnight, and the empress has dismissed us because she and Ivan Shuvalov need private time. It is still light with the mother-of-pearl radiance of the White Nights.

"Will you send my regards and blessings to Her Imperial Highness for me?" I ask.

The count smiles, and I cannot help mentally compare him to a loveable teddy bear. "Of course. Anything else?"

I bend down, ostensibly in a curtsy, and reach into the secret pocket inside my hem. "This is for her." I hand him the little snuff-box I decorated, covered with little emeralds arranged in the shape of two books. "For her collection."

He reaches for his satchel as if to rummage for coins, and I put up my hand. "No, it is a gift. A token of my esteem for Her Imperial Highness, who I consider a friend." I made it for her over a year ago but haven't found an opportune moment to sneak it to her.

"My Catherine also has mentioned she feels close to you. To Igor, as well. You must also realize that we are both admirers of your work. And with Bernardi now gone . . ." He does not finish the sentence, though I sense what he might be trying to say: that he and Catherine need loyal allies, and occasionally someone to transport messages.

"We are always at your command, Count Poniatowski." I dip another low curtsy before preparing to resume my walk.

"I shall remember," he replies, his pale eyes twinkling.

Before he rides away, I bid him take care. Only a few weeks ago he was attacked and held prisoner for most of the evening by Peter and his men. Now the count fears above all being sent back to Poland and away from the love of his life if the empress believes the rumors. There are no secrets in imperial Russia that are not uncovered.

Except, I hope, for mine.

I dress with extra care, insisting Liza use birch-bark rinse on my hair before arranging it into a swept-up style my husband favors. She then uses hot tongs, the fashion being to let a single curl dangle beside my ears. After that, I direct her to fasten the opal necklace I received on my wedding day, and lastly sweeten my breath by chewing parsley sprigs.

By five it is light, the sun shining on the cupolas of Peterhof's imperial church as my carriage leaves the palace. I am incredibly nervous.

Aunt Gina is awake when I arrive, her bones seeming brittle as a bird's when I hug her. She receives me as warmly as ever, looking so drawn, underweight, and pale that I fear she may not be with us much longer. Yet she has the energy to serve me a plate of pasta and a chianti, ignoring protests that I am not hungry. "*Mangia*," she insists. Seeing her often brings tears to my eyes since she reminds me in many ways of my lost Aunt Roberta.

Sipping the wine gratefully, I am, however, nearly unnerved when Igor comes downstairs to the kitchen behind the shop. He looks so handsome and so serious I yearn to jump up and throw my arms around him.

We greet each other somewhat formally, and Aunt Gina whisks away my uneaten meal, refills my wine, pours for Igor, and quietly disappears.

"What have you told them? Your family? About us, I mean."

He shrugs. "They are kind enough not to press me, but obviously very unhappy. You are loved," he adds, and I am unsure whether he means only by Uncle Giuseppe and Aunt Gina or by him, as well.

Based on this uncertainty, I ask questions about his business. About his clients. About his cameos.

"I wish for you to see my progress," he agrees, "but not yet. Today we must begin to discuss us. Our marriage. Our future. Is this not true?"

"*Pravda*" It is true.

He settles across the table, toasting my good health.

Yet when he begins to speak, it is about court matters. "You must know about the great escape that Count Poniatowski made from the grand duke's men? It is the talk of Petersburg."

"I met him upon his return to the palace that morning," I admit.

"Did you also hear that Count Poniatowski has been recalled to Poland? The order from the empress is that he depart immediately."

"Her Imperial Highness will be lost without him."

"As I am without you," he says quietly.

"Igor . . ." I reach for his hands, strong yet smooth ones that craft so many wondrous treasures. "I cannot lose you," I whisper.

In seconds he rises, crosses the space between us, and pulls me into his arms. I cuddle there, content as a baby kangaroo in its mother's pouch, feeling as if I could stay in those loving and firm arms forever.

And then we are kissing.

"I need you," he says urgently as he removes his lips from mine.

"Now?" I ask, my body tingling.

We end up upstairs in his—or our—bedroom, and if he is afraid of making love to some sort of freak, he does not show it. We cannot get enough of one another, staying there for two hours. I did not know a man could be ready and hard so frequently but am grateful he wants me as badly as I do him.

Later, nibbling at his ear and then nestling against the sweet scent of his neck and shoulders, I feel as if I have regained the world. No more quietly sneaking around the palace in fear of being noticed. No more avoiding the empress's eye lest she remember I am allegedly unwed. No more restless mornings taking turns around the gardens because I cannot sleep. No more desperate maneuverings to discourage men who watch for the different meanings assigned to the rapidity and placement of my fan. The messages I send of my availability versus lack of interest all depend precisely and intricately on whether one uses the fan to touch one's cheek or chin just so with a closed fan or unfurls it in a certain direction.

And no more anxiously scanning the halls and grounds in a desperate attempt to spot my absent husband. No more brooding about turning thirty in this other world in which I have landed.

Igor still loves me, and that is everything.

We do not speak of my futuristic self that day, as if nothing ever happened. As if I never confessed such a thing. Yet I know that we will, and whether or not he accepts the truth, I cannot leave him. Perhaps not even to return to where I *thought* I belonged.

It is a wonderful summer! Even Catherine has made overtures of friendship to Peter's mistress in a bid to save her own lover, and oddly enough, the two couples have started to socialize, albeit uncomfortably. At the same time, the empress has loosened the reins that kept Catherine from her children. Now she is permitted to travel more frequently to Peterhof to see them. Anna, who has mastered crawling, now struggles to stand and take her first steps. Even Paul, a four-year-old blond with brown eyes and an overindulged temperament, does not entirely ignore his real mother. I've never seen Catherine so happy.

Yet nothing stays constant in this court, where at any given moment a player might cheat or make an unexpected checkmate, and thus a tragedy could alter everything.

In August, General Apraksin is court martialed for high treason. All summer a commission has examined his case, eventually concluding he had no choice but to lead his troops in the famous retreat.

"He had a worn-out army," Igor tells me when he arrives home from the trial. "His soldiers had few clothes, no boots, and no bread or meat. Although Apraksin repeatedly called for supplies and rein-forcements, his pleas were all ignored."

"He is exonerated?"

"He would have been," Igor says sadly, burying his head in his hands. "But just before the judge pronounced the sentence of not guilty, the general collapsed. He died instantly."

"What happened?"

"Perhaps heart failure, perhaps apoplexy. He never even heard that he had been freed."

This is not the only tragedy to befall Catherine's allies that year. The next blow comes when Stanislaus can no longer avoid his orders to return to Poland. and as Igor warned, he must go immediately. Catherine, helpless to forestall this or to hope for his return, appears inconsolable.

Watching the count board the carriage to begin his long journey, I cannot foresee how he will survive without the love of his life. "Tell her again," he whispers to me as I curtsy one last time, "that I will love her until the day I die. God willing, we will be together again."

I somehow doubt that, feeling sad for the parted lovers. They've always seemed so perfect for one another, and I cannot imagine another man who will be to Catherine what Stanislaus was.

The third blow comes in October.

There had been hints Sir Charles was having some mental problems when he left Russia the previous autumn, such as when he altered his itinerary a dozen times and then accused his servants of stealing the very same china he forgot he'd packed already; still, no one foresaw what would happen next. Soon after his arrival in Hamburg, he was declared insane and brought back to England and locked up.

"He is gone! Sir Charles!" Catherine weeps when she summons me in late October.

"Surely not back to Russia?" I know the empress would never countenance such a thing, although I, too, have missed the Englishman. I also enjoyed speaking English with him when no one was around to overhear my inexplicable fluency.

"He meant the world to me—and to Stanislaus."

"How can he be gone?" I ask, puzzled.

"He committed suicide."

"No!" Not that sweet man. Not that man who firmly believed someday Catherine would rule, and who shared his books, experience, expertise, funds, and political savvy so generously.

"At least they buried him in Westminster Abbey. He was a fine diplomat and deserved at least that."

Now she has no real political allies; she has lost Bestuzhev, Apraksin, and Sir Charles, not to mention her beloved Poniatowski, and who knows when someone with power will come along again to aid her cause and defend her from her enemies.

But by the first of the year, I have my own serious problems. The empress has set my wedding for spring, when some Sergeant of the Guard away at the front will return to become my "husband." It is time to confess to the empress that I already have one.

CHAPTER 31

(CATHERINE) 1759

"She had a habit of writing memorandums and notations to herself: reminders, anecdotes, insights, ideas and sudden inspirations, items of self-criticism and self-congratulation, character sketches, fragments of old memories—all sorts of serious and random jottings . . . and in an age famous for the volume and polish of personal correspondence she was among the most prolific."
— Robert Coughland

She wrote Stanislaus daily, pouring out her love yet careful not to mention anything political in the smuggled letters. Fortunately, the palaces all seemed to shelter hundreds of hiding places, ranging from false-bottom trunks to concealed drawers and escritoires with locks that could be picked with a hairpin if you could spot subtle changes in the wood grain. Catherine possessed her own hollowed out books, a moving bookcase that concealed an open space, and a secret compartment in her favorite clock.

She also had initiated epistolary exchanges with European authors and leading thinkers of the day, although still dared not approach the proponents of the Enlightenment Movement she so admired. She did continue her memoirs, as well as jotted page after page of notes on her vision of Russia.

Occasionally she slipped Igor a letter folded into the binding of a mineralogy book. One day when he returned the book containing a letter from Stanislaus, she discovered a note from Igor's secret wife, Maria, tucked in with it: *It is time. Your Highness, I need your help.*

They had worked out some details weeks ago, although Catherine knew it was risky. If she interceded on Maria's behalf, Her Majesty's wrath could just as likely fall on Catherine. Yet she more than owed it to her former maid of honor, who was now a young woman who put her life on the line by spying and smuggling for Catherine.

She waited four days for the empress to grant an audience. When she finally was admitted, the empress's mingled scents of orange blossom and rose oil nearly overwhelmed her. Just like her nephew, the empress always had her fingernails stained pink with rose-hip oil, and each night the Lady of the Toilette softened her hands with fragrant attar of roses.

As usual, cats arranged themselves on most of the furniture, each wearing an embroidered velvet coat or top hat that threatened to fall off when they lapped from silver dishes filled with milk and fried chicken breasts.

"What is it?" the empress demanded curtly, and Catherine's heart sank at this indication of her bad temper. Yet she wore a *shlafrok*—an informal English morning dress—which hinted she might be in a relaxed mood.

"It is about your maid of honor—formerly mine—Maria Sergei-evna."

"What about her? We found her a decent husband. What more

does she want?"

"I fear he is not the right man for her, Your Majesty. There is another who—"

"She'll marry the man we have selected! We are quite certain that we made that clear to her. The ungrateful thing!"

"If she is in love with another and if by some fortuitous chance he is acceptable, perhaps Your Most Gracious Imperial Majesty would reconsider. You are our Little Mother," she hastily added, hoping to remind the empress of her reputation for love matches. At least when they coalesced with her own wishes.

"Who is it?"

"He is not a nobleman, Your Majesty, but a respected artisan and merchant."

"A merchant? I want a name. He will never sell to this court again!"

Hastily crossing herself, Catherine told her.

"What? Igor Blukhov took advantage of Maria's position of handling my jewels to seduce her?"

"No, not exactly. They fell in love!"

"Love? What do these girls know about love!"

"She is now past thirty, Your Majesty. Hardly a girl."

"Thirty? You are mistaken."

"I admit she looks young for her age . . ."

"I forbid this relationship. I forbid this scoundrel jeweler from darkening the doors of my palaces."

Catherine had hoped and prayed she would not have to use her final bluff, but apparently there was no choice.

"She is pregnant," she lied quietly, and then stared hard into those steel blue eyes to await their transformation to black.

"Ah, I see. I certainly do see." The empress seemed a bit too restrained, and thus Catherine was more afraid than ever.

"And she told *you* this? You? A woman whose affairs scandalize my court and set an awful example for our ladies? A woman who carries on a *ménage à quatre* with her lover, her husband, and her husband's mistress? No wonder she has come to you with her sin!" And suddenly she reached across the arm of her chair for one of the cats, appeared to think better of it, and instead threw her gold hairbrush across the room.

Catherine realized then how right she had been in suspecting that the empress had not only been aware of the get-togethers with Peter, Elizabeth Vorontsova and Stanislaus, but indeed had used that socializing as the primary rationale for Poniatowski's dismissal. The evenings the four of them had shared over meals the previous year had always made her nervous, although Peter, far from seeing himself as a cuckold, seemed proud to sit across from his wife while draping an arm around his own sloppy, big-breasted mistress. It was as if for the first time he had felt himself an equal to his intelligent wife. For Catherine, however, those nights had been pure torture not just because of Peter, but in part due to being forced to spend hours in the company of his mistress, *das Fraulein*, who apparently shared Peter's dislike of bathing and could barely speak without spitting or cursing like a drunken sailor.

She must try to shake away those memories and her loss of Stanislaus to help her friend. "My most humble apologies, Little Mother. I believe she feared losing her position with you, the kind Imperial Majesty she so admires and loves."

Apparently, this was the correct approach, as the empress began to pace the carpet.

"Send her to me," she commanded at last.

"Yes, of course, Your Imperial Majesty. Might I inquire as to how you will handle this situation?"

"Dismissed!"

Catherine backed out, wondering if she had found a solution or devastated the lives of two people she had come to love.

Whether Maria had seen the empress that week in early March, Catherine didn't know, and the events of the following day took precedence over her thoughts. She was out riding in Petersburg in pouring rain when a message arrived that her daughter, precious little Anna, was seriously ill.

In the downpour, she risked her horse and her safety to gallop hard back to the palace, arriving in the nursery wearing her drenched riding habit and boots.

She was too late.

The fifteen-month-old toddler had succumbed minutes ago, and the empress appeared inconsolable. Torn between grief and fury at the way the empress had purportedly taken care of the little girl, Catherine swallowed her anger and was permitted to touch the tiny pearly fingernails, to stroke the already cold porcelain-like face. Now at last no one stopped her when she reached down and scooped up the baby who had never really belonged to her. Only in the previous six months had the empress permitted rationed visits to Anna.

The court went into mourning, and six days later a shaken Catherine attended the burial at Alexander Nevsky Monastery. She'd said her goodbyes by crying for days in her room, where she concluded her own situation was totally out of control. Paul certainly would become even more spoiled and estranged from her, Peter habitually had ignored both children, and any chance she had to become a real mother was gone, at least for now. Even if she could stomach the possibility of sleeping with Peter, there seemed little chance of her bearing another heir. Despite all his affairs, not one of his women had gotten pregnant. For all she knew, he was sterile. Even if he weren't, she wondered if one more heir would be enough to protect the kingdom and ensure its future.

Straightening up from the miniature casket, she climbed back in the carriage. She must not give herself up to grief. Must not allow this awful death of a baby she'd barely known to spin her out of control. She would pour out her grief in letters to the baby's father, Stanislaus, but after that she would never speak of it again.

She did what she always did in times of despair: buried herself in her studies. It was during this time she developed dozens of ideas for altering Russia, many based on Montesquieu's writings, as well as plans for reducing tariffs, making laws more humane, restructuring cities, and founding schools, universities, and cultural centers.

She studied maps intensely. Recalling her pilgrimage to Kiev while still an obscure fourteen-year-old grand duchess, she recognized the geographical and agricultural importance of the region. She also confided in her notes a desire to join the Caspian and Black seas, linking them through a system of riverways to the Baltic and White seas. This would not only grant Russia control of the eastern commerce route once dominated by China and India, but make it the largest empire in the world. As she sketched out plans, she never stopped cherishing dreams of ending Russia's stagnation and achieving it even more glory than that of which her predecessor Peter the First had dreamed.

Elizabeth had accomplished virtually nothing in twenty years, even neglecting to attend the weekly War Council and finding creative excuses for not being able to hold a pen to sign documents. When she simply refused, her ministers manufactured stories about how she had bruised an arm or wrist. She also left letters unanswered, going so far as to ignore two written by France's Louis XV himself. She had become a volcano, normally dormant but occasionally exploding in fiery lava over something insignificant.

If someday Tsar Peter would leave Catherine alone—or let her rule as more than a consort—her own ideas had an excellent chance of implementation. She dared not think about the hundreds more ideas she would put into effect if she somehow ended up ruling by herself.

CHAPTER 32

(MARIA) 1759

I have been demoted, albeit temporarily. After my alleged pregnancy culminates with a child, I am to move out. Her Imperial Majesty allowed me to stay here and be tended by court physicians, only after arranging a hasty wedding scarcely anyone dared attend.

"After the baby arrives, you and *it* shall go live as a merchant's wife," the empress said coldly. "Then you shall see all that you will have given up for your stupidity and immorality!"

Despite yearning to shoot back something about all *her* lovers, I don't want to end up flogged or minus a body part. Thus I acquiesced quietly, even acting grateful.

Igor is happy I ended up reassigned to the Imperial Wardrobe, with its wide rooms of large wooden tables, rather than elsewhere. I suspect this is partially because he grew jealous of all the men I met at the balls, theatrical performances, and other functions for which my former duties required me to look glamorous and act politely toward courtiers and soldiers. Had I not been disgraced, for example, I would have surely been elegantly coiffed and gowned for Catherine's thirtieth birthday celebration the previous month.

"I spend my days sorting through baskets of buttons and ribbons," I complain, but Igor laughs.

"This is a promotion, no?"

I grin wanly, recalling my first month under Madame Vorahova, the head seamstress who oversees our atelier: the main design studio.

"Begin at the beginning, and then we shall see," Madame insisted, and meant it. My first day I joined the newest and youngest servants to thread needles, sweep up fabric scraps and tinsel bits, and keep irons heated. With my abominable sewing skills, I didn't expect to be assigned to do exquisite stitching, such as the kind done on petticoats, chemises, bodices, and men's waistcoats. I was pleased the third week to be moved up to draperies.

One afternoon Anya, a fellow seamstress, sneaks me up to the attic rooms where previously worn gowns are encased in dust-free Venetian glass panels. "Why do we keep all of these?" I ask, having wondered often what happens to the elegant gowns the empress refuses to wear more than once.

"Well, I doubt Her Majesty is fully aware that we preserve so many, yet she is loathe to part with her favorites. Most the time we don't ask, just request her ladies to return the gowns to us."

I gaze around in awe. "How many are there?"

"About fifteen hundred, although thousands were destroyed in the fire at Moscow. But she still possesses about five thousand pairs of shoes and at least that many gloves."

As I've noticed previously, the empress tends to favor unique embroideries with elaborate embellishments over the watered silks, sable-trimmed velvets, and rich silver and gold brocades.

"The brocades are only for the imperial house," Anya explains. "According to Romanov tradition, no one else is permitted to wear them."

Dazzled by the opulence, I return to our room to snack on cheese, fruits, and biscuits. I am barely hungry, though my fellow seamstresses savor their cold lunches. Many were serfs or family members of serfs, and undoubtedly this constitutes a treat. The women, I've also learned, are not counted in the landowners' estimate of wealth. The more male serfs owned, on the other hand, the richer the landowner.

"It is something like slavery," I observe to Igor.

"It has always been so. It would take a revolution to change things."

"Which there will be," I murmur under my breath, but he hears me.

"I'm happy to learn this. I know many serfs get flogged for insignificant errors, and this is grossly unfair. Perhaps someday your beloved Catherine will be able to effect some real change to a situation long engrained in our culture."

It is nearly time for our weekly visit to end when he adds, "Soon we will awaken together every morning and fall asleep each night in one another's arms."

"I hope so," I say fervently. "But who knows for certain what the empress might do if she discovers I am not pregnant—or at least no longer pregnant?"

He wrinkles his brow. "You are correct to worry. It is only great fortune that she hasn't followed up on her orders for send a doctor, who would surely discover the truth."

We—including Catherine—have already planned that I will suffer a fake miscarriage soon, which should free me from the palace much faster.

"She is too sick herself to think of such things," Tatiana assures me, "and Grand Duke Paul has just recovered from colic. Of late, however, Her Majesty seems healthier. It must be all the remedies her new French specialist has prescribed."

Dr. Francois Poissonnier was summoned to examine Elizabeth late in the summer, about the time I started to tuck a small pillow below my stays.

Tatiana relays all his prescriptions to me with glee. "He gives her purgatives dipped in marmalade to make them tastier. He blames it on her age, and says her humors have become slower, but everyone in the room knows he is more concerned about her diet."

I remember well countless nights when she and her ladies ordered trays of sweetmeats and pastries, and Elizabeth's diet of dairy foods and meat surely contributes to her frequent disabling bouts of constipation. "Yet she is only about forty-five, is she not?"

"Dr. Poissonier claims her sedentary life is responsible, as well, although Her Majesty refuses to exercise." Tatiana adds, "It is difficult to remember all those years of trying to keep up with her on the ballroom floor, let alone tramping around to shrines and cottages. She even stopped hunting."

"I hear she prefers to be wheeled everywhere now. Did she take care of everything for your wedding?"

"It was heavenly," Tatiana gushes. "Even the grand duke and duchess were in attendance, without exchanging a word, of course."

"Tell me about the desserts," I ask hungrily.

We are meeting in one of the lesser used wardrobe rooms in the basement because I no longer have freedom to wander. I am on duty round the clock, and the Mistress of the Wardrobe's eagle eye misses nothing and no one. I live with over two dozen other women, as well as rows and rows of silk-wrapped dresses. Most of the latter, however, are stored in enormous leather trunks, as are thousands of paper flowers Elizabeth orders to adorn them.

As if reading my thoughts, Tatiana stops discussing gingerbread confections and cakes topped with sparklers and asks kindly, "How are you surviving?" Her glance encompasses the collection of wooden dolls and dummies—the pandoras—used to adjust or model dresses. Strong women haul the largest, draped in ceremonial gowns and robes, all the way to the Imperial Bedroom whenever Her Majesty needs to decide what to wear for part of the day.

"It stinks," I admit. "Literally. The ladies are clean enough, but no one wants to change the chamber pots, so the rooms reek. Not to mention that we sleep three to a bed." I don't add there are nearly a dozen of us in each sleeping chamber, squabbling like crows fighting over a piece of shiny metal. Nor do I burden her with my fear of mice, which day and night scurry around the room and even occasionally over the thin mattresses passing for beds.

"You should leave, Tanya," I suggest, "before you are discovered and get in trouble."

"Or before you do," she says sympathetically, perhaps judging by the pinched look on my face how much the circumstances of my life have deteriorated.

I long to tuck our feet up on the sofa the way we used to do, sip tea and eat candies while contemplating whether or not to play cards. I miss the special card tables with a net in each corner sconce for holding a goblet. Now I don't have enough space to lay the magnifier that I must use for needlework.

"I find it incomprehensible," Mistress Vorahova says to me the very next day, "that they would send me such an incompetent seamstress. You should be working in the kitchens, not with fine silks, brocades, and velvets."

"Yes, Mistress," I murmur meekly, terrified she might indeed find a way to get me transferred to the galleys. "I will improve with practice. You will see."

"Humph." She grunts and wheels around, only to return minutes later with bins of threads to be sorted by color. Apparently, I am now on my way down rather than up the ladder of sewing success.

Anya, an extremely talented albeit seldom recognized seamstress, speaks only broken French and gratefully accepts my language coaching. Should she fail to master the language, she might never advance in the sewing world, since so many of the nobility refuse to speak Russian. With Elizabeth in power, it is less of a problem, but everyone knows without saying it that those days are numbered. The future tsar abhors the Russian language and will undoubtedly insist upon French or, more likely, change the national and court language to German.

As I sort threads and Anya carefully stitches pearls onto caps and bodices, we practice French. When no one is around, however, we chatter in Russian. Anya adores hearing stories about what goes on in the main parts of the palace and within court. She especially enjoys my discussions about jewels, since now I am publicly acknowledged as the wife of Igor Blukhov, jeweler extraordinaire.

I see my husband once a week, on my free afternoon each Tuesday. I am permitted by Mistress Vorahova to stay overnight only when there is no ball or performance, which so far has occurred rarely.

"You look worn," Igor complains as usual. "I thought the entire purpose of keeping you in the palace was out of concern for your health."

"I don't think that was true, darling. I've had time to think—way too much time—and it seems to me Her Majesty merely wanted to make a point. No doctor has even called. I eat the same meat pies and noodles the other women do in the evening, and there is no special treatment or time for rest allotted to me. No one asks, as if I am not pregnant, so I have stopped faking morning sickness or even wearing my pillow when I sleep."

"You must not do that!" he protests worriedly. "If Her Imperial Majesty ever discovers she was duped, who knows what she might do?"

Anya's family are brewers, and she delights in relating various methods of making beer from barley, hops, rye, oats, and wheat. "We sell many flavors, too," she says proudly, and I can always tell she is homesick when she describes how her father infuses brews with honey, juniper, cinnamon, lemon rind, anise, or even St. John's Wort. "Last year my uncle started creating mead by fermenting honey with yeast and then after he brews it, adding nutmeg. Sometimes even cherries or raspberries."

"How did you end up here?"

"When I was a child, my mother worked in another sewing room in the palace. I was tasked with crawling around the rooms and picking up stray pins and sometimes matching up strands of silk thread by size and color. This was hers," she explains, stroking the heavily embroidered sewing box she always carries. I'm one of few needle-women who does not possess her own sewing box of favorite thimbles, needles, and French trimmings. Now I understand why Anya reaches out to hers so often, almost as if for comfort.

"And your mother?"

"The pox. Several years ago."

"So you stayed on here even after your mother died?" My eyes sweep the cutting and pressing tables, as well as the smaller alcoves. These contain candle-lamps with reflectors fastened to them so embroiders can work for twenty-four hours when necessary. "In this place," I add slowly, "where it is rumored that even a misplaced stitch could get us all punished?"

She shrugs, stabs a needle into her pincushion. and snips a thread. "We need the wages. My family is hoping to supply the imperial palace. Until my father can convince Her Majesty's staff of that, we sell only locally. And as much as our people love beer, no one seems able to afford the best ones."

I confess things have not been successful in my own little family lately, either. The nobility routinely act as if an invoice or request for money is rude—as if it is a privilege to work for them. "It is nearly always a year before I get paid," Igor once told me. "If I—or any other merchant or craftsman—gets too demanding, all orders cease."

"Igor sells very little to the imperial family anymore," I confess to Anya. "And many noble families have stopped commissioning jewelry for fear of angering Her Majesty."

"Surely they will buy again. Other women have told us about the jewels he handles. Your husband Monsieur Blukhov has a wonderful reputation."

"He does. And so does his uncle. But Uncle Giuseppe can barely move his hands anymore, and he is far away in Moscow. And until I return to assist, Igor and his apprentices cannot manage even the little bit of repair business they have."

"Someday it will not matter," Anya whispers. "Someday there will be a new empress."

I nod in agreement, and then, as if she has not spoken, we resume conjugating French verbs.

At long last Mistress Vorahova allows me to handle the pearls, while Anya has been promoted to stitching on satin and velvet, at which she immediately excels. Thanks to Igor, I already know a hole bored even a hair off center can ruin a necklace. The sorting, however, requires a keen eye. The pearls must be similar in size, shape, color, and lustre—difficult enough with earrings or necklaces, but even more challenging, I soon realize, when trying to compare tiny ones for bodices and hairpieces.

Finally I have found a way to please the Mistress, who cannot seem to find fault with my ability. On the other hand, my head and eyes ache from countless hours of close work.

This is so unlike other winters, when I accompanied Catherine's court to Oranienbaum, where we spent countless hours sledding. Often the grand duchess ordered grounds men to build the same kind of snow mountain they had in the capital, just for herself and her entourage. It reached perhaps eighty feet high, propped by timbers that also supported a wooden staircase leading to the top. Once we were up there, we flew down on blocks of ice lined with a pad to keep our bottoms from freezing. A hole in the ice block made room for a rope we could grasp, although I occasionally saw people fall off and suffer serious injuries.

Afterward we often rode sledges up another hill to Catherine's dacha, where servants served us fresh black bread and churned butter, as well as a selection of Italian liqueurs. Peter, his Holsteiners, and his opera troupe stayed inside the entire time with their cigars and brandies, so they bothered us little.

In my new role this year it is nearly time to begin preparing for the holidays, and the fine ladies with whom I once shared a life will need new gowns. I vow if I'm ever again permitted to go to court as one of them, I won't take my servants and seamstresses for granted. I berate myself for years of being selfish and blind to the lives of those around me, especially that of my own servant Liza.

My life now is basically that of a servant, although ironically the women I work with are much tidier and even cleaner than some of the nobility, once you ignore the odor of often overfull toilet receptacles beneath the beds. I recall how the same magnificent and bejeweled noblewomen who dance at balls and eat off gold plates seldom wash, possess terrible table manners, chug vodka out of perfume bottles, and could easily while away an afternoon engaged in nothing but swatting flies. Under that painted veneer of Europe's most lavish court also resides a very different world that both fosters and suffers servility.

"At least it's not yet Easter," Anya sighs.

"Why? How could it be worse than Christmas or New Year's celebrations?"

"Because, as you must have forgotten already," she chides gently, "every single lady of the court is commanded to order a special new dress then."

I *had* forgotten, immersed in my certainty of being in my new home with Igor long before that. Already summer has passed, meaning while I no longer sweat in the timber palace, I've lost my weekly opportunities to stroll outside with Igor. Most of the seamstresses have returned from Oranienbaum with the grand duke and duchess or from Peterhof with the empress. Without the cover of leaves, anyone could spot us outside. Instead we sneak meetings in basement rooms, though it is a risk that the domestic quarters will be locked and bolted before my return. "I'm guessing the locks are to keep us all inside," I say bitterly to Igor. "Why in the world would we want to gain entrance *into* this place?"

"Don't make too many waves, my dear," he reminds me. He is right, of course, and having lived beside Catherine for so many years

I should take a lesson from her in patience.

Since I've neither been seen by a physician nor grow any larger, most of the women assume I am no longer pregnant. Unfortunately—or perhaps fortunately—the empress seems to have forgotten my existence.

In early fall I casually remark in front of several ladies how I still feel sad over "losing my darling child."

After that no one mentions the topic. I can only pray word of my presumed miscarriage reaches the empress and she will soon release me. As much as I would like to see and speak with Catherine, on the other hand, no such opportunities present themselves.

When a few more months pass, I decide I've had enough. I feel somewhat guilty, as this is one of our busy seasons. Even Anya has her own project for the grand duchess: a gown embroidered with peacocks, with a matching pattern on the slippers and real peacock feathers for Catherine's hair.

"Suggest that she wear the sapphire necklace," I offer, but Anya is probably too shy to do so. Privately I fear for Anya, as I feel confident that when the empress sees the grand duchess's gown, she will rage with jealousy.

Around me women exist with little sleep. Although some noblewomen employ local seamstresses, others pay for (or at least commit to paying for) the services of the imperial sewing rooms. Many order adjustments that not only give a dress the look of an original design, but hide a variety of physical flaws. All of us stay busy doing everything from removing the bones of bodices and replacing them with a more pliable stiffening to removing or adding ribbons, ruffles, lace frills, fringes, and clusters of paper flowers. These can go a long way in increasing the size of a bosom or decreasing the girth of a posterior, and I learn how to fashion button loops that can be used to expand one's breathing or stomach space. This task reminds me of Catherine, who is still so slim no such subterfuge is necessary. Not yet, anyway.

Since no woman wants anyone else to preview what she will be wearing, individual clients demand a series of smaller rooms. Sequins, seed pearls, shiny beads, and snippets from a rainbow of silk embroidery threads constantly litter the floor. Madame Vorahova and the head embroiderers slip in and out armed with swatches of French silk in large presentation folders.

On New Year's Eve, when the ladies we've labored for finally show off their finery, we seamstresses are permitted to spend the evening outside. Splendid fireworks drop giant bouquets of glittering stars over the Neva River. At times, the sky comes alive with groupings of allegorical and mythological figures, lighting up in consecutive order. I have seen this before, but never in my own time. How is it possible that a lake can appear in the sky, its banks illuminated by moving animals and carriages and orchards of waving trees?

"Someone who works with the pyrotechnicians confessed that he is close to perfecting rockets and stars in the color green," Igor murmurs in my ear. "They say the other imperial courts of Europe would kill for the secret methods we have."

"I don't care," I murmur back, nibbling on his neck.

While Igor and I kiss through most of the grand finale, we also silently come to a decision.

We simply climb into his carriage and go home.

CHAPTER 33

(CATHERINE) 1760-1761

"In Grigory Orlov Catherine found what unconsciously she had always been looking for—a primitive strength, a natural life force sweeping all obstacles aside and taking her by storm. He was not a seducer like Saltykov or a sentimentalist like Poniatowski. He was at once brutal, tender and strong, simple and uncomplicated."
—Joan Haslip

For months Catherine had been writing Johanna in Paris, where her exiled mother had settled after her son lost the Anhalt-Zerbst throne. There Johanna dabbled in alchemy, though not enough to cure her own severe case of dropsy. Catherine sent her packages containing the latest cure-all from the Russian court: Chinese tea and rhubarb.

Nothing worked, however, and in June 1760, Catherine's last link to the past was severed when Princess Johanna died. She left behind nothing except debts to be settled by Catherine and partially by the empress. Although Johanna had never acted as a true mother, Catherine grieved for her.

She did take some comfort when a messenger arrived confirming Johanna had burned all her daughter's correspondence before her death.

Around the same time, Catherine couldn't avoid noticing a military hero who'd drawn a great deal of admiration since his arrival at court the previous year. Lieutenant Grigory Orlov, the handsomest of five brothers, belonged to the elite Izmailovsky Guards. He was only in his twenties and found the thirty-one-year-old Catherine still at the height of her beauty. In many ways, Grigory was the opposite of Stanislaus: a battle-hardened, non-intellectual soldier with a matching physique, as well as an avid gambler, bear hunter, boxer, and womanizer. He was the talk of Petersburg for his bravery, having been wounded three times and now assigned the dull duty of overseeing a Prussian officer who had become a pampered prisoner of war on Peter's orders.

The two did not fall in love immediately, but the grand duchess noticed him at every court event. For his part, he could not take his eyes off her. When they spoke, she did so cautiously. Catherine's experience with Stanislaus had put her in great danger, and with Elizabeth often ill and Peter and his mistress ever watchful, she dared not act on her impulses.

She tried to resist her attraction to Grigory, telling herself she did not need a man in her life. She had an active intellectual agenda, a full schedule of mandated appearances, a bevy of ladies she barely knew who could be counted on for a card game or a garden stroll, and a son she had permission to see more often.

In the meantime, she continued to look out for Peter's interests, still linked by marriage to hers. When he referred to the guard regiments as "chocolate soldiers" lacking in substance and talent, Catherine mentioned to him that someday they might need to depend on those same soldiers.

"At least don't alienate the officers," she pleaded. He agreed reluctantly.

At her insistence, he also started to fake a dozen signs of the cross at mass so he would not offend dignitaries in attendance. "Someday we may need them, as well," she commented, and after giving her a more thoughtful look than usual, he complied.

With Elizabeth's health as unpredictable as her personality, Peter knew his time to rule was close. Although making it widely known he did not intend to do so with Catherine at his side, he at least recognized that danger abounded from other factions. For her part, Catherine firmly disassociated herself from her husband's treasonous love for all things Prussian.

"They say you are more Russian than your Russian husband," Grigory Orlov commented to her as they danced.

"Sadly true," she laughed, at the same time admiring him in the elegant uniform he wore after being appointed aide-de-camp to Peter Shuvalov, Grand Master of Artillery.

"Except," Grigory added, "you are more lovely than any Russian woman I have known."

"You are too much the flatterer, Lieutenant."

"I am serious." He leaned his six-foot frame closer to her ear so that his head touched hers. "You will make a phenomenal empress, as well."

"Whenever that day comes, I hope still to be somewhat young," she replied lightly.

"It may come soon, and I fear then I will be denied the opportunity to look at you from more than a distance. Unless," he continued to whisper, "you would deign to welcome me into your life."

Laughingly she promised to consider this without committing to exactly how she would welcome him.

That summer at Oranienbaum, Peter Shuvalov spent a great deal of time with the Grand Duke, and thus his aide-de-camp accompanied him. Delighted, Catherine took advantage of every opportunity to show Grigory her gardens, go riding with him, and invite him to late night suppers with her own ladies and gentlemen. Here they could talk quietly, often earnestly, since the later the hour the fewer people lingered.

"My brother Alexis and I discuss you often," he said as they shared a bottle of wine after nearly everyone had departed. The oldest Orlov brother was known as the toughest, and although middle aged and tipping the scales with his heftiness, still commanded respect and fear.

"I have only met your brother once, and he seemed very kind, though I have heard of his fierce reputation."

"He is only fierce in war and in all things important to the country we both love."

"We appreciate your sacrifices."

"We are willing to sacrifice much more for Russia," he said, glancing around to note that one chambermaid was asleep near the door and the other had discreetly left to order more wine over thirty minutes ago.

"One hopes your sacrifices are not needed again, and that we will be at peace soon."

"This is not what I mean, Your Imperial Highness. I want you to understand that we are here for you. Not just myself, but my brothers and the guards. You may always count on us."

Under cover of the chambermaid's snoring, Catherine murmured, "I am grateful to know this, although I hope not to have to demand a great sacrifice from all of you."

"It is what we want. Just tell me when the day comes you require assistance, and it will be yours."

This was not about romance, they both knew. It was about the future of the country they both loved.

⌘

Certain she and Peter would never sleep together and that he planned to put her aside for another wife, Catherine nevertheless was gratified he still turned to her when he became worried or upset. He had done so a few times when rumors surfaced about the succession, and when it happened again a few months later, she obeyed his summons.

It was difficult to move anywhere in his apartments, particularly because he was again building a set for a play he'd written about a drunken charlatan who tried to pass himself off as a great and wise man. She finally had to admit that Peter's productions seemed to be the one area in which he exceled. Although often making fun of him, she secretly admired his energy and enthusiasm.

He had recently acquired an entire cast of large wooden puppets from a street troupe, and was making them costumes when she entered.

"*Bravo!*" she clapped, grateful Vorontsova was absent. Peter was tinkering with the puppets' joints and pulleys, making each one scratch its head, twitch its nose, move its cheek, and open its mouth in what appeared to be a belly laugh.

She could tell he was pleased, but as soon as she settled onto the sofa, he left his puppets and sat beside her. "We must do something!" he said urgently.

"What is it?"

"There are rumors. About that baby. You know, Ivan."

Ivan VI, the infant whose rule the Empress had interrupted by kidnapping and locking the child up with its mother in order to assume the throne herself, was certainly no baby anymore. His mother had since died, and the boy, now a man, remained where he had been since childhood: in solitary confinement at the impregnable Schlüsselburg Fortress.

"There are always such rumors, Peter. Yet we know he is a sickly man, both physically and especially mentally. He is incapable of ruling."

"But they would depose my aunt, then me, and set him up as a legitimate tsar even though they would rule for him. Don't you see?"

"Who do you suspect?"

"The Shuvalovs. They do not respect me." He looked as if he would cry.

As was her habit, Catherine spoke to him soothingly yet firmly. "I have told you what we will do if such a calamity strikes. We have friends, Peter."

"Perhaps *you* have friends, wife, but I do not." He jumped up and started his usual pacing, panic reflected in the creased features that sometimes made his face resemble a crumpled napkin.

This was not the first time the issue of an attempted coup had arisen, most recently when rumors had surfaced that Peter Shuvalov had raised a private thirty-thousand-man army to capture the imprisoned Ivan VI and set him up as a puppet ruler.

"We *both* have friends," Catherine reassured him. "And I've explained how we will handle this. The first thing we must do is secure young Paul; as long as we have the legitimate heir with us, no one will be able to challenge our right to reign."

She lowered her voice even more. "You and I both know Ivan Antonevich is feeble, nearly an idiot. Most of the Russian people have forgotten his existence." In fact, as soon as she became empress, Elizabeth had ordered every coin minted with the likeness of the baby melted down.

"They would not be able to convince the people to back him under any circumstances," Catherine added.

There was every reason to believe this, as those guards who had talked reported he was a sorry specimen of a man who, denied both education and companionship (let alone physical contact) for over a decade and a half, lacked the ability to communicate. Another rumor had circulated that the empress herself had secretly observed him from behind a hidden screen to satisfy herself he was not capable of inspiring—let alone instigating—a revolution. Relating such rumors came with extreme risk, since when Elizabeth had seized the throne, she had also issued an imperial ukase forbidding all mention of baby Ivan's name throughout the kingdom. The penalty for defiance was loss of a hand.

There was no question, however, that the scramble for power upon Elizabeth's death had started long ago, and no one knew for certain who would win. Most likely the Shuvalovs might continue to fool Elizabeth with their apparent support for Peter, although Catherine suspected they must have doubts about making the besotted, inexperienced grand duke an emperor.

"Let us review this again," Catherine said patiently. "We will fetch Grand Duke Paul. Simultaneously, my informants who command a small cadre of soldiers will summon the captain of the guard. He will take an oath of loyalty, as will the imperial council and the general. He is not Apraksin, yet I still believe him to be loyal. Before the Shuvalovs or someone else arrives, we will present them with a *fait accompli*."

"A what?" He nervously picked up a puppet and began to stroke its hair.

"We will be on the throne. I also have lieutenants who have sworn to arrest anyone who interferes."

"Where do you get such ideas, and how do you know this could work?"

"An ancient writer named Tacitus, actually."

He stopped pacing and looked at her suspiciously. "Who?"

"Never mind. Just someone very intelligent who wrote about such things. We are going to be fine."

Leaving him to his puppetry, she returned to her rooms and ordered coffee. No matter how often she reviewed their plans with her husband, each time it was as if he could not remember what to do—or doubted her power.

I'm glad he doubts it, she thought. It wouldn't do to have her husband suspect she was on anyone's side except his.

Over the past year, no new threats surfaced. Given that Elizabeth's health could take another turn for the worse anytime, however, Catherine knew she must be observant and ready every day.

Grigory, she thought with some satisfaction. She'd already met all his brothers, and Alexis in particular inspired confidence in her own and her son's safety. The five brothers kept her well informed of court and military matters, often passing her messages kept in secret pockets sewn into their belts or traveling sacks. In this way she learned as soon as the gleeful empress did that Berlin had fallen to the Russian army. She also received secret missives from the Austrian and French ambassadors, who feared Elizabeth might die soon and Peter could take the throne and undo all of Russia's military success.

Other tongues or spies tucked their notes into her chimney or even stove vents; before she had left for a convent, Irina favored windowsills and inside cushions. Catherine smiled, remembering how the jeweler Igor Blukhov used to hide letters in his shoe linings.

She wondered for the dozenth time what had happened to Maria Sergeievna Blukhova since revealing her alleged pregnancy to the empress. Although each had feared a harsh punishment, Catherine had no way to reach her former maid, and Igor no longer plied his art at the palace. One servant told her that Maria had been sent to the laundry rooms and then disappeared one day, but Catherine could not be certain.

Resolving to get answers through Grigory, she also determined to recall the couple as soon as she and Peter held the throne. Fiercely loyal, Catherine never forgot a friend or a favor.

Grigory didn't give up his pursuit of her, albeit discreetly, and at last Catherine admitted she wanted him as much as he apparently did her. They came together just before the holidays, when she once again disguised herself as a soldier and slipped out to his waiting sleigh.

For months every inch of her body had craved him, and now when they were finally in a bedroom together, she did not think she could wait another minute.

Yet Grigory was not Sergei, who was always in a hurry after that first seduction and took his own satisfaction first. Or Stanislaus, who gently let her take the lead. Grigory knew how to torment her, nibbling her neck, then licking and sucking her nipples for so long she thought she'd scream out of need.

At last his large body finally settled over her diminutive one. By this time she was so moist as she strained towards him she feared he would slip right back out.

This was sex the way she had never really experienced before, and she allowed Grigory to explore her body in ways no one had previously. At thirty-one, she was learning at last what she had only suspected: that the sexual act could involve so much more than coupling in the traditional manner.

She excitedly opened her legs to his tongue, arching her back, her whimpers and then groans replaced by cries. When he flipped her over and took her in the manner that she had seen stallions do mares, she found herself laughing aloud with glee.

Despite the fact they were both insatiable in their affair, they carefully doled out their times together to avoid detection. "Katinka," he called her when they were alone, "I promise no one will discover our love. Especially the grand duke. Let him flaunt his mistress. The people must think *you* are their virtuous Imperial Highness."

"I know it well, my love. What about your own brothers? Are they informed?"

He looked at her with that grin that melted her. "That, I'm afraid, would be difficult to hide. Plus, we need their help if we are going to keep our relationship secret."

Somehow this didn't bother her, as she had gained respect and admiration for the five Orlov brothers, continuing to trust them above all.

She had another ally now, one with whom she could share things in which Grigory had no interest. Catherine's newest friend, Princess Catherine Dashkova, perhaps the most loyal admirer she'd ever had, had moved to her father's dacha midway between Peterhof and Oranienbaum with her new husband and two children. Only seventeen, she nevertheless had received a superior education under the tutelage of her uncle. Known for staying up all night studying philosophers and foreign languages, she quickly developed a fierce attachment and loyalty to the grand duchess. Surprisingly, the princess was the younger sister of Peter's mistress, Elizabeth Vorontsova, although the two were exact opposites in appearance and intellect. Predictably, they detested one another.

Sundays after Catherine rode to Peterhof to see her son Paul, she stopped on her way home to visit the princess or invite her to Oranienbaum. In Catherine's apartments or the gardens, they talked all afternoon about politics and books. Not only did the princess idolize Catherine to the point of writing her a laudatory poem, she viewed the grand duchess as a potential "savior of the nation," as she put it bluntly. Catherine, both flattered and enchanted with her young friend, nevertheless sometimes grew nervous at such idealism.

Princess Dashkova not only hated her own vulgar sister, calling her a "concubine," but Peter, as well. "I do not understand how you can tolerate the grand duke," she said one day. Brave, outspoken, and impetuous, the princess never seemed afraid of offending anyone, let alone overstepping her bounds.

"He has his life and I have mine."

"He is an awful man, Your Imperial Highness. I have heard things . . ."

Catherine looked amused. "Such as?"

"Such as the time he court-martialed a rat right in front of you! They say you walked in and discovered him hanging the rat on gallows!"

"It was many years ago."

"Forgive me, Your Imperial Highness, but your husband is a cruel man."

There was really no denying this, although once she and Peter had been allies and playmates. It had been a long time since she had attempted to fool him into thinking they'd been intimate together, and she knew such a deception would never work again. Besides, her husband remained besotted with Elizabeth Vorontsova.

"You don't think he is cruel?" the princess interrupted her reverie.

"He can be, of course. But don't forget your sister loves him. And I think he loves her."

"Love! What do they know about it?" Dashkova then launched into a tirade about love in novels, talking rapidly and incessantly.

Today Catherine was content to listen. She valued her admirer, who cared more about intellectualism than things such as elaborate clothes that occupied most noblewomen. Princess Dashkova dressed simply, refused to rouge her face or powder her hair, and, with the exception of sharing every bit of information she heard with her mistress, did not gossip. But she was also prudish and would've been shocked to learn about her idol's affair.

By now Catherine had learned to compartmentalize her relationships with allies, particularly unexpected ones such as Grand Duke Paul's new tutor, Count Nikita Panin, who had rejoined the court at Elizabeth's behest. Panin greatly disliked his little charge's father but seemed to be fond of the grand duchess. Whenever convenient, he found some pretense to bring Paul outside when Catherine and her ladies were taking air. Although these "accidental" meetings accomplished little in terms of drawing mother and son any closer, Catherine and the brilliant, dedicated Panin often found themselves of similar minds.

Fortunately, there was plenty of time to spend as she liked due to a new architect, Antonio Rinaldi, recently appointed to the grand duke's court and commissioned to build at Oranienbaum. The first thing he oversaw was construction of a miniature but realistic fortress for Peter, complete with bastions and real cannon. Inside stood a small palace made of stone and intended as a barracks for Peter's "troops." Known as Peterstadt, it kept the whole racket well out of

Catherine's sight and hearing.

One afternoon as Paul and his tutor strolled the grounds with Catherine, Panin lowered his voice. "Someday, Your Imperial Highness," he offered secretively, "our little grand duke will rule, but he will need much guidance and a firm hand."

He also admitted more than once that he could easily envision Paul as the tsar and Catherine as regent. As if he were one of the Fates, Panin implied he wanted to cut the thread binding her to Peter's future in favor of Paul's.

Catherine listened, despite the danger. Painfully aware of the need for discretion, she also recognized that Panin genuinely had her son's needs and future in mind—and not just as the son of the unpopular heir to the throne.

Panin admired her levelheaded, sophisticated political mind. Dashkova saw her as an intellectual proponent of the Enlightenment. Grigory knew her as an ambitious but warm-blooded woman. In truth, she was all of those, plus a lot more.

She was also very pregnant.

CHAPTER 34

(MARIA) 1761

On the way to the market with Anya during one of her rare visits, I find myself singing. It is as if I have lived several lives here, including the opulent life of the nobility, the servitude of life under Madame Vorahova, and now a member of the hardworking yet relatively well-off merchant class. In this last incarnation, I'm heady at the chance to stroll Petersburg's already snowy yet still attractive streets without fear of being reported to the empress or to a head seamstress.

I know I'm fortunate to marry for love, as well as to have a husband who does not expect me to perform only the traditional female role. Together we make decisions, work throughout the day and often into the night, relax in our modest home, make occasional visits to clients, find time to socialize, and spend free evenings talking, reading to one another, and making love.

Anya and I wear heavy coats over long wool dresses. The cold also means there is less to purchase this morning, and I will not get to select fresh vegetables or fruits. I do buy two loaves of bread, butter, and enough flour to make pasta and dumplings. The food stalls also boast salted fish, dried meats, frozen joints of meat and fowl, and frosted game. Once frozen, everything seems to stay that way in this climate.

In another section, stallholders hawk everything from second-hand clothes to furs and household goods, all overseen by a pathetic-looking dancing bear. Behind the stalls reside the semi-enclosed archways where shopkeepers grind knives and scissors, bake gingerbread, fashion wigs, trim beards, make gloves, and sell all manner of supplies.

No matter how hard I try, I still cannot figure out the logistics of what passes for a cash register: rows of wire strung with beads that rattle as they are casually shoved about on the wires to calculate a price. I vaguely recall studying these things in grade school and that they are called abacuses but have long since forgotten how to use them.

Sometimes we haggle, with varying results. Today Anya gets a decent price on a new sewing hoop and a pair of gloves.

Noticing how thin she appears, I suggest we duck into a tavern that serves brown bread and warm soups, as well as salads made with all manner of dried vegetables and something that could be mayonnaise. We wash it down with tasteless kvass.

"This is a special treat," Anya claims, rolling her eyes in ecstasy over the borshch. I recall then how we never got to eat hot food during the day in the sewing atelier for fear food odors would be picked up by the fabrics and garments. Even our own clothing had to be kept free of greasy smells, not to mention possible spills.

"I've missed you," I tell her. "How are things at home? Have you seen your father lately?"

"Not good. Papa has not been paid by so many customers he can barely afford to stay in business."

I can sympathize, even empathize. Only recently Igor admitted, "Jeremie Pauzie tells me he's contemplating leaving Russia."

"But Pauzie is the official diamond expert for Her Majesty! And the grand duke considers him the best jeweler in court. I'm sorry, my dear one," I added as he winced. "You know *I* think you're the best, but he seems to have this hold over the imperial family. All except the grand duchess, that is."

He's told me previously how much Pauzie resents his own position, which requires him to be at the empress's beck and call. "Sometimes she sends for me in the middle of the night," he told Igor. "Then she keeps me waiting for hours or simply forgets she summoned me so I go home. And it's not unusual for me to go and get sent for a few hours—and sometimes even minutes—later!"

Igor added, "I know how talented he is, and the empress's whims are just part of what one must endure. But more importantly, all the prestige and commissions do no good whatsoever if you never get paid. And his patrons are the richest and therefore the worst at ignoring their debts. He claims he will return to Geneva soon if he does not get paid by certain imperial clients. Even the grand duke still has not paid him for the jeweled telescope he ordered years ago."

Now I mention this to Anya, who only shakes her head. "This is why it is perhaps best to be poor. What if my father supplied all the beer to the palace? He still would be broke waiting for the money. No," she says, frowning. "At least at the palace I draw a small salary and have a bed and meals."

After we separate, I stop at the apothecary, where elaborately carved gargoyles, cupids, and other mythological beasts decorate wooden shelves that climb in tiers to the ceiling. Each shelf contains an array of bottles, metal cans, stoppers, and glass alembics filled with herbals, potions, and liqueurs. When I ask the plump-faced proprietor for the birth control herbs I use daily, he doesn't blink or indicate he has any idea why such wares should be on the shopping list of Maria Sergei-evna Blukhova, a respected married woman.

"Any news on the empress?" I ask when Igor arrives home earlier than usual. He has just visited one of the Orlov brothers, all of whom have indicated their intent to commission jewelry from him. This afternoon I am attempting to re-glue tiny garnets onto a bracelet. Business has started to pick up, as if no one fears Elizabeth's wrath when she is in this ravaged state.

"No change," he replies, setting down his large leather traveling wallet and tearing off his wig before planting a kiss on my forehead. He leans over to examine my work. "Nice!"

"Thanks. I should be finished tomorrow."

"I don't think her illness is any more serious than last time," he comments, his mind obviously still on the empress. Last year she was not seen in public from late November until nearly this past Easter, even during the six weeks of mourning imposed in memory of His Majesty King George II of England, who died late last year. Somehow all through that illness she managed to arrange for entertainment in her apartments and found time to sit for her portrait in February.

I cannot help recalling old television commercials I once saw—in another life—for a certain battery that allegedly never loses a charge, just as Elizabeth goes on and on regardless of all her illnesses. It is the first time in months I've thought of the future. I am tempted to share my analogy with Igor, though then I would have to find a way to explain batteries.

He looks at me oddly, as if able to read my mind. "Can't you just tell me what is going to happen?"

Startled, I drop one of the garnets on the floor.

"What do you mean?"

"You must have some idea approximately when she will die and when or if Peter will take the throne." He says it casually, not looking at me as he pours tea from the always simmering samovar.

We've been home together for well over a year, during which we've had limited conversations about my "identity." If anyone had asked me this morning if my husband truly believes I come from the future, I would have said, *probably not.*

"I honestly don't know," I answer at last.

He taps his fingers on the kitchen table and takes a sip of the steaming tea, which he drinks from a glass with a brass holder in the traditional Russian manner. "There should be some advantage to being married to a seer."

"I'm not a seer."

"I know that." He smiles ruefully. "It's just what I tell myself to deal with the fact that I'm married to someone who hasn't been born yet."

I lean over to retrieve the garnet before sitting across from him. "I love you," I say softly.

"Why? Because I believe you?" he asks, but I can tell he is joking. "How could I not be in love with an auburn-haired beauty with mesmerizing eyes, delicate hands, a brilliant mind, and skin soft as a baby's?"

"Igor!"

"What did I say wrong?"

I toss a sugar cube at his chest. "I'm far from brilliant, for one thing. And my skin is not all that soft now that I am in my thirties."

"Accept the compliments, my lovely wife. They come from my heart."

He crosses to the door he just entered, and conspicuously locks it.

"*Zakrit!*" he announces. Closed. He takes off his frockcoat and looks at me in that sexy manner that tells me exactly why we are unexpectedly *zakrit.*

An hour later, we are curled up atop our goose-down quilt, the fire stoked higher than usual during the afternoon, although we really do not need it. My nipples stand erect, but not from the cold.

"By the way, your skin is plenty soft," he whispers, cupping my breasts before he starts to nuzzle my neck again.

"Thank you, my dear husband. I like yours, too." It is always such a delight not just to feel each other's bodies and to stroke his smooth, almost coppery-looking chest and arms, but to sense the freedom of getting rid of all the layers of clothing we wear year round. In fall and winter, it takes forever to get undressed, and I luxuriate in bed with my husband, warmed by a flimsy linen shift, the hearth, and Igor's perpetually warm body.

"Are you hungry?" I ask, and when he nods, I throw on a wrap and sneak downstairs to find a hunk of cheddar, cold meat pies, and a half bottle of wine. In the room behind the pantry, I can hear Aunt Gina's loud snores.

We have finished eating in bed and are sipping wine from cups when I cannot resist asking: "You really do believe me? About where I came from?"

"I have no choice. You're not like any other woman I've met in *this* world." He raises his cup in a toast.

"I'm so glad," I respond softly, and my heart seems to fill with more peace than it has since I left the palace and settled into this new and satisfying life with Igor.

"Sometime, my mysterious wife, we will need to talk more about this. I'm particularly interested in inventions of the future." I have told him already what I can, postponing more challenging concepts like electricity and power tools. When I tried to describe airplanes, I'm not at all certain he believed me.

"What do you miss most?" It seems to be his favorite question.

"Air-conditioning," I reply promptly, "only in the summer, that is." Summers in Petersburg, not to mention Moscow, can get muggy, and after being trapped inside the palace with Madame Vorahova throughout those steamy months of 1759, I remember how much I fantasized about cold air blowing on my skin.

"The machines you said magically cool a house?"

"Exactly. I don't mind the cold, you know that, but I do hate hot days wearing a corset, stays, a shift, a dress, a hoop, an overlay, a chemise, stockings, and tons of lace."

"You do look marvelous in all those things."

His next question comes unexpectedly. "Would you go back?"

"Would I go back?" I repeat. "You mean if I could?"

"If you could find the statue." He lights a cigar, which he usually does only when nervous.

"I don't know," I say finally, trying not to cough. "I don't—I don't think . . ."

"Never mind," he squashes the cigar out and stands. "We can talk of these things when we have more time." He winces then, as we both do at the last word.

"But we have—"

"We don't have it now, my love."

"Why not?"

"Did you forget we have been invited to Grigory Orlov's supper? Her Imperial Highness will be there, and it is at her request that we were invited."

I *have* forgotten, primarily because since Uncle Giuseppe died last month, I've been looking after Aunt Gina. When not asleep, she spends hours in the small back room tackling my least favorite task: stitching. No longer does she hobble into the main work room to talk while I work. Nor does she smile—or even eat unless I serve her something.

"I'll look in on my aunt," Igor says, anticipating my response. "You get dressed."

It should take me little time to make myself presentable, except for tightening those wretched whalebone corsets. I select a sea green satin gown that Igor insists matches my eyes perfectly. My hair has grown quite long, and I carefully fix it into a simple chignon and set out my silk stockings.

After slipping into the makeshift tub Igor has created out of a huge barrel, I examine my body carefully. There are definite changes that I assume accompany the aging process, but nothing major. Fortunately, I've escaped any disfiguring illnesses thus far, although I still fear smallpox, not to mention other diseases eradicated in my time.

My belly is still flat and I am definitely not pregnant, thanks, I presume, to my herbal birth control. Yet one never knows. Each month when my period arrives, I imagine I can sense the disappointment in Igor's voice and eyes. He has never made an issue of my desire not to have a child, but I know nothing would make him—not to mention Aunt Gina—happier.

Perhaps I should stop taking the herbs. Perhaps we should have a child, I think now, washing myself with French soap. Last year I thought about it all the time, but lately I have been hesitant due to something I heard when Tatiana visited recently—something that makes me feel guilty at the conversation Igor and I just had.

"You should see the public rooms of the new palace," she gushed. "We all took a tour last month because the grand duke wishes to move in soon. The grand duchess, however, refuses. Yet everything is ready, even the ballroom, or it will be soon."

I recall seeing it during construction, when the huge room was coated with dust and crowded with building materials. Everything up to and including the ceiling had been covered to protect gilded walls, glittering chandeliers, and marble or parquet floors.

"What is left to be done to the ballroom?" I asked, only idly curious.

"Not much, although all the new statues are still wrapped in burlap. They won't be unveiled until the empress gets well."

"Statues?"

"A collection of alabaster and marble gods and goddesses, or so they say. Her Imperial Majesty ordered them sculpted to match the decor, although Monsieur Rastrelli has been having arguments for years with the artists. Of course, he argues with everyone."

I stopped listening to Tatiana, who threw me worried looks until she departed.

No. I cannot risk a pregnancy, not while there is a chance that one of the new sculptures is *my* sculpture: the goddess who could return me to where I belong.

I am not at all certain that the future *is* where I belong, I realize once again, listening with a smile as my precious husband attempts to sing opera in the adjoining room. For some reason I just yearn to have the choice.

Catherine and "Little Catherine," as everyone has started calling Princess Dashkova, arrive together, the princess as lovely without the obligatory rouge and white paint on her youthful face as her sister Elizabeth Vorontsova (*das Fraulein*) is ugly. Immediately she begins chattering like a very intelligent magpie. It is rumored she maintains a personal library of over nine hundred books and has read each. She also has gained somewhat of a reputation for standing up to Peter, who on occasion sticks his tongue out at her.

Beside me, Igor is resplendent in a dark green, tightly fitted knee-length frockcoat with white breeches and high stockings that flaunt his fine male figure. Like most men, at his neck he wears a ruffled lace jabot pinned with an emerald; in keeping with his profession and the style, his shoes sparkle with matching emerald buckles. His long hair is laced with a green ribbon and unpowdered, the way I prefer it.

This is our first invitation to Catherine's inner circle as a couple, although we have each managed to see her separately over the past few months. I can only attribute her boldness in summoning me for such visits to the fact that the empress is no longer aware of court intrigues and events. Throughout summer and now fall rumors persist that she loses consciousness for hours at a time.

Tonight a sleigh pulls us to a modest house on Vasilievsky Island owned by Countess Praskovia Bruce, who has remained friends with Catherine since her arrival in Russia as a girl and now facilitates the assignations between Grigory and Catherine. Even now, their relationship remains a secret, including from most the guests at this intimate gathering.

"Igor, my friend," Grigory pats him on the back and winks as we all head into dinner. "We must talk soon about some new orders when all this war nonsense is over."

"Of course. And I shall show you my collection of opals, which I promise you very much resemble the Northern Lights."

We are seated near Little Catherine, who does not make it to the second course before voicing her opinions about the war and Peter. "He is passing information from the war councils to the enemy; I am certain of this, and I suspect the new English ambassador is his conduit."

"Princess Dashkova." The grand duchess places a warning hand on that of her mentee. "Enough."

"She is correct," Alexis Orlov growls from across the room. "There is no other way the King of Prussia could so often have knowledge of our operations even before Russian field commanders have been told!" Alexis is a formidable figure, his large size and long facial scar from a saber slash only adding to his reputation.

I sense that he, not to mention all the Orlovs, would do anything to stop Peter from taking the throne.

As conversation about the war turns heated, everyone skirts the main issue: that its outcome dangles on the fate of one woman. If the empress's doctors can prolong her life for another year, even six months, Frederick's army will certainly fall. Russia will win the prize of Prussia—but only if Grand Duke Peter is denied his inheritance for a little longer.

Meanwhile, I concentrate on the food, as the tables nearly sag beneath the weight of stewed lamb with saffron, lamb pie, roast goose and swan, chicken livers seasoned with thyme, and lemon grouse stuffed with hazelnuts. Footmen in formal livery serve from trays loaded with smoked pork-belly slices rimmed with grapes and *pirozhki* pies filled with wild mushrooms and cabbage.

Although the grand duchess has always been thin, I notice she polishes off nearly every course. She wears a samara, a loose dress with a pleated back fitted over a corset. An underskirt decorated with the mythical firebird is supported by a hooped pannier, which, despite its width, provides much more comfort and gives every woman a similar figure. Catherine usually delights in showing off her own slimness, although for the past few years Elizabeth also has favored this looser attire, perhaps to disguise her own thick figure. I notice, too, that Catherine's cheeks have a natural rose glow, although her eyes betray weariness. She also is quieter than usual.

When I venture to approach her after supper, she beckons me to sit while others play cards and a small orchestra appears.

"Will you be moving soon into the new palace?" I ask after we exchange pleasantries.

"Not yet," she says, almost evasively.

"I understand it is impressive and sumptuous."

"Quite. I wish the empress would move there now, as she has so many years invested in its design and decor. She and Rastrelli must have met hundreds of times already."

"Yes, it would make her very happy."

"You should return to my court," Catherine says unexpectedly.

"I should?"

"I would be delighted to welcome you back into the position you held previously," she says matter-of-factly, referring to those early years when I served in her court. "Although with more status than you had," she adds.

"But the empress . . ."

Catherine waves a hand, as if dismissing this as immaterial. "She will never know."

Uncertain how to respond, I attempt honesty. "I am quite busy in my husband's shop now, although I am very honored, Your Imperial Highness."

"That is easily remedied. You could have all your weekends free. And other days as you desire. Nor do you have to stay overnight all the time."

"You are very generous, Your Imperial Highness. May I have some time to think about this—and to discuss it with my husband?"

"Igor is welcome back to court as well," she says, smiling, and I am grateful that, unlike the empress, she does not command me to serve her. "Of course, we have official jewelers now, but his work is unique and I prefer to examine it first when I select gems. Is that a possibility?"

"I cannot speak for my husband, of course, but I believe he will be delighted and honored—as long as he can work from his own shop."

"Of course. Do let me know." She turns as Grigory, looking every inch a Roman god, approaches and reaches out his hand to her.

As they move casually and unobtrusively into the billiards room, I marvel at this uneven relationship. Grigory is far beneath the grand duchess in status and rank. He holds no official court position or title except military ones. Yet one only has to look at their faces to read the love there. I am amazed more courtiers and tongues have not noticed and reported it to the empress.

As Catherine has pointed out, however, such things are of minimal interest to a woman everyone believes is on her deathbed.

As weeks progress, it seems as if the entire nation holds its collective breath. Although the empress and grand duchess attend a French comedy together the second week of November, the empress has not been seen in public since. Elizabeth misses even her own name day, not to mention the celebration of her accession to the throne. Surely she must have heard the traditional 101-gun salute across the Neva.

Her Imperial Majesty's fifty-second birthday festivities are canceled on December 18. This strong, confident woman who parties until dawn yet fears nothing so much as the palace shadows is no longer a presence in the opulent setting and court she has fostered. The only noises heard in the halls are the murmur of nervous voices and speculative suppositions, like a background of crickets.

One woman seems to remain calm. Just as an oyster defends itself from the irritating pearl by secreting layer after layer of nacre, Catherine encases her true feelings in a silky crystalline coating of tranquility and beauty. Although the equally lovely and lustrous grand duchess soon will be yanked from her shell-like home, the lining below will emerge in a shimmer of rainbows.

I return to this amazing woman's court a few days per week, and no one protests my presence. There is virtually no chance Elizabeth will know—or care.

Nor will she notice what I have finally figured out: that the outwardly composed Imperial Grand Duchess Catherine is pregnant with Grigory Orlov's child, and this time there will be no way to convince Peter to claim paternity.

The timing could not have been worse.

CHAPTER 35

(CATHERINE) 1761-MARCH 1762

"Her political supporters, ready to mount a coup on her behalf, remained in the shadows, waiting for a signal from her—a signal she dare not give until she had delivered the child and recovered from the birth."
—Carolly Erickson

For months the farce has gone on, necessitating that her personal maid smear Catherine's undergarments with fake menstrual blood every four weeks. Barking dogs and loud manufactured laughter muffled the sound of morning sickness. Just as she had once disguised her breasts to sneak out dressed as a man to meet her lover, now she wrapped her belly just enough to keep her figure looking petite. And every few weeks, overseen by her newly returned maid of honor Maria Sergeievna, a trusted seamstress released a few more stitches from her gowns.

Catherine could not risk discovery. As she sat through interminable gala suppers and theatrical performances, she stifled each yawn. Her desperately needed naps had to be stolen, with Maria standing guard in the antechamber with a ready-made lie about how her mistress allegedly was busy with her toilette or engrossed in an important document.

Fortunately, she had few callers at this time, as courtiers and ambassadors did not know for certain which way to turn. Should they curry favor with Peter, the heir apparent, and risk the empress's displeasure if she recovered per the usual pattern? Should they look toward the obviously more competent Catherine as the future consort of Tsar Peter III or even the future regent of baby Tsar Paul I? Should they lean in the direction of the Shuvalovs and thus stay where the power appeared to be shifting? Or should they be wary of the suspected loyalty of the military and the guardsmen to the Grand Duchess Catherine, a woman perhaps capable of mounting her own coup? Most did not, however, suspect that the latter was a real possibility.

In this atmosphere of uncertainty, court business ceased. Nearly everyone waited in the shadows, unsure who would emerge into the light.

Exceptions came in the form of secret messages from the grand duchess's supporters, who urged her to prepare to act. Only one person dared to sneak into her chambers: Princess Dashkova, who arrived, candle in hand, via the aid of a servant who guided her up the secret staircase one December evening.

Catherine, already almost asleep, did not rise.

"The empress could die at any moment," the princess said urgently. "Have you formed a plan?"

"Thank you, my dearest friend. I am grateful, yet I assure you I have formed no plan and can attempt nothing at the moment."

"Then your friends must act for you!" the princess insisted. "I have enough courage and enthusiasm to arouse them all. Give me orders! Direct me!"

Alarmed, Catherine removed the hand that she had laid across her young friend's heart. "In the name of heaven," she told her, mustering as much calm as possible. "Do nothing. Do not even think about placing yourself in danger. Your misfortunes on my account would subject me to everlasting regret."

An enthusiastic Princess Dashkova nevertheless heeded her mistress, kissed Catherine's hand, and withdrew.

Thankfully, she failed to notice that beneath the covers, the woman she idolized was very, very pregnant.

"There is another note from Count Panin," Maria Sergeievna announced the morning of December 25. It was a brisk cold day, with crushed ice clouds in a palette of grays streaked across an otherwise clear murky sky. Bells clanged from the churches in celebration of what were presumed to be the final two victories over Prussia.

"What does he say?" Catherine was stitching, the needle dipping in and out of the fabric in an almost musical rhythm. It was a skill she had mastered so well she was now begged to embroider ecclesiastical robes.

She and Maria often sewed together, since as Maria admitted, "it's not so bad when it is not your job." The two took turns practicing French knots and a variety of stitches, including satin, stem, fishbone, and fly varieties.

Catherine set down her hoop and luxuriated in being able to yawn without fear of judgement or suspicion.

"Count Panin says to prepare to be summoned to see Her Imperial Majesty. The grand duke has just left her sickbed."

Catherine groaned, then immediately hoisted her thickened body off the divan and yanked a bellpull to summon her maid to help her into a bulky caftan.

"Does Count Panin know what Her Majesty said to my husband?"

"No, but there is another message from Princess Dashkova, who seems to think that the succession has not been altered."

Catherine watched as Maria turned to the stove and dropped both pieces of paper into the fire.

The empress, apparently still lucid, made no comment when Catherine entered the royal stateroom with its massive, canopied bed, no longer moved from place to place each night. Elizabeth's silence did not bode well for the future, and as Catherine contemplated what was to come, she feared the only woman with the power to change it would do nothing to stop the nephew she recognized full well as being incapable of assuming her throne. Less than a year ago, the empress had vowed to "give up half my dresses and diamonds" if that was what it took to defeat Frederick of Prussia. Now she appeared not to care what happened after she departed this world.

Although she attempted to speak with the woman who had brought her here nearly eighteen years ago, Elizabeth merely averted her eyes and turned her head.

It was midafternoon when a nervous Grand Duchess Catherine stepped out of the room while the priest and confessor spoke alone to the empress, took her confession, and administered extreme unction.

Catherine paced, longing for air. It was difficult to grasp that after so many years of intermittent illnesses, the woman she'd tried to please for nearly two decades would soon be gone from this earth—and without the two of them ever truly growing to love one another. She asked herself now what she could have done differently and still remained true to herself? She had tried to please, had tried to stay in her "place," but at times the stakes had seemed too high. What was important now was this nation, and the empress's impending death at this critical time would do nothing to strengthen or stabilize the empire.

That task would have to fall to someone else, and God help us, Catherine thought, if the reign of Russia were turned over to her husband.

She knew she had limited options, even though a stream of messages arrived urging her to take control. She must demur, as the timing was all wrong. Any hope that little Paul would be named tsar and his mother regent waned literally by the minute.

At midday the intricately carved doors opened and the announcement they all had dreaded yet expected was made by the senate's president: "Her Imperial Majesty Elizaveta Petrovna has fallen asleep in the Lord. God preserve our gracious sovereign, Emperor Peter the Third."

Mere hours later, elated by the celebratory cannon fired from the St. Peter and Paul Fortress and the oaths given to him by the guard regiments, Peter hosted a dinner for one hundred and fifty; he ordered everyone to don light-colored clothing rather than mourning black. Catherine, forced to sit beside him, could not fathom how the empress's favorite and lover, Ivan Shuvalov, could have gone from raining tears at the dying empress's bedside only hours ago to joking and toasting as he stood behind Peter.

The following evening the new tsar ordered all the ladies to appear richly dressed for an even more lavish dinner. A tearful Catherine refused, pleading illness, as did "Little Catherine," yet the latter was not so fortunate. Two of Peter's men showed up to force Princess Dashkova to attend, threatening to destroy her husband if she refused.

When the princess belatedly arrived, Peter warned, "The time may come when you will have good reason to repent of any negligence shown your own sister. You have no other way of making yourself of consequence in the world than by seeking her protection." He wrapped an arm sloppily over Elizabeth's plump shoulders.

A seething Princess Dashkova for once remained silent, although later reported everything word for word to Catherine.

While the dead empress was being washed, disemboweled, and embalmed, her nephew—the emperor who had hated her—continued to celebrate. Detesting the idea of wearing black, Peter hosted these parties wearing the full-dress uniform of a Prussian lieutenant general.

Peter III announced repeatedly that the war was over, ordering as many toasts to Frederick of Prussia as to himself. The very night of his accession, he had ordered courtiers to carry messages to field generals commanding they cease all hostilities. All prisoners of war were to be treated with gifts, banquets, and a free pass home.

Catherine cried and worried in her rooms, staying out of sight as much as possible. Only a few were admitted to her chambers, including Princess Dashkova, who kept her updated.

"Our poor troops," she wailed to Catherine. "So many years of suffering and bravery, and now they are reduced to this!"

"What this time?" Catherine asked wearily, trying to ignore the baby's rigorous kicks.

"He has issued order to our soldiers to wear those dreadful Prussian uniforms. My husband says even all drills, formations, and commands must now be changed to Prussian versions."

"They must loathe him."

"They do. He is trying to turn them into his German puppets. Just like the ones he plays with."

Grigory, the one time he was able to sneak in to see her, echoed these sentiments in a much stronger manner. "This is sacrilege!" he yelled so loudly Catherine feared he would be heard.

"I know, my love, but for now—."

"They detest him! This is a travesty. We must act soon!"

It was not easy to calm her lover down, although he, unlike the princess and the entire court, knew exactly why Catherine could not act.

"Hush," she reminded him again.

"But Katushka, even some of our own guards have been replaced with Holstein troops."

"The baby is due very soon, Grigory. Then we shall see."

In the meantime, it was necessary to attend the empress's body, now arrayed in a virginal white gown with an elaborate silver tunic and fine lace sleeves and laid out in the imperial stateroom. Catherine held vigil as much out of responsibility as out of love and genuine grief. Even after all that had been done to her, her feelings toward Elizabeth Petrovna were complex.

Three weeks later, the once proud empress was carried in an open coffin to a darkened state room by a dozen Chevaliers Guards, who laid her on a dais draped in black and gold. Above this perched a giant canopy decorated with ermine and emblazoned with a golden crown with the double-headed eagle. Elizabeth's lifeless fingers grasped a scroll on which a confessor had inscribed the customary commendation of her departed soul to Saint Peter, and beside her body rested a traditional plate of boiled rice and raisins.

It was here for an entire week that people could file past their former empress and express grief and respect while two archimandrites stood at the foot of the coffin reading day and night from the Bible.

Only Peter III was conspicuously absent.

Aided by her accommodating hooped skirts, Catherine spent as much time there as possible. When the body was moved to Kazan

Cathedral, she continued to make the trip back and forth from the palace each day. She kneeled on the stone floor for hours, minus jewelry or a crown, wrapped in heavy black robes and a veil. The crowds who streamed past to bid farewell to their beloved Little Mother—their *matushka*—couldn't avoid taking note of the mysterious figure, and those who recognized her marveled at her apparent devotion and humility.

For ten days Catherine repeated her vigil of obeisance, endangering her own health but capturing the hearts of the people as she paid daily homage to her late empress. Not only did she kneel for hours beside the sarcophagus, at times she would lie prostrate. Despite her advanced pregnancy, she continued to endure the nausea engendered not only by the corpse's smell, but by the unwashed bodies of the mourners, the candle grease, and the cathedral's stuffiness.

No one could miss the contrast: Peter, on rare occasions when he finally showed up, made a mockery of not only his aunt's life, but Orthodox Church customs. In addition to refusing to stand respectfully or kneel at the bier, he paced the cathedral while chattering loudly. He also laughed, cracked jokes, made pathetic attempts to flirt with female worshippers, and even stuck out his tongue at the priests.

In the fifth week Catherine had the odious duty of placing a gold crown inscribed with the words "Most Pious Autocrat" on Elizabeth's swollen skull. She never betrayed the agony of this task, assisted by court jeweler Jeremie Pauzie, who'd had the foresight to insert screws in the band so it would fit and then utilized tweezers to keep it attached. Not even the smoke from six thousand candles or the liberal use of fragrances could mitigate the stench. Only the swinging incense censers of priests in richly embroidered vestments who chanted prayers as they circled the biers somewhat masked it.

The funeral was marked by a long procession from Kazan Cathedral all the way across the Neva River to the Peter and Paul Cathedral, where the empress's father and the cathedral and city's founder, Peter the Great, had become the first tsar buried.

"I don't know how I shall get through this," Catherine complained to Maria that morning.

"Perhaps His Majesty will not show up," Maria half smiled. "After all, lately he seldom leaves his apartments during the day."

"He will be there. He cannot help but want to demonstrate his merriment." For weeks Peter had acted out his joy at escaping the looming shadow of his aunt and the possibility of being cut out of the succession. Giddy as a schoolboy released from his tutor's lessons, he did little except drink and throw parties.

"He has accomplished a few things," Maria offered hesitantly. "Albeit some despicable ones," she added quickly, noting Catherine's frown.

"Indeed. He has recalled everyone Her Majesty ever exiled. Except, that is, for Chancellor Bestuzhev. For my husband this is the end of a nightmare. For me," she added softly, "it is just the beginning of another one."

"Do not despair, Your High—I mean Your Imperial Majesty. This will not last."

"If only I could be certain of that," Catherine murmured.

Maria Sergeievna dared to put a hand on her arm. "Believe it or not, Your Majesty, I *can* be certain of it."

Regardless of Maria's firm optimism, Catherine could not shake her fears. Already Peter had found time to return all of Prussia to Frederick the Great. Rumors reached them that he planned to issue a manifesto exempting the nobility from compulsory military and government service, as well as to issue another decree secularizing all church property. In the case of the latter, he would be moving toward his long-term goal of forcing Protestantism on Russia's venerated Orthodox Church. The only one of his proposed acts she welcomed was the abolishment of Elizabeth's secret police force, the much hated and feared Secret Chancery.

"We must go now," Maria urged her, and Catherine sighed heavily as the two of them, followed by the remainder of Catherine's ladies, moved through the rooms of what remained of the old Winter Palace and out into the icy cold.

The coffin, drawn by eight horses festooned with black ribbons, slowly and solemnly moved from cathedral to cathedral. Peter and Catherine, the new tsar and tsaritsa—now referred to as emperor and empress—walked behind, followed by two Holstein princes and three hundred grenadiers. Whereas a sedate Catherine, clasping a burning taper and wearing a long black robe carried by her maids of honor, was fully aware of the grief of those lining the route, Peter seemed oblivious.

The thirty-three-year-old new emperor shocked the mourning crowds by indulging in grotesque buffoonery. Intentionally lagging behind, he would suddenly stop walking until the hearse was about thirty feet ahead of him. Then, laughing, he dashed to catch up, leaving the twelve elderly men responsible for holding his long mourning train scurrying to stay with him. The sight of the black train flapping wildly like a berserk flag in the wind, not to mention the usually prim and proper old noblemen huffing and puffing in consternation, made Peter snicker even more in delight—so much so that he repeated the prank a number of times.

Crossing herself again and again, Catherine somehow endured the ceremony. Inside the cathedral, she could not keep her eyes off Peter the Great's tomb rather than the elaborate catafalque just erected for his daughter Elizabeth. Nor could she watch without a shudder. How many years before this would be her fate? And how would she herself be remembered? Was there any possibility she would be beloved by the people and able to accomplish even a fraction of the things she hoped to if she could not influence her husband or even reign in her own right?

They were grim thoughts, and she resolutely pushed them aside in a burst of optimism. Somehow, she *would* find a way to overcome the destiny that providence appeared to have meted out thus far.

As if the return of all Prussia's lands to Frederick and the empress's funeral had freed him, Peter at last abandoned his room and initiated some kind of a routine, devoting mornings to hearing reports and visiting a few offices in the palace. At promptly eleven, Catherine could hear him outside conducting a mandatory drilling of all troops and reluctant officers, after which he was said to eat lunch, take a nap, play his violin, and make one of his two daily visits to the new Prussian envoy, Baron von Goltz, whom he adored. Peter would then take an early dinner as a prelude to hosting a late-night party.

On those rare occasions when Catherine was invited, she could barely smother her laughter as her husband strutted around sucking on his ivory-handled pipe and trailed by a servant toting a basket of extra clay pipes and assorted tobaccos. If he were in a particularly good mood, Peter would lead his men outside to play hopscotch in the courtyard.

Unfortunately, hopscotch and pipe smoking gave way each night to brandy and vodka, and into the wee hours Peter and his cronies drank until they were inebriated. It was always toward dawn when he would lose his temper, stomping his foot and issuing irrational and harsh orders and punishments. Even his mistress Elizabeth did not escape his tantrums.

Stung by Peter's behavior and apparent attachment to a new hunchbacked favorite, Elizabeth Vorontsova accused him of everything she could think in foul oaths that came naturally to her tongue. For an hour they hurled insults from one end of the table to another. At last, fed up with her accusations and epithets, Peter stood unsteadily and ordered her home.

The battle of wills did not end there, particularly when a few days later Vorontsova publicly accused her lover of impotence and infertility. Peter sputtered denials, and although this must have rankled, it did end the quarrel. Not once did Peter defend himself by pointing out that after all, Paul was his son. It was an omission lost on no one. Finally, the two made up, and things between him and *das Fraulein* continued as before.

Regardless of the ongoing quarrels with his mistress, Peter celebrated his birthday by bestowing the coveted Order of St. Catherine, usually reserved for empresses and grand duchesses, on Elizabeth Vorontsova. This was not the worst insult: he demanded that his wife pin the ribboned sash onto *das Fraulein's* dress. Catherine bore the offense with dignity, never betraying her loathing and anger as she politely leaned over the squat, shapeless figure with the puffy pocked face.

Although this very public affront won Catherine much sympathy amongst the nobility and the foreign ambassadors, she did not know how much more she could endure.

"When will the coronation be?" was the question now on everyone's lips.

Later that week, Maria Sergeievna asked the same thing.

Catherine managed a faint smile. "He does not believe it is necessary."

"Why not?"

"Because his idol was never crowned."

"The great Frederick II never had a coronation? How strange."

"Indeed. His Imperial Majesty refuses to even discuss the subject."

Maria, carefully polishing one of Catherine's favorite amethyst necklaces, said shyly, "I have heard some very odd rumors."

"Do tell."

"They say His Imperial Majesty has decided all of the courtiers should divorce their spouses and remarry."

Catherine laughed. "And I suppose I will be first on the list." Yet she did not seem visibly upset. "What else have you heard lately?"

"That gentlemen are now permitted to hunt ravens in the city, and that all dogs found in the vicinity of the palace should be shot!"

The latter astounded and upset Catherine in a way that the spouse-trading rumor had not. "I will kill him," she said grimly. "If he harms one hair on any of my dogs, I will shoot him myself."

"Yes, Your Imperial Majesty," Maria murmured.

"Do you know," Catherine said thoughtfully, "that my husband refuses to see our son? He wants nothing to do with him."

"That *is* strange. You would think he might at least want to train the new heir to drill with the troops."

"One might think so. What bothers me most, though, is that he has placed my uncle at the head of the army. Imagine, the man has absolutely zero military experience."

"Did you know him well?"

Catherine frowned. "Quite." She did not add that she had once thought she might marry her young uncle, now Prince Georg Lewis. Thank God she had not done so.

Yes, she had made mistakes. Plenty of them. Now, however, she must tread carefully. It was not easy to ignore the bloating and slight kicks in her belly. She patted it often, silently asking the child within to arrive soon. Before it was too late.

CHAPTER 36

(MARIA) APRIL 1762

I'm exhausted from dashing back and forth between home and the palace. Yet I must be there for Catherine, who is suffering so much and has few options at the hands of that skinny, ugly fool she married. The emperor, I remind myself. Peter the Third. The little man who threatens the future of Russia and the reign of the woman I know is destined to become one of the most powerful and important leaders in world history. This *will* happen, I assure myself, no matter what I do. I dare not interfere, even if I had the ability.

Attempting to share this with Igor is not easy now that Peter rules and Catherine is ignored and disrespected by half the court.

"Are you certain?" he keeps asking, his features wearing the same worried, pinched look I see everywhere. In the city. At the market. At court. In church. It is as if the nation has become collectively ill, with people sharing one another's angst but helpless to do anything about this insidious sickness gripping us.

Already Peter has made good on his promises, not only nationalizing the churches, but secularizing huge tracts of church property. For over a month his troops have marched into the countryside, grabbing farmland owned by the church for centuries. On their vengeful emperor's orders, the military ransacks the homes of priests and high clergy and conducts raids on every chapel, church, and monastery, including the monks' bare cells. Even the nobility's private chapels are confiscated.

No one should have been surprised, as Peter's contempt for the Russian church is widely known. He hates everything about Orthodox Christianity, from its rich vocal music and lengthy liturgy to its panoply of saints and jewel-encrusted icons enshrining their likenesses above dozens of flickering candles.

One night at dinner with her ladies Catherine remarks casually, "I have never known a more perfect atheist in practice than my husband, although His Imperial Majesty often fears both the devil and God. Mostly," she adds, reaching for a plum tart, "he despises them both."

Besides attempting to destroy the Orthodox Church, Peter has done other less serious but more strange things. One of the oddest has been to recall the exiled Sergei Saltykov from Paris. None of us, not even Catherine, knows exactly what transpired when her first lover met with her husband for hours behind closed doors. Yet she does discover that Sergei steadfastly denied the two of them had been lovers, and presumably thus denied that he had fathered the young Grand Duke Paul. Whether he did so out of loyalty or fear for his life, since the punishment under Peter III could have been execution or at least life imprisonment, no one would ever know. The two meet twice more before etiquette demands that Catherine herself receive him.

Catherine confides to none of us what the conversation between them entailed, though I suspect it must have been a tense, awkward meeting.

My one glimpse of Sergei in the corridor reveals how his former good looks have deteriorated, although I assume it is not his sagging skin marred by age lines or his thinning hair that leaves the new Imperial Majesty in a bad mood when he departs. Regardless of any residual feelings between them—and I doubt that any exist—Sergei must now find himself in a position to do her substantial harm. Beneath any surface pleasantries, surely the two of them know that any mention of the blond, brown-eyed Paul would be dangerous. For both of them.

"Saltykov's visit was frightening enough," I observe now, as Igor and I can scarcely avoid hashing over recent events.

"I've heard some other disturbing things," Igor says quietly, even if there is no one to overhear us except Aunt Gina.

"Such as?" I glance up from the belt buckle on which I'm gluing a scattering of diamonds shaped into twin roses.

"Well, he has declared *eternal* peace with Prussia. That's not the most disturbing one: he has visited Schlüsselburg Fortress."

"Truly?" It does seem surprising that Peter would visit the one person he must realize poses the greatest risk to his rule, even more than his wife: the deposed Ivan VI.

"They say he ordered the guards to build the prisoner a house in the courtyard."

"But why? Wouldn't that make it easier for someone to free him?"

"So the boy—man now—can have more air and some room to walk. There has even been talk of releasing him."

"Hmmm." I don't know what to think, as admittedly the once baby emperor has done nothing to deserve his imprisonment. Nothing except getting in the way of Elizabeth's ambitions. Perhaps he deserves his freedom.

"Is he . . . is he *normal*, though?" I emphasize the word, since despite the ban on saying his name, the court ladies always brought up the topic whenever Elizabeth would get sick or seem particularly displeased with Peter. The words they used varied from milder epithets such as *fool* or *idiot* to stronger ones: moron, crazy, lunatic.

"I do not believe so," Igor confirms. "Still, few people alive have seen him over the past twenty or more years."

I shudder at the injustice. It is impossible to imagine being locked up for nearly two decades in one room—and if the rumors are to be believed, with virtually no human contact or diversions.

On the other hand, Catherine has survived a different sort of misery. The last time I saw her, she confided, "I have lived a life for eighteen years from which ten others would have gone crazy and twenty in my place would have died of melancholy." Having shared those years with her, I cannot disagree.

"Will you have time to work on the cameo?" I ask in an attempt to change the subject.

"Absolutely," he grins, both dimples that I love on full display whenever he mentions his beloved project. He has decided the cameo definitely will be a gift for Catherine, now made specially to celebrate the coronation he desperately wants to believe will occur.

His eyes sparkle as he moves to his workbench, where he carefully sets up his tools. He has carved several practice cameos that have sold, but this will be his masterpiece.

Secretly we refer to it as the Catherine the Great cameo, this miniature oval portrait executed on a Colombian emerald that demands all of Igor's highly refined artistic skills. The cameo is two-layered, with the emerald surrounded by onyx and set in a gold framework. "I will surround it with brilliants," he muses now, using the current term for diamonds. "Do you think one layer or two?"

"Definitely two," I insist, knowing how much this will cost. Just one layer will require approximately fifty tiny cushion-shaped or round diamonds, but this is a piece I know will delight the empress. And with Elizabeth's influence now a moot point, business has been excellent for us. Not only have we been able to hire another apprentice named George, Igor has made an offer to purchase two rooms adjoining the shop so we will have more living and more working space.

"I want to surround the cameo with waves of gold so that it resembles an eight-petaled flower," he adds now, and I murmur approval.

We will spend the night working on our individual projects, occasionally stopping to share a meal or wine. Often Aunt Gina makes her way into the workshop with her embroidery or a basket of dried fruits to sort through. It is Easter week, almost the end of Lent, and soon we will both be busy decorating eggs and making the traditional Easter breads and cakes.

The room is illuminated by extra candle-filled sconces so we can work late, and sometimes I look up to feast my eyes on my husband. With his dark locks tied back with string, Igor's features glow in the golden candlelight. He is a man who only gets more handsome with age. I hope he thinks the same of me.

It is indeed a good life, I realize particularly on nights like these. I cannot wait to turn in and cuddle together in our featherbed, where we never tire of making love and whispering about our day to one another as the banked fire burns lower and lower.

A few hours later, however, a messenger bangs on the door. Igor returns to tell me I am needed urgently at the palace. We also have a full-time coach and groomsman now, who sleepily emerges in the entryway to fetch me. Wrapped in a loose gray gown and felt boots, I hastily climb into the carriage, knowing exactly what might be demanded of me tonight. The night when Catherine must bear her secret child.

Labor pains are well under way when I arrive, and Catherine appears wan but determined. As much as she might want to keep Grigory's child and even raise it herself this time, there is no question of what she must do. Both her life and a kingdom depend on the covertness of this event. Already it is amazing neither Peter nor his ministers suspect, even after all these months during which her shape has ballooned from petiteness to something that beneath her loose caftans resembles an overgrown mango. And after so many weeks of claiming the new empress has a sprained ankle, we all concede that she cannot fool anyone much longer.

I am here solely as moral support. It is Countess Bruce, the midwife, and one of Catherine's trusted servants who hold the future of the kingdom—Catherine's life—in their hands.

Fortunately, all goes well, and the wife of the emperor grasps my hand throughout. She does not cry out.

It is still early in the evening by court standards, and I share the responsibility of watching the halls for any sign of the emperor. It would be unlikely for Peter to make an appearance, although if one of his men were to get suspicious, all would be lost. There is no way he would acknowledge this child as his own, and Catherine would certainly be sent away, locked up, or even executed for treason.

With the stakes that high, none of us relaxes until a little cry announces the arrival of a baby boy.

Anticipating the need for a diversion tonight, Catherine's servant Shkurin has created it by sacrificing his own home. Since it is well-known that Peter has a passion for pyrotechnics and never misses a local fire, Shkurin's house has conveniently caught fire soon after the labor pains began.

Receiving word Peter and his entourage have indeed departed for the fire, Catherine looks up with the first genuine smile I've seen in months. "Let me hold him."

Never before has she held one of her own babies, and it nearly breaks my heart to see her five minutes later reluctantly hand him to the countess. "He shall be christened Alexei Grigorevich," Catherine announces firmly, and then, as if transformed from mother to empress in a matter of minutes, she sits up.

"Go in peace and safety, my love," she whispers to the baby.

There is precious time to waste. While Moscow fires might consume entire city blocks of wooden buildings and evolve into a long-lasting conflagration, most of Petersburg has been constructed of stone and brick. Peter will return soon.

An hour after the clandestine delivery, baby Alexei is wrapped in a beaver skin and spirited away by Countess Bruce to the family who will raise him. Henceforth he will be known as Alexei Grigorevich Bobrinksy.

Peter does not stop by Catherine's apartments after the fire; just in case he does, his wife has herself gowned, coiffed, and powdered. If anyone were to visit, all suspicions would be allayed.

This is not only an end, but the beginning she has awaited, and all in attendance are keenly aware of that. We exchange smiles, I kiss her hand, and before dawn I am home again with Igor.

We have been invited to a party at the new Winter Palace to celebrate Catherine's thirty-third birthday, although Igor is reluctant to attend.

"The less we are seen right now, the safer it is," he warns.

"You may be right," I respond reluctantly, "though I really want to be there. It could happen any day now, and we should be close in case she needs us."

"The Orlov brothers will be on call."

"But what if they cannot get to her and something happens?" I protest.

"My darling," Igor says gently but firmly, "this is exactly what you told me can never happen."

"What?" I am enjoying witnessing the always fascinating ritual of Igor trying to get his wig on straight.

"You told me you may never interfere with events. With *history*." He still says the last word with a sense of surprise.

"I'm not planning to *do* anything. Just be there in case she needs something. Perhaps a message delivered." I reach over and tuck a few brown curls under his wig. "After all, if I were not here, *someone* must have helped her. Or will help her."

He sighs, fastening an amethyst stick pin to his lace jabot and then leaning over to adjust the matching knee buckles. Tonight we have decided to dress in honor of Catherine's love for amethyst, as well as to advertise the shop's wares by donning jewelry and decorations we have made. For me, this means a parure of green and purple: a matching necklace, earrings, bracelet, brooch, and ring all fashioned from peridot and amethyst and designed by Igor to resemble clusters of green-leafed violets.

"We will be there, my love," he assures me, reaching over to attach a tiny black crescent beauty mark near my lips. "I just want you to be safe, and I worry your association with Her Imperial Majesty could put you in danger."

"I will be fine. Now tell me, how do I look?" I spin around, wishing for a full-length mirror so that I can see myself in a lavender gown embroidered with violets and a bodice sprinkled with bits of green and purple gems. Aunt Gina has managed to stitch the entire gown, and that afternoon Anya sneaked over with the fan-shaped headdress I secretly hired her to make. Aunt Gina now fastens it to the back of my lightly powdered hair, where I cannot see the tiny amethysts and diamonds with which Aunt Gina herself adorned it even though her eyesight is failing. The other ladies at court will drool with envy.

As we prepare to leave, Aunt Gina proclaims me *"Bellisima*!" I hug her carefully. Standing before us with her silvery hair hanging loose almost to her waist rather than in its usual bun, she resembles an angel. *Don't go to the other angels just yet*, I pray silently. *I have already lost one aunt, an uncle, and two parents.*

"You should be asleep," Igor chides his aunt. "You have worked way too many days to transform my already lovely wife into the woman who will surely outshine every other female at court."

"*Si, si.*" Then, smoothly switching to Russian, she cautions, "Don't dance too close to any of the gentlemen. You'll cover the ballroom with gemstones if they crush you."

"And you assume I would permit her to dance with anyone except me, Aunt Gina? Never."

We depart somewhat reluctantly from this woman I've grown to love. Yet I'm eager to get there: to our first ball at the new Winter Palace, not to mention our first of the new reign.

The building that will someday be known as the Hermitage is freshly painted in the golden hue of spun straw, and I wonder idly when it will become the pistachio hue of the future. Inside, I try to be unobtrusive as we stroll past each of the new statues. For his sake, I would rather Igor not realize how keenly I've awaited this moment.

None of the marble women resembles "my" goddess, and I shrug, concentrating instead on what is going on around me. Somehow it no longer matters that I am living two and a half centuries in the past.

This is where I belong, and this is the life I love.

One of the courtiers stands on an elegant chair to read aloud birthday congratulations, including a letter from the new King George III of England that delights Catherine.

A palpable sense of relief engendered by the conspicuous absence of the new emperor seems to pervade the sparkling atmosphere. However, the only thing those of us standing nearby will remember is what Her Majesty says when she cordially receives the Austrian ambassador, Count Mercy.

"Your Imperial Majesty," the count bows deeply. "Thank you for receiving me in this time of difficulty between our two nations."

"I assure you, Count, that my goodwill toward your country remains unchanged."

The count, whose nation, as a former ally, fears nothing so much as a Prussian-Russian alliance against Austria, kisses her hand. Almost casually she adds, "You know, I, too, detest the new treaty with our mutual sworn enemy, Prussia."

She says it lightly and not too loudly, yet I catch myself from gasping.

Those of us who heard her words know that the die has been cast. The new empress not only has criticized her husband's proudest military accomplishment publicly but pronounced Frederick the Great—the man with whom she once shared dinner in Berlin and chatted with about literature as a fourteen-year-old Prussian princess—her enemy rather than Russia's new ally.

In the circle of diplomats around her, the comment is met not with the shock of hearing what could amount to treason, but the silence of approval. Very few civil or military officials support the treaty with Prussia after so many Russian lives have been sacrificed, and almost unanimously they find the rumors that Peter plans a new war with Denmark abhorrent. The tsar has ordered the minting of over two million more rubles to finance this war to recover an insignificant portion of his beloved Holstein, and it is common knowledge that the national deficit now stands at well over one million more. Virtually no one can countenance the strain of yet another costly war for such a non-specific cause.

With less need for restraint, the British ambassador is heard to comment from across the room later, "Even his advisors are throwing pitchforks into the fire to stop His Imperial Majesty Peter III from doing this thing."

Catherine surely hears him, too, and evidently it is a complaint she has heard expressed before. Had I not been watching her closely, I would have missed it: the bluish-violet eyes blinking once at him. Then, as if the sun has briefly peeped out from behind a cloud, she also sends her beguiling smile in the ambassador's direction.

The fight, I realize, has officially begun. I cannot wait to watch it play out—and to be part of it.

CHAPTER 37

(CATHERINE) APRIL-JUNE 1762

"The whole country was seething with discontent, and the poor, mad emperor was every day adding another nail to his coffin."
—Joan Haslip

"He allowed himself to be dethroned like a child getting sent to bed."
—Frederick the Great

For the hundreds of Russian subjects invited to the newly constructed imperial residence for another celebration of peace with Prussia, it meant an endless evening at banquet tables weighted down with over a hundred dishes and an equal number of liqueurs and wines. They did not suspect as they sat in prearranged seats that this capitulation presided over by a Russian emperor dressed in a Prussian blue uniform and wearing the Prussian Order of the Black Eagle around his neck—this humiliation of their nation—was soon to extend even more publicly to their beloved new empress.

Before they began, Peter drained his silver goblet in honor of Frederick of Prussia and the new Prussian envoy Baron von Goltz, the latter, along with Chancellor Vorontsov and the Prussian ambassador, seated with him. At the opposite end of the hall, Catherine sat with her face frozen. The faces around her, too, stayed stiff with the effort to smile, the lifting of glasses tentative and forced. Nor could she hear well, although it seemed as if Peter also raised his glass to the woman beside him: *das Fraulein* or Elizabeth Vorontsova: Catherine's replacement, if Peter had his way.

She sensed looks in her direction as His Majesty prepared to make the first of three official toasts. "To the health of the Imperial Family!" he bellowed, pausing delightedly to hear cannon fire a salvo.

While everyone except her and Peter eased chairs back and rose with glasses in hand, Catherine sat quietly and sipped, wearing that winning smile so beloved by her subjects.

In the sudden silence that descended, she dared glance down the table, where she could read Peter's lips. "Why is she not standing?" he demanded, eyes bulging with anger.

Moments later, a visibly shaken Peter sent his adjutant, General Godovich, down the table to inquire as to why Catherine had not risen.

"Please advise Your Imperial Majesty," she replied coolly but loudly, "that I—and his son the Grand Duke Paul—*are* part of the royal family. Naturally I remained seated."

As her hands shook, she folded them out of sight in her lap.

This back-and-forth exchange continued a few more minutes, with the general struggling to repeat exactly each of their full responses as he shuffled up and down the hall.

"His Majesty," he told Catherine, "says Her Majesty is a fool and that she should have recognized that the emperor's two uncles are members of the royal family, as well."

Before Catherine could reply, not to mention remind him that the recently appointed military leaders were Prussian and not Russian— and actually *her* uncles rather than his—a harsh voice reverberated through the silence.

"*Dura*! Fool!"

It took a few seconds to register that now Peter was screaming insults directly at her.

"Idiot!" he could be heard muttering, and even at this distance she could see his face flaming redder than usual.

This was too much. She could handle no more. Yet she would not depart the banquet; she remained teary-eyed but firmly seated in the shocked silence.

Determined to hide her anger, not to mention fear, she sought respite from her humiliation by turning toward Count Stroganov, in attendance behind her chair. "Do you have any funny stories to relate today?" she asked bravely.

Taking her lead, the guests settled back to their next course, and the loud buzzing of voices refilled the room.

For most guests, this incident was clearly a throwing down of the gauntlet, and they waited in curiosity and trepidation to see what would happen next.

As Catherine feigned interest in one of the count's anecdotes, she could feel herself trembling. What, if anything, could she do if her husband ordered the guards to seize her?

Until today, it had been mainly petty insults and punishments, such as Peter canceling some of her jewelry orders and forbidding gardeners to deliver her favorite fruits.

The kingdom, too, faced new threats. The Khan of the Crimea had launched an invasion at the Russian frontier. Peter, however, paid no attention to this. He had continued to stress his intention of launching a military campaign against Denmark to preserve the integrity of his beloved Holstein lands. "I shall lead it myself!" he announced in German, warning the military they must wear German uniforms and follow a German commander.

The banquet insult was different. And venomous. She realized with no uncertainty that it was almost time: time to act, not to be locked away.

A few days later she learned her drunken husband had gone so far as to order her arrest after the banquet that night, dissuaded only by her own Uncle Georg. For now.

The threat of arrest was no secret at court, and Her Imperial Majesty did not sleep soundly.

At the start of summer, the sun glowed tangerine and cherry long after midnight. Its tints reflected on the Neva's waters visible from the new three-story Winter Palace's myriad windows for four hundred sixty rooms. It also glittered on the one hundred seventy-six mythological statues stretched end to end across the rooftop balustrade. In June Catherine left her son here in the care of Count Nikita Panin, who has remained deeply invested in a bright imperial future for the boy. Peter had ordered her to Peterhof while he and Vorontsova and their retinue went to Oranienbaum. He made no secret, however, of his intention to return to the city soon before leading his troops into battle.

It was in this atmosphere that the need to act reached the pinnacle of necessity, and at last Catherine began a series of secret meetings with the goal of accomplishing a successful *coup d'état*. The conspirators, most with different motives and even objectives, separately began to water the seeds of discontent that hopefully would take root and blossom into a fresh new reign. If some rumors were false, at least most of them were true.

On June 19, Catherine endured watching her husband play violin in a court opera at Oranienbaum before gratefully heading through the opalescent perpetual daylight back to Peterhof.

A week later, husband and wife, tsar and consort, met at a dinner hosted by Count Alexei Razumovsky. The two barely spoke to one another, and each time she saw Peter and the despicable *das Fraulein*, she wondered if it might be the last—and prayed it would.

The following day, with Catherine happily avoiding her husband by staying at Peterhof, Grigory Orlov received a message that one Captain Passek had been arrested for making "treasonable speeches." It was clear to Catherine's supporters that all plans must be activated immediately before the inevitable arrests that could follow as soon as the next day.

Catherine rested at Mon Plaisir, a small red brick villa on Peterhof's grounds. It wasn't so noisy at night when the fountains that cascaded down from the Grand Palace all day were shut off. She felt safe a mere hundred yards from the Gulf of Finland, with its secluded landing beach for secret messengers.

Her husband was expected at Peterhof soon to check out the preparations she was supposed to be making for his and Paul's name day celebration, and she'd fallen asleep dreading the inevitable confrontation.

She was drowsing peacefully just before dawn on June 28 when Alexis Orlov, accompanied by his lieutenant, arrived unexpectedly at her bedchamber.

"*Matushka*," he whispered.

"What is it?" she demanded, instantly awake.

"It is time, Your Imperial Majesty," Orlov assured her. "All is ready to proclaim you Empress of all the Russias."

Catherine grabbed her gown and rose wordlessly.

Because officially she was still in mourning for the empress, her women dressed her in simple black. With Alexis impatiently pacing just outside the chamber and whispering loudly for her to hurry, the women had no time to bind her hair or powder her face.

As she emerged, he rapidly explained they had to act earlier than planned because one of their own key spies has been arrested.

"Then we must in fact go with haste," she agreed. Still wearing house slippers and a lace night cap, she climbed into a rickety hired carriage accompanied by one maid and a servant, thus ensuring no one could ferret her location out of them.

Through endless daylight, the driver whipped the horses to breakneck speed. Alexis perched atop the box beside him, waving a pistol in each hand. They were racing to secure the capital, and regardless of what the outcome might be, Catherine felt exhilarated. The original plan to arrest Peter first, so carefully planned and coordinated, had been thwarted by circumstances. That did not mean all was lost.

She should have as many doubts as there were ruts and stones in the road; instead, she longed to jump out of the carriage and gallop on horseback to seize Petersburg on her own. After all, she now had only two choices: courage or cowardice. And she had never been one to follow the latter path.

In the thickly floral-scented dawn, the sun was high in the sky, which had evolved from frosted gray to pearl, its clouds hemmed with pink. Catherine barely noticed as her thoughts whirled at the possibilities for the day. Even with a stiff breeze from the Gulf and the speed of the carriage, she was too warm and flushed with excitement for a cloak.

When the horses, overworked from galloping to and from Peterhof at such a pace, began to falter, the driver ordered a halt. It was then that a peasant cart pulled by two farm horses fortuitously ambled by. After much argument won over at last by a hefty weight of coins, Alexis commandeered the fresh farm horses, resuming their race to secure Petersburg.

Encountering yet another equipage traveling in the opposite direction, Alexis Orlov recognized Catherine's French hairdresser, summoned to dress her hair for the planned event at Peterhof that day. Orlov, never one to miss an opportunity to orchestrate a show, insisted they do it now, disregarding momentarily the necessity for speed.

Catherine waved him off. "Later!" she dismissed the idea, and Alexis did not protest.

No matter the pace, the remainder of the journey proceeded too slowly for Catherine and Alexis, although at last they lurched to a stop. In full dress uniform, Grigory awaited: her love, her light, her champion. Laughter bubbled up as she and the two Orlov brothers climbed into a newer coach and the horses galloped straight for the Izmailovsky Guards' regimental barracks.

Alighting in the courtyard, they were met by a sleepy drummer boy and a host of half-awake soldiers, who'd either not expected anything like this to happen or had anticipated it days later.

Grigory immediately called the men to arms, and as Catherine descended behind him, a great cry arose from the guards: "Little Mother, *Matushka*!" they called out for her before swarming to take turns kissing her skirt, her hands, even her feet.

She did not need to present her cause, but did so after additional soldiers swelled the ranks, some still fastening on sword belts and all smiling broadly.

Her voice rang out steadily across the compound. "I am compelled to throw myself upon your protection. My life and that of the Grand Duke Paul have been threatened by Emperor Peter III, and I ask for your protection not for our sakes alone, but for the good of our beloved nation and our holy Church." It was a slight exaggeration, but no one who had lived in Russia for the past several months could doubt it.

More cheers and the sound of drums greeted this plea, and the regimental commander came forward to kiss her hand. Seconds later, the regimental chaplain stepped up carrying a cross. "We must take an oath of allegiance to our dear Catherine the Second, Empress of all the Russias!" he declared, and more cheering and chanting of "Matushka" erupted.

She knew she must press on to have this auspicious beginning sanctioned by the church and the people. Exhilarated and buoyed up by the chanting, cheering, and yelling behind her, she and the Orlovs climbed back into the carriage. Soldiers formed a procession behind.

The group moved just as quickly to the next regimental headquarters, where the Semyonovsky Guards, joined by some from the neighboring Preobrazhensky unit, provided even more enthusiastic supporters. Before joining the procession, most tore off and then trampled their new Prussian blue uniforms as they raced to their quarters to redress in Russian bottle green.

"The city is alive!" she yelled to Grigory over the noise, as he urged the driver to even greater speed. Indeed, as they entered Petersburg, the streets seemed to swell as if by magic to accommodate thousands of horse guards, priests, disbanded imperial bodyguards, soldiers, and citizens.

"Look who is leading them!" Grigory pointed to Father Alexei, visible at the front of the crowd beneath the tall silver cross he hoisted over his head.

Word soon arrived that the entire government had capitulated with barely a whimper of defiance, and it took just minutes to reach the heart of the city where the regiments ahead of them were hastening to secure the palace.

"The senators have incarcerated themselves inside to await the outcome," Grigory explained after a messenger galloped back to them, "although I daresay they will join us within minutes."

He was right. Three hours after leaving Peterhof, Catherine found herself inside the magnificent thirty-year-old Cathedral of Our Lady of Kazan, where a lifetime ago she and Peter had married, and where only months ago Empress Elizabeth Petrovna Romanov had lain in state. Now, standing beside the two Orlovs and Colonel Cyril Razumovsky, she barely noticed the stunning iconostasis as the Archbishop of Novgorod blessed her and proclaimed her *Gosudarina*, or Sovereign Autocrat of All the Russias. Grand Duke Paul Petrovich was named heir.

Emerging from the cathedral's incense-filled darkness, the newly appointed empress was greeted by deliriously joyful crowds. For most, the past few months had seemed like a nightmare of capricious rule from which they had awakened happily, and it was difficult to determine what was louder: the cheers of the Russian people or the ceaseless tolling of the city's church bells.

Catherine alternated between striding up Nevsky Prospekt on foot and riding in a two-seater with Grigory on the running board, as masses of supporters shouted her name.

They met only one pocket of resistance when several officers of the Preobrazhensky Regiment, the elite guard established by Peter the Great and now replaced by a Holstein unit, seemed dubious. Many of their fellow guardsmen quickly and bloodlessly subdued them before belatedly joining the march. "We've arrested the dissenters among us and apologize for having joined the procession late," a spokesman yelled passionately. "We wish the same thing for our country as the others here."

Catherine nodded and smiled gracefully. If ever she'd doubted her ability to rally her people, she did not now. The entire city, it seemed, was in a frenzy of joy.

Meanwhile, the archbishop circulated in the crowds, administering the oath of loyalty. One of the men still beside her, Colonel Razumovsky of the Izmailovsky Guards, also served as president of the Academy of Arts and Sciences and had been an early loyal supporter and co-conspirator. He had mobilized the academy's printing press in preparation for this moment, and copies of a freshly printed manifesto announcing and justifying Catherine II's assumption of the throne rapidly passed hand to hand.

They reached the Winter Palace by ten a.m., and Catherine strode inside to meet her destiny. Grand Duke Paul, who had been under protective guard while asleep, was hastily brought to his mother and while he was yet in his nightclothes, the two of them made a balcony appearance to deliriously happy crowds below.

Throughout the day, the new autocrat and Imperial Majesty never stopped scribbling orders, receiving reports, ordering arrests, and administering oaths to officials as she secured her throne. There was neither time to sleep nor to eat. Nor was there time to argue with Panin, who appeared quieter than usual. Even after being neatly outwitted in his plan to establish Catherine only as a regent for Grand Duke Paul, he reluctantly accepted this new direction.

There was time, however, for the empress to review over fourteen thousand troops. Proudly attired in the green and red gold-braided uniform and wearing tall black jackboots and a sable-trimmed black tricorne symbolically adorned with oak leaves, she presented herself to be proclaimed colonel of the Preobrazhensky Guard. Princess Dashkova borrowed Nikita Panin's ribbon of the order of St. Andrew (typically awarded only to males) and pinned it onto Catherine's unform.

The newly anointed empress then rode in a wide circle around the troops, historically signaling her intent to assume command.

Despite the late hour, the evening maintained total daylight. Although no rumors or news of a counterattack arrived, Catherine nevertheless was anxious to do something to ensure continuation of the control she now had of the military and of the government.

Shortly thereafter, she flung herself back into the saddle of her dappled gray stallion, Brilliant. With a dig into the stallion's withers, she galloped off to arrest her deposed husband.

Princess Dashkova, attired in another borrowed uniform, rode at her side, and together they assumed control of the rear guard.

In front of and behind the newly proclaimed empress, the ebullient soldiers marching with her could almost envision her as a living incarnation of the goddess of victory. For her and for Russia, they were prepared to die. Yet almost to a man, they were confident of victory.

Just before exiting the city, they were met by a bold Chancellor Vorontsov, who attempted to talk the newly anointed empress out of her coup. It took him only a minute, however, to realize Peter's cause was a lost one, and unhampered by arrest, he refused to take the oath of loyalty and went home to stay. Although Count Alexander Shuvalov and others also tried briefly to rally some resisters, their opposition abruptly failed.

The army, one of three detachments on the road following the

Gulf of Finland toward Peterhof and Oranienbaum, continued on its way with no great need for urgency.

By two a.m., the entire troop halted for a rest at a cheap hostelry at Krasni-Kabachek. Here they would await the latest reports on the deposed emperor's movements, as well as build campfires, feed and water the horses, and bivouac in the surrounding fields.

Forced to share a bed at the little inn with Princess Dashkova, Catherine lay down without removing any of her clothing. Unable to sleep, however, she sat back up, ordered candles, and began to draw up more manifestoes in preparation for resumption of the march at 5 a.m.

At last news from the advance guard reached them. Peter had arrived as scheduled the previous day at Peterhof with Elizabeth Vorontsova and a group of partygoers prepared to celebrate his Name Day.

"Tell me exactly what he did and said," Catherine demanded.

The story, which would have made the new empress laugh if it were not so pitiful, was that Peter and a retinue consisting of *das Fraulein* and sixteen maids of honor had dawdled on their way from Oranienbaum. Pausing for games and picnics, they didn't arrive until long after noon. Finding zero preparations for his party underway and frightened servants knowing nothing, he'd sought out his wife at Mon Plaisir. Initially he'd treated Catherine's absence as if it were a grand game of Hide and Seek; he poked around in every closet, wardrobe, and chamber, even crawling on his hands and knees to look under beds. Pouting like a spoiled child, he then ordered lunch served beneath the larch trees. As the afternoon progressed, he peacefully downed several glasses of wine and vodka.

"His Majesty—I mean his former Majesty—did send off a number of couriers to inquire," another messenger confirmed.

"And does he not know that he is no longer emperor?"

"He does realize that now, Your Imperial Majesty. Most of his couriers never returned, but the few who did reported roads into the city blocked."

"He wasted precious time," Catherine mused. "He had hundreds of his Holstein troops at Oranienbaum."

Peter had vacillated until his messengers could get him to believe what was happening. By the time he had counselors to advise him, he had become too hysterical to know which advice to take. Persuaded that evening to seek refuge at the island fortress of Kronstadt, home of the Russian fleet, he'd insisted that his mistress and an entourage of fifty accompany him. He had refused to embark without his kitchen equipment, a large supply of liquor, and excess baggage—the latter crammed into a small yacht. On board, he sipped brandy all the way until they arrived at 1 a.m.

"They say," Princess Dashkova was only too happy to relate the news from yet another messenger, "that the former emperor hid in the ship's hold clinging to his mistress all the way there and slept in her lap all the way back."

Thankfully, Catherine had had the foresight the previous day to appoint a new commandant at Kronstadt and to authorize him to secure all naval units. When Peter had climbed unsteadily into a very small boat and had himself rowed within yelling distance, he expected a welcome. Hailing the watchman, he commanded him to open the locked harbor chains.

The unexpected reply floated loudly back across the water: "There is no emperor—only an empress."

Peter had been turned away before his ship could land. Disregarding advice, he then refused to flee to Finland or to regroup, insisting that the captain of the ship return to Oranienbaum so Peter could open negotiations with his wife.

"And where is he now?" Catherine asked sharply.

The consensus was that he was in custody of Alexis Orlov, whose troops had secured both Peterhof and Oranienbaum.

After stopping to arrest some of Peter's Hussars and to welcome others who had deserted, Empress Catherine received a letter containing a pathetic apology from her husband, as well as a request for reconciliation.

"Does he still not realize this is no mere marital spat?" she wondered to Princess Dashkova.

"He is not, Your Imperial Majesty, the brightest star in the heavens." Little Catherine laughed—something she had been doing off and on ever since she had been able to make her way to the palace the previous day. At last they'd succeeded in seizing the throne, and she credited herself in no small part.

Finally a penciled letter renouncing the throne arrived.

Immediately Catherine dispatched a formal Act of Abdication, requiring only Peter's signature.

By the time Catherine rode into Peterhof to great acclamation on her thoroughbred stallion, she was more than ready to grasp the reins of state. No longer, she knew, would she be eclipsed by Empress Elizabeth I or Emperor Peter III. History had been forever altered.

She suddenly recalled Countess von Bentinck, the intriguing and independent woman she had admired so much while still a teen in Prussia. Henceforth she, too, would be a woman not only emerging from her shadow, but one who would "make some noise."

A lot of noise.

Notes

The Russian mile at that time was divided into 7 versts or approximately 7.5 kilometres. The metric system was not introduced until 1925.

In Russia, a patronymic is a middle name that identifies the person's father by his first name; women's names are then followed by "ovna" or "evna" (i.e. Maria Sergeievna means her father was named Sergei). Men's patronymics end in "ovich" or "evich" (Igor Igorevich means his father was named Igor). Both are the English transations/transliterations rather than the Russian or Romanized versions (both of which would have required me to use Catherine's Russian name, Ekaterina).

Tsaritsa or царица is the Russian word, whereas tsarina is the English version of it.

Similarly, there are various non-Russian spellings and transliterations of the soup *borshch*. The "t" on the end refers to a Jewish-American import of the famous soup, although there are other ways to spell it based on Ukrainian, Polish, Bulgarian, etc. versions. Many words also altered their spellings over the centuries (i.e. puds vs. poods referring to a measurement).

The Cathedral of the Dormition, which Catherine so admired on her trip to Kiev, was blown up during World War II (recreated early in the 21st century).

Author's Note

M y research for the novel not only required long years, but consistently ran into conflicts and contradictions that slowed things down. These included discrepancies in chronologies, dates, specific dignitaries in attendance at important events, details, etc. While all errors ultimately are my own, I did find the dozens of scholarly sources often frustrating in their disagreements, contradictions, and sometimes outright errors. Occasionally I had to draw my own conclusions as to which account might be correct. To take one example of many, biographers differ on whether Catherine had her hair dressed enroute to the coup or, as I have chosen to believe, waved her hairdresser's carriage away.

This judgment call based on available evidence and sources, as well as a variety of theories, was especially challenging when it came to coming up with my own interpretation of some key unanswered historical questions. One of the most contentious is the question of Paul's paternity (and thus the truth about Catherine and Peter's physical relationship). My own theories are just that. Indeed, as Virginia Rounding so keenly puts it, "Whether

Paul Petrovich was indeed the son of Grand Duke Peter, or that of Sergei Saltykov, is a question that will never be satisfactorily answered unless and until DNA tests are carried out on the remains of Peter III and Paul I."

Several TV series and films have, alas, not only sensationalized Catherine's life, but skewed it out of all proportion to the truth. Similarly, too many authors of historical fiction and fictionalized biographies of Catherine apparently saw nothing unethical or suspect about alternating facts and chronologies for the sake of the plot. This is something I tried to avoid at all costs, particularly since Catherine's life was exciting enough that it needs no embellishment or manipulation.

I was and am determined to ensure authenticity in terms of the details of Catherine II's life as much as they are known in sources available to me, and regret any mistakes that may have slipped by. Most incidents and many of the conversations recounted here actually occurred. With the aid of so much available information, documentation, and correspondence on her life, I was even able to quote Catherine directly in some dialogue.

The portrayal of Peter III is perhaps more negative than some scholars (especially in Russia) would prefer. However, I did not rely solely on Catherine's memoirs regarding his childishness, meanness, and ineptitude in so many areas. Plenty of evidence exists to back this up, most notably correspondence, writings, and reports by other witnesses and diplomats from throughout Europe who met and observed him. Perhaps given time he might have become a tolerable emperor, but certainly Catherine's seizure of the throne resulted in primarily positive changes and developments in Russia.

The spellings of names of actual persons and places always present problems in the transliteration of Russian. I chose not to try to follow a specific one religiously, opting instead to go either with the most familiar or recognizable versions or those that seemed to me to be closest to the Russian (as well as sometimes German and Polish) spellings. In some cases I followed the leads of the most recent Catherinian scholars and biographers.

A very similar Catherine the Great emerald cameo does exist, although no records remain as to the name of the jeweler who crafted it.

Fireworks in Russia during this period did indeed include massive figures marching across the night sky, although much of the art of this animation seems lost thus far to posterity.

For those fascinated with the Hermitage's large and well-known collection of cats, please note that they are not necessarily descendants of the Empress Elizabeth's cats, who lived in the old Winter Palace. Most of today's feline population arrived at the museum in the 1990s.

Finally, readers might note that for the key fifty-plus years of her life from adolescence through her death, Catherine took only approximately twelve lovers—and the promiscuity and tales of bestiality attributed to her especially in her later life are lacking in evidence and even logic; most historians dismiss them as ludicrous attempts to mar her reputation at home and abroad. In terms of numbers, Elizabeth, on the other hand, appears to have had too many lovers for historians to count. Throughout history it has been far from unusual for powerful women with powerful enemies to suffer attempts to discredit them both through and after their lifetimes via salacious, scandalous, reprehensible, and totally fabricated rumors (i.e. Elizabeth I, Alexandra II, Eleanor of Aquitaine). This was especially true since Catherine II reigned during both the American and French revolutions, as well as the sectioning off of Poland and countless other wars and controversies (see my forthcoming sequels).

One of my favorite assessments of Catherine II's personality comes from Gina Kaus, who rightly points out that "[her] posthumous image in the panopticum of semi-educated public opinion has been painted in . . . garish colors . . . For [centuries] this monstrous picture has tickled the imagination of the middle classes. It is utterly false. Catherine was as tender and loving as any other woman of warm and natural desires."

I hope you'll join me for *Out of the Shadows*, the sequel that will trace the next portion of Catherine's life (and Maria's), after her accession to the throne.

Special thanks to Dr. Elena Kalnitskaya, Director of Oranienbaum and Peterhof Palace museums.

Special thanks to Ms. Olga Filiminova, Director of Public Relations, Catherine Palace.

Additional thanks to the marvelous students at Leningrad State University in Pushkin for lending a hand with some of the research translations and museum visits.

I'd especially like to express my gratitude to my dear friend and journalist Sue McMillin for her always astute advice and professional editing—and above all, a close friendship that goes back to our undergrad years at Michigan State University—a time that fueled my interest in all things Russian.

The following main sources were consulted while researching this novel:

Alexander, John T. *Catherine the Great: Life and Legend*. NY: Oxford University Press, 1989.

Alexander Palace Time Machine. <http://alexanderpalace.org>

Almedingen, E. M. *Catherine the Great.: A Portrait*. London: Hutchinson, 1963.

Anisimov, Evgeni V. *Five Empresses: Court Life in Eighteenth-Century Russia*. Trans. Kathleen

Carroll. Westport, CT: Praeger Publishers, 2004.

Anthony, Katharine. *Catherine the Great*. Garden City, NY: Garden City Publishing, 1925.

Berdnikov, Lev. "Empress Elizabeth: The Iron-Fisted Fashionista." *Russian Life* 52, No. 6 (November/December 2009). 54-59

Chekhonin, Oleg and Svetlana Chekhoninina. *Oranienbaum*. St. Petersburg: Prepress Kitezh Art Publishers, 2006.

Cone, Polly, Editor. *Treasures From the Kremlin*. Moscow: State Museums of the Moscow Kremlin: 1979.

Coughland, Robert. *Elizabeth & Catherine: Empresses of All the Russias*. NY: G. P. Putnam's, 1974.

Cronin, Vincent. *Catherine Empress of All the Russias: An Intimate Biography*. London: William Collins Sons & Co.,1978.

Dixon, Simon. *Catherine the Great*. England, Profile Books, 2009.

_____. *Catherine the Great: Profile in Power*. Harlow, Longman, 2001.

Erickson, Carolly. *Great Catherine: The Life of Catherine the Great, Empress of Russia*. NY: St. Martin's Griffin, 1994.

Figes, Orlando. *Natasha's Dance: A Cultural History of Russia*. NY: Picador, 2003.

Forbes, Isabella and William Underhill, ed. *Treasures of Imperial Russia: Catherine the Great from the State Hermitage Museum, St. Petersburg.* Leningrad: The State Hermitage Museum, 1990.

Garrard, J. G., Ed. *The Eighteenth Century in Russia*. Oxford: Clarendon Press, 1973.

Grey, Ian. *Catherine the Great*. Philadelphia, Lippincott, 1962.

Haslip, Joan. *Catherine the Great: A Biography*. Toronto: Longman, 1977. 1st American Edition.

"The Hermitage." Wikipedia. (July 15, 2014)

   http://en.wikipedia.org/wiki/Hermitage_Museum (19 August 2014)

Hodgetts, Edward Arthur Brayley. 1859-1932. *The Life of Catherine the Great of Russia*. London: Methuen & Co. Ltd, 1914. Archived Empress of All Russia." (July 2013).

   <http:www.catherinethegreat.org> (09 March 2016)

_____. "Catherine the Great." <http://www,catherinethegreat.org>

Kaus, Gina. *Catherine: The Portrait of An Empress*. Trans. from German by June Head. NY: Viking Press, 1935. The Literary Guild edition.

Kelly, Laurence, Ed. *A Traveller's Companion to St. Petersburg*. NU: Interlink1981. Reprint 2003.

Kennett et al. *In the Russian Style*. Edited Jacqueline Onassis. NY: MJF Books, 1976.

Kochan, Miriam. *Life in Russia Under Catherine the Great*. NY: G. P. Putnam's Sons, 1969.

Kliuchevsky, V. O. *A Course in Russian History: The Time of Catherine the Great*. Trans. and Ed. Marshall S. Shatz. Armonk, NY: M. E. Sharpe, 1997.

Lawrence, John. *A History of Russia*, 7th Ed. NY: Meridian, 1993.

Lentin, Antony. *Russia in the Eighteenth Century: From Peter the Great to Catherine the Great (1696-1796)*. London: Heinemann Educational Books, 1973.

Longworth, Philip. *The Three Empresses*. NY: Rinehart and Winston, 1973.

Madariaga, Isabel de. *Catherine the Great*. New Haven: Yale University Press, 1990.

_____. "Catherine the Great: A Personal View. *History Today* 51.11 (Nov. 2001): 45-51.

_____. *Catherine the Great: A Short History.* New Haven, London: Yale University Press, 1990. Reprinted Yale Note Bene 2003.

_____. *Russia in the Age of Catherine the Great*. New Haven, Yale University Press, 1981.

Mason, Mary Willan. "The Treasures of Catherine the Great from the State Hermitage Museum St. Petersburg." *Antiques & Collecting Magazine* 106, no. 3, 62.

Massie, Robert K. *Catherine the Great: Portrait of a Woman*. NY: Random House, 2011.

Massie, Suzanne. *Land of the Firebird: The Beauty of Old Russia*. NY: Touchstone, 1980.

Montefiore, Simon Sebag. *The Romanovs*. NY: Knopf, 2016.

Murat, Princess Lucien Marie. *Private Life of Catherine the Great*. Trans. Garnett Saffery. NY: Louis Carrier & Co., 1928.

Oldenbourg, Zoe. *Catherine the Great*. NY: Pantheon, 1965.

Palmer, Alan. *Russia in War and Peace*. NY: Macmillan Co., 1972.

Piotrovski, Mikhail B., Ed. *Treasures of Catherine the Great*. London: Thames and Hudson, 2000.

Pipes, Richard. *Russia Under the Old Regime*. New York, Scribner's, 1974.

Radishchev, Alexander. *A Journey from St. Petersburg to Moscow*. Trans. Leo Wiener. Cambridge, MA: Harvard University Press, 1958.

Riasanovsky, Nicholas V. *A History of Russia*, 4th ed. NY: Oxford University Press, 1984.

Romanov, Catherine. *The Memoirs of Catherine the Great*. Trans. Mark Cruse and Hilde Hoogenboom. NY: Modern Library, 2005.

Rounding, Virginia. *Catherine the Great: Love, Sex, and Power*. NY: St. Martin's Press. 2006.

Troyat, Henri. *Catherine the Great*. Trans. Joan Pinkham. NY: E. P. Dutton, 1980.

_____. *Catherine the Great*. Reprint. London: Phoenix Press, 2000.

Van Der Post, Laurens. *A View of All the Russias*. NY: William, Morrow: 1964.

Waliszewski, Kasimierz. *The Romance of an Empress*. New York: D. Appleton and Company, 1894. Trans. from French 1905. Reprinted 1968.

Zwingle, Erla. "Catherine the Great." *National Geographic* 194, No. 3 (September 1998). 94-117.

COMING IN 2023

From Book Two:

OUT OF THE SHADOWS
WITH CATHERINE THE GREAT

(Catherine)

She dared not ring for someone yet. Not even Grigory.

Then she started to shake. First her hands, which had dropped the letter after a fourth reading. Then her legs.

She must have made a sound, even a cry, because two ladies emerged from where she had sent them and started to fuss.

"Leave us!" Catherine managed to say sharply, relieved she still had command of her voice. When they did, she sank onto the divan and let her tears flow.

An hour passed. Then another. At last she rose, resolved that she had wept the last tears over him that she should ever weep. She kept a key around her neck, and moved slowly into her chamber and to the small desk beside her bed. Carefully unlocking it, she then folded the parchment with its offending, hideous news and placed it inside before turning the key.

There, she vowed, the letter should remain: unseen, unread, and unjudged by anyone. She did not wish to read it again. Perhaps ever. Nor did she wish to share it with anyone.

She rang for coffee, then changed her mind and ordered a cordial of brandy. She must have all her wits about her, although she needed to cease this residual trembling.

For a long time, she drummed bejeweled fingers on an agate table that held her quills and ink pots. There were decisions to be made. She held not only the futures of the parties involved in her hands, but that of the Russian Empire.

Convinced she was sufficiently collected, Catherine returned to her own papers. There was much to be done.

She refused to have this awful and unexpected death shortening—or shadowing—her reign.

(Maria)

There are risks no matter what I do. If I give up this opportunity, the statue might be hauled off to Moscow, cutting off future access to it.

I thought that long ago I'd resigned myself to living out my life in the eighteenth century. Now I realize that is not necessarily true.

By the third glass of wine, I'm worrying about what might happen if the statue *does* work. Would I be able to return here? To return to my beloved husband and my life here in imperial Russia?

And if this statue is indeed a conduit to the future—or even an alternate past—what if I end up in yet another time? I could find myself in the Napoleonic wars. Or World War II. Or further backward to Peter the Great's time. Or ancient Russia. Or the Roman era. I could not adapt again to another historical period, of that I feel certain.

The candles in the sconces are waning, and all the statues slipping into shadow. I should leave. Should retreat upstairs and take the carriage home.

I nearly empty the bottle and, clutching the glass, stand up.

About the Author

Judith Rypma's previous novels include *The Amber Beads* (time travel to 1917 Russia released by Black Opal Books) and *Mrs. Fleeney's Flowers* (family mental illness). In addition to publishing nine collections of poetry, she has taught Russian Studies, World Literature, and Youth Literature at Western Michigan University.

Made in United States
North Haven, CT
23 March 2025

67141576R00276